a DUEL with the VAMPIRE LORD

a MARRIED TO MAGIC novel

ELISE KOVA

D1502122

Silver Wing Press

a DUEL with the VAMPIRE LORD

a MARRIED TO MAGIC novel

ELISE KOVA

This book is a work of fiction. The names, characters and events in this book are the products of the author's imagination or are used fictitiously. Any similarity to real persons living or dead is coincidental and not intended by the author.

Published by Silver Wing Press
Copyright © 2022 by Elise Kova

All rights reserved. Neither this book, nor any parts within it may be sold or reproduced in any form without permission.

Cover Artwork by Marcela Medeiros
Developmental Editing by Rebecca Faith Editorial
Line Editing by Melissa Frain
Proofreading by Kate Anderson

ISBN (paperback): 978-1-949694-40-6
ISBN (hardcover): 978-1-949694-39-0
eISBN: 978-1-949694-35-2

Also by Elise Kova

Married to Magic

A Deal with the Elf King
A Dance with the Fae Prince
A Duel with the Vampire Lord
A Duet with the Siren Duke
More to Come

Air Awakens Universe

AIR AWAKENS SERIES
Air Awakens
Fire Falling
Earth's End
Water's Wrath
Crystal Crowned

GOLDEN GUARD TRILOGY
The Crown's Dog
The Prince's Rogue
The Farmer's War

VORTEX CHRONICLES
Vortex Visions
Chosen Champion
Failed Future
Sovereign Sacrifice
Crystal Caged

A TRIAL OF SORCERERS
A Trial of Sorcerers
A Hunt of Shadows
A Tournament of Crowns
More to Come

Loom Saga

The Alchemists of Loom
The Dragons of Nova
The Rebels of Gold

See all books and learn more at:
http://www.EliseKova.com

for all the book lovers
with daggers and crowns
on their bookshelves

Table of Contents

one 1
two 9
three 17
four 28
five 34
six 39
seven 46
eight 58
nine 70
ten 78
eleven 85
twelve 95
thirteen 106
fourteen 118
fifteen 130
sixteen 139
seventeen 149
eighteen 159
nineteen 169
twenty 180
twenty-one 189
twenty-two 200
twenty-three 210
twenty-four 220
twenty-five 228
twenty-six 235
twenty-seven 242
twenty-eight 251
twenty-nine 266
thirty 271
thirty-one 281
thirty-two 288
thirty-three 296
thirty-four 303
thirty-five 312
thirty-six 323
thirty-seven 334
thirty-eight 344
thirty-nine 355
forty 362
forty-one 368
forty-two 376
forty-three 385
forty-four 391
forty-five 396
forty-six 406
forty-seven 411
forty-eight 415

Mer Waters
Lake of Anointing
Fae Wilds
Dreamsong
The High Court
The Bleeding Woods
Carron
Westwatch
Elf Kingdo
N

Vampir Mountains
Tempost
Castle Tempost
Sea Gate
Midscape
Quinnar

one

"Marry me and I will give you such strong babies." He slurs the words almost to the point of unintelligibility.

I cringe and shove—Walt? *Waldor?* I can't even remember his name—I shove what's-his-name's arm off my shoulders. He stumbles back with a laugh, almost bumping into a group of women dancing in the street and howling at the moon. They're down to their silken nightgowns, a haze of red and orange glowing on their skin from unnatural moonlight and the open doors of the smithy.

They can twirl and dance. They can sing and cry. They're as free as the hems that graze over their thighs. What would it be like to be one of them? What would I do? I don't even know. The bonds around me are as tight as the clasps on the sturdy leather apron I wear. Keeping me buttoned up. Contained.

What's-his-name reaches for me again.

I slap his hand away. "That's enough." Touching me could get him lashed at best; the drink is keeping his better sense at bay. He couldn't even claim that he doesn't know who I am. *Everyone* in this small hamlet knows who I am. I'm easy enough to spot by my rough, soot-stained hands. By my rolled sleeves and arms of dotted scars. My duty is seen as more sacred than that of many of the hunters themselves. For I am the one who will arm and armor them for years to come. I know the secrets of the forge.

I am the keeper of steel and silver.

He, like all of Hunter's Hamlet, knows the only one

permitted to touch me is the man the master hunter decides will be my husband. No exceptions.

Not even on what might be our last night alive.

"Is there a problem here?"

Last I saw, Drew was in the smithy, speaking with a young woman in the corner. But my twin and guardian is never far. He must've stepped out when he noticed I hadn't returned from my errand to the back shed promptly.

"Not a problem, just a drunk." I adjust my grip on the bucket of charcoal. The fueler lives down by the marshes—he's one of the few laymen permitted past the line of salted earth and into the land of the vampire. He brought up a fresh delivery tonight before the revelries started. I'm sure he'll be staying with someone in town tomorrow. He does for regular full moons; he definitely will for the Blood Moon. We all look after each other in the hamlet, especially when the vampires attack.

There are three fundamental truths of the mysterious and bloodthirsty vampire:

The first is that they subsist on human blood for sustenance and for their dark magics. Because of this, the war between vampires and humans has been raging since the dawn of time. Without the fortress and its thick walls that surround all of Hunter's Hamlet, they would overrun the world with their thirst for blood and death.

The second is that the vampire have only one true weakness—silver. All other tools are merely meant to slow them, or give their victims clean deaths. Catching a vampire's flesh with a silvered blade kills them instantly. It's our only defense, and why those who know how to smith the silver are revered in Hunter's Hamlet.

The final truth is that the vampires share one mind. The beasts that torment us month to month are little more than living golems that heed their lord's will. If the vampire lord is felled, the rest of his spawn will follow. But he is protected by the Fade, coming only once every five hundred years with his dark knights to attack on the night of the Blood Moon when the Fade is weak and he can lead his armies in force.

Tomorrow the Blood Moon will rise in full and the hunters will try to use my weapons to kill him and save humanity. Everything could change in a single night, for better or worse, and no one beyond Hunter's Hamlet has any idea.

The hunter that has been bothering me is aghast. "I'm not a drunk, I'm a noble hunter!"

"You can barely stand up," I retort.

"Enough, Wallice." *Ah, that's his name.* "You shouldn't be caught alone with the forge maiden," Drew scolds.

"We're, we're not *alone*." Wallice sways and hiccups. "See, all our friends are here!" He jumps into the group of dancing women, who accept him with open arms as if he really had been dancing with them all along.

In an instant his hands are on a brunette, running over the curves of her thighs, up to the swell of her stomach. Even the hands of a trained killer like Wallice can look elegant smoothing over silk. It pools between his fingers, spilling over as he hikes up her dress.

I can't stop myself from wondering what it would feel like if it were me. My own thighs tingle, heat rising to my core. I don't want Wallice. But I do want to know what it feels like to be touched. To be desired for more than my skill with a hammer and position in the hamlet. Wallice bites the woman's neck as a vampire would. She moans, head rolling back, and I turn to the smithy before a flush rises to my cheeks. At least inside I'll be able to claim the redness is from the heat.

"He didn't do anything untoward, did he?" Drew gives a final scowl at Wallice and then catches up to me.

"Nothing other than being so drunk that his better sense has vanished." I have no interest in getting Wallice in trouble. The hunters live hard enough lives as it is and tonight is a night of revelry, recklessness, and indulgence. Besides, he didn't do anything worse than throwing an arm around my shoulder. "I doubt he even knew who I was."

"He'd have to be pretty drunk to forget that."

"He seemed it; you saw him with the other women." I glance back over my shoulder. Wallice is stumbling off with one of the dancers.

"Thanks for not being too hard on him, Flor." *Flor*, short for Floriane. Only my brother and mother use the nickname. "It's just how things are the night before the Blood Moon."

"Should all the hunters be drunk to the point that it might impair their ability to hunt tomorrow?" I arch my eyebrows at him. Drew mirrors the movement. We're almost the same height and of similar build. We share the same black hair and eyes as our mother. Looking at him is truly like looking into a mirror and seeing a more masculine version of myself.

"We have until sunset to nurse our heads and stomachs, *and* the Hunter's Elixir to aid us. No second day ache is stronger than the elixir."

"Tomorrow isn't like a regular hunt."

"No one knows that more than us," he says with a note of severity.

I shrug rather than arguing further. Drew lets it drop. We enter the smithy side by side.

The smithy is one of the larger buildings of Hunter's Hamlet, set off slightly from the rest of the clustered cobblestone structures cramped together like too many teeth in a vampire's mouth. Unlike the other thatched roofs of the hamlet, its roof is slate, like the fortress's. Wooden awnings cover the front, welcoming us inside. The forge is at the center of everything, wooden tables stretching out from it. Usually they're covered in tools and blades. But tonight they're covered with food and flagons.

This is the hub of Hunter's Hamlet, as everyone needs the work of a blacksmith, at some point, and tonight is no exception.

The brewer has brought a cask of ale and tapped it fresh. Farmers have gathered around, sipping on the fruit of their labors. The milliner is spinning stories to children up far past bedtime. And thrumming underneath the din of it all is the beating heart of Hunter's Hamlet—the smith matron, the shield of Hunter's Hamlet. My mother.

Mother's hammer rhythmically rises and falls. Her dark hair escapes the tightly braided bun she wears at the nape of her neck, clinging with sweat to the sides of her face. Even now, late in the night before the Blood Moon, we're still hard at work. There's still much to be done.

"By the way, who were you talking to before?" I ask Drew as we weave through a gaggle of gossiping elders.

"When?"

"Earlier. Over there." I gesture toward the corner. Whoever the young lady was, she wasn't waiting for Drew to come back.

"I've spoken with a lot of people tonight; you'll have to be more specific." He knows exactly what I'm talking about and is being obtuse.

"Fine, keep your secrets. But if I saw then Mother did, too, and I can *promise* you'll have a harder time dodging her questions."

"It's just a woman, nothing serious." Drew rubs the back of his neck.

"Mother is going to lay into you if you keep up this 'nothing serious' business with every lady in the hamlet." I drop the bucket by the forge and shovel in some of the charcoal, moving to work the bellows to alleviate a burst of frustration. Drew can touch, and dance, and feel all he wants. But me… I pull the bellows even harder.

Mother spares me an appreciative glance before promptly returning to her conversation with the tanner. Whatever they're discussing must be important, because her expression is severe. Could it be there's something wrong with the last batch of leathers we sent for the hunters to wear tomorrow? I'm instantly trying to recall every clasp and buckle I made, every pauldron and needle. Did I hammer a defect into the metal without realizing?

"I've no complaints from anyone I've been with." Drew shrugs. "I'll settle down eventually, whenever I decide."

"Must be nice to just decide whenever you want to be with someone or marry them," I mutter under my breath. I might gracefully accept my role for the betterment of Hunter's Hamlet around everyone else. But Drew is the one person I don't need to be graceful in front of.

"I shouldn't have phrased it like that. I'm sorry, Flor."

I shake my head and sigh, trying to ease the tension in my shoulders. "It's true."

"But it might not have to be for long."

My heart skips a beat. "What do you mean?"

"I'll tell you later."

"But—"

"Normal time."

"Nothing about tonight is normal," I hiss. Our voices have dropped to a whisper. I can't believe he's talking about our midnight training within earshot of so many. "Look at how many people are here; we're not going to have time to—"

I don't get to finish because I learn what made Drew so confident we'll be able to sneak a moment alone.

The smithy falls to a hush. Even Mother's hammer is silent as she rests it on the anvil and plunges the iron she was working into the almost white-hot coals I've stoked in the forge. All eyes have turned to the silhouette in the doorway, outlined by a pinkish, festering moon.

This gnarled and fearsome man is Davos, the master hunter, the man whom our world would be lost without.

His clothes are finely made of velvet. A rare material reserved for the master hunter himself as it can only be procured outside the hamlet. His hands are folded atop a walking stick adorned with the silver head of a raven—one identical to the large bird perched on his shoulder. I fight a chill that runs down my spine at the sight of the raven.

The black eyes of the master hunter.

That's what the townsfolk refer to the bird as. It has a name; Drew told me it once. But I promptly forgot it. The name was as uncomfortable as the bird's gaze. A fitting name that sounds like shrill cries and sharp nails on stone.

The old stories say that not one master hunter, dating as far back as the fortress itself, thousands of years, has been without a raven. When one master hunter dies, the raven takes to the skies. Then, when it is time for a new master hunter to be masked, a raven returns to perch on their shoulder. Some claim it has been the same raven for every master hunter since the first stones of the forge were laid. Drew says the raven is so revered in the fortress that *it* is usually the one to choose the next master hunter from worthy candidates. Others in the hamlet go so far as to think that the creature is an ancient god in the shape of a beast, defending Hunter's Hamlet against the vampire scourge.

If that is true, the old god does a poor job of it. Because even though the vampire lord himself can't come through the Fade, he still sends monsters every full moon to attack, to remind us that he is there, waiting. And the rumored divine could clearly do nothing to prevent the impending Blood Moon.

"Hail, Hunter's Hamlet," Davos says in that weary way of his.

"Guide and guard us," the room intones in response.

"Tonight's revelries seem to have been a delight." Davos smiles. I think the expression is intended to be fatherly, but to me it always looks wicked. There's a gleam to his eyes that deeply unnerves me. Drew has never found my unease surprising.

Davos is baptized in the blood of our enemies, he says. *The man has seen more vampires, more of his kin live and die, than any of us.*

And none of us are strangers to bloodshed in Hunter's Hamlet. Death keeps a summer home in this forsaken place.

"But the night is growing thin," Davos continues. "And I must recall my hunters to me."

Men and women slowly step away from the crowd, as if in a trance. They are the hunters and have the scars, both visible and not, as a testament to their bloody work. I want to grab Drew's hand. To ask if he's sure he'll be able to come later. I can't stomach the thought of him marching out tomorrow evening without a chance to speak to him alone just one more time. Even though I don't know what I want to say yet.

What do you say to someone before they march off to certain death? What could I tell him that he doesn't already know? What words would be enough to encapsulate everything? He was always the clever one with finesse. I'm useless if I can't hit my problem with a hammer.

But I let him go.

I have no other choice.

He has his role and I have mine. They were given to us before we were born, determined solely by our family name and sex. No matter how much we might hope, or dream, or begrudge, neither of us can escape the path laid before us.

"Is there anything more you need from the forge?" Mother asks Davos.

"No, you have already done more than enough to protect Hunter's Hamlet. Without your weaponry, wall fortifications, and assistance with our leather armor, the hunters would be going out underneath the Blood Moon in a sad state," Davos says as the hunters gather round.

"It is our family's honor to see the hunters and the hamlet prepared for every hunt, this one especially." Mother lets her eyes drift to Drew with a sad smile; it's an expression I've seen her give him often, one of both pride and worry, fear and joy. Even though we knew becoming a hunter was his destiny, as much as mine is the forge, neither of us looked forward to him embarking on that path. It is not a life with longevity. But we knew why he had to leave the house and join the fortress. We understood.

That is the way of things in the Runil family: the eldest daughter is the forge maiden and the eldest son heads to the fortress. Every family has their traditions and their role to play in Hunter's Hamlet. There is security when we are all in our place. It is the promise and sacrifice we've all made. So after Father died it was merely a matter of time until Drew assumed his position in society.

From that moment on, Mother and I have been waiting each month for Davos to arrive and tell us that the vampires have claimed another member of our family. But, miraculously, month after month, Drew has returned. Maybe this month, even with the Blood Moon, will be no different. It's a fool's hope and I know it. But all hope is foolish in Hunter's Hamlet.

"Speaking of your family's honor…" Davos's eyes drift to me as he trails off. His eyes shine and the taste of bile rises in the back of my throat. "Following tomorrow night's hunt, there will be even more cause for celebration. It is time to cement our forge maiden's future, so that the smithy continues to run hot for generations to come."

"I will do as the master hunter bids." I dip my chin and keep my face as blank as the masks the hunters wear when they go out to the Fade Marshes.

"May the bell toll for a wedding in the coming week." Davos taps his walking stick for emphasis. Drew is fighting a scowl. I think he hates this topic even more than I do.

I can imagine what he'll say later. *How dare Davos speak about you like you're not there, in front of everyone. How dare he speak of marrying you off like you're some prized mare.* But my fate is no secret. The forge maiden is always married before twenty. That's just the way of it, the tradition, the necessity since any of our lives might end come the next full moon. I'll likely be with child before the end of the year and the idea has me cold, even standing next to the forge.

There's excited murmuring among the eligible male hunters. They leer at me. I grab one of the hammers by the forge on instinct, keeping it at my side.

I might be the forge maiden, but I am no delicate flower. I am as cold as silver. As strong as iron. I will bend for destiny, but not for any man.

two

No one notices my white knuckles; they're too busy cheering. The wedding of the forge maiden is a huge affair in Hunter's Hamlet. We have precious little to celebrate, so when there is an excuse, the hamlet indulges deeply.

I keep my panic, my worry, within. I won't be the one to squelch their joy. Not due to childish notions of getting to choose my husband for love, or desire, or attraction, or any of the other reasons someone is drawn to a partner. I have my duty. I have an obligation, and all of it is far more important than anything I would *want*.

"Into the night," Davos says, turning.

"Good hunting," the rest of us respond as the master hunter leaves with his loyal soldiers.

"The bellows, Floriane," Mother says, gentle but firm. "And since you have a hammer in hand, help me with a few sickles; the fortress can never have enough." Her eyes dart from the tool to my face. Her expression softens into a sad smile. She knows what my future holds all too well. It had been hers too.

And she had fallen in love with Father, in time.

I can see them together in the forge. Sweat shines on their cheeks. They share a smile reserved only for the two of them. Father is nimble and light. Mother is strong and sturdy. He was her shield, her his sword. They were two parts to one being, one entity.

The image is briefly replaced by the shell of my father

stumbling unnaturally toward the smithy without his sickle—that was how we knew he was dead.

I shake my head, scattering the thoughts, and set to work.

Before I know it, the last reveler has wandered away. It's just Mother and me left, as it always is at the end of a long day. The coals are turning orange-red and the shadows are lengthening.

"That's enough for tonight." Mother pats the horn of the anvil, returns her hammer to its peg, rolls her shoulders, and then stretches her wrists. No matter how long we do this job, there are still aches and pains that come with it. Every strike reverberates up through the elbow and into the shoulders. The core is worn ragged. Knees ache. The smithy demands every part of the body.

"I'll clean up."

"Thank you." Mother rests a hand on my shoulder. "What Davos said earlier about your marriage…"

"I thought nothing of it."

She smiles. She knows I'm lying. "I wanted you to know that I had no prior knowledge he would bring it up. If I had, I would've told you."

"I know," I say softly. For years it's felt like it's just her and me—ever since Father died and Drew left for the fortress. We work together every day. Share dinner every night. She's the only one who really understands my circumstances.

"After we survive tomorrow, if the vampire lord is not slain, then we'll talk more about your nuptials. I won't send you in blind. And I'll do what I can to find you a smart match."

"Thank you," I say earnestly.

"Of course." She leans forward and kisses me on my forehead, even though I know it's coated in metal dust and soot. "Now, take your time. We'll be cooped up tomorrow night and have preparations come dawn, so enjoy this time for yourself."

Mother knows me too well.

I run my hand along the smooth top of the anvil after she leaves. My nails stick on the grooves of the softer metal of the horn. It's still warm from her work.

Home.

Every month the vampires come to try and take it all from us. But, according to the old stories, the infiltrations month after month are just glancing blows. The real fight is tomorrow. Drew has been telling me not to dwell on my possible demise for the past few months, but how could I not? Just like the old stories warn, the moon grows ever more ominous, a faint pink darkening with each night. It can't be ignored.

I set to cleaning. First, I sweep up the scale, then rake the coals, piling them toward the back. It's odd to think we won't be stoking them in a few hours come dawn. Then I head to the back.

In the back of the forge is a vault built into the thick walls. I check and count the silver within, making sure all the bars are stacked in the particular way that Mother likes them. Then, I lock the door with the spinning dials smelted onto its front. The numerical lock is a strange contraption designed by my great-great-grandmother. She kept its workings a secret to the grave. Every forge maiden has left their mark—a great work left behind. Mine still remains a mystery.

Perhaps I'll figure out how to make my own unique lock and replace this one. No one alive knows how to fix the one smelted into the door. But the benefit is that no one but our family has any idea how it works and how to open it. *Fear marries desperation to breed poor decisions*, Mother always says. *We must protect the silver, for it is our only defense against the vampires*. A defense that grows more finite by the day.

Those who enter Hunter's Hamlet by way of the fortress gate and join our community are never allowed to leave thereafter. That is part of our sacrifice to keep the world safe from the vampires. No one goes in or out, vampires included. Space for humans to slip through means spaces for vampires to pass. The single path through the fortress is the only, tightly guarded, connection to the outside world.

The only exception to sequestering is for the master hunter. He is permitted to leave through the outer gate to engage with the traders the other hunters call from the walls. There are some things we cannot produce on our own, namely iron and silver.

According to Drew, the Applegate Trading Company that transports rare, raw silver from the distant north has not come to the port town near us for almost a year now. Mother and I have begun to worry that they might not ever return. There have been many dinners spent discussing what we will do if the veins of silver in those faraway mines have run out. She has already begun consulting the old family records for ideas on how to more efficiently smelt down the existing, but broken, weapons and recast them into the crescent moon sickles that the hunters wield without losing the silver's potency.

The door of the forge opens. Moonlight dances with lamplight as a cloaked figure slips in. I do not sound an alarm because I know the man at a glance.

"Everything looks good," Drew appraises.

"I'm glad to have your approval." I hop up onto one of the tables. "I really didn't think you'd be able to come tonight."

"I had to." He sits next to me and we linger in comfortable silence for a few minutes. "Listen, we don't have much time, so tomorrow—"

"Don't. I don't like that tone."

He continues anyway. "Tomorrow, it'll be up to you to protect Mother."

"I know."

"Do you still have them?" He sticks to the point. Relentless, my brother.

"Of course I do. One here—" I nod toward the forge tools "—and one in the house, just like you told me." I shift uncomfortably. "But wouldn't it be better to give them to the fortress? Couldn't the hunters use all the weapons you can get?"

"Thanks to you and Mother, we have more than enough." He pushes off the table and crosses toward the racks of tools. The wood on the side of the rack is loose where it meets the wall. Wedged behind it is a sickle. Drew had told me to make it in secret.

Then he insisted I learn how to use it.

He holds out the hilt to me. "Keep it on you in the coming hours."

"Mother will see."

"It'll be too late for her to do anything."

"She's just going to *love* us breaking the law." I roll my eyes, fingers closing around the cool metal. Drew releases the familiar weight of the sickle into my palm. I wonder if any other forge maiden has been so comfortable with a weapon in her hands. I doubt it. We're to be protected and kept off the battlefield at all costs. Resources are too precious for everyone to have weapons. Everyone has a role and is given enough for them to fulfill the duties of that role. No more or less.

"She'll be grateful if the need arises."

"She will be cross with both of us the second she sees it." *The hunters have claimed both my children*, I can hear her saying. Lamplight glistens off the wicked-sharp blade. I've been honing it for weeks leading up to tomorrow. As if I could make it so sharp that I could cut away my worries.

"I have something else for you." Drew hovers, looking both uncomfortable and intense at the same time.

"What?"

He fishes into his pocket and produces a small, obsidian vial. "Here."

"What's this?" I turn the strange vessel over in my hands, placing the sickle on the table next to me.

"The reason I was late to sneak out and the reason I had to come." Drew inhales slowly, as he always does when he's working up the courage to say something he knows I won't like. "If the vampires reach the town, things have gone awry. The remaining hunters here will need all the help they can get. And…and I can't go out into the marshes tomorrow without knowing you and Mother will be safe."

"*No one* is safe in Hunter's Hamlet." I huff bitterly. Our lives are spent locked in combat, trying to fight away vampires and our own fear.

"This is why you have been training."

"And I'm still not good enough to face a vampire."

"You're better than you think. And with this, you'll be unstoppable." He nods to the vial.

It dawns on me what his gift actually is. Chills run up my body, starting from the hand holding the vial. My skin puckers to gooseflesh.

"No." I thrust it toward him. He takes a step away. "No, *no*." I jump off the table; he steps back. "You cannot—"

"I have."

"If you—if anyone—if it's discovered that you took this from the fortress and gave it to me you will be *hanged*."

"If you and Mother aren't here for me to return to then I'll wish I was dead anyway," Drew says severely.

I stare at the vial in my palm and whisper, "Hunter's Elixir." It feels forbidden for me to even *say*. It is very illegal for me to be holding.

"A powerful brew at that." He shifts his weight, looking briefly uncertain. But it passes before I can try and capitalize on it enough to give back the vial. "Davos said this particular elixir was rare, stronger, something he was saving only for tomorrow. It came from a special font deep below the fortress. So I know it will make you strong enough to defend Mother and the forge."

"And if I'm discovered with this, or having drunk it, *I'll* be hanged, too." I shake my head and give him a glare. He's gambling with our lives.

"No one would ever hang the forge maiden. Plus, how would they know? Only drink it if you're staring down the dead eyes of a vampire. Otherwise, keep it secret and give it back to me the morning after the Blood Moon." He says it like it's so simple.

"What about the hunter's madness?" I ask.

"One drink of the elixir will not cause madness. It's built up over time." Drew's eyes become distant. He has seen his brothers- and sisters-in-arms succumb to the madness of the Hunter's Elixir, a bloodlust and thirst for battle unlike any other.

Over the years, he's hardened before my eyes, hammered into a man I hardly recognize sometimes. It makes me all the more desperate to be close to him. It's part of why I agreed to let him train me at all. I didn't share in his notions that we might be able to escape, or even bend, our fate if we became strong enough, as tempting as they might be. No, these nightly trainings have happened because I missed my brother.

He continues, "Besides, I suspect the madness has nothing to do with the elixir at all, and more with what we see and must do in the Fade Marshes."

My knuckles turn white as I grip the vial. All our combat practice suddenly seems so foolish. I'm a forge maiden, not a hunter. I'm supposed to make weapons, not use them. This has all gone too far. "Please, don't go tomorrow. Stay here in the city and protect us. Don't make me have to use this."

"I'm going so you won't ever have to fear the vampire again." My fool of a brother steps forward and places both his hands on my shoulders. "I'm going with the vanguard so that vampires won't make it here."

The vanguard. Drew will be on the front lines. My heart begins to race.

"Don't, Drew," I say hastily. "Davos loves you—"

Drew snorts softly.

"You're the brother of the forge maiden; he will let you stay as part of the town's defense if you ask to defend me. You don't have to go so deep into the marshes."

"I *have to*." His voice has dropped to a whisper. Even though we're alone, he glances around. "Davos wouldn't let me stay in town because he has prepared me for this night since I joined the hunters. I've been chosen for a special mission, Flor. I can end this."

"End it?"

"End it all." Drew hugs me tight. It's like the hugs Father would give before the full moon. But this time… I know this is the last I'll see my brother. *He's saying goodbye*.

"Please don't go," I beg. My throat is gummy. Eyes are burning. "I don't care about any special mission or old stories. There will never be an end. We will always be hunted. So stay here and live with me." My insecurities and fears are multiplying. I am the fool Mother always warned of and I give in to desperation when I say, "Don't make me get married off to whatever hunter Davos pleases. How will I know it's someone decent if you're not there to intervene?"

Drew releases me. "I will *never* let you live a life of misery."

"But—"

"Tomorrow," he says softly. "When the Blood Moon thins the Fade and the vampire lord himself leads his legions through it, I will be ready and waiting. I will kill the vampire lord—the mind of the hive—and *I* will put an end to this endless war."

My heart seizes in my chest. My throat is too tight to say anything else. I knew the vampire lord would come. But…I never imagined my brother would be the one poised to attack him head on.

"You can't," I whisper.

Drew wears a sad smile. "Not even a bit of confidence for your older brother?"

"Older by minutes," I say on instinct. He chuckles. "Please, I—"

"The decision is made. I'm doing this for all of Hunter's Hamlet. But also for you. If the vampire lord dies, then you won't need to be a forge maiden any longer. Hunter's Hamlet will be like any other town. You won't have to work here every day. You won't be married off. You and I could finally go to the sea." *The sea*, the symbol of that all-encompassing dream of the world beyond the walls.

"I have all I need here; I don't need the sea." It's a lie. One I've told myself so many times since I was a girl that I believe it more and more the older I get. Time has a way of snuffing dreams. "I need you and Mother safe and the forge hot."

"You wanted to go to the sea when we were children," he counters.

"We were seven. Things were simpler then." I shake my head, wondering just how we could be so alike and yet so different at the same time. Drew was always fighting—fighting for more, for Hunter's Hamlet, for dreams I stopped dreaming long ago.

"You could be so much more, Floriane," Drew says softly.

"All I want is not to see another one of our family die."

"Then promise me you'll protect Mother, so the only thing I must focus on is keeping myself alive and killing the vampire lord."

When he puts it like that… "Fine. But you must come back."

"I will."

"Swear it. Swear that when the sun's light hits the bell tower following the night of the Blood Moon you will be marching home."

"I swear I will come back."

I grasp him tightly. As tightly as I'm holding on to my emotions. He's sworn it to me. He'll come back.

Yet, my heart knows the truth. Maybe it's because we're twins. Maybe because he's a hunter like Father was. Maybe I just know from being born on the soil of Hunter's Hamlet that death is already in the air.

He might swear he'll return, but…

He's lying.

three

TODAY'S THE FIRST DAY IN MY LIFE THAT THE FORGE WAS NOT LIT.

Usually, every morning, Mother is the first to rise. She heads downstairs and puts the kettle on for tea, then she heads to the smithy and begins to wake the slumbering coals in the hearth, stoking them into high flames to create a bed of heat for us to work from. The forge glows an angry orange as if in contempt that it must wake before even the sky. By the time I make my way downstairs, I can feel the heat all the way at the kitchen window, and Mother is already working the bellows. Before the sun rises, we are ready to melt silver and steel together to make the special alloy that only we can craft.

But today, the house is quiet.

All of Hunter's Hamlet is filled with the most horrible, deafening silence.

I'm up before Mother. Not utterly unheard of, but on top of everything else it's a reminder of how strange the day is. I stare out my window at the quiet streets. There's no smoke from the baker's chimney. There aren't laborers trudging out to the fields that fill the gap between town and the Fade Marshes. The only people outside are before their doors, beginning to hang on their eaves the delicate silver bells we have spent months smithing.

Mother and I join them.

We don't say much. The hunters have told us what to do to prepare and it is not so different than any other full moon.

There's only so much we can do to prepare for vampires, even less for the vampire lord himself. The old stories are vague on what to expect from the ruler and hive mind of the vampires—some say he's a winged monstrosity, others claim him to be able to draw the blood from all living creatures within his sight with a mere thought. I'm not sure what I believe, other than that he's certainly the cause of every bit of hardship and loss in Hunter's Hamlet.

What Drew said weighs on me as the hours tick on. His words—his lies—were sharper than the sickles I forge. Sharper than the weapons I have hidden in the main room downstairs. I look to the fortress, as though I could catch a glimpse of him, but he's behind those high, thick walls. Not for the first time, I wonder what's going on within all that stone.

But hunters' affairs aren't meant for me. I haven't taken the vows of a hunter. I will not wear a mask tonight. I am the forge maiden and my place is here as much as his is in the Fade Marshes. We can't change our roles, no matter how badly we might want to.

The bell tolls.

The bell tower of Hunter's Hamlet stretches up from the center of the main square. It is as old as the fortress, said to have been built thousands of years ago, at the same time as the walls that surround all the land of Hunter's Hamlet. One of the hunters serves as the bell ringer. I always thought it was a pointless task. None of us forget when the full moon has come. We certainly don't need a ringing reminder each dusk before full moons to be in our homes. Every toll is worse than the last.

I lower my hands from the silver bells stretched over our door and look to Mother. She stares at the bell tower. At three stories tall, it's the second tallest thing in the hamlet. The tallest is the fortress at four, which I'm certain is the highest structure ever built by human hands. Mother's features are as hard as the iron we hammer and betray no emotion. I mirror her expression. We cannot be delicate.

"Do you want to go see the procession?" I ask.

"Of course." She shakes her head, as if trying to banish the worried thoughts that I know are there. There will be no banishing them, not tonight.

We join the rest of Hunter's Hamlet, heading for the main road that cuts through town. I've never seen so many people in one place being so silent. There's only the sound of our boots on the cobblestone streets. I hear weeping coming from one of the windows we pass underneath. It does not quiet.

The main road stretches from the fortress to the center square and bell tower, and then on past the lower wall of Hunter's Hamlet. It cuts through the farmers' fields and heads north through the salted earth. Then, it goes past the realm of my knowing and into the Fade Marshes. No one knows what's at the end of it. No one has made it that far into the lands of the vampire and lived to tell the tale.

Drew has said that the road is ancient and connects all the way to the vampire stronghold at the far end of the Fade Marshes, farther than any human has ever gone and returned. He claimed to have read it in one of Davos's books—a secret and ancient tome that only *he* was permitted to read. All the special privileges my brother got suddenly make sense in a way that I wish they didn't. Davos has molded him into what the master hunter thinks is the most ideal killer of vampires. And because of it, he will send my brother to attack the vampire lord tonight.

My stomach is uneasy as Mother and I come to a stop along the road. I don't know if I want to see my brother in his hunter's garb. Not tonight. Not this full moon. It will all be real the moment I lay eyes on him and then the last sight I'll have of him is Drew the hunter, in his leather armor, and not Drew the brother I knew last night.

But it's too late to turn back now.

The mighty portcullis of the fortress slowly opens with a deep clanking. Behind it is the might of the Hunters' Guild. Every hunter wears the same armor—heavy leather and thin plates, designed for fast movement. It's the only way to keep up with the unnatural speed of the vampire. They all wear blank masks with only a thin slit for their eyes, and collars around their throats.

Drew showed me the inside of his once when I asked why they needed such delicate thorns made. There are hidden points within, laced with a deadly poison. The tips of the needles are tucked into leather flaps. But if a hunter hits their throat in the right way, the needles will pop free and they will die a clean death. More importantly, the poison will render their blood too putrid for the vampire to consume. It's a risky design, but worth the few accidents that happen. The alternative would be to cover the hunters in silver, and it's too precious a resource for that.

The tough leather and high collars, the masks, the poison, it is all designed to prevent vampires from performing their darkest and rarest magic. With blood, they can steal the faces of those they drink from and infiltrate the town as our loved ones.

As happened with Father.

I banish the thought into the void left behind by his death. The same void widened by Drew leaving for the fortress. I won't let myself think of Drew in the same way. He will return home. I have to believe it or I might give in to despair all too soon.

The procession passes, led by Davos. Of course that means Drew is at the front, at the master hunter's right hand, helping lead the vanguard. I can tell him by his armor, even though it is an identical design to everyone else's. I made all the clasps that line his fittings. I made the silver ring that he wears on his right pinky, identical to mine.

His head turns. Our eyes meet. I can feel his stare through the mask.

I am overwhelmed with the urge to run to him, to grab him, shake him, hold him back, scream at him for what he is doing. I admire him endlessly for the sacrifices he has made and continues to make and the hope he somehow manages to muster despite them.

Don't forget your promise, I mouth.

His right thumb reaches underneath his palm and spins the ring on his pinky. It's a movement that everyone else certainly misses, but I don't. There's no explicit meaning to that movement, just a feeling—a reminder of the bond we share and the tether between us.

I dip my chin. He looks forward once more.

Drew is gone. The rest of the procession continues onward, obscuring my view of him. Mother and I stay with all the other townsfolk, hovering in our place until long after the vast majority of the hunters have left. Only a few remain stationed at the lower wall that rings the town proper.

When we arrive back at our home, Mother picks up the bucket of salt just inside our door and carefully pours out a thick line on every windowsill, and over the threshold of the door. We then lock ourselves inside, ready to settle in for the long night.

"Come." Mother calmly motions for me to follow her upstairs. I do so silently. I don't quite trust myself to speak yet. My heart is still in turmoil that wants to escape as screams or sobs. "In here."

Mother leads me into her bedroom. She opens the chest at the foot of her bed, taking out the blankets we use in winter and the linens that were a gift from the milliner when she and Father wed. At the very bottom of the chest is a set of leather armor identical to the hunters'. "Put this on."

"How do you have that?" I look between her and the armor. "We're not permitted to have any hunter's tools as citizenry." Everyone in the hamlet has their place, and no one is permitted the trimmings of another's station. But everyone is always promised to have enough. Worthy rewards for worthy sacrifices—yet another teaching of the hamlet.

"Neither is your brother permitted to teach you the skills of a hunter between full moons."

I freeze. My mother's eyes, dark as the coals of the forge, the same as her hair, the same as mine, pierce me. "You knew," I whisper.

"I knew from the first night." She gives an exasperated chuckle. "You two didn't really think that you could keep something like that from me, did you?"

"We didn't— We weren't— We— Why did you never say anything?" I have a thousand questions, yet I can barely seem to formulate one.

"Why would I prevent my children from learning how to defend themselves?" She puts her hands on her hips. "Old gods forbid, if you were attacked by a vampire, I would want you to know everything you could. The hamlet needs its forge maiden. I always thought it was foolish we never learned how to properly use the weapons we made just in case."

"That isn't the role of the forge maiden."

"Sometimes roles should change." The sentiment is counter to our entire way of life.

"Even if…" No, I can't even think an agreement with her even though I want to. My objections are still buried underneath all the words of the town elders, of Davos, of even Mother herself about our stations. Instead, I say, "But I'm not as good as Drew." I continue to regard the armor uncertainly. I doubt it'd fit, and not just because of my curves. That's not the life I'm made for.

"Of course not. Your days were spent in the forge. He can't hold a candle to your smithing." She smirks. "But if you had gone into the fortress, and not him, I have no doubt that you would've been just as good as your brother." I doubt it, but don't say so. That wasn't my destiny. "Now, let me help you into this."

"What about you?" I ask as she holds out the armor. Even though I've never worn it, I know it well. I've forged thousands of these clasps. Checking each one several times.

"I could only make a deal with the tanner for one set of armor. It took years to collect all the pieces, enough to cobble together a complete set without the Hunter's Guild noticing anything was amiss." Stealing from the guild bears the same punishment as Drew sneaking me the elixir. We're a family racing to the gallows, it seems. "We began working on the arrangement not long after Drew told me of the impending Blood Moon."

"What did you give the tanner in return?"

"Silver daggers, three of them, small ones."

"Where did you get the silver?" I already know the answer. This solves a long-standing mystery my brother and I have wondered about for years. I know what she'll say before she says it.

"I smelted your father's sickle." A rare gift from the fortress to a mourning widow and forge maiden, a bending of the rules intended solely to honor the dead.

"Mother—"

"Don't feel guilty for a moment." She punctuates the firm sentiment with a jerk of the armor straps. I inhale, chest fighting against the constricting leather breastplate. "This was my choice, Floriane." She uses my full name. That's how I know she's serious. "I assume you still have the other one you managed to forge?"

"Yes."

"And the one your brother got for you?"

She really does know everything. "Yes."

"Good." Mother finishes tightening the belt around my waist. "Go and get them."

I'm in a daze as I head back downstairs. Drew and I were so careful, so thoughtful. We tried to keep Mother out of this. And yet she knew.

She was making her own preparations just as we were—also skirting the law for our family.

For me.

My chest tightens past the point of pain as I get the two sickles and slide them into the hooks on the belt. They've risked so much for me. My shoulders suddenly are pulled down by an invisible weight. Mother folds her arms, leaning against a support column in the main room. The sky has turned angry behind her, illuminating her black hair with streaks of gold, like fire in a hearth.

"You look like a proper hunter."

"I don't have a mask or collar." I rub my throat. I might *look* like a Hunter, but I'm not one. I will never be. I do not know if I could take my own life, not even with the vampire staring me down, not even knowing that it would be the best for Hunter's Hamlet. That's why Drew was destined for the guild, and I was made for the forge.

"Let's hope you need none of it." Mother sits at our table and folds her hands. She closes her eyes and I can see her lips move in a silent prayer. I hope her old gods are listening. I can't pray to gods that have clearly forgotten about us.

I go to the window. The sky is turning purple. The sun is bleeding out. I watch as it disappears completely and we are plunged into a brief darkness before the moon rises from the ashes of its sibling. Angry and red.

The Blood Moon hangs above the earth, tinting everything crimson. It's the largest moon I have ever seen, inflamed like a festering pustule. It creeps over the rooftops and charges the air with a restless energy. I place my hands in the sickles, adjusting my grip.

"You should come away from the window," Mother says softly.

"I will go mad if I can't see what's happening." I don't know what I expect to see. But I do know that not knowing is far worse.

"Hopefully nothing happens."

"Hopefully," I echo.

For the first part of the evening, my heart is in my throat. I cannot tear my eyes away from the empty streets. Every shadow is haunted. Every corner hides a secret vampire that exists only in my mind.

My mind steps away from reality, back to that night…long ago… the night Father died.

I remember him leaving. He kissed us both goodbye and held us tightly as he always did. Unlike Drew's embrace, it did not feel final. I wonder if things would've been easier if it had. If we had known that that was the last time we would see him and say goodbye, would it still have hurt so much? Could I have begun to form that yawning void within me in advance so my descent into it wasn't so sudden?

He left and the next time we saw him…he didn't have his sickle. His face had been stolen by a monster.

Screaming fills my ears.

But this screaming is not in my memory of the day Father left. Mother hears it too. She jumps up from her seat, sprinting to the window, ignoring her earlier warning.

"Do you see anything?" she whispers.

"No." I try and shake the ghosts of the past.

"It sounded close…"

"It did." I tighten my grip on the sickles. If the vampires are here, it means the vanguard fell. It means Drew is—I can't even think it. Because something in me tells me he's not dead. *My brother lives*. It's foolish optimism, nothing more. And yet I'm so sure I would know deep within if he died. "Go upstairs."

"Flor—"

"Mother, please," I say, quiet and firm, locking my eyes with hers. I've never ordered her to do anything. Perhaps it's Drew's confidence in me—the one thing he asked of me, to protect her—that gives me the strength to be stern. "Go upstairs and hide."

"If there is a vampire, they will find me even if I'm hiding."

"That's why we have the salt. And I will not let the monster come even that close." I shake my head. "Isn't this what you got this armor for? Isn't that why you let Drew train me in secret? To protect you?"

Her hands fall on my shoulders, and she shakes me lightly. "To protect *yourself*."

"I can do both, if you let me." Drew as well, *I can protect him also*, at least that's what my heart says. I know better logically. There's no way that I could help him now. And yet, as the screams begin to grow closer and closer, I know with more and more certainty that he needs me. Things have gone terribly wrong. The Blood Moon is hungry and we are the prey. "Go upstairs and hide, salt the threshold of your door, don't make a sound, and don't come out till morning, no matter what happens."

Her eyes are shining; her mouth purses. She wants to fight me. I know she does. But she won't.

Because this is who we are.

This is who we've always been.

Everyone in Hunter's Hamlet has one foot in the grave and one hand on a silver weapon. We don't go down without a fight. We are the only thing standing between our world and the vampires that would consume it.

"Be safe. Don't make any rash choices," she whispers and pulls me in for a tight embrace. "I will see you in the morning."

"I'm just going to guard the door." I don't know why it sounds like a lie. That's all I should be doing; all I can be. And yet my heart is racing. My feet are antsy to do so as well. "I'll see you in the morning." I pat her back and she pulls away.

Mother takes the bucket of salt and leaves.

I am alone with my worries and distant screams. I rest my hands on the hilts of the sickles and go to twist them out of their hooks. Movement makes my hands go slack with shock. I almost fumble my weapons, quickly recovering before they can clatter to the ground.

A lone shadow cuts through the night. *Not human,* I can tell that much by its movements. It's too fast, too fluid, yet somehow frantic and irregular. The monster comes to a halt and it swings its haunted eyes from left to right. They're completely black orbs, only the smallest fleck of gold at their center. Teeth line its gaping maw—pointed and deadly. With one bite it can carve out the throats of its victims and engorge itself on blood.

Judging from the explosion of crimson down its front, it already has. It hasn't even bothered stealing the faces of its prey. It knows it doesn't need to tonight.

Slowly, I reach into my pocket and retrieve the obsidian vial that's there. Hunter's Elixir. A powerful, ancient draught to grant strength and speed equal to that of the vampires so that we might go toe-to-toe with them. But it's so potent that it's forbidden for any but the hunters to consume because of the hunter's madness—a state of frenzy that old hunters descend into.

Drew said it would be all right.

I look back to the vampire. It stalks across the street to another doorway while sniffing the air. Its brow brushes against the low-hanging bells. They chime softly, but it does not flee at the sound. Panic and doubt make fast friends in my heart. Were the hunters wrong? Will the bells or salt help at all?

Flicking open the vial, I look at the meager few drops of liquid within. Even in the red moonlight it's black as pitch. I inhale its unique scent as I bring it to trembling lips. My whole body aches; an urge I've never known wrests itself from the depths of my being at the aroma alone. It is as if I've been waiting for this freedom, this power to make my own destiny, my whole life and have never known it.

I drink.

The thick, clotted liquid goes down as one lump. It slips down all the way into me, lining my throat, falling into my stomach like a lit bottle of liquor smashing against the ground. Fire erupts within and I fall to my knees.

Images flash before my eyes. Of the fortress. Of eyes as bright as sunlight. Of starlight and mountain cities only drawn in picture books. They are gone in a blink.

More, my muscles scream. The burdens and pains and aches of reality drift away to nothingness. *Give it to me*. Rush through my veins and turn me into a hunter. *Transform me into someone who can protect all that I love. Everything I've ever known. Make me strong enough to defy all that everyone thought I could be, if only for one night.*

I push myself away from the ground, trying to keep from doubling over and throwing up the gift of strength that Drew has given me. The world blurs, vibrating, faster and faster until everything is illegible. Air has never tasted so sweet, so sharp. I have never smelled so keenly—the night's dew, the charcoal in the forge, the tiniest amount of residue of last night's dinner in the cooking pot, I can smell it all. Feel it all. The world is suddenly more than it has ever been and I am ready to take it all.

The door slams open. The whole earth quakes.

Moonlight hangs over the vampire's shoulders like a bloody halo. The creature hisses softly through its elongated teeth.

"Die," I snarl. My voice does not sound like my own. It is deeper, tinged with a hunger that is gnawing my insides. *More*, the elixir urges, *give me more. Give me power and give me blood. Finally bring an end to the long night.*

I leap, becoming a whisper of death on the wind.

four

The vampire lets out a primal screech and reaches with its claws. I dodge from the monster's grasp. Its movements seem to be slower and more telegraphed than they previously appeared. Though it's still fluid and silent, it seems to move only on instinct. It's nothing like my brother and the disciplined steps of someone trained in combat. I see every strike before it comes.

The vampire tips forward when I'm not where it expected me to be and I sidestep around while it's off-balance. In one motion, and with a firm grip, I hook my sickle between its ribs and pull, unbuttoning its chest with sickening plops of black and grayish innards. The vampire lets out a cry and writhes as the silver purifies its mottled blood. Life leaves its body. The sensation is more than it going limp over my blade. It is a distinct awareness of existence suddenly vanishing—a void where there was once *something*.

I free the sickle with a jerk, unable to bear its weight, panting softly. *I did it. I actually did it*. My hands tremble. A few steps and it was over. I moved just as Drew told me. He'll be so proud. If he believes me. I'll have to tell him first thing when—

A scream reverberates through the air from far, far away.

The sound is different from all the others I've heard, all the others I *shouldn't* be able to hear. The sounds of battle, near and far, reverberate in my ears. There are distant shouts and cries, orders given from one desperate hunter to another. It is as though, with the elixir flowing through me, the whole world has opened up to my senses to an almost unbearable degree. Hunter's Hamlet is a din of noise, hammering heartbeats and frantic commands. I can smell the blood spilled on distant battlefields. Every sensation is lit up on my senses, fear and panic of all humanity thrumming against mine on this forsaken night of sinister, red moonlight.

I try and shut it all out until the scream cuts above it all again with its low resonance. I've never heard it before. And I hoped I never would.

It's Drew.

I know so in my very soul. My brother is in danger. I glance back toward the stairs.

"Forgive me," I whisper to Mother, even though she can't hear. I don't know if she would tell me to stay or go. But this is my brother and I'm not going to let him die alone in the Fade Marshes. Not when I have all this unbridled power.

I dash into the night.

An invisible tether yanks on my navel, as though I am being pulled toward something—*someone*—in the distance. It guides me down the main road and out of town. Hunters and monstrous vampires fight in the field. The night is stained crimson with moonlight and blood. I keep running.

I'm faster than any man or monster. None pay me any mind. Or, if they do, they're gone in a blur.

The sensation of damp earth under my feet mingles with the crispness of the night air in my lungs. I feel like I've made this run before, even though I know I never have. As the forge maiden, I am hardly permitted on the edge of town. Entering the Fade Marshes is strictly forbidden.

The farmers' fields stop abruptly at another wall. This is the true end of Hunter's Hamlet, and the beginning of the war front. The road continues, cutting through barren earth—the land has been burned and salted over the years to ward against the vampire.

Little good it's done.

The ground around the road becomes sodden. Skeletal trees reach up through wetlands, hazy silhouettes in the fading light. The mists curl across the water, wisps released from the barrier of fog that extends to the hunter's wall in either direction behind an ancient stone archway.

At the top of the arch is the symbol of a diamond with a V shape arcing underneath it, two crescent moons reflected on either side. Drew has drawn me this shape before and called it the mark of the vampire—a warning built by our forefathers at the edges of their land. The Fade Marshes embrace me with their misty arms as I pass beneath the archway.

I am in their land now and the only thing offering me calm is the elixir racing through my veins.

A long, winding, stone road snakes through rotted trees and dark waters. I am a streak through the fog. I run faster than I thought possible, moving on the undercurrents of wind.

I quickly discover that the fog plays tricks on the eyes. More than once, my gaze is pulled in a direction as I think I see movement. But when I examine closely, there is nothing there. I blink several times, willing my sight to sharpen. I will not allow myself to be distracted by a trick of the light.

There's another grunt. A wheeze. My ears are trained on the strained sounds of my brother. *Hang in there*, I beg with every panting breath. I can feel the vampire all around me—around him—disrupting the balance of our world.

The fog suddenly parts and I emerge onto a large, circular platform. It looks like the remnants of some great tower. Crumbling walls prevent the marshes from overflowing and claiming the worn stones. Whatever urge pulled me through the night snaps the moment my eyes land on the carnage.

Davos, master hunter…is dead.

His body is mutilated. A deep gash has nearly cut straight through his neck. His eyes are wide and soulless. Blood pools around him, meaning the vampire did not drain him. As if his death was for sport.

My nostrils flare at the scent of blood. Overwhelming, almost to the point of unbearable. More images of golden eyes and mottled flesh assault me. I shake my head, trying to banish them, to focus on the here and now. I will not allow the hunter's madness to claim me.

A trail of red splatter leads me to two others.

Drew has been beaten badly. He hangs limply, supported by the steel claws that are gouged through his shoulder, pinning him to the wall of the ruins. His black hair, the same as mine, as Mother's, has fallen around his face in wet clumps as his chin hangs toward his chest.

The vampire that has him pinned is like nothing I have ever heard of or seen before, not even in my darkest nightmares.

Unlike the other monsters, who roam in tattered clothing, he dons plate of polished iron. Every intricate fold has been hammered with more care than the tailoring of the finest Yule ball dress.

The plate is trimmed in gold; woven strands cover the armor in shapes I do not recognize but I appreciate the immense skill it would take to create despite myself—I've never had the resources available to make anything half as fine. The vampire has plumes of raven's feathers, oil-slicked and gleaming in the red moonlight, jutting like horns on either side of his helmet—I wonder if they are trophies off the hunters his scouts have killed for him. Hunters wear feathers of the raven of the master hunter for luck; the stolen tokens churn my stomach. A crimson cape, also trimmed in gold, drifts through the air behind him. Unseen hands reach from the mist, pulling at its hem, fraying it slightly, as though something is trying to pull him back to the world from whence he came.

I grasp my sickle tighter. I think the only thing keeping my grip steady is the elixir in me.

"If *he* was not the anchor, are you? Tell me where it is. *Tell me how to break it.*" The voice is like plunging hot metal into water. Surely it cannot be from the creature before me… That voice…that primordial *sound* seems to have come from everywhere at once. It was not spoken so much as willed into existence. The words enter through my ears and curl in my mind like a serpent making my skull its new den. I can almost feel it—feel his raw power—sliding against the backs of all my innermost thoughts.

The vampire leans closer to Drew. His collar has been ripped off. The monster is going to kill him. I imagine the vampire drinking my brother's blood and taking his face. I will not be able to slay the beast if he wears Drew's skin.

"Let him go!" I shout, pulling the attention onto me before the vampire can act.

Drew jerks at the sound of my voice but he does not raise his head. He's lost too much blood for that. Through our bond as twins, or the elixir, I can feel he's alive, but only barely.

A huff of air. Amusement. The vampire lets out a low chuckle that sounds more like the distant roar of some beast, long forgotten, prowling the wetlands. "Another hunter come to avenge her fallen friends?"

So that voice truly was the vampire? They're capable of speech? I've never heard of such a thing before. If it can talk, does that mean it's capable of reason? And if it does have the capacity for higher thought then…then that means…

Everything has been a choice.

They do not hunt us as beasts. They hunt us because they have *chosen* to. Because they see us as nothing more than sport. I clutch my sickle tighter and don't ask for the creature to free my brother a second time. There are only two things a creature like him knows—bloodshed and death. And I will give them to him.

"I am your quarry now!" I close the gap between me and the vampire, jumping. He tries to turn, but he's too slow. The steel gauntlet covering his clawed hands is embedded too deeply in the stone. I wedge one sickle into the visor of his helmet and yank.

Steel meets iron with a clamor. His helmet flies, my sickle going with it. He staggers and I am thrown off-balance. I dig the tip of my other sickle into the stone, using it to pivot around, finding my feet. I tuck them under me, freeing the weapon with a twist. I might not have trained with the hunters, but Drew taught me the skills Davos passed on to him. And by day I was honing my body by hoisting coal, hammer, iron, and silver.

The vampire spins and, as I meet the hollow eyes of the monster, I remember too late what Drew told me:

Tomorrow, the vampire lord himself will lead his legions through the Fade… I will kill him.

This creature of nightmare and pure evil…he is the source of all our pain. He can speak because he is the mind of the vampire. It is because of him the people of Hunter's Hamlet have fought and bled. It is because of him we are walled in, struggling to survive for the sake of the world beyond.

Because of him, my father is dead and my brother is dying.

His eyes are sunken against his cheeks. Folds of flesh sag underneath, leathered with an age that must be ancient. A deeply furrowed brow hunches over them, carving wrinkles between. What would be white in a human's eyes is black for him, making the deep recesses they sit in on his face all the more pronounced. At their center is a gleaming yellow iris, like a wolf's eyes caught in the lamplight of a dark night.

His nose is hooked and sharp, as though it is made of wax and was pressed too close to the inside of his helmet. His skin is sagging and gray, lifeless and worn. Two yellowed fangs protrude from his slightly parted lips as he gasps for air.

The lord of the vampires is a walking corpse, embellished with every frightful story passed down in Hunter's Hamlet.

Monster. Yes. The word suits him. He is every nightmare and more. He is the wind that raked against my window as a girl. He is the shadow that lingered too long in the corner of my room. He is what I feared beneath my bed. What stalked me in my nightmares into my adult years.

The vampire lord freezes as he looks upon me. His haunted eyes widen slightly, shining ominously in the bloody moonlight. Those hungry eyes study me, as if already consuming my soul.

"What *are* you?" he rasps.

What am I? A strange question coming from a beast like him. I smile wildly. "I am your death."

five

I SWING THE SICKLE UP AND TOWARD THOSE HAUNTED, HORRIBLE EYES. One jab is all it would take to end this. My strike nearly connects with sagging flesh when the vampire collapses into nothing more than mist. I fall through the dissipating shadows, bracing myself.

There's a whisper of movement. I can feel his essence re-condensing with a whorl of shadow and blood magic. Mist gathers and the vampire lord emerges.

"You are an abomination," he snarls.

I say nothing in reply, lunging forward to close the gap. The vampire dissolves again. My senses tingle and the hair on my right arm raises. The vampire lord materializing feels like the air right before a lightning strike. Shadowy haze collects and his red cape billows around him as he reappears.

He grabs for me and I drop to a crouch. I twist the sickle in my hand, rotating it so that I can stab with a pull. I try for the small space behind his knee. The chainmail should end at his hips. Greaves end just below the knee. I know enough about making armor to know there should be a vulnerability here—my blade sinks in but doesn't find flesh before he reaches for me.

I abandon my sickle, still wedged in his armor, to grab him by the shoulder and use his awkward positioning against him. We tumble on the cobblestone. My nails crack as I rip up a rock to smash against the lord's temple. He reels back.

I scramble for my weapon, but am too late. A plate-covered

greave steps on it and kicks it back, sliding the sickle into the muck of the swamp. I go to grab for my other sickle as the vampire lord reaches down for me, hand wide. He's going for my neck. I twist away. Our eyes lock once more. Breathless.

"They have made you a monster." Disapproval—*hatred* bleeds into his words. An emotion we share.

"If I must be a monster to kill one then so it shall be!" I leap up.

He's faster. Angry black mist follows his movements and when he stops before me it radiates off of him, enveloping my face with unseen hands. The lord grabs me by the throat, slamming me into one of the crumbling walls. I grab with my outside arm for his hand, gripping over his thumb. In a swift movement, I've peeled his hand away.

Usually I would bring my knee to his stomach, but it would do little against his plate. Falling, off-balance again, we grapple, rolling across the ground. I swing for him, but he disarms me once more.

Blow for blow, we match each other. One strike after the next, neither of us can seem to land much more than grazing hits. My knuckles meet the hard cobblestone, cracking and splitting as he dodges a punch, rolling me off of him and pinning me down with both hands.

The gnarled, living corpse of the vampire lord hangs over me. The bright red moon frames his haunted face as he stares down with those burning, unnatural eyes—all black save for the bright, yellow irises.

"You're a truly tenacious beast," he growls, the words spoken around those razor-sharp fangs. His mouth is not like a normal vampire's. Most of his teeth are humanlike. Only his canines are elongated.

My mind races as I try to think of a way to escape his hold. The time is drawing near. I can feel it. He will take me into his arms and will drink from me until I am dry. Then, he will use my face to infiltrate Hunter's Hamlet.

Mother, forgive me. I don't even have a collar to stop it.

"But, damn it all, Callos was right. You will serve for what we need," he proclaims.

Before I can process what he's said, mist envelops us.

I inhale and choke, sputtering, coughing. It tears at my lungs, rips through my veins and threatens to explode out my flesh. I am undone and remade in a blink.

We are no longer in the ruins, but back on the main road of the marsh. *Are we closer to or farther from town?* I barely have time to wonder before I am ripped apart again. My ears pop, the night collapses on me, condensed by magic. I am nothing more than a thought in a void.

Red light once more. We're elsewhere again. We stand on the crest of a foothill, the fogs of the marshes thinning. It swirls around us like an ocean. We must be at the highest point in the Fade Marshes. Far, far in the distance is a lonely point of light. It is Hunter's Hamlet, made small by how far we are. Everything I've ever known, every comfort I've ever had or scrap of hope I could even dream of, is being swept away as I'm pulled farther and farther by this monster.

Yet again, just as I catch my bearings, we move. I grit my teeth to keep myself from letting out a shout. Every time he drags me through space with him is more painful than the last. Every time I am more winded. Living magic surrounds me, an endless tunnel of night. We pass by faintly glowing stone markers that look like a graveyard before it all becomes too much.

I press my eyes closed. The air shifts and I inhale sharply. The lord glances back as we materialize at the foot of a mountain I have never seen.

Where are mountains? I have never heard any of the hunters speak of mountains. I spin, looking behind me. A splintered coast dots a tempest sea. Waves crash foam against jagged rocks that dot between islands like stepping stones. Ocean spray mingles with the low clouds that carve against the horizon, blocking everything beyond from view.

I'm at the sea. Finally, at long last…and it's because of this monster.

A lonely, crumbling bridge stretches across the waters, suspended on those islands, connecting the wall of magic smoke to a heavy portcullis blocking the tunnel before me.

The walls of Hunter's Hamlet extend toward the sea to keep the vampires in their lands. Seeing this ocean has only ever been a dream—now turned into a nightmare. I look back up to the mountain, outlined by a crimson moon that hangs low.

"We're not far now," he murmurs, almost reassuringly. The tone is a jarring contrast to the monster I have been fighting.

Not far from what? I'm reeling. It doesn't matter where I am. I have to—

I'm plunged into darkness once more and ripped through time and space by the vampire lord's magic, pulled along at his side, kidnapped. Yanked deeper into what I know with certainty, despite all odds, is the land of the vampire.

The world rematerializes and frigid wind rips through me as we stand in almost knee-deep snow on a mountain ledge. *Snow, in summer*. We only spend a second before moving again. Every step the vampire takes feels longer than the last, the darkness more permanent. My muscles scream with an agony I have never known.

Will he pull me to the edge of the world just so that he can push me off of it? I must escape. The next time we blink back into existence I yank myself from his grasp. The vampire lord lets out a startled grunt as he spins to face me. We are higher still up the mountain. My feet are instantly numb and slide on the ice hidden beneath the layers of thick snow.

He reaches for me, and I dodge out of his grasp. The elixir is still in my veins, numbing what must surely be excruciating pain. Keeping me sharp. The lord purses his lips, eyes shining with anger as I reach for an icicle hanging off a nearby ledge. My skin burns at the brutal cold, fusing to the ice as I yank it off.

The lord arches a pale brow at me. "Do you think you can kill me with that?"

I stand my ground wordlessly. My weapons are long gone. He has taken me to an arena of his choosing and I have no other options. But I am *not* going down without a fight.

"You couldn't kill me when armed with two of your precious silver sickles. What do you honestly think you could do with that?"

I hold up the icicle in a silent threat.

"I'll grant you that with the blood lore, you're strong. Tenacious, certainly. But you clearly are not quick-witted." Let him think what he wants; all I need is for him to take just a few more steps. I brandish the icicle a little higher. "Let's say you actually do manage to kill me, *hmm*? What then? Where will you go? You can't escape this place without my help. I am going to present to you a unique opportunity, stop threatening—"

The lord moves to rip the icicle from my grasp. I pull it toward me instead and, thanks to the elixir, I have the strength to pull him along with it. I wrap my arms quickly around his armored shoulders and tighten the muscles in my lower back. I hoist him like a massive bag of coal. We tip backward, and I push off with both legs, using every last bit of my strength.

My teeth rake against the shell of his ear as I snarl, "I wasn't trying to escape." The wind howls around us, nearly stealing my words. There is no coming back for me now. If it's not the madness of the elixir that gets me, I will certainly die at the hands of the vampire lord. And if I somehow manage to kill him, his legions will take me. There's no way out for me now, not when we've come this far. "If I'm going to die, I'm bringing you with me!"

We fall into the open air. My arms are around him, holding him as tightly as possible. The moon spins overhead. The air screams in my ears.

With a clamor of steel and flesh, we meet unyielding stone.

six

All the wind is knocked from me. Stars explode in my eyes as my head cracks against the hard ground. A splitting headache rips through my skull instantly, threatening to make me retch. The weight of the vampire lord is atop me, the sound of his mail ringing in my ears. It's too much; my senses revolt.

Luckily Drew and I grappled constantly from a young age. Even before he became a hunter. Instinct kicks in.

I bend my knee to get leverage and twist the vampire off of me, releasing my grip on him. The movement sends me over the edge. My stomach clenches around my ribs, upturning its contents, as though that would expunge the pain from my mind at the same time. My bile is as black as the elixir I drank and I wonder if I just expelled the only thing keeping me alive.

Everything begins to hurt. A pain beyond any I've ever known. My muscles tremble with weakness as exhaustion descends upon me.

I won't... I can't... This monster…

I think of him pinning Drew against the wall. I imagine my brother bleeding, dying on the ground, deep in the Fade Marshes where no one will find him. I'm no healer. But I know a bad wound when I see one. His life was fading and this monster took me from my brother in his final moments. The rage is almost enough to numb the pain.

"You…" A dark chuckle cuts through the air. "They have certainly made you a wicked beast." The vampire lord lets out a groan. Plate clanks. He's on his feet.

I push myself off the ground to match, nothing other than hate and fear propelling me. The world spins, finally settling into another unfamiliar place. He must have moved us as we fell. *Damn it all.* He can even use his magic mid-fall.

We're at the back of a room that reminds me of the great hall of the fortress that Drew described for me after joining the hunters. Threadbare tapestries and fans of swords adorn walls of stone. Two long tables stretch parallel out from a hearth larger than that of our forge. A smaller table is perpendicular to them, before the dark fireplace.

"You thought you could kill me?" the vampire lord seethes, spinning to face me. His red cape looks more tattered than before. Armor dented. If I'm right about how the armor is forged, then I might be able to make some joints lock up with a well-placed strike or two and severely limit his mobility.

Rather than responding, I dash off to the side toward one of the racks of ornate weapons. Their blunt edges weren't meant for anything more than decoration, but a dull sword is better than no sword. My fingers close around the steel hilt just as he moves right behind me. The vampire lord catches my wrist, yanking me away. He hoists me in the air by my arm. My shoulder pops and the quick jerking motion threatens to make me sick again.

"You can't kill me with that. You know you can't," he snarls, leaning in with his horrifying face. "Enough resisting."

I try to jerk my arm free. He drops me and I'm back to holding in sick. My muscles are beginning to strain with the effort to just keep me upright. I definitely think the retching removed the last of the elixir I so desperately needed.

The vampire lord looks down on me. "If I wanted you dead, you would be, you know."

"If you were smart I'd already be dead," I growl, baring my teeth at him.

His lips curl back in reply, revealing the two sharp fangs I saw earlier. "You don't even want to know why I have yet to take your life? You're not even curious?"

"To serve you." The words taste fouler than the elixir the second time around.

"There are those who would be honored by a chance to serve me."

"I'll never serve a monster." And if he thinks different then I must reevaluate my opinions of his intellect.

"Ah, yes, *I* am the monster, when you are the one who has been transformed into a test subject."

I ignore his words—the lies he spins for distraction—instead lunging for the sword once more. Yet again, he's faster, already behind me. My strength is waning but I kick and squirm against the viselike hold he has around my middle anyway. I claw and push at his arms, but it does little good against his gauntlets. My arms are pinned to my sides and it's hard to get leverage.

"Would you listen to—"

I hang forward, brace myself for the agony this will be, and rear back. The back of my head slams against his nose and he drops me out of pain or shock. I fall to the ground, trying for the sword again, but the soft spot at the back of my skull is ringing. I slump against one of the tables, falling unceremoniously into a bench.

If you're ever face-to-face with a vampire, fight! I can hear Drew's voice in the back of my mind. *Fight with everything you have. Fight like your life depends on it.*

"But what if I can't?" I'm not sure if I say the words or if I just think them loudly. My eyes are burning. Everything hurts. Drew was the hunter, not me. How am I the one who ended up here? This is why everyone in Hunter's Hamlet is taught to never question their place. The elixir is gone and my old doubts rise to fill its place.

If you can't kill it, take the bloody monster down with you. That was what Drew told me. That was how he lived. I can't let him down. I can't. Won't. I push myself up, stumbling for the weapons once more as though they are my only lifeline.

For once, the vampire lord does not lunge for me. Even though my movements are sluggish and clumsy. I pry a sword from the wall and its tip falls to the floor with a deafening clang, nearly falling from my grasp. My muscles are giving up. I feel worse than when I've been smithing for days on end with little rest.

"Enough of this," the vampire lord says. His voice has softened. I draw up my eyes. Blood, nearly black, streams from his nose. It mingles with the crimson of my own blood. He licks his lips and his gold eyes seem to shine slightly brighter. "You are in no condition to fight me and you're throwing the life away that I've so generously allowed you to keep by trying."

With a grunt I hold up the sword. The muscles in my back scream. The weapon trembles in the air.

"I will not…die…without taking you with me," I manage to say.

"Why do you defend the people who have committed such horrors against you?"

I grip the sword with both hands as my only reply. I will not heed the words of a monster. Of the source of all my hardships.

He sighs and steps backward toward a tapestry hanging on the wall. The vampire lord grabs it, ripping it from the stretcher bar. The tapestry frays half to dust as he pulls, exposing a mirror. The reflection catches my eyes and I can't look away.

He is not the monster that is before me, but a normal man of flesh and blood. From what I can see of his cheek, his skin is not wrinkled and sagging, but taut against his angled jaw and rounded cheekbones. Hair that I see as greasy, clumped, and matted hangs around the back of his head in loose waves in his reflection.

I wonder how his face might look but all wondering ceases when I catch sight of what should be me.

"What trickery is this?" I whisper. The monster that stares back at me moves her mouth in time with mine. But I cannot make sense of her. The woman has dusky, bloodshot eyes with irises ringed in gold. Dark purple veins bulge from paper-thin skin that is sunken against the bones of her face.

She looks…*I* look…*almost like one of them.*

"What is this?" I repeat, louder. A sickness that has nothing to do with my throbbing head is rising in me.

"The truth of what you are becoming."

"You lie!" I scream and raise the sword higher.

"That is why I have brought you here. The hunters are turning you into one of us—more or less—so that you might be able to stand a chance at killing us."

"I am *not* one of you and I will never be." *The elixir.* This must be some function of it. A side effect, perhaps. But Drew would've warned me.

Unless he didn't know this could happen. Hunters only drink when they're out in the marshes on the hunt and their masks are on. Perhaps he had no idea. Or perhaps this is happening because I am not a true hunter. I wasn't meant to take the elixir and somehow the draught knew.

The vampire lord continues as though I said nothing. "They have knowledge that should not exist and with it—"

"Lord Ruvan!" a man's voice cuts through the air. I glance from the corner of my eye, not daring to take my attention off the lord for more than a second. Sure enough, there is another yellow-eyed vampire standing in an archway.

Yet, he too is different from the other vampires I've encountered. And not just because, like Ruvan, he is also capable of speech. This new vampire doesn't wear any kind of plate or leathers, nor is he in tattered clothes like the vampires that attack during regular full moons. Steel has been replaced by velvet of the same shade as the lord's cape. Ruffles extend from the thick cuffs of his sleeves, accented by highly polished brass buttons. He would seem well put together, were it not for his leathered skin and sunken eyes. The vampire looks just like Ruvan does—a dressed-up corpse.

His eyes dart from the vampire lord to myself and back.

The vampire lord gathers himself and commands, "Quinn, take our guest to the western tower, if it's still clear. She is weary from the journey here and is in no condition to converse meaningfully. I will wait until she has a better head about her."

"Our *guest*?" Quinn echoes my sentiment. Perhaps the only time I'll ever find myself agreeing with a vampire.

"Our guest," Ruvan repeats, more firmly than the last. "See her attended to. She needs mending. We're going to need her."

Need me? I imagine them strapping me against a table of torture, plunging their fangs into me. I can almost feel the ghost of the vampire lord's tongue running up my breast, my collar, my neck. I shudder.

"Yes, my lord." Quinn bows and turns toward me. I see his movements from my periphery and feel his attention. But my focus remains solely on the vampire lord. The sword I'm clutching with both hands continues to waver in the air, threatening to fall at any moment. "If you would please?"

I don't move. Lord Ruvan levels his eyes with mine. I can feel as much as hear the silent invitation. *Kill me, if you can. If you dare.*

My grip tightens on the sword and I shift my weight slightly. I assess my balance and remaining strength. I'm strong enough. I refuse to believe anything else.

All those years training in secret. Everything Drew and Mother risked to try and keep me safe. The foolish decision I made in engaging in the Blood Moon hunt even though it was forbidden for me to.

If I am going to die, I must take the vampire lord with me. Killing him might have been Drew's destiny, but it is a job my brother was not able to finish, a mantle I will assume for him. All of Hunter's Hamlet is depending on me in this moment.

Why can't I *be enough?* I've tried so hard. I've come so close. But it's not enough…the vampire lord still breathes.

I'm going to be sick again. Blood drips off my shattered, tightening knuckles. It runs down my back. I am held together with little more than hatred and a need for vengeance.

One life.

All I have to do is take one life.

The vampire lord standing before me is the source of all our pain. All the anguish. Without him the Hunter's Hamlet would be free of its obligations, its walls. My family would be whole. Drew and I would've gone to the sea long, long ago. How can one man be the source of so much despair and hope? How can one man be so hard to kill?

I fray and begin to rip. Seams I didn't know were holding me together buckle and come undone; I explode with pain I've been ignoring my whole life. Fury I've never allowed myself to feel dredges up from a forgotten place deep within me and erupts with violent force. My father's death. My brother leaving. Every longing glance I never let anyone else see because I was not permitted a moment of happiness that a normal person would have. Years of pent-up hurt smooths over the breaks in my flesh and ache in my muscles. This anger gives my feet speed.

The world blurs and I charge toward the vampire lord. I shift my weight, putting one foot forward, rearing back with my arms. I swing the blade with all my might, bringing it down like a forge hammer in an arc of hope.

He doesn't even flinch. The lord lifts a hand and catches the sword easily by the blade. It's so dull that the steel can't even penetrate the leather of his gauntlet. Ruvan heaves a monumental sigh.

"The hard way, then."

He rips the sword from my grasp and swings it through the air. The strength that filled me is evaporating. I don't have time to dodge before the pommel meets my temple.

The world goes black.

seven

HAZY TWILIGHT MUTES THE CRIMSON OF BLOODSTAINED SHEETS.

Tunnel vision. Slowly blinking. Filtered scenes of the withered visages of vampires hovering above me. Their haunting eyes shining as they speak. Inspecting my battered body. I can almost see myself through their gaze.

Shattered, pitiable thing. Pathetic. The words start out in the deep resonance of the vampire lord, but evolve into my own. I was not strong enough.

I was a forge maiden. Not a fighter. I wasn't supposed to have even been here. That was made clear in the end. A true fighter would've been able to end it.

What had I been thinking? With a vial and a drink, I stepped into Drew's shoes and assumed the obligation of killing the vampire lord.

Where is my brother now? Does he live? Something in me says he does…but I worry I can't trust that hopeful, foolish corner of my heart. I have to fight, for him. But want is not enough. My will has severed from my body, leaving me like a puppet whose strings have been cut. The elixir took all I had and then some. I cannot move any longer.

Darkness once more.

A man with long, silvery hair sits at my bedside. "You pushed yourself too hard," he says, sounding somewhat exasperated.

I did? *I want to say. But instead, "I know" slips from my lips with an almost coy sigh.*

He leans forward and I can see his face clearer than anything else. I feel like I've seen it before, many times. And yet I would remember a face as handsome as this. I would remember a man who smells of evergreen with eyes like sunlight.

"What am I going to do with you?"

"Love me forever?" My mouth moves on its own.

"Careful, or I just might."

I drift through not-quite consciousness, odd, fleeting dreams, and heavy, smothering nothingness. My mind retreats to a place very far, and very detached, from my body. I have been in this dark, internal nightmare before. This is the same void I went to when Davos killed the vampire that stole my father's face, exposing the horrific truth underneath.

I lived here while I drowned in that pain. The pain of knowing Father was gone. That nothing more could be done for him or my family. But that maybe…maybe if I had been old and strong enough to forge him a sharper sickle…if I had not wanted him to be home for so many dinners that he skipped training…maybe he would still be with me…

How did I get out of this pit of despair, then? How did I find the strength to move during those days of endless grief?

Ah, that's right… I smothered everything. Thoughts. Feelings. Unnecessary and dangerous. Instead, I worked. I hammered until my hands were raw. That's what I must do again. I must smother the pain. I must pound the frustration from my bones. If I feel nothing and treasure nothing, then I cannot be hurt. I will be immune to their blows. Once I do, my mind will be clearer.

I can get back to work.

But what can I work on?

Work. Endless. Always much to be done. But we're close.

A woman walking through darkened halls. Passing through like a ghost: present, felt, but unseen. Arms laden with three journals. A raven-haired man is on one side of her, a golden-eyed man on the other.

"We must tell them," the raven-haired man says.

"They won't accept it. Not yet," the other man objects.

"Perhaps in time," she says.

But, for now, I work...

I have no duty here. No job. The smithy is far…so far. I cannot feel its warmth. Hunter's Hamlet. Mother. Drew… What can I do for you now?

Please tell me what to do.

More strings cut from within. My tethers are fraying. I am adrift in too many thoughts—all different, all overwhelming. These emotions will smother me beneath them until I cannot breathe. Until there is nothing more than darkness…and failure.

Cool rivulets flow down my hot face. Hot with shame, or fever? I don't know. Delirium has set in on me. There are hands tending my wounds, strong and sure, numbing the pain almost to the point of being bearable. There's more talking, more of that deep voice that threatens to tear me apart. More of the silver-haired man in my dreams.

What do they want with me?

With the right ritual, I can help him, help all of them. The cost needn't be so high.

We can do this without unnecessary bloodshed.

Since when are we on opposite sides, brother?

My eyes finally open and stay open. A bedroom comes into focus.

There's a heavy velvet canopy in an already familiar crimson shade overhead. The curtains are pulled back and tied around the four posts that support them. A thick duvet covers me, yet my body still trembles. I am the forge in winter—cold and hot at the same time. Fevered, likely.

Pushing myself into a seated position hurts far less than I would've expected. I reach behind my head and my fingertips brush against bandages. My skull is still tender but it's been tended to. The monsters have tried to heal me.

Why? Because they need my blood fresh? Drew would know. And the thought nearly makes me sick. My brother would know what to do. He wouldn't have even allowed himself to end up in this position. He would've killed the vampire lord.

We changed destinies with the hand-off of a vial, and now we will both suffer for it. Drew might have already paid the ultimate price. My chest squeezes, my heart skips a beat. *No*, it seems to say.

"You're healing as well as can be expected."

I jerk toward the source of the sound, instantly regretting the quick movement as it takes my vision a second to catch up and nearly turns over my stomach. The vampire lord stands before a single window. It's larger than any single piece of glass I've ever seen and yet it somehow still seems small in the vastness of this lonely room.

"We've done what we could for you." The vampire turns to face me, silhouetted by pale, normal moonlight streaming through the open window. A regular moon. That means it's no longer the night of the Blood Moon. How much time has passed? The moon's still large—perhaps only a day? Two? I hope no more. "But taking a human through the Fade is a dangerous and forbidden endeavor under normal circumstances. Doing so when that human insists on wounding herself speeds up the natural decay."

As he speaks, I scan the room. There's precious little. One table at my side of the bed—empty. A bookcase surrounds a hearth opposite the foot of the bed that holds cobwebs instead of paper and leather. Other than the symbol of the vampire etched into the stone of the hearth, this place is a void. Soulless.

"There's nothing in here you could use to attack me," he says.

"I wasn't—"

"Spare me." He rolls his eyes. "I have records detailing how you hunters are trained. You can turn anything into a weapon." He motions to the small, empty hearth flanked by the bookcases. "I even had the fireplace tools removed."

I swallow thickly. He still thinks I'm a hunter. That means…maybe he fears me? I try and summon all the bravery I ever witnessed in my brother.

"What do you want with me?" My words are even and level.

"I want to speak with you."

"What makes you assume I want to speak with you?" I dare to say, even though my insides are liquefying still at the mere sight of him. Without the elixir I am helpless before him.

"Do you have something better to do?" There's a glimmer of amusement in his bright eyes.

"Fine, go on," I relent. He's right, I don't have a choice. He has kept me alive thus far, and provoking the lord of the vampires further seems like a poor idea when I no longer have an elixir to back up my threats.

"I will be plain and direct, as we have precious little time. You're dying," he says gravely.

I stare at my palms. I've been patched up. But my hands ache in a way they haven't in years—like the first time I was in the forge. No, worse. With every movement my fingers go numb, my hands threaten to lock up, refusing to open.

"All right," I say, finally. I'm not sure if I'm ready to fully believe him. But something does feel different in me, down to my marrow. Arguing with him might also prevent him from giving me further, precious information.

"You don't seem bothered by that."

He *almost* sounds like he cares. What does the monster who's hunted me and my kin care about my feelings toward death? He doesn't. It must be a trick to lull me into a false sense of security.

"I imagine it's hard for you to relate to the emotions that surround one's own mortality." Hatred seeps into my voice.

"You don't think I know of mortality?" He raises his brow, haunted eyes shining.

"The eternal vampire lord?"

He snorts softly. "Eternal…if only," he murmurs and looks to the window, wrinkled and cracking lips slightly parted to display his horrific fangs. Am I to believe the vampires are not long-lived?

"Why am I still alive?" I ask pointedly. "Your kind has always been very good at killing mine."

"I'm willing to keep you alive long enough to let you leave." *That* gives me pause. "If you agree to help me."

"Help you?" I echo. "What could a vampire possibly need a human's help for?"

"*Vam-pie-err.*" He sounds out the word slowly, echoing me with a bit of a sneer. "You humans butcher our kind in name and body."

"Are you not a vampire?" I don't know why I'm asking. His nature is as apparent as his yellowed teeth, all-black eyes, and withered flesh.

"We are vampir. *Va-m-peer*." The word jumps from his lips with a flourish I've never heard before. It's softer, more rounded. As though the sound comes from the back of his throat and then fades softly off the tip of the tongue. It's a more elegant sound than I would've thought he could produce. "Vampir*e* is a human mispronunciation."

"*Ah*, but you're still life-draining monsters, regardless of name."

He's at my side faster than I can blink, looming over me. "We are not the ones who drain life," he snarls. "If you want to know who the monsters are, you should look no further than your precious hunters. You saw what they did to you."

"What *you* did to me," I insist.

He scoffs. "I met you in the state you were. You saw yourself in the mirror. Your precious hunters turned you into an experiment. If anything, what I am offering to you is a kindness by comparison."

I ignore his remarks. He's trying to confuse me—to turn me against my own. The mirror in the hall must have been tricked with vampire magic. After all, it had made his hair look silvery white, not greasy and clumped as it is.

"Forcing me to serve you is not a kindness," I say.

"You will serve me in one area alone."

However that is, I'm not sure I want to know. Yet I ask anyway, "And that is?"

He levels his eyes with mine. "Help me break the curse. Do so and I will free you."

Curse? I've never heard anything about curses. "Inventing curses is quite the elaborate way to convince me to your cause."

He scoffs. "I'm shocked you don't already know." He leans away, looking down on me. "I speak of the same curse that your hunters placed on us and that has plagued my people for centuries."

"And you think *I* can break an ancient curse?" I decide to play along with his delusions. He's keeping me alive because he thinks I might be of use to him. But if the hunters actually possessed the ability to lay a curse on the vampire, they would've done so long ago, with an affliction far worse than whatever he thinks is ailing him.

"There is a door, deep within this castle, that can only be opened by human hands. I need you to get me inside, for within is the anchor of the curse."

"Very well." I continue to pretend as if I know what he's talking about. Why would the anchor of a curse be within the vampire castle behind a door that only opens to human hands? How does he really think that, after all he's done to my people, I'd actually help him? I don't have the answers, but if I allow this ruse to continue long enough, I might find a way to kill him or free myself in the process.

"Very well?" he repeats. "You're going to help me?" He's cautious and on guard. Perhaps I should have shown more ignorance. Perhaps I should have hesitated more. I'm not made for this and am leagues out of my depth.

Drew would know what to do, my mind laments. *Drew is*— Don't even think it.

"I'm rather fond of breathing and if helping you is the only way to continue doing that then consider me your new assistant." It's partly true. Partly a brave face. I knew I was dead from the moment he took me.

"Do you think I will take you at your word?" He dips his chin slightly to look me better in the eyes. His gaze is shadowed, two gleaming orbs set on a night sky. Relaxed and outside of battle, he looks at me with the eyes of a much younger man; they're striking, even. But painfully juxtaposed on his ancient visage. They're the eyes of a man in his prime, brimming with masculine prowess trapped in the body of a walking corpse. I find myself unable to look away.

"You must want to, or you wouldn't be talking to me right now." I speak around the lump in my throat.

"I want many things I do not have," he says solemnly. The words are as heavy as stones sinking to the bottom of a well, echoing with a dull note of yearning. "But I cannot let wants cloud my judgment when the fate of my people hangs in the balance."

"Then what will you do with me? If you cannot trust me, what's the point of any of this?"

"That is something I have been debating while you slumbered and healed. And I think I have come up with a solution—solving one problem with another, as it were. I do not know if I can trust you. Rather, I know I *can't* trust you."

The feeling is mutual.

"And we return to the problem that you are dying as well." He pauses and briefly considers his next words. "How much do you know of the Fade?"

Very little, in truth. The Fade exists in the myths and legends of Hunter's Hamlet. It's as old as the fortress and even more mysterious. Drew told me stories of it, but every one seemed more impossible than the last.

"I know it stems from the first hunter—a protection to keep your kind from overrunning my world." Perhaps *that's* the "curse" of which he speaks? If it is, there's no reasonable way he could imagine I would help him undo it.

He snorts and folds his hands behind his back. The vampire lord turns, stalking to the window. "Clearly, you know nothing."

"I know enough."

"The Fade has nothing to do with our squabbles," he says.

"Then what is it?"

He glares at me. I seem to be rather good at frustrating the vampire lord. A wonderful talent, that. Which makes me all the more surprised when he answers.

"Just over three thousand years ago, there was a great war of magic. Humans were caught in the fray, unable to contend with those like the vampir. The Elf King made a treaty with the Human King. He took a bride and severed the world in two with the Fade. On one side lived the humans in what we call the Natural World. On the other side, in Midscape, lived the rest of us."

Elves. *Rest of us?* No…there's only ever been the humans and the vampires. There's not…more. My head aches, and not just from my wounds.

"It was not long after the world was split that the curse was laid." His voice becomes as sharp as a sickle. "And we have been weakened by it ever since." Ruvan's—the vampire lord's hands tighten at the small of his back. It's hard to imagine that the vampires we face are *weakened.* "But what you need to understand, from all of this, is that humans are not made for Midscape. Only the Human Queen can live in this world. All other humans from the Natural World wither and die. That is the death chasing you now. That is why our healing is dulled at best. We can slow its progress, minimally, but we cannot stop you from withering."

He could be lying to make me desperate. I stare back at my hands.

I curl my fingers into a fist. I can still feel the unnatural ache that was there from the moment I first woke. The exhaustion in my body is deeper than muscular, deeper than skeletal. I know what those injuries and pains feel like. I might not be a hunter, but I've had my share of hardship and toil. I've lived in the smithy—through all the burns, scrapes, bruises, and breaks. I know how I should be healing and this isn't it.

I'm still aware that he could be lying to make me desperate. But I can't shake how my body feels…different. Wracked with pain and an unabating exhaustion.

"How long do I have?" I finally ask. I'm still not sure if I fully believe him, but this would all be a rather long, drawn-out ruse to be entirely a lie. If all he wanted was my blood, he could've already had it. And then there's the aches in my body.

There's more to all this, there has to be.

"A week, two at most." He faces me once more. His eyes drift from my head, down to the blanket, and over my covered legs. "But in a few days you won't be able to even lift your head. A few days after that you will lose the strength to chew and swallow. You might still breathe, but you will already be dead long before your eyes shut for the final time."

"Then let's go open your door now." I've been gone from the hamlet for too long. I must get home, even if I'm returning in shame. The thought of Mother searching for me makes my chest ache with yet another pain. Does she think she lost both her children to the Blood Moon hunt?

He laughs again, deep and rumbling. The sound reminds me of the taste of lemons. Bitter and sharp…yet not entirely unpleasant, if you have an inclination for it. "If only it were that simple. We will need to move fast, yes. But there is no way we will be able to accomplish in one week what vampire lords before me have been trying to accomplish for centuries. The door is deep within the old castle and difficult at best, deadly at worst, to get to. Impossible for you to make the journey with your condition deteriorating the entire time."

"Couldn't you transport us there with your mist?" I ask.

He inhales slowly and pinches the bridge of his nose as though he's holding together every scrap of his patience. "No, the castle is warded. If there was an easy way to get to this door you would already be there."

"Well, if I cannot be transported there and it will take great effort to get to—more time and energy than I have remaining—what is your plan to get to it?"

The air grows thick and heavy with silence. My eyes are drawn back to him, attention away from assessing my condition to hanging on his next words. He seems uncertain.

"We will exchange blood."

"Exchange…*blood*?"

"Yes, you will consume my blood, and I will consume yours."

I can feel my lids widen. A cold, invisible hand grips my spine around my neck, sending chills throughout my entire body. Every vertebra shudders. My stomach churns. Fear and disgust drench me in cold sweat.

"I am *not* a vampire. I do not consume blood."

"Oh? You attempted to gain the powers of one."

"That is the last thing I would ever do."

"The state in which I found you says differently." He chuckles darkly, the yellows of his eyes shining brightly at my grimace. "But you're right, you are not a vampir. Nor would I ever give you the rites of such a blessing." His upper lip curls slightly in a displeasure that mirrors my own. "I would only give you enough of my blood to strengthen your body, to help ground you in Midscape enough that it will ward off the withering."

"And you would consume my blood in return?"

His lips pull into an almost vicious smile. I work to keep myself composed at the sight. "Yes. To accomplish our goals, we would become bloodsworn—two who have consumed the other's blood. A vow made on our lives that if broken would result in the death of the other."

"You would be able to steal my face." My voice has become hushed by shock. My ears are ringing with remnants of his words. I see the vampire that wore the visage of my father, its corpse mottled and burning in the sunlight after Davos killed it.

"Yes, I would be able to assume your form so long as your blood is in my body, if I desired. But I assure you I have no interest in *your* body." His nose scrunches slightly in a sneer of disgust.

I pointedly ignore the remark. "Would I be able to take your form?"

"You are not vampir and know nothing of the blood lore. So, no."

He seems to be delighted by this. It must be a reminder of just how helpless I am before him.

"Then what benefit do I have?"

"Your benefit would be to have the vampir lord bloodsworn—bound—to you. I could not lie to you even if I desired to, nor you to me. Neither of us can break the terms of our arrangement once set. As I said, this is the best solution I could think of that would solve all our problems. If you know I cannot deceive or harm you, then you will know you can trust me, and the same works in my favor."

I narrow my eyes slightly. In my silence, I weigh my options. If he speaks true…I don't have long before I am helpless and cannot fight back. It already hurts to sit upright; every breath is more labored than the last. *He could be lying*, my skepticism persists. But if he wanted to kill me and steal my face, he could have by now—he still could if I refuse. While I am not so naive as to think he is telling me *all* the details of this arrangement, I do believe some of it must be true. That's the only explanation that makes sense. Why else would he be keeping me alive?

But, to drink the blood of a vampire. To be *bloodsworn*, bound in some magic fashion, to the lord of the vampires… My stomach clenches as though my body is physically trying to reject the idea. The only solace I can find is that it is better me than Drew.

For all I would rather be anywhere else…if I traded fates with Drew underneath the Blood Moon and spared him of this, then that will be my consolation. So long as my brother is still alive…

"I will leave you to the decision." The vampire lord breaks my thoughts as he starts for the door. "But do choose quickly, because soon enough you will be too weak to accept the blood."

His footsteps ring out like the solemn bell toll that reverberated through town on nights of the full moon. Twelve tolls. Twelve steps.

Time is running out for me.

But my life has always been on borrowed time. All of ours in Hunter's Hamlet. We were born into a harsh world of survival. All my life I've been working to try and make my breaths mean something—for my family, my town, the world.

If I can kill the vampire lord all this ends, I hear in Drew's voice. All the pain will finally end.

"I'll do it," I say loudly, summoning his attention back to me.

He stills and the air becomes thick once more. This time I cannot read the emotion he wears. I did not even realize vampires were so capable of an array of feelings.

"You, a hunter, will become bloodsworn to a vampir and help me break the curse on my people?" Even though this is what he wanted, surely what he had been calculating, he still seems surprised.

"If that is what I must do to stay alive"—*so I can spare my family and every future generation from your ilk*—"then yes."

The muscles of his throat tense as he swallows, sinewy tendons and ligaments straining already under this foolish agreement. "Then I will begin the arrangements and return shortly. Before the moon sets, it will be done. You shall be my bloodsworn."

eight

AN ICY FROST CLAWS ITS WAY INTO ME AND A VIOLENT SHIVER OF FEAR AND DISGUST RAKES THROUGH MY BODY.

After the vampire lord leaves, the room is darker, colder. Every shadow is more sinister. I never thought I might actually miss the Blood Moon and its unnatural hue. But somehow the steely light of a normal moon is worse. It's a reminder that time has passed and I think again, *How long have I been here?*

Perhaps I was unconscious for multiple days and that's why I feel so weak. But even if I was…it cannot have been *much* more than two days at most. Such an inconsequential period of time and everything has changed.

I stare at my hands, my arms, my legs, feeling that deep and undeniable ache in all of them; it's an exhaustion unlike any I've ever known. I want it to be reassuring. I made the right decision, didn't I? If my choices were death by withering away, or a pact with the vampire lord, then I chose correctly. As long as I'm alive I can do *something*; I can keep working toward a brighter future for Hunter's Hamlet.

When Drew first announced he would join the hunters, Mother said, *Don't throw your life away*. She had been telling him that if this was the decision he was determined to make, if this was how he wanted to spend his life, then he should make sure it meant something. That he gave his life to a worthy cause.

That is what we all do in Hunter's Hamlet. I just thought my cause would be forging silver weapons. Not wielding them myself.

I grip my head and curl into a ball. Tears try to squirm from my eyes, threatening to drown me if I let them loose. Was this how my brother felt when he joined the hunters? Did he know it was the right decision and yet was torn asunder by it because he was terrified at the same time? No, he must've been calm, so I will be, too.

Drawing shaky breaths, I fight for my composure. *The vampire lord thinks you're a hunter, act like one!* I scold myself, thinking of Drew's stoic, immovable strength. Absolutely nothing seems to shake him. He can take anything in his stride. If that power is within him, then it is within me, too. I bring my hand to my chest, spinning the silver ring that matches his around my little finger until I'm calm.

Pushing the blanket off, I'm determined not to wallow in worry and self-doubt. I must strike sure and true in the forge, mere seconds and heat between perfection and scrap. I try and channel the same confidence here and now.

Blood has crusted against my leather armor, but doesn't seem too old. It's another odd comfort—another assurance that not *much* time has passed. I make my way toward the window, sinking lower in my knees with every step to test my muscles. My legs shake in ways they shouldn't. But there's still strength there, enough for me to walk tall for a bit longer yet.

At the window, I behold the land of the vampire.

Expectedly, given our journey here, I am in a mountaintop castle. Frosted peaks circle a low caldera, the tips reminiscent of the sharp-toothed mouths of the vampire. The basin is packed tightly with buildings. It's a moonlit city of bridgeways connecting towers with spires. The city stretches so tall that I cannot see the ground. And even if I could, I am too far up to see any creatures, vampire or otherwise. Most importantly, I cannot spy any way down to the city below. Which leads me to believe the mountains are hollow and there are internal tunnels. Or, the only way in and out of this castle is through a vampire's mist stepping.

Didn't he say that the castle was warded? He must've been lying. We entered using magic, after all. The vampire are pure evil and I can trust nothing they say. I can't even be sure about the terms of the bloodsworn. I'll have to find everything out for myself and trust only my own instinct. Anything less could mean my demise.

I wonder if he put me in this particular room so I would try and find a possible way to escape this castle and the vampire's territory—to assess my options and find none. I bet he is hoping I panic at the sight of my helplessness and truly submit to him. He assumes me to be afraid, easily manipulated, and cowering at the thought of being trapped or alone.

He doesn't realize that I have always been trapped by his kind. I was born into Hunter's Hamlet and will die there because it is my sworn oath to all of humanity to protect the world from his scourge. This is not materially different. I am just in closer confines with my sworn enemy.

At least, that's what I tell myself. I'm not going to let him break me down with mind games and doubt.

"If I kill him, it all ends." My breath fogs the glass. The door opens, interrupting my thoughts. I hope the sentiment wasn't heard.

It is not the vampire lord but the man from the hall we landed in. Quinn, was his name. Strange, I didn't think any but the vampire lord would have a name. Though I didn't think any, the vampire lord included, were sentient enough to talk, either. Perhaps if I do somehow manage to escape with my life, and fail to kill the vampire lord in the process, I can take useful knowledge back to the hamlet.

"I am to take you to the altar." As he speaks, I also notice that he only has two elongated fangs. Another similarity with the vampire lord and difference from vampires I'm familiar with.

"Very well." I'm grateful he didn't come sooner. If he'd arrived immediately after the vampire lord left, he would've found me a mess on the bed. Luckily I've managed to gather myself enough to project as a strong hunter.

He's skeptical of my calmness. I can tell by how he glances at me from the corner of his eye. How he lingers, waiting to see if I say or do something else. I can almost hear the unsaid whispers that burn the other side of his wrinkled lips. But the man is an obedient servant to his lord and says nothing, merely steps aside in the door frame and motions for me to follow.

I wonder if he cannot say anything else, even if he wanted to. Drew's stories from the hunters' books made it clear that all the vampire come from a single lord—they share the old blood of the first of their forsaken kind. That is why, if someone kills the lord, the rest will die. They will be mindless monsters, incapable of thought without their leader, a directionless horde rather than a thinking foe.

Will becoming bloodsworn also make me a mindless slave to him? I inhale slowly and keep my head level. No, it won't. The vampire lord seems to think that he needs me as a *human.* If this pact were to change my humanity—thus giving him any kind of control over me—then I doubt he would go through with it. Moreover, as he aptly put, I am not a vampire. The effects of this ritual likely won't affect me in the same ways as the others of his kind.

Even if I can't trust what he says…I can trust my own logic. Or, can I? Pain stabs my temples and I rub them lightly. All this thinking and scheming and debating has me going in circles; I'm not cut out for this in the slightest.

The halls of the castle are drafty, dusty, empty voids. It's a massive and mazelike place. I follow Quinn through a series of rooms and onto a balcony. Snow has piled high. A single path of footsteps cuts through the blanket of white. The tracks step off the edge of the balcony, past a section of broken railing, and continue along a buttress that supports this wing of the castle. The narrow walkway stretches across the dark abyss of cliff and castle like a pale, unfurled ribbon.

I pause at the edge of the balcony and swallow hard. The world tilts slightly. Quinn is several steps ahead down the path he clearly intends for us both to use.

"Afraid, human?"

"No," I lie. I've never even *seen* anywhere this high up. But to be perched at the edge…

He sniffs, as though he can smell my deceit. I hope he can't. The cliffs below the walkway—*Who am I kidding?* It's not even a walkway. It's a decorative element of the castle at best. *Why are we not going through the inside?* I want to ask but I don't want to sound like a coward.

"Are we not using the castle interior for the same reasons your lord can't take me right to his special door?" I try phrasing my question to sound like I'm probing for information.

"You should focus on not slipping instead of worrying about the old castle." *Old castle?* "Unless you *are* afraid, after all?"

"Of course not." This test isn't something a hunter would fear.

"What are you waiting for, then?" Quinn halts his stroll, as though the narrow, icy path is nothing to him. Vampire speed, strength, balance, accuracy, all things hunters struggle to compete against without the elixirs. An elixir I no longer have in me.

"I'm thinking it would be a shame if your lord's new—" I struggle to think of what to call myself "—assistant tumbled to her death. I want to make sure he's all right with you taking such a risk."

"He knows the pathways we must take," Quinn answers enigmatically. "Besides, this should be no trouble for a hunter such as yourself. I've read about how you're trained."

"What have you read about my kind?" The vampire lord mentioned something too about having record of the hunters' training. No doubt brought back by his minions every full moon.

"Enough." It seems that being painfully obtuse is another vampire trait I had never been taught. "Now, hurry up."

You can do this, Floriane, I tell myself. *You must be confident and sure-footed in the forge. This is nothing. Just a drop to your death. You'll be fine.*

I suck in a breath, hold it, and step forward.

Underneath the snow is a layer of ice, thicker in some places than others. I move my feet slowly, making sure the soles of my boots have found their grip before continuing onward. I continue to study the darkened windows and archways. There's not a single sign of life here beyond us. I'd expected the whole vampire horde to be wandering these halls. But they feel empty. Lonely, even.

A particularly violent gust of wind threatens to knock me over. I let out a yelp and fall to my knees, clutching onto ice and stone for dear life. The world beneath me blurs, becoming even more distant, shrinking away as if to swallow me. I press my eyes closed. My vision darkens and I feel faint.

"We don't have all night, hunter." Quinn makes a small leap from the buttress to the open window of a tower. He doesn't even care if I die. Of course not, he's a vampire.

The only person keeping me alive is myself. *You can do this*.

Keeping my center of gravity low and ignoring the biting frost, I crawl to the other end of the walkway. The window ledge seems so far away; it retreats more the longer I stare at it. I gather my legs under me and my courage at the same time. If I don't move, I'll be frozen to the spot forever.

Do it! the part of Drew that lives within me shouts. He always knew just how hard to push me during our midnight trainings.

I leap and stretch both arms forward.

It's a bad jump. I land awkwardly—face first, tumbling. But all of my limbs are inside and I can't hold back a monumental sigh of relief. Quinn's monstrous face appears over me.

"I expected more from a hunter."

"Maybe I'm luring you into a false sense of security?" It sounds ridiculous given my showing, even to my ears, and judging from Quinn's smirk, it does to him as well.

"Maybe they should train you more with heights rather than letting your kind wallow in the dirt." He starts down the stairs, leaving me to collect myself and scamper behind him, biting my tongue with a scowl.

We pass several doors, each barred with a heavy padlock. Are they designed to keep something or someone out? Or in? After a long stretch, I begin to hear a soft wailing. At first I think it's the wind. But then realize it is far too close and far too…*I dare not think human*—vampire.

"What's that?" I ask.

"Nothing for you to concern yourself with."

I can't bring myself to ask again.

As we reach the bottom of the stairs and step into the castle's inner sanctum, I lay eyes once more on the vampire lord. He stands at the far end of a chapel before a semicircular altar. Rings of stone radiate out from it like ripples on the floor. At varying intervals, candelabras illuminate the carvings and statues of contorting men and women, fanged mouths open in ecstasy, that climb up the pillars on either side, supporting the lofty ceiling.

Sculpted over the altar is the statue of a man with outstretched arms, holding a book. Carved and etched rings of power originate from its pages and swirl around him. He has his stony eyes turned skyward, lips slightly parted as if in prayer. On his brow is a crown made of black metal that arcs like a web of fangs away from his brow, a large ruby set in its center.

"Good, you made it," the vampire lord murmurs, continuing to fuss with what I can only assume are magical tools on the altar. He moves a goblet several times back and forth between candles.

"No issues, Lord Ruvan," Quinn reports. I glance at him from the corners of my eyes. Sure, I made it here. But I certainly wouldn't say I did so without issue. Is he being nice by not sharing my embarrassment? No, this is another ploy to get me to lower my guard.

"I'm glad you're still strong and steady on your feet." The vampire lord brings his attention to me.

"It's good we didn't wait for a few more days. Then I might be too weak to use the outdoor shortcut and would have *had to* go through the castle. Maybe I could've opened your door on the way."

Ruvan rasps dark amusement and doesn't rise to my bait, refusing to elaborate further on why I didn't go within the castle and turning back to the altar. His bitter smile carries endless unsaid words.

"Good, indeed," he says finally. "Let's not waste any more time and proceed with our communion." With an open palm, he motions for me to stand by his side.

This close to him, I can see every gnarled, ancient groove of his face. Bags hang underneath his eyes, folded down over his cheeks. Yet his eyes—for as horrifying as they are—remain bright and sharp. Clever. They're the eyes of a hungry scholar…or a ruthless military strategist.

They're nothing like the expressionless eyes of the vampire I've known.

The vampire lord faces the altar. "Blood of the old kings, bathed in moonlight," he intones, bringing my attention back to his movements. He cups a goblet filled with thick, black liquid. I fight a cringe.

"Fresh blood of the descendant, freely given." The vampire lord raises his hand to his mouth, and bites at the soft flesh around the base of his thumb. Equally inky blood drips out into the chalice. He speaks with soft reverence and moves with purpose, confident and strong despite the state of his body. "I bring forth the lineage of old, the king I have sworn fealty to, and the oath to my people on which to make my vow. I come before the place of blood lore's origin, to pay homage, offer reverence, and empower my magic."

He puts the chalice between us at the altar's edge. Reverently, he hands me a silver dagger. "Blood must be freely given. A bloodsworn vow cannot be entered under duress, or coercion. You have to do this willingly or the magic will not take."

"Your kind has no problem *taking* it normally."

"We always give an option for it to be handed over willingly," he counters. I bark laughter that hammers on the cold walls of this cavernous hall. Give us an option? Does he really think I'll believe that? Ruvan swells slightly, as though he's trying to inflate himself like some predatory bird. "You mock me and my kindness."

"You know no kindness," I snap back. "How is any of this willing on my part?"

"You're welcome to leave." The words are firm, but his eyes are desperate, and almost…sad. It only makes me angrier. How dare he be sad in this situation after all he's done to me and to my people?

"And die." I shake my head and wait for the sour taste he's put in the back of my mouth to pass. He seems as if he's about to speak, but I cut him off. "Fine, yes, I'll finish your bloodsworn oath *willingly*. What must I do?"

The tendons in Ruvan's neck strain. He forces through clenched teeth, "Offer your blood to the chalice and say you enter this vow of your own volition."

I hold my forearm over the chalice and nick the back of my arm with the blade. Puncturing the skin of my palms would be foolish; it would prevent me from gripping effectively. One thing the forge has taught me is to preserve my hands.

"I enter the vow freely." I barely keep the sarcasm from my voice as blood drips down into the chalice below.

"Say it like you mean it. Bind yourself to me." The words are almost growled from deep in the back of his throat.

I inhale slowly. I have a lot of things I want to say to him. But pushing my luck before this bloodsworn oath is finished is likely a bad idea.

"In blood and body, I bind myself to you, Lord of the Vampires." My voice starts strong and then fades into a whisper. A rush sweeps up my body and tingles the back of my neck, causing my chest to flush at the sensation.

As soon as I finish speaking, a rusty plume rises from the contents of the cup. It smells of blood and metal, yes. But it also smells somewhat…

sweet? Like morning's first dew just before the sun has risen. Perhaps even floral. Honeysuckle, perhaps? Orchid? It's the first time I've ever seen anything related to vampire magic that didn't immediately disgust me.

Ruvan lifts the chalice, holding it between us as he continues to pin me in my spot with his stare. "Place your palm on the other side."

I do. My fingertips nearly touch the base of his wrist. Cool, sticky blood runs down the chalice between our hands. He still hasn't healed? I thought that vampires could heal in mere seconds. I wonder if I could've killed him, if I should try. I quickly scan for anything that I might be able to use as a weapon, but there's nothing, and Quinn still lingers as a solemn guard. He'd be on me if I took one step out of line. I've lived my entire life hunted within walls and yet I've never felt so trapped.

Did I miscalculate the risks and benefits of this oath? Everything is happening so fast.

What have I done?

"I vow that while you are in my care you will be a guest of Castle Tempost. All manner of protection and hospitality shall extend to you. None under my control shall bring you harm in the lands I protect." His words are slow and deep with purpose. They sink into my marrow, as though I am being encased in the magical oath which he is forging. "And when you have fulfilled your vows to me, I will bring you back to the world where you belong. You shall return the way you came, free of harm."

"And neither you nor the vampire under your control will *ever* cross the Fade to attack humans again," I add hastily.

He blinks, three times. His mouth curls into a slow smile, one more threatening than kind. "And neither I, nor any under my control, shall come to your lands to attack humans forevermore *once* the curse has been broken," he adds. "Now, your vow to me."

"I vow to help you, however I am able, to break the curse on you and your people." My mind whirls, trying to think of what else I might need to say. He seems to be asking for so little. But it can't be that simple—

"And, while you do…you swear to not lay a finger in harm on me or any who are loyal to me."

My muscles tighten. I work to keep my breathing slow and even. He had said this vow, once made, could not be broken—if it were, we would die. Which means, if I say these words, I will not be able to attack him without also attacking myself.

But if I can find a way to kill him, I will gladly give my life for that. I doubt I'll find a way to escape this place alive. This vow will give me time to find a silver weapon. It will help me learn his movements and powers. At worst I will sacrifice my life to take his. At best, I will be ready the moment the curse is broken.

"I swear to not harm you or any loyal to you while I am working to break the curse."

His eyes flash. He knows my intent. He knows that as I stand here, making vows to him of protection and fidelity, I am plotting his death. He might be able to prevent me from acting on these wants, but he can't stop me from thinking them, and that's how I know my mind is still my own. The chalice quivers between us as we both clutch it tightly. Holding onto our secret hopes and plots with all the desperation we can muster.

"I accept your vow," he says, finally. The vampire lord wrenches the cup from my grasp and brings it to his lips. He drinks deeply.

Ruvan's flesh fills out, muscles straining against his clothes where they previously hung limp. His skin turns from lifeless to luminescent. It is radiant underneath the moonlight streaming through the massive circular window over the statue. The darkness falls from his eyes as inky tears. He blinks the impurities away, revealing whites, as any normal human would have. His irises are still yellow, but they take on a deep, swirling, golden hue. Hair that was previously greasy and matted now shines as though it has been freshly washed and relaxed, white framing a suddenly ethereal face.

He has gone from the monster of my worst nightmare to a man straight from a daydream. Death made beautiful is somehow far worse, far more sinister, than his original form.

The vampire lord looks down on me as if to say, *Behold, look upon me in all my glory*. I wonder whose face it is…perhaps it was one he stole long ago. I had thought vampires could only steal the faces of the hosts freshly consumed, but that could be as wrong as so many other things are turning out to be. But it doesn't matter, for I have seen his true form. And I know underneath that suddenly achingly handsome exterior is the truth of the monster he is. Black mist follows his movements like angry, sentient power as he holds the cup toward me.

"Now, you drink."

"I accept your vow," I echo his words and take the goblet with both hands. I meet his molten gaze as, for the second time, I brace myself and drink an unexpected, magic draught thrust upon me, forcing myself not to gag. And like the Hunter's Elixir that Drew gave me, this one burns the entire way down. I let out a gasp and clutch my chest as my heart pounds louder than a hammer and faster than a hummingbird's wings. My breathing is suddenly noisy. I have never been more aware of the sounds air makes as it passes through me. I can hear the blood rushing in my veins and my tendons groan as they strain between bone and tightening muscle.

I slam my hand on the altar. Golden coins and daggers rattle against other gilded chalices. I keep my eyes locked with his, teeth clenched. I will not give this monster the satisfaction of seeing me on my knees.

The well of my throat burns as if a white-hot dagger is being thrust through my neck. The invisible weapon curves and drops to my chest. Without warning, my heart stops. It might only be a second, but time exists in the hollow of my chest where a beat should be. *Beat*, I will it.

My breath hitches.

The world spins a full revolution and comes to a screeching halt.

"Remember to breathe," he says softly.

Inhale. Exhale. The burning within begins to subside. As it fades, it is replaced with a surge of raw power. The weakness in my muscles vanishes. I stare at the back of my forearm, watching with fascination as my skin knits back into place. My strength has returned, and then some.

This is the power of the Hunter's Elixir…but deeper. Richer. More profound and complete. I glare up at the vampire lord. A crescent smile cuts his lips at my displeasure, his teeth as pale as the moonlight that outlines his shoulders. Of course he would choose the most painfully beautiful face to wear out of all he's stolen. But if he thinks it will make me any less inclined to loathe him—to kill him—he is sorely mistaken.

He leans forward but does not touch me. His breath moves the strands of hair by my ear and sends chills down the back of my neck.

"My power is intoxicating, isn't it?" he whispers. "Do you want more? Break the curse on my people, dear hunter, and I can keep you drunk on my power until your body can no longer handle me." He eases away, hair falling into his eyes, shadowing them with the evil I know is real, for he has imprinted it on my soul.

It's hard not to throttle him. But my body revolts at the mere thought of doing so. I push the notion from my mind, unable to handle the dizzying, nauseous feeling just *thinking* of harming him suddenly fills me with. My earlier fear returns: *What have I done?*

"Now, come along… I will show you to your quarters and then the real work can begin."

nine

THE THREE OF US LEAVE THE CHAPEL. I expect us to come back the way we came, but we do not. Instead, we head farther down the stairway with many locked doors. Ruvan lifts a massive keyring off a peg from the wall and attaches it to his belt as we begin our descent.

I keep my focus on the path he's taking me on, trying to stay oriented in this mazelike castle. But it's hopeless. I find myself continually distracted by the oddest things. The faint smell of meat sizzling brushes against my nostrils. There are currents in the air, whipping around my ankles, tangling with my fingers, as though there's a life to this place that I hadn't felt before.

Vampire magic still flows in me, threatening dizziness with every step from being so overwhelming. I brace myself for each wave that crashes over me so I don't stumble. I am stronger than ever before, like I could forge for a day straight without stopping and still have energy left over to haul coal or hoist remaining smelt iron into storage. Yet I might also be torn apart at any second.

Ruvan stops at a door, unlocking it before stepping through. I notice the line of salt that covers the doorjamb on both sides. He takes a careful step over it and I follow the movement, heart sinking as I do.

"So, salt does nothing to actually ward off vampire." It did little to protect my mother and I from the rogue vampire that attacked us. I wonder how many homes in Hunter's Hamlet were invaded; the flimsy protections we thought we had were rendered worthless. What was the point of any of it? Did we actually know anything about the vampires at all?

I didn't expect my dejected musing to be heeded.

"Yes and no." Ruvan locks the door behind us. "Salt dulls a vampir's senses; it hinders our innate ability to track and seek out blood, even blood still in the veins." He stills and I wonder if he's reconsidering giving me this information. Maybe he'll continue to make such errors and tell me the secrets of the vampire. Should I ever see Hunter's Hamlet again, I'll bring it back to Drew and the fortress. To my surprise, Ruvan continues, following his hesitation. "So the salt works to an extent—if a vampir doesn't know a person is behind a door, they won't sense them or seek them out. But if they can *see* people within then the salt does little."

"Why do you have it here?" I ask.

He flinches. Ruvan is good at keeping his composure, I'll give him that, but I don't miss his brief wince. And I note the suddenly distant quality to his eyes.

"For protection."

"You need protection from vampires?" I arch my brows in disbelief.

"*Vampir*, and contrary to what you might believe, there are monsters far worse than us lurking in the darkness." He motions back to the salt. "The salt helps."

"I see." Something is not adding up. He says the salt dilutes a vampire's senses, but that doesn't explain how the vampire sensed me when I was within a well-salted home; it hadn't seen me. He wants me to think of him and his allies as weak, or sympathize with them. I resolve again that I won't fall prey to his mind games.

"You have more questions," he says softly as Quinn passes.

"Things I doubt you'll tell me," I retort.

We regard each other warily as Quinn opens a second set of doors that lead out of this sparse antechamber. I wonder if Ruvan is engaging in the same calculus as I am. The bloodsworn oath prevents us from lying, allegedly, but I don't know if it would prevent half-truths. And Quinn has already proved that the vampires can be good at dodging questions.

"Come, hunter." Ruvan breezes past me and through the door Quinn has opened.

He leads me onto a mezzanine that overlooks a gathering hall below. A few vampire are gathered, but they don't notice us. Or, if they do, they don't look our way. Ruvan quickly ushers me through another door that Quinn holds open. But the servant doesn't follow behind. He instead remains on the other side as it closes.

"These are my chambers," Ruvan explains, leading me through another set of doors and into a sitting room. "You will stay here."

"*Here?*"

"Yes, where I can keep an eye on you personally. Do you really think I'd let you out of my sight?"

"Oh? Worried about me attacking your minions? Don't have faith in your bloodsworn oath?" I jut my chin out at him, hoping he'll rise to the bait and tell me if there's a way I could harm these vampires.

"I have faith in the oath staying your blade. But it won't do much to your tongue, and I don't care to deal with the tensions a brute like you could create." He frowns slightly. I choose to ignore the insult.

"Why don't you lock me up in a room somewhere, then? I would be happier not to spend time with *any* of your kind."

"Too bad, hunter. You're going to have to manage working with all of us if you want to see that hovel you call a home again." He sneers slightly. It is far less fearsome now with his fresh, handsome face. When his skin was leathered, and his fangs bared, he looked like an ancient beast. Now, he looks like any other human would.

No…that's not quite true. He still moves with the impossible grace of the vampire. His hair is moonlight and his eyes are molten gold. And his fangs are still present, though not as pronounced. Even the subtle things about his appearance aren't quite human; he's like a living portrait, too fine to be completely real. Too enchanting to be normal.

"Or…" Ruvan continues. "Is your protesting because these accommodations aren't comfortable enough for a *delicate* hunter?"

"Truthfully everything about this arrangement is uncomfortable," I say outright.

"Excellent. Wouldn't want you to get comfortable and stay too long."

"No chance of that," I assure him with a tone that I hope conveys how obvious it is. I gather my height. Which isn't much. I'm somewhat stocky in stature and the muscles the forge has hammered into me emphasize the physique. "But what about you? Will it be uncomfortable to have a human in your midst?"

He doesn't back away; instead, he puffs his chest slightly. "You could never do anything that would make me uncomfortable."

"Is that a challenge?" My lips split as I bare my teeth at him, trying to speak to him in a language he understands—threats. He mirrors the expression. His fangs are easily far more fearsome to behold.

"By all means," he invites, holding out his arms. "Make me uncomfortable. I welcome you." He takes a half step forward. I blink quickly and lean away. *I didn't expect him to actually…* He laughs. At me. "I didn't think so."

I attempt to salvage my composure. "I've no interest in playing games. I'm here to kill."

"Good." Ruvan dips his chin slightly. A shadow falls over his eyes and his expression darkens, growing in intensity. We're a breath from each other. He's so close that I can see the streaks of gold so bright they're nearly platinum, star-bursting around the black of his irises. He's close enough that I could reach up and strangle him. But the mere thought sets my hands to shaking. "I know you will spend every day of this arrangement plotting my death." His words are slow. Voice low with what sounds like an earth-shattering sorrow, so deep it rumbles my ribs. "Recognize I made this vow with you, knowing the dangers, knowing what you are—that I will hold the leash of a very dangerous creature, one that will bite my throat the first moment I slip."

What I am... A very dangerous creature, he says, as if I'm the monster here. "I have already beheld your true form. I know the monster you are as well, vampire."

He scoffs and pulls away. The tension that ignites the air between us is alleviated some. Though the promise of death is still whispered, just waiting for one of us to make good on it.

"What I am…" the vampire lord murmurs, stalking over to the wall. He grabs a blanket that has been thrown over a frame, yanking it to reveal a mirror. The beautiful lie that is his face stares back at him, myself in the background.

My gaze shifts.

I am once more the woman I've always known. My skin is back to its naturally tawny hue. There are no dark, angry veins writhing underneath its surface. No flush or pallor to my cheeks. However, I notice a marking in black at the base of my throat, in the hollow between my collarbones. It's a diamond shape with a long, slender teardrop underneath it. What looks like two stylized bat wings gracefully arc around either side. I touch it lightly.

"It's my mark." He approaches, staring thoughtfully at it. "A signature of my blood, of my magic. It signifies that you are bound to me."

I inhale slowly, watching as the muscles of my neck strain against the marking. It moves with my skin as though it has been tattooed there. He chuckles.

"Don't fret. Once our deal has concluded and the vow has been upheld, it will fade from you."

"Good." I lower my hand and frown up at him.

He leans forward, nose almost touching mine. "Fear not, the loathing of wearing the other's mark is mutual." He reaches for his collar, unfastening the top button deftly, even one-handed. My eyes are drawn instantly to the motion, and a flush rises toward my cheeks despite myself. My fascination with a man undressing is instantly quenched as he yanks the shirt aside, revealing a diamond outline with a smaller diamond in its center. Two sickle shapes envelop it from either side, hooklike points jutting off their ends.

"What is that?"

"Your mark."

Mine… "But I am not a vampire."

"Vampir," he corrects pointlessly. I will never make the adjustment, especially not on his behalf. "And I did not say they were a mark of the vampir, but a signature of an individual's blood. Your blood holds the power of your life itself, made richer by every experience you've ever or will ever carry with you. No two marks are alike."

That is my mark, I think as he leans away. My eyes are affixed to it even as he buttons his shirt once more, re-situating it. I am in the world of the vampire. I have sworn a blood oath with the vampire lord. But what finally shakes my core is this:

My blood.

My very human blood.

Has magic.

"There's magic in *me*?" I whisper. I hadn't intended the thought to escape.

He turns, a crescent brow rising. "Of course there is. Others might have assumed humans to be completely non-magical, but the vampir knew the truth of it: Everyone has power, if they claim it."

Power is made, not born, that's what Drew told me long ago when I asked him why Davos had chosen him to take on as a special student. Anyone could be made powerful. All it took was hard work and guidance. That was why Drew sneaked back to me, almost every night. *We are twins*, he would say. *If I can become strong, so can you*. Together, we became more than what we were—than what we ever thought we would be. I wonder if Davos knew that he was really training us both. Likely not. If he had, he never would've continued teaching Drew.

I cross toward my reflection. The vampire lord continues to watch me as I gently rub at the mark on my neck. His expression remains guarded and impossible to read. I've no idea how I, a humble forge maiden, have ended up *here*, marked by a vampire lord and wearing the guise of a hunter. I still have my black eyes and dark hair, the familiar scars and burns up my arms, on my right cheek from a forge accident when I was twelve, but I hardly recognize myself otherwise.

"Do you want to harness it?" He jars me from my thoughts.

"Harness what?"

"The untapped power in your blood that your ancestors never did." Ruvan smirks slightly. He's smug. So self-satisfied that I might be fascinated by something in his world. I stifle my musings. Those will be for me alone.

"Of course not. I'm no vampire and I don't want to have anything to do with them."

"Oh? Being bloodsworn to one certainly is 'anything to do' with a vampir." His smugness intensifies.

"This is an arrangement, nothing more." I ease away from the mirror, fastening my armor all the way. I wish I could tighten down my racing thoughts with the same effectiveness.

"Yes, of course." Ruvan turns for the door. "Now that you have seen your quarters, I will introduce you to the rest of my covenant."

"Your covenant?"

"Yes. My loyal knights—those who have sworn an oath to me, to this land, and to our kin. My own group of hunters, if you will."

"Are you sure you want to? No longer worried about my sharp tongue?" I'm not sure *I* want to meet them. I would be very happy to hide in this room as long as I'm able while I try and catch my breath. So much is changing and I've hardly had a chance to keep up. "Besides, what will they say when they discover that their illustrious vampire lord has made a deal with their sworn enemy?"

"Do you question your hunter lord?"

I purse my lips. I've no idea what happens in the fortress and that makes answering dangerous since I still don't know how much information these vampires have about Hunter's Hamlet or where they got it from.

"I thought not." He opens the door. "Now come."

We backtrack through the doors and past Quinn, who waited dutifully. The hall is slightly noisier now; the chatter of multiple people echoes above the plucking of what sounds like a fiddle. Even though the mezzanine of the room is high above, I can almost make out every word spoken—something I'm certain I wouldn't be able to do before becoming bloodsworn.

Yet another reminder of what I've done and how I've changed. *It was the right decision*, I try and remind myself. But my internal voice is weaker than before. Nothing feels right. My own skin is uncomfortable and my senses play tricks on me. A seed of loathing works its way into me for my own blood. For the power that has always been there but I never wanted, never asked for. At most, I wanted to keep my family safe and maybe see the ocean with my brother.

How did I end up here?

"They're bolder than before," a man grumbles.

"Bolder. Stronger. More stubborn time after time," another man with a soft, dreamlike voice adds.

"At least we have their blood," a woman says lightly. That's when it hits me with an icy chill: they're talking about Hunter's Hamlet. My ears begin to ring to the point that I barely hear the rest of their conversations, as if my body is physically trying to block them out.

"Precious little given freely," the second man laments. "We'll have to purify the rest as we're able."

"Purify? Blood by force is rubbish," the woman mutters.

"I'll do my best," the soft voice says.

The plucking pauses. "Will it be enough?" A second woman.

"It will have to be," Ruvan says as we descend the staircase that wraps around the back of the hall, connecting the mezzanine to the meeting area below.

They're all on their feet the instant they see me. I swallow thickly and focus on my feet to keep myself from tripping. I am a hunter right now, not the forge maiden; I will not allow myself to show my fear. We lock eyes with each other and the air goes thick, as it does right before a fight breaks out.

ten

I CLENCH MY HANDS INTO FISTS. Even with this new strength, all it would take would be two of them, *at most*, to have me pinned. They could break me like a toy if they wanted.

Ruvan must be able to sense it, too, because he steps forward, physically placing himself between me and the rest of them. "This is the newest member of our covenant."

"My lord…" the man with the deep gravelly voice starts, and then loses his words along the way. He's as pale as the snow-capped mountains outside, and just as massive. All his dark brown hair left his head and has taken residence on his chin.

"*That* is a hunter," a woman finishes, easing her fiddle to the table. Long strands of pale blonde hair slip over her shoulder with the motion. It's almost the same color as her eyes—as all of their eyes.

"And she has become bloodsworn with me." Ruvan folds his hands at the small of his back.

The woman I heard laughing before lets out an incredulous blurt. She pushes her long, dark brown bangs behind her ear. Her hair is short, like mine, on one side. The other half of her head is shaved and marred with scars that trace down her neck, ghostly tracks across the sepia hue of her skin. "You can't be serious."

"Deathly."

So much for his fold not questioning him. I glance at the

vampire lord from the corner of my eye. His jaw is clenched. Smugness floods me but I don't let it show. Doing so would be foolish.

"You…are bloodsworn with a *human*?" The large man balks.

"And a hunter at that?" The man with the soft voice and dark skin adjusts his circular spectacles as if trying to see me better. His black hair has been tightly braided against his scalp, the remaining pulled into a plump bun at the back of his head.

"I did. She is going to help us break this curse, once and for all. It's not as if we're going to take her into the depths while she's withering from simply existing in Midscape."

"I admit, it's logical," the bespectacled man murmurs. "I just hadn't calculated it."

"*You* didn't calculate something?" The blonde gasps.

The soft-spoken man rolls his eyes, glancing away and quickly back at her before away again.

"Hunters look out only for themselves." The pale man with the gravelly voice glowers down at me. He might be built like a small mountain, muscles bulging, threatening to swallow his neck and ears whole, but I often find muscle like that is just for show. Then again, I don't think I want to find out in this instance.

"She is looking out for herself." Ruvan's eyes dart back to me with almost an expectant look. Does he want me to say something? I smile thinly and leave him to flounder among his knights. Ruvan huffs. "I vowed that should she help me break the curse on our kind, we would never cross the Fade to hunt her people again after."

"You're going to let them go, free of punishment, after all they've done?" The petite woman isn't laughing anymore. She almost looks like she could cry, or murder something. "Ruvan—"

"It is done," he snaps. "I would swear more if it meant our people would be free of this blight. We've lost too many and only have a few cycles left, otherwise we're dead, all of us." Frustration radiates off his shoulders as he half turns to face me. "This is my covenant. You will be working closely with them so do try to be polite, if you can manage the mere basics of decorum. None of them will harm you, per the conditions of our vow." Ruvan proceeds to introduce them, his palm motioning to each one by one.

"Our fiddle-playing siren is Winny."

"*Quarter*-siren," she says, somewhat coyly, but her eyes are as hard as the gold they resemble.

"Ventos is our muscle."

The burly man folds his arms over his chest, accentuating his biceps.

"Should you need anything of tactics or knowledge, there are none better than Callos."

The bespectacled man raises a hand to his right breast, bowing low. Every fold of his clothing is carefully pressed. Not one bit out of place. He is clearly someone who appreciates form over function and doesn't strike me as being threatening…unless that's his plan.

"Lavenzia is…"

"The practical one." She grins widely, fangs on display. The shorter woman is full-bodied. There could easily be untold strength under her curves and, given her scars, there likely is.

"And you have met Quinn."

He hardly looks at me as he crosses to the table. He fills a golden chalice—not unlike what was on the altar—with water. Then he fills it with three drops from an obsidian vial. The vial is similar to the one Drew gave me. Unnervingly so…

"What's in the vial?" I ask.

They all share a look. Callos is the one to answer, "Blood."

Taken from the hunters on the night of the Blood Moon, no doubt.

My thoughts are interrupted as, right before my eyes, Quinn's flesh fills out. His tawny skin is a shade darker than Ruvan's and Ventos's pallor. His eyes regain clarity, the darkness dripping down his cheeks in rivulets. The wisps of hair fill out on his head, replaced with rusty-brown locks—short cut and slightly upturned in the front. His lips plump into a pout, complemented by his sad, intense eyes.

They drink human blood to conceal their monstrous forms. That must be why they need to hunt humans on the full moon and why they look like shambling corpses when they do. Perhaps drinking the blood consistently is what allows them to speak and think—why these vampires are sentient compared to the ones who usually attack us.

"And, my covenant, this is…is…" Ruvan pauses, blinking several times at me. "I don't have your name."

I smile triumphantly. I had been waiting for him to realize this. It might be a small, insignificant victory to have concealed this from him for so long. But it's a victory nonetheless. I have something simple now to use as a test for the bloodsworn oath.

"My name is—" The fake name I had been planning to give sticks in my throat. I clear it with a cough. So what he said was true. We can't lie to each other. Or at least *I* can't lie to him. I'll have to find a way to test that it's the same for him, just for safety. "Riane," I manage, proving half-truths can be said. Another good piece of information.

"How many vampir have you killed, Riane?" Ventos asks, stroking his beard, a deep shade of umber.

"One," I answer honestly, then immediately wish I had inflated the number to sound more threatening.

"One?" he scoffs. "Lie."

"Think what you will." I shrug.

"She's a young one." Winny sits back down, pulling the fiddle to her chest. She plucks it gently, not playing anything in particular. The notes are sharp and high-pitched, grating in comparison to her earlier melody. "There's no way she could've killed many."

"She's telling the truth," Ruvan says with conviction enough that it reinforces his ability to sense truth from lie.

"I take it by the fact that you brought a human here at all that the anchor was not the master hunter, as you suspected." Callos shifts the topic of conversation away from me and speaks directly to Ruvan. The others quiet themselves. There's a knowing gleam in Callos's eyes. Ruvan stiffens at my side.

A sudden, oppressive sensation settles on my shoulders. At first, I think it's mourning for Davos, but I hardly ever felt love for the grizzly old hunter who guarded our town and was ready to marry me off like a broodmare. No, this is different… I can almost feel my stomach sinking as if I'm the one on the spot. I glance at Ruvan. His face is passive, but… My nerves are aflame. I can almost see under the surface of his expression. I think I can feel *his* panic.

"The master hunter was slain by my hand, but the curse still stands," Ruvan begrudgingly admits.

"I told you so." Callos sighs. "I've read every book on the early blood lore written by Jontun and I'm confident that the anchor of a curse must be a *thing*, not a person. Especially a curse as long-lasting as this. If it had been a person, they and the curse would've died long ago."

"Then we will find the anchor in the room you've identified," Ruvan says curtly.

"If she can make it there." Lavenzia glances between myself and Ruvan.

"She'll make it. She held her own against me," Ruvan says solemnly.

"You would try and kill the human we needed." Winny rolls her eyes.

"She wasn't about to come peacefully—no human would. Moreover, as soon as I saw her, I knew it had to be her. She wasn't like the other hunters."

Ruvan's words spin a small ball of warmth in my stomach. One I instantly try and douse. I will *not* be flattered by him.

"You mean that as more than her combat prowess," Callos asks in that quiet, knowing way of his.

"They had used the blood lore on her, and for it, she could go toe-to-toe with me." The room goes still. The silence fills the space easily, highlighting just how large and *empty* the room is. This hall could fit fifty. No, one hundred. Surely the vampire lord has a more fearsome retainer? Are they not back from across the Fade? Or…perhaps…did the hunters slay the rest?

Pride swells in me. Maybe Hunter's Hamlet is all right. Maybe Drew was found in the mists and saved by other hunters who reclaimed the night for humanity.

"There's no way." Winny pauses her playing.

"I know what I saw. Her eyes were gold-ringed and bloodshot. Her veins bulged. You might not know what the transformation rites look like, but I do. I have seen the old drawings and rituals, and she looked halfway through them while still being completely human and yet…" His eyes swing back to me. I continue to remain silent. Anything I say right now might be used against myself or the hamlet. "She radiated the great power of our kind. I could sense her coming as easily as I could any of you."

Sense me… Perhaps that's how the vampire knew I was in my home despite the salt? If that's true, then there's some hope that Mother remained safe through the night. But if it's true then it also means that I really did have some kind of power. How I looked in the mirror when I first arrived...was that truly me?

"Fascinating." Callos stalks up to me, looking at me from head to toe. I hate the feeling of a vampire inspecting me as if *I'm* the one who's the oddity. "How did they do it?"

"I..." *What do I tell them?* I have to do anything to keep up the charade. I know I can't outright lie to Ruvan, but what of the rest of them? "I'm a hunter"—so I can lie to the others—"not a scholar. I don't ask questions of my superiors."

"Ah, because the true measure of loyalty is not questioning," Callos says sarcastically, rolls his eyes, and returns to the bench.

"You found a real useful one, Ruvan." Lavenzia sinks back into her seat.

"She *will* be useful. She will get us inside the door. And if she can't, then she will still know of the hunters' attempts at blood lore. That might give us some clarity on how they made the curse in the first place—she might know something without realizing it."

I look up at Ruvan from the corners of my eyes. The way he speaks makes it sound like he's been as diligently planning on contingencies as I have. Maybe he's right and we both need each other. But if we are of similar mind then that begs the question, how is he planning to kill me once this has run its course?

If he truly is like me, he's thought of several ways.

"You know the Succumbed will frenzy at her scent," Winny says.

"Callos can find us a path of least resistance through the old castle," Ruvan counters.

Old castle? Succumbed? Curse anchors? I've no idea what they're talking about but I try and mentally take note of it all.

"I think it could be amusing to watch the Succumbed tear her limb from limb." Lavenzia leans forward in her chair, eyes gleaming. She looks ten times more deadly and now competes with Ventos for the most terrifying person here. Perhaps it's the bloodsworn, but Ruvan is solidly third and I almost want to tell him so just for the sake of a jab.

"She is one of us now. No wishing for her death," Ruvan reminds them.

"No." Ventos stands, chair toppling over with the force by which he does. He's clearly a hot-headed fellow. "She might have sworn an oath to *you*, and we might have a duty to honor your commands and oaths you make. But she is not, and will *never* be one of us. She is a hunter. She is the enemy." He thrusts a finger at me.

Vampires act so much like humans. Emotional. Capable of speech. Vampires *feel.* And if they are all so loyal to Ruvan…why do they speak out against him?

They seem to think their own thoughts rather than being a hive-like group… But they *are* monsters, I've seen as much, just not the kind I was always told. They are monsters that wear the skin of humans, drink blood to gain human feelings and emotions, masquerading close enough to humanity that it's *almost* confusing. They want me to sympathize with them, to see them as not so different from me. Well I won't be fooled.

"I would *never* want to be one of you," I say quietly. All eyes are on me instantly. "I will fulfill this oath for all of humanity and rid myself of this place and the vampire forever."

"Well said," Ruvan appraises. "The sooner we break the curse the better, on that much we can all agree."

Ventos reluctantly nods, righting his chair and falling heavily into it. It's a wonder the thing doesn't crack under the weight of all that muscle.

"Which means, tomorrow, we're headed into the old castle," he declares.

Worry and apprehension flash in their eyes. I think back to the dark windows Quinn and I avoided. "What is the old castle?" I dare to ask. None of them seem prepared to answer. A few open and shut their mouths. Finally, it's Ruvan who speaks.

"The place where the rot of your curse festers. Where you will see the true horror of what your dear hunters have done to our kind."

eleven

"To descend into the old castle, you're going to need your strength," Ruvan continues. "So you should eat while you're able." He looks to the rest of them. "Have you all had your fill?"

"Yes, but there's still some left," Lavenzia says.

"Hold on, I'll get it." Winny hops up and dashes down the hall, quickly returning with food—normal, human food—that she sets on the table.

No matter how much of a hard exterior I want to project, my stomach betrays me with a mighty growl. Ruvan startles, eyes swinging my way. He's the only one who seems to notice and, much to my surprise, doesn't draw attention to it.

Instead he says, "Please, help yourself."

"So I can eat the poison?" I counter.

He sighs heavily. "It's not poisoned. I couldn't kill you if I wanted to, remember?" *If* he wanted to, as if it hasn't been the primary thing on his mind this entire time.

"You might not be able to, but she could." I point to Winny, who's procuring eating vessels and utensils. She blinks several times, startled to suddenly be the subject of my attention. "I'm not bloodsworn to her."

"They've sworn their own oaths to me and I swore none under my command may harm you. No one will hurt you." There's an impatient edge to Ruvan's voice. "Now, *eat*."

"Yes, my lord." I force the words with every stone of

displeasure that has sunken to the pit of my stomach. Winny bringing over the cutlery gives me an idea.

"She is *not* sitting with us," Ventos grumbles.

"Let her sit," Lavenzia counters lightly. She rests a hand on Ventos's large forearm. "You're going to have to fight alongside her come morning. I think that's far worse than sharing a table. You might as well grow accustomed to her presence sooner rather than later."

Ventos glares at Ruvan but says nothing else.

"I have no interest in sharing your table," I say plainly. "We have all made it quite clear that this is a tenuous alliance. I am not one of you and I have no desire to be. I will eat on my own and we will interact as little as possible."

"At least *you* have some sense." It should be a compliment, but the way Ventos says it makes it clear that he doesn't think humans have sense in general. I ignore the offense and focus on the meager spread before me—salted pork and pickled vegetables.

I know hardship when I see it. There's generally enough to go around in Hunter's Hamlet, thanks to everyone living such regimented lives. But there have been times of bad drought, or heavy rains, that have limited our food stores to the point of aching stomachs. Why is the lord of the vampires eating the food of paupers in an empty, decrepit hall with only a few knights at his side?

It's one of many questions, but all I can seem to muster to ask is, "Vampires eat regular food?"

"What else would we eat?" Quinn asks.

"Blood? Human flesh?" I would think it obvious, but when the table erupts with laughter I realize I'm wrong. A hot flush burns my neck and I purse my lips to keep it from overtaking my face.

"Humans truly know nothing about us." Lavenzia helps herself to a pickled brussels sprout.

"We use blood for magic, Riane, not for sustenance." The alternative name sounds odd, but I force myself to quickly grow accustomed to it. I've already given him magic I didn't know I had and an oath I never wanted… I won't give him my name, too. A heavy weight follows Ruvan's statement, accompanied by a contemplative stare that I can't decipher. I wonder if, somehow, he's sensing my discomfort as I've sensed his. "At least, true vampir do."

"True vampires?" I ask.

"Those who haven't Succumbed to the curse. You'll see tomorrow." There's something about his tone that reminds me of a metal support about to snap. Grumbling. Groaning. A sound that you feel—that tells you if there is any extra weight placed upon it, it will split.

Deeming the conversation finished, I grab a plate and carefully select my food—choosing the largest hunk of meat available and hoping it's not of suspect origin. Then, I take cutlery, resisting glancing from the corners of my eyes to see if they're going to stop me. They don't. I try to keep the motion fluid and simple, folding up the napkin in such a way that its contents can't be seen. They're not paying attention to me, but rather talking amongst themselves again.

"Should we awaken more soldiers if we're going into the old castle?" Lavenzia asks Ruvan.

"No, we've already lost too many, we can't afford to awaken more."

"The Lord of the Keep is supposed to have seven vassals, at least."

"I don't want to wake anyone else," Ruvan insists. I wonder what he means by "awaken." Perhaps it is another term for the rites they spoke of to make vampires. "And even if I did, we only took enough blood for ourselves and to sustain the long night. It'd be too much to support another's magic."

"Is this really a conversation we should be having in front of her?" Ventos jerks his head in my direction.

Fortunately, I've already pressed the fork and knife against the bottom of the plate. "Don't mind me; I'll take this upstairs."

"No, you won't." Ruvan narrows his eyes at me. For a second, I'm worried my intentions have been uncovered. "We already have enough of a problem with vermin. I don't want anything attracting them to my bedroom." He turns back to Ventos. "She has made a blood oath with me. She is *not* your enemy."

"And what about when the blood oath expires?" Ventos hums after his question. "Will she be our enemy then?"

"She will have secured safety for her people; she will not see us as an enemy any longer." Ruvan's words are pointed and we lock eyes as he speaks for me. I can feel him trying to probe for the malice I still hold toward him.

I keep my face as blank as a hunter's mask. "Exactly as you say. Once this is over with, I've no reason to concern myself with you."

"Once a hunter, *always* a hunter." Ventos is going to be a problem. He suspects my true intentions and could just as easily become suspicious that I'm not quite all I claim; I'm going to have to keep myself alert around him.

But for now I shrug and head to one of the far tables, putting my back toward them.

Lavenzia assumes her earlier line of questioning. "So we're really going into the old castle, just the five of us?"

"We'll have to be strategic," Ruvan says gravely.

"Callos, you better consult all your books and records to come up with a good path," she murmurs.

"Do you really doubt my abilities?" Callos asks incredulously.

As they speak, I force myself to eat. They've already dined of this food, so I don't think it's poisoned. Plus, I'm supposed to be safe as long as I have the blood oath.

The conversation carries on, oddly normal. The six of them sound like old friends—like humans, not monsters.

"Do you really think that we can put an end to this long night?" Ventos's voice has gone softer, more thoughtful.

"I wouldn't have bet my life on it if I didn't. I wouldn't have brought a hunter here if I didn't." I can almost feel Ruvan's eyes on my back. I'm keenly aware of him, more than I've been of anyone before. I continue eating, ignoring the sensation. It abates when he begins speaking again. "The hunters *are* engaging in the blood lore, even still—we have confirmation of it at last. I'd bet they're using it to fuel the curse year after year since they can no longer reach its anchor. With the right blood tools, we might be able to undo it entirely…or at least combat it more than just feeding the casings."

Lavenzia laughs, but it is not a joyous sound. There is a twinge of sorrow running through it. Sadness and heartache. "An end to the long night," she muses softly, her tone almost songlike. "I don't even know what I would do first. No, I know. I would eat one of Lamir's famous cakes. I would eat *seven*."

"You would make yourself sick," Ventos says.

"And what a delightful sickness it would be." I can tell there's a smile in her voice.

A vampire talking about cake… The world has flipped itself. Down is up. Blood is ink. I'm sitting on the wrong side of the Fade. And *a vampire is talking about cake.*

"I would trade all the cakes in the world to have a city that Julia could return to." Heavy silence fills the room behind Ventos's words.

"Have you visited her since we came back?" Lavenzia asks softly.

The long pause draws my attention over my shoulder. Ventos stares at nothing. He doesn't look sad, but he exudes sorrow. There's a loss there that I know all too well from the hamlet. I want to revel in it. To think of how wonderful it is to see a vampire in even a fraction of the pain that they've caused us.

But…I see myself in that pained expression. I see Mother searching the flames of the forge. Staring at nothing as she sank further into her own void following the death of our father. I see my blank eyes in the mirror after Father died, after Drew left.

Ventos stands and the scraping sound of a chair over the stone floor fills the air. "It's getting late, I'm going to bed," he declares, firmly ending the conversation.

"You're right, we should get some rest," Lavenzia agrees.

As they are each departing for the night, I carefully wipe the knife I lifted with the rest of the cutlery and slide it into my sleeve. The flat of the blade is cool against my skin. Reassuring. I secure it into place by tightening the leather strap around my cuff with one hand. Hunters' clothes and armor are designed to hide weapons wherever possible. Even though I've never worn the leathers before, I know their designs well enough from working with the tanner for clasps, light plate, and other modifications.

I take their cue and stand as well, wrapping up the other cutlery as I did when I carried my food over to the far table. I set the plate down with the rest of the remnants of dinner.

"I can take care of it," Lavenzia offers.

"No, no, it's my turn." Ruvan waves her away. It's hard to believe that all the grace and elegance he projects now was wrapped into the miserable-looking husk of a man I first met. "The rest of you, off to bed."

I take my leave of them, returning upstairs. What luck that the vampire lord decided to stay behind. But I wonder what it was he was "taking care" of… It almost seemed as though he was staying behind to clean up. Worry seeps into me. If he's cleaning up dishes, will he notice the missing knife?

But surely a vampire lord has attendants to do such basic tasks. Even if I haven't seen them…they must be making themselves scarce.

I shake my head as I enter the quarters that are now my temporary home. *I am worrying for nothing*, I try and reassure myself.

The chambers are empty and Quinn isn't at the door this time. I am alone. It's a curious decision, leaving me without any kind of supervision in his personal quarters. One that I quickly learn isn't as foolish as it appears on the surface. All the cabinets are locked. I take a turn about the sitting area, investigating everything within reach.

The furniture is old, and mostly moth-eaten. What remains is bare and fraying. These don't look like the lavish chambers of the vampire lord I would've expected. Not that I ever gave much thought to how the vampires lived. Until now it was almost as if the Fade Marshes birthed them for the sake of terrorizing us. It didn't matter where they came from. All that mattered was stopping them.

There are three doors from the main room—one I entered from, the second is locked, but the third opens for me. Inside is a washroom. Just like everything else, it has the veneer of luxury, covered in a thick grime of neglect. The spigot over the sink has turned green with age, calcium coating its nozzle. I am astounded when the handles turn and mostly clear water sputters out. At least I will not die of thirst.

Back in the main room I begin to take stock of the things I can control, the supplies that are available to me, and everything I have access to. There's a loose board on the floor, but there's only stone and bugs beneath. I find one of the baseboards nearby to be loose as well; the plaster behind has been cracked and eaten away by some rodent. I could store food there so they can't starve me as motivation to do any bidding I don't like. But I'm reminded of Ruvan's words at dinner about vermin. I don't want whatever creature that made this hole to consume my emergency rations before I have a chance to. It could be a spot for weapons, however.

I pull up the cushions on the settee. Sure enough, the seams are soft and I can pry them open with ease. It's another good hiding place for a small weapon. I store the knife there and settle the cushions in place before lying down. The weapon is just within my reach, pinned between the cushion and the back of the couch, hidden within the folds of the fraying seam.

Expectedly, sleep avoids me. I stay awake, watching as the silvery glow of the moon begins to weaken and fade, replaced by a softer, more natural haze of dawn. If I were home I would be just waking to head downstairs and put on the kettle for tea before heading to the forge so both would be hot by the time Mother rose.

The ache of loss settles into my bones. I know this sensation well. The cause is different, but the touch is the same. It's the same icy embrace my father gives me from the Great Beyond.

How is the hamlet? What is Mother doing? Where is Drew? Is he even alive?

If I manage to kill the vampire lord and survive long enough to return home, what would I be returning home to? If Ruvan is dead… then we're free, whatever's left of us. I could go to the sea. I could smith with metals I've only ever heard of. I could marry whomever I please or maybe even not marry at all. All the choices in the world would be mine for the making.

It's a waking dream so delightful it hurts. The life that I could've had, but that was stolen from the moment I was born.

I blink up at the ceiling, trying to replace my sorrow with anger before it can slip into the void of nothingness that lies within me. The questions threaten to smother me. My ribcage is suddenly three sizes too small.

If not for the vampires, I wouldn't be here. Hunter's Hamlet would be whole. Mother, Father, Drew, and I might have long since moved to the sea. It's the vampire's fault. I can't lose sight of that. Even when the wondering of back home becomes deafeningly loud in the silence of night. My hatred for the vampires can be my guiding light.

The door opens just before the sun crests the horizon.

The vampire lord crosses the room. The hair on the back of my neck stands on end as he passes me. I keep my breathing even and low. Eyes closed. The metal rungs of the curtain scrape against the rod as he plunges the room into total darkness. Shuttering out the light.

Sunlight burns away the carcasses of vampires. Maybe I don't need silver at all. Maybe I just need to rip off the curtains at the right moment.

"I know you're not asleep."

I cease my pretense and sit. The vampire lord is at the window, back to me. Hands still gripped around the curtains.

"I know you took it," he continues. I remain silent and he turns to face me, eyes shimmering in the low light. "At least you don't deny it."

"Did you find out when your attendants were cleaning the dishes?"

"Attendants..." He scoffs softly. "Don't insult me. I knew it would end up in your sleeve from the moment you lifted it off the table." I swallow disappointment in myself. I am transparent. "What do you think a steak knife could do against me?"

Nothing...I knew it from the moment I took it. A slim piece of steel is nothing against a vampire. But I had to. "I don't feel comfortable being unarmed here."

"And you won't be." He folds his arms over his chest. "You just couldn't trust me enough to wait for me to give you a weapon—or to even ask."

"You would give me a weapon?"

"Why wouldn't I?"

I level my eyes with him. He knows why; we both know why. The same reason why Ventos will never trust me. Why Lavenzia watches me with such attentiveness. Perhaps they all knew I had the knife.

"*Ah,* you think I would not trust you with a weapon because you would turn it against me." He stalks slowly over, coming to a stop right before me. As he moves I ease my legs down onto the floor, ready to bolt, ready to attack if need be. Even if I'm helpless to his vampire abilities, I won't die without a fight. Not ever. I'm born and bred of Hunter's Hamlet. We do not die peacefully in our beds. "Do it then."

I tilt my head slightly, eyes narrowing.

"You have your weapon, turn it against me."

"Steel will do nothing to you."

"And yet you risked the goodwill I was attempting to build with you by taking it." He leans forward, placing both hands on the back of the settee, on either side of me. I'm framed by his arms. Pinned without a touch. The vampire lord's face is so very close, close enough for me to smell the scent of moss and leather on his clothes and feel the heat of his breath. The last time it was this close I still had a silver weapon. He was a husk, not a breathtaking creature of death and moonlight, and I still had a chance to end him. "So use it."

I don't move. I just glare at his stolen face and lying eyes.

"*Do it*," he urges harshly.

All the hatred I'd wound up earlier around my heart snaps. I reach for the weapon, yanking it from its hiding place. With all my might I thrust forward, going right for his throat—as though I am trying to stab through, and carve out the mark at the base of his neck. The mark that is supposedly mine.

Thousands of invisible hands wrap themselves around my limbs, holding me in place. The knife quivers in the air as I strain against the unseen restraints. Using every muscle I have, I bring my left hand to my right and grip the knife with both, trying to force it forward. My heart hammers as if it is about to explode from the effort.

But it doesn't move.

A hair's breadth away from the vampire lord's neck, and the knife won't move forward any more. *I* can't move. An invisible wall holds me back from him. No, it actively pushes me away.

With a frustrated grunt, I fall back. The knife clatters to the floor as my muscles release, exhausted by the effort. A smirk slides across his face. Horrible and exceedingly self-satisfied. The vampire lord reaches down and grabs the knife, turning it over in his hands, making a show of inspecting it.

"Do you see now? Do you understand *why* I will arm you? Why I do not fear you and neither will my kin?"

"The oath." I've never said a word with such disdain before.

"You swore on your blood that you would not harm me or any loyal to me—you marked yourself with your vow to me."

Until the curse is broken, I add mentally. I am only trapped in this arrangement so long as this curse exists. The second it is lifted, I will be free, and he will be dead.

"So, steal all the weapons you want, Riane. Squirrel them away, keep them in your clothes, in your bed. Hide them wherever you think they will be safe. But know that you will not use them on me, or my covenant. Not now, not *ever*."

He hovers, looming over me, golden eyes shining, waiting to see if I will try and argue. Maybe he's waiting to see if I will try and attack him again. But I am a fast learner, adaptable. He's made his point clear and I will not throw myself against that wall again.

I will have to be clever. Maybe, if I cannot do it by my hand, I can force the hand of another. Or perhaps it could be as simple as an accident, a silver dagger, tiny and unnoticeable, stabbed upward to the base of his pillow. And when he lays his head upon it, he will be skewered dead. A trip of my clumsy feet and the curtains are yanked off as he stands right before the sunlit window.

Yes, there are many things for me to try. And if he thinks that I am only deadly while a weapon is in my hand then his life will be the cost of underestimating me.

"Now go to sleep. You'll need your strength. The nightmare begins at sunset."

twelve

Sleep remains elusive. I can't commit myself to slumber. Not when I'm in the lair of the vampire.

I should be further investigating my surroundings. Finding possible escape paths. Something of use… But I am exhausted. My want is overshadowed by the more practical knowledge that I am, to an extent, safe at present. I can't harm the vampire lord or his kin. They cannot harm me. His display was clear enough evidence of that. And I need to keep my strength.

I don't want to rest. But I should. *I need to keep my strength.*

When my eyes do close, I'm haunted by the Blood Moon.

The crimson fog curls around me. Hidden beasts move through it. Ready to pounce. I see my fellow hunters sprinting through the mists. Drew is a blur, gone before I can even call out his name. His scream is quick to follow, cut short with a gurgle of blood.

Deep within me is a spinning thread, pulling me forward. I have to get to Drew. It's pulling me to my brother, my twin. Pulling me to—

Him.

The vampire lord stands in the center of the ruins where we fought, screaming to the sky. Drew is nowhere to be seen. Dark power radiates off the vampire in waves that crash against the fog, competing with it. His hair is as pale as bone, hanging down to his mid-back in a single sheet. Ruvan's hair is not that long, *my mind rebels. Ruvan's hair spills over his eyes but tapers at his neck, unlike this man's. Though, this could just be another face Ruvan can wear.*

Everything goes silent.

"A curse of vengeance," the vampire lord whispers. "A curse wrought in blood..."

A curse.

A curse...

The dreams slip around me, shifting, changing. I'm no longer in the marshes but the smithy. Mother and I are lighting the fires. Dawn has just broken.

"Get inside, Floriane," she urges.

"Mother?"

"Inside, now."

The sound of the charcoal hitting the ground rings in my ears. It deafens the groaning coming from my father's lips. Animal growling hissing between two fangs.

A blur of movement.

A flash of silver.

A scream.

My father crumples and his skin sinks into his bones. No. *As the sunlight hits him, the body of the vampire that stole his face begins to steam and burn away. Its screams match my own.*

"Wake up!"

I jolt awake. Ruvan looms over me, his golden eyes wide and frightened, almost comforting. Almost human. Until my attention drops to his slightly parted lips and I see his fangs.

I'm back in the dream and I violently shove him away. Ruvan tumbles back, head over heels. I stare at my hands, surprised by the force. Shaken by it. By the dream. My fingers tremble as if trying to release the energy and I grab my head as a flash of pain splits through it, vanishing as quickly as it came.

"Are you all right?" he asks, composing himself, as though he wasn't just turned into a living tumbleweed. He runs a hand through his disheveled hair and tugs on a worn velvet dressing robe, loose trousers and shirt underneath. It almost looks as if he just bolted out of bed.

"What do you care?" I glare at him.

"You are my bloodsworn, it is my duty to care," he tries to say, having the audacity to look concerned.

"I don't want your lies."

"I can't lie to you." Ruvan shakes his head, silvery hair in the lowlight falling into his face. "Was it a nightmare?"

"I'm fine." I look away from him.

He snorts. "You don't look fine."

"I said I'm fine!" I snap, clenching my hands into fists to stop them from shaking. The last person I will let console me is him.

"Very well." Ruvan's upright once more, looming over me. I don't look up at him. It's his fault my father is dead. It's his fault… "I'll let you suffer in silence, then."

I stay on the settee long after he leaves, thoughts of my father leaving aftershocks in their wake. "Get yourself together, Floriane." I grip my head and try to force myself to stop shaking. It takes a while, but I manage.

Shaking my head, I reorient myself and head to the washroom, settle my morning ablutions, and check the status of my armor. Only a few straps need to be tightened. I pull on the straps as far as they will go, leaving no room for any fears or trembling.

Inspecting the clasps gives my mind something to do. There's a few that got dented in my initial scuffle with the vampire lord. If I can find a chance to fix them before I see any combat, it'd be a good idea.

Finally emerging into the main hall, I immediately pick out Callos's soft voice.

"I think I have it entirely covered."

"Good, I don't want a repeat of last time." That's Ruvan. I pause, waiting to see if I hear anyone else. There's a long moment of silence. "Good morning, Riane." Ruvan's voice fills the cavernous space. He speaks as though our previous interaction hadn't happened at all. I doubt it's a kindness, more like he doesn't want his other vampire friends to know that I put him on his rear first thing. But I'm content letting the matter be forgotten.

"Isn't it dusk?" I ask as I descend. I expected they would wake at sunset. All I saw was light bleeding through the curtains.

"Not quite," Ruvan answers, straightening away from the table to look at me. I pointedly keep my eyes on his face when I notice that the ties on his shirt are mostly undone. I've seen a man's bare chest before—in the fields, or sometimes even in the forge, when it got too hot and the young men Mother and I would hire as strikers to take some of the physical toll off our bodies would strip their shirts. But none of the men in Hunter's Hamlet can hold a candle to Ruvan's physique. The man is practically carved marble. My throat is dry. "Afternoon."

"And you're awake?" I try and sound casual. "Don't vampires sleep all day?"

"Vampir*es* might. Can't say I know much about them. But *vampir* do not," Callos answers. "Though our group does tend to keep odd hours, given our circumstances."

I can't figure out how to ask if sunlight burns a living vampire's skin or not so I give up trying for now. Instead I assess the journals and maps that are laid out across the table. Rooms are carefully sketched out in ink on the yellowed parchment. On fresher looking paper are similar sketches, with accompanying notes.

"What's all this?"

"The most likely path to get us to the anchor of the curse," Ruvan says.

"A relief to hear you finally agree with me," Callos murmurs. Ruvan ignores him.

There are lines and Xs drawn all over the papers, red ink marring the black outlines of rooms and hallways. Individual places mean nothing to me. But on the whole…it's massive. Far in one corner is a room marked "workshop" and circled in red ink—at least I hope that red is ink and not some kind of vampire blood magic.

"In the workshop there?"

Ruvan nods. "That's our destination." It's clear why we couldn't just walk there when he first brought up my helping him. The castle looks larger than all of Hunter's Hamlet.

"With any luck you'll make it," Callos says. I wish he sounded more confident.

Ruvan clasps him on the shoulder, almost causing the man to lose his eyeglasses from startling. "If anyone can get us the best path there, it's you."

"No one has gone that deep for centuries…" Callos removes his spectacles and cleans them on his shirt. "I'm working with old information pieced together from Jontun's records with a prayer."

"Jontun?" I ask.

"He was the royal archivist during the time of the first king—when this workshop was built and the blood lore began. Lord Jontun was the one to preserve our history of the time. Our first king wasn't much of a writer," Callos explains.

"Why would a curse anchor be in a workshop in the oldest part of the vampire's castle behind a door that only a human can open?" None of it makes sense. Surely they have to see that, too.

"I was hoping you could tell me." Ruvan folds his arms and I notice his biceps straining against the cotton of his simple coat. He would have to be strong to move in all that plate, even with vampiric powers. "Maybe some hunter's secret passed down?"

"Don't look at me for answers. I'm just here to open a door." I shrug and turn back to Callos. I'll give Ruvan nothing more than I must, lest I say something that might be able to be used against Hunter's Hamlet. "What type of workshop is it?"

"One of the original blood lore studies," Callos answers. "There were two, originally, but one was destroyed shortly after the Fade was made. By all records we can find, this is the only one left."

"Is the original 'blood lore' different from the current?"

"Yes, and no. Blood lore is merely the act of drawing out magic from the blood through item and ritual. There are some rituals every vampir can perform and some that are imprinted on our own blood." Callos flips through the journals. "Others are unique to individual vampir. Innate abilities that come forth over time that allow them to use blood in ways no others can. Blood lore, like any study, has evolved over time for all vampir and for every individual."

"What kind of innate abilities?" The idea of every vampire having unique powers is disheartening. It means they're all more dangerous than I thought—than can be tracked or traced.

"It's different for every person." He glances up at me. "Take Winny, for example. If her dagger has a drop of her blood on it, she can never miss her mark."

"I see." I had been hoping for more concrete information on what I was up against. I had always thought the vampire could use blood lore just to steal faces. But it sounds like they can do almost anything with it on top of these "innate abilities."

Callos arches his brows at me. "Are you genuinely curious about the blood lore?"

"I'm more trying to make sure you're not taking me there to break the oath and carve me up," I retort quickly to hide my genuine curiosity. If I ask too many questions, they might become more suspicious and stop giving me useful information.

"The oath will not be broken until it is fulfilled," Ruvan says tiredly. "Stop thinking a threat lies around every corner."

"A threat has lain around every corner my whole life," I snap. "If anything, it's stranger to be able to look danger in the eye rather than it lunging at me from the shadows."

On my words, I lock my gaze with his. He dips his chin slightly. Those luminescent eyes threaten to swallow me whole. I can almost feel the depths of thoughts swirling behind that gaze. It's as if a bridge has been erected between us, one I can never—will never—cross… But with it I can see and feel things I shouldn't in him. I sense the ebbs and flows of his emotion. Strength radiates off of him, caressing me like the whisper of a dangerously good dream.

"You are not the only one who lives with danger lurking in the shadows," he finally says, words as cold as the air of the castle. "You are not the only one who has spent their entire existence in fragility."

I have never thought of anything about the vampires as "frail." But the way Ruvan says so gives me pause. There's genuine pain there that manifests as a dull ache in the hollow of my throat.

Ruvan stands. Before I can say anything else, he continues, likely for the best. "Come. We should outfit you properly for going into the old castle."

He leads me through the double doors at the front of the hall, which connects to an antechamber that has been turned into an armory. The moment I see an armor rack, piled haphazardly with bloodied, all-too-familiar leathers, I cease all movement. I simply stare at the leather armor, void of owners to fill it. It mirrors the growing emptiness within me—the void into which I've attempted to throw all feelings…all thoughts of home, Mother, and Drew…just for the sake of survival.

"Does it enrage you?" he asks.

There's only so much one can feel before emotions begin to numb, and I have passed that threshold. But I'm not about to be that open, that vulnerable, with the lord of the vampires. So instead I retort, "I did not take you for someone to be concerned with my feelings."

"You wound me."

"I strike true."

A thin smile works its way across his lips. "That is one of the reasons I chose you, after all. To be a hunter, to strike fast and true, to be ruthless."

"I thought you wanted me for access to this door and information on the hunters?"

"I am purposeful. Everything and everyone around me have multiple functions." Ruvan crosses to the armor rack I've been staring at. He motions with an open palm to the pile of armor. "Take whatever you need."

"I'm already fitted with armor."

"Is there nothing better here?"

"No, every hunter is given the same armor." With the exception of the master hunter. Davos always had the finest armor of the entire fortress…little good it did him. Still, I approach the racks, encroaching on Ruvan's space. Lightly, I run my fingertips over the leathers. I press them into the buckles and fastenings I remember making. It was a small job that even a child could do. Goodness, it was *easier* when my fingers were smaller and nimbler.

A fourth of the armor here, I helped make. And it's all stained with blood that looks far too fresh for my liking. Phantom heat from the forge tingles my fingertips as I think of working on Drew's armor, armor that was just as bloody as this when I last saw him.

"The man you were killing, when I first saw you, in those ruins…" The words escape me as a whisper. I should keep them in. But this ache is too deep, threatening to overwhelm me if I'm not careful. "He… We left him…" I swallow thickly. The vampire lord merely watches me. Silent. Waiting. Allowing me to struggle. I bet he's enjoying this turmoil. I wonder if he can feel my senses across that invisible bridge between us as keenly as I can feel his. "Was he still alive?"

Ruvan is horribly silent. Made worse when he doesn't give me a direct answer. "What does it matter to you?"

"He's—" The word *twin* sticks in my throat, choking me. I can't talk about my family. Doing so would be a danger to Drew if Ruvan ever decided to steal my face. I will not be a repeat of my father. "Someone I care about."

"A lover?"

"*No!*" I gag. "We've been…for a long time we were…very close…"

"You're family." Ruvan folds his arms. I purse my lips and it's all the affirmation he needs. "I didn't kill him, and I heard his heartbeat when we left. But whether he bled out before help arrived, I cannot say."

I exhale a small sigh of relief and touch the ring on my pinky. There is a chance Drew survived. It's better than nothing. Drew is strong. He'll be fine. *I would know if he wasn't*, I try to tell myself.

"He's my brother," I admit it despite myself, compelled by an unknown force. Perhaps it's because Ruvan already sussed out that he was family and, given his age, it's clear Drew isn't my uncle or father.

"I'm sorry."

"You're not." I glare up at the lord. Jerking my face toward him puts our noses almost touching as he leans in. My heart hammers and I can feel tension in the air. I wonder if one of us is going to give into futility by trying to attack the other. My insides squirm at the idea of tumbling with him again against the stone. Of exchanging blow for blow. Of pinning him down and looming over him, triumphant.

"I am." Ruvan gives me a firm stare. Oddly…I sense sincerity coming from him. But why? "You and your brother are as victim to this circumstance as I and my covenant are. None of us laid the foundation for all this bloodshed, all this death. But we are the ones who must continue to bleed for it."

"Your people thrive off it."

"Do we look like we're thriving?" he says coolly, leaning closer. I can feel angry power vibrating the air around him. "Tell me, from what you have seen, is this the mighty *vampire* horde you were expecting?"

I open my mouth to retort and come up short. I want to say *yes*. But

I don't know what to make of this strange world and the few vampires within it. The old stories, passed down longer than time has been counted in Hunter's Hamlet, tell of the bloodthirsty vampire lord and his legions of mindless death bringers, ready to lay waste to humanity every five hundred years when the Blood Moon rises if not for the hunters.

None of the stories unfolded around a small group of friends in a lonely, decrepit castle.

"Tell me…" His attention returns to the armor as he leans away, tension evaporating. "What have your hunters done with our fallen following the Blood Moon years past?"

Now is my chance to learn about them. "We've left them to burn away in the sun."

"Ah, of course, not a proper burial." He grimaces.

"We do not bury monsters."

"Do I look like a monster to you?" The question is quiet, filled with sorrow, longing—yearning, even. But for what? *What does he keep wanting from me?*

I study his face, the high swell of his cheekbones, his thin but firm lips. The sharp hook of his nose and the square of his chin. He's almost…*too* perfect. Uncomfortably so. Unbearable to look at and for it…I can't look away. I can hardly fight the urge to touch him.

"I have seen your true form. I know how monstrous you are," I whisper.

"My true form? That—that—" He seems at a loss for words and shakes his head. "How are you so dense? *That* is not my true form. This is. Were it not for the curse, sapping my strength, my power, my body itself, this is how I would look." He runs his hand down his front, his long fingers catching on the open lacings of his shirt, pulling them open slightly more. Never have I been more focused on the length of a man's body. Never have I been *alone* with a man at all for this long. The second I realize it my insides are squirming. "It is the curse *your kind* placed upon us that turned us into monsters."

"We don't have that kind of power," I manage to say.

"Humans did once. And it seems your ilk has stolen some of our blood lore to preserve it."

"I didn't even know I had magic in my blood," I counter. The fallacies in his logic are adding up to be too much to stay silent on—

even if I know I likely should. "How do you think all of Hunter's Hamlet is sustaining some kind of secret curse? And if we did have that power, why wouldn't we use it to fight back against you monsters?"

"Ah, *monsters*, there's that word again." He takes a step closer, into my personal space. It's a small movement, but enough to make my senses alight. "Those who have Succumbed to the curse might seem that way as they have sunken below the threshold of cognizance and have resorted to base instinct. Yes, *they* are monsters, as you say. But they are also victims. Your hands are just as bloody as mine. And we were both born into cages not of our making." His brow softens slightly and his lips part, just barely giving me a glimpse of his wicked-sharp fangs. He would look almost human in this moment of emotion, were it not for that reminder of his wickedness. Ruvan continues to search my face. What does he want? My sympathy? My forgiveness for all he's done? "But we can fix it. You and I. We can find our freedom from this unyielding nightmare. If you can just put your blind hatred aside long enough to see the truth before you."

Freedom.

That almost forbidden word of yearning. Of want. The thing that I craved so desperately from birth that I had to teach myself not to so I wouldn't go mad. Could such a thing really exist for me?

No. *No*. He's lying. There is no freedom for any of us. Only death. To think there could be would be ripping open a new wound.

Nothing cuts deeper than hope.

"You have nothing to say?" He shakes his head in disappointment. I am adrift, washed away into an ocean of sorrow originating from him. "Why did I expect anything more from you?" He motions to a table of silver sickles, daggers, and swords. "Take what you need to defend yourself. Anything you want is yours. Prepare for the battle of your life so we may be done with each other as quickly as possible."

His words of battle should make me afraid, but my focus is solely on the weaponry. *Swords*… My family hasn't forged swords in centuries. The sickles are lighter and require less material. And what the hunters sacrificed in range with sickles, they gained, and more, in speed.

But I do wonder what I might make if given the choice…if I had all the resources in the world. If I didn't have a town to protect. What would *I* make? I've never asked myself that before.

"These are old," I whisper.

"Old weapons are still good weapons." He rolls his eyes.

"Not always true." I lift a sword, eying down the fuller and inspecting the edge. "Age alone can dull a blade. And if you took these off the battlefield, they were already nicked and damaged to begin with." I show him the subtle dents in the weapon. "See, here."

Ruvan seems mildly impressed, but the emotion is fleeting. "A dull silver sword is still a silver sword. All it needs to do is break a vampir's flesh."

"It's far more effective when sharp. The blade does more of the work so the fighter isn't slowed down. Plus, old, dented blades will get stuck in bones rather than slice clean, which creates opening for attacks. Do you have a smithy?"

"A smithy?" He blinks, clearly startled. "What could you possibly need a smithy for?"

You are pretending to be a hunter right now, Floriane, not a smith. Keep the illusion. "I…I could make an attempt at honing them," I murmur. Figuring out how to dance with my words is more difficult by the moment. "I've seen it done enough times. Sometimes I worked on my own sickles." Which a hunter would never do. But I can't resist. I can't leave these weapons in the state they're in. Doing so would be a dishonor to all the forge maidens who came before me.

Ruvan considers this for a long moment and I worry my ruse has been destroyed. He starts back for the main doors. I begin trying to find which is the sharpest weapon, quickly hoisting sickles that I think will be my best bet.

"Leave them. Ventos will bring them to you."

"Pardon?"

"He'll be delighted to put to use all that muscle of his by carrying them to the smithy," Ruvan clarifies. "But we haven't had a smith in the castle in centuries. So your time will be better spent clearing the cobwebs than lugging metal."

"You actually have a smithy…" I slowly set down the sickle. And here I thought it was just blood *everything*.

"Of course we do. But you only have a day to do whatever it is you need. I won't delay going into the old castle longer than that."

thirteen

BACK IN THE MAIN HALL, THE OTHER FIVE VAMPIRES ARE SEATED AROUND THE TABLE, ALL TEN EYES ON US IMMEDIATELY ON ENTRY.

"Ventos, I need you to bring the weaponry everyone uses to the smithy."

"Weaponry? Smithy?" Ventos rumbles, sharing glances with those at the table. "We have a smithy?"

"I do believe there is one attached to the true armory," Quinn responds. "Though as far as the path to get there—"

"It's clear," Callos says, adjusting his spectacles. "I took that route earlier to access the library."

"Those corridors have been walled off for years, nothing is getting through." Lavenzia picks at her plate. Breakfast is as uninspired as dinner was. I miss the fresh biscuits the baker would bring every morning for us—*a special treat for the forge maiden*, he would say. "But what do you need the smithy for? Our weapons not good enough for you, human?"

"Not in the slightest," I say plainly. Lavenzia's eyebrows raise at my directness. "Those weapons have been left in neglect and aren't worth wielding in this state."

The table seems stunned I would say anything of the sort. I hear a soft huff come from Ruvan. Amusement, perhaps? But it couldn't be. Certainly not, given that the entirety of our interaction has been nothing but contentious until this point. Then again, he had mentioned last night that I was throwing away the goodwill he was attempting to give me. Perhaps there's still traces of that goodwill left, restored from our conversations this morning. Not that I care about the goodwill of a vampire.

"This way." He leads me through the side door at the base of the stairs that stretch up to the mezzanine his rooms are on. I saw members of his covenant go down this hall last night. These must be their quarters.

At the end of the hall is a staircase behind a barred door. Much like the circular stair that led to the chapel, the majority of the doors along this passageway are locked. The patina on the bolts and bars betrays just how long ago they were put in place. These locks aren't here for my benefit.

"What's behind these doors?" I ask. Ruvan glances my way, arching one perfect eyebrow. I assume it to mean, *how dare you ask,* but I'm wrong. Yet again, he answers my question.

"Passages we no longer use, or need, or can protect."

"It seems like a lot of barricades to keep people in certain areas."

"Less about keeping us in and more about keeping them out," Ruvan says solemnly.

"Them?"

"The Succumbed."

At the base of the stairs, as mentioned, is an old armory. Large weapons racks are lined with spears and swords. But they have not been lifted in centuries, judging from the thick layer of dust and cobwebs lacing them.

"Steel." I run my fingertip down the fuller of one of the swords. It's of good make. Or was, at a time. Now it's as useless as the decorative sword I attempted to use against Ruvan when we first arrived.

"You can tell that quickly just by looking?" He seems surprised.

"I've grown up with silver weapons; I know the difference." It's just a quickly thought-of excuse, but then excitement gets the better of my tongue. "You can see it when you look closely, here, see?" Ruvan approaches. He hovers over my shoulder as I point at the metal of the sword. "This is tarnished and rusted, of course, time does that. But you can see the grooves of the grindstone worked out by the whetstone to create that smooth finish. If it had silver in it, there would be subtle grooves, waves, or blooms." *As Mother would call them.*

"Yes, your silver weapons are unique indeed." Ruvan leans away, inspecting me more than the sword. I quickly turn away from the weapon and he continues on. I stay a step behind, scolding myself for my eagerness for all things metal. "That's why we must steal them, along with the armor and whatever other resources we can scavenge during the Blood Moon. There was only ever one smith among us who could have a chance at reproducing your silver, and he's long gone."

"I'm not surprised," I murmur under my breath. If Ruvan hears, he says nothing. My family, generations ago, were the ones to come up with the process of smelting silver with iron in a special process to create an alloy as strong as steel and as deadly as silver. All that work, all the smithing, my mother's, my grandmother's…being wielded by vampires. It's almost enough to make me sick. I continue talking in an attempt to distract myself. "What do you need silver weapons for, anyway?"

"Why do you think?"

There's only one explanation for why they'd need silver, specifically. Steel is just fine for humans and beasts, silver is for— "You hunt your own kind?"

He pauses at a back archway, shoulders rising to his ears, head hanging. "They are not 'our kind' any longer," he says solemnly. "The best thing we can do for them is to offer a clean death."

Any further thoughts leave me as we enter a smithy twice the size of my family's. Windows have been shuttered, though beams of light punch through breaks and missing slats. Tables of stone are dotted throughout the room. A pedal-powered grist wheel is in the far back corner, more replacement stones of different grits than I have seen in my life stacked behind it. Hammers of all sizes and heads are racked neatly along the wall next to tongs and other necessary tools, as if someone intended to return, but never did. Now, they're as forgotten as the weapons in the armory.

The forge itself is shaped like a mighty, fearsome maw. Almost lizard-like. Sharp teeth bared in the archway over where the forge fires will be lit. The sparks of hearth embers will illuminate two, currently dark, eyes. Built into the floor are mighty bellows, intended to be pumped with the power of legs over arms.

Like the altar before its god rests the anvil in the center of it all. I approach reverently, my breaths shallow. There's still life in this place, in this anvil. There's still heat, for those who know how to feel it. "Hello," I whisper, running my fingers along its top and edges. The grooves and indentations are different than any I've known, the mark of a forger whom I will never meet.

"Is it all right?" Ruvan is suddenly at my side. I don't remember him approaching. His long fingers trail over the anvil as well. Our pinkies brush and the silver ring on mine catches my eye.

I quickly ball my hand into a fist. I'm suddenly imagining Drew seeing me brushing hands with the vampire lord.

"It's more than 'all right,' it's magnificent." I can't even lie. The ghosts of the blacksmiths who came before me still linger here, silently begging for noise and heat. For the clang of metal and the relentless hammering of creations not yet realized. "Why is it not used?"

"You heard Ventos, most of those awoken in the long night don't realize we even have a smithy. The smiths all died long ago." Ruvan's attention drifts out the windows to where the ice-covered city lies beyond. "We only wake so many at a time, just enough to keep our people alive and protected. Those who wake have a function—usually to fight. Or to keep records. Forging was deemed unnecessary."

"If you're fighting, you absolutely need an active smithy." *And a dark forge should be a crime, especially one this pretty.*

"It's simply not something we have the numbers for."

I don't argue and instead am drawn to the hearth, inspecting the charcoal still tucked within. There's enough stocked off to the side to sustain months of work. Without a thought, I get to lighting the forge by looking for the tinderbox. Before I know it, I'm stoking the flames.

For a glorious moment, I forget where I am and who I'm with. There's only the heavy breaths of the bellows. The crackle of fire that casts everything in a familiar orange glow. There's the clanking of metal as I set up my tools just as I want them. My heart is full. I am where I belong.

Here is the one space where I can express myself—where I have power. In Hunter's Hamlet I am a prize to be gifted. I am the representation of generations of protections against the vampires. But in the smithy, I am creation itself. I am mighty.

But only for a second.

Reality crashes down around me when Ruvan speaks again. "You seem…rather confident in the smithy." He sounds almost skeptical.

I pause and quickly resume my preparations. A hunter wouldn't be so confident, would they? I quickly craft a half-truth and keep my hesitations to myself. If I'm going to make this believable, I must speak with the utmost confidence.

"I've spent much time in a smithy while weapons were being worked on." I glance his way, trying to see if he's reading between the lines I'm drawing. His face is impossible to read, but I don't feel any doubt stemming from him. To my knowledge the fortress has never been breached, so the vampire shouldn't have any in-depth information on what happens within or how practical what I'm explaining is. "*We* have a smith, of course." I intend it as a light jab but he doesn't react. The silence agitates my nerves just enough that it prompts me to speak a little faster. "The smithy was always warm. Bright, even in the darkest of nights. The fire never goes completely out. It always burned too hot for that and would be needed again too soon to ever snuff it completely. It was a place of power, creation, and life. Where people could gather and tell stories. Where men and women would gossip as they waited for their tools to be mended. It was the heart of everything."

He folds his arms and leans against a table. I can feel his gaze on me, looking me from top to bottom, assessing my words. I imagine he's searching for a lie but his stare doesn't feel…it doesn't feel like he doubts me. There's an underlying gentleness to him that only puts me more on guard.

Nothing about a vampire is or ever could be gentle. But just as I think that, I'm reminded of his finger brushing against mine. Of the way he looked at me in the upper armory, begging for me to see things his way without outright asking.

I worry my pinky ring around my finger.

"You're not what I expected of a hunter."

I snort. "What did you expect? I made it a point to try and kill you."

"That you did. And, goodness, with the magic you had surging through you, if any hunter could've killed me it was you." He chuckles as if he finds it amusing now. Though it just settles a rock in my core. *Kill the vampire lord.* If Drew had kept the elixir, with all his training, maybe he really could've killed Ruvan. If I could hold my own, Drew could've won.

Does that mean we damned Hunter's Hamlet and all of humanity by him giving me the elixir? What if this war could've finally been over? At best, Hunter's Hamlet will kill the vampire lord during the next Blood Moon in five hundred years but…*this* is why I was told to never step out of place. To accept my lot in life. The consequence of abandoning my post as the forge maiden ripples beyond me.

I have to get home, one voice in me pulls. *You have to kill the vampire lord, first*, another retorts. There is no future for me in Hunter's Hamlet if Ruvan breathes. I am torn in so many directions my head aches.

"What is it?" He notices my hands have stilled.

"Nothing." I shake my head.

"No, it was—"

"Where should I put this?" Ventos arrives with a clamor, unknowingly saving me from my own tormented thoughts. The various weaponry are piled in his arms. A heavy canvas tarp separates the silver blades from his flesh.

Ruvan must have the same thought as me about the risk. "What do you think you're doing?" He rushes over, carefully taking the weapons one by one, ensuring that he only handles them by the leather wrapped around their hilts.

"I was doing what you asked; I'm bringing the weapons."

"I didn't expect it to be like this." Ruvan pinches the bridge of his nose with a sigh. "Expected you to take multiple trips to be safe. What if one of them cut you?"

"Multiple trips are for the weak." Ventos chuckles.

"But the silver."

"I can manage." Ventos puffs his chest.

A snort of laughter escapes me, distracting me from my preparation of opening the smithy back up.

"Is the human laughing at me?" Ventos is somewhere between shock and anger.

"I wouldn't dream of laughing at the fearsome vampire." I roll my eyes away from Ventos. Ruvan sees, judging from his huff of amusement.

"You, too, my lord? You wound me more sharply than a silver blade."

"If my words were silver blades you'd be long dead." Ruvan leans against the anvil. The fire highlights the sharp lines of his jaw with striking orange lines—as if he's glowing from within like a blisteringly hot piece of iron. I tear my gaze away from his stolen face and cross to the weapons Ventos brought.

A large hand covers mine as I reach for a sword. "You're really going to improve them?"

I stare up at Ventos. "Unhand me."

"Answer me."

I grit my teeth but manage to say, "Yes. Sharp enough to cut that hand clean off if you don't remove it from my person."

He releases me. I take the sword with a glare, return to the forge, and plunge it into the coals. This one is particularly bad; the whole thing is off-center from the grip. I'll hammer it back into rough shape before it meets the grinding wheel.

"I don't trust you," he says to my back. He's just itching for a fight. I can feel it. An ill-advised part of me wants to give it to him, even though I can't thanks to being Ruvan's bloodsworn.

"And I trust none of you," I say.

"Good, why would you? After all, we killed dozens of your kind on the night of the Blood Moon."

"Enough," Ruvan says firmly. We both ignore him. Ventos has struck too much of a nerve for me to see reason. I'm just seeing the same red as my brother's blood.

"How many did you kill?" I whirl in place, my knuckles white around the hilt of the sword.

"A good many." Ventos tilts his head back smugly. "And we didn't lose one of us."

I think of the armor I saw earlier, void of bodies. "What's the point of it all? Why do you hunt us?"

"To survive."

"We should not have to die so you can live!" My voice echoes off all the stone and metal.

"Then to punish you for all you've done to us."

"I said that's enough," Ruvan says firmly, moving to stand between us. "Both of you."

Ventos continues to ignore him. "I hope you lost important people. Either to that forsaken guild, or to you personally. I hope *you* hurt. I hope you all bleed. I hope you feel an ounce of the pain that you have caused my kind."

As Ventos speaks, he slowly approaches me. Even though Ruvan is still wedged between us, that mountain of a man tries to loom over me, poisoning the air around me with his hatred. Hatred that is mirrored within me and growing.

"Worry not, I have known pain every day of my life," I assure Ventos. My voice is more frigid than the mountaintops that surround us.

"Your suffering is hardly the equivalent of a day compared to what our kind has endured and will endure. You could live in agony for a hundred lifetimes and it would still not be enough to atone for the long night."

"Ventos, stop. You get us nowhere by alienating her."

"I never asked for her help to begin with!" Ventos glares at his lord. "When you thrust this arrangement upon us, did you even think of how your covenant might feel? Or did you even care?"

"I am doing what must be done to save our people." Ruvan's words are desperate and all too familiar.

"The salvation of our people cannot come from the hands of a hunter!" Ventos slams his palm on the table, rattling the weaponry.

"I will do whatever it takes to save the vampir and end the long night."

"You are a fool," Ventos seethes.

"That is my choice—though I see myself as an idealist rather than a fool." Ruvan draws his height; even though he's a good head shorter than Ventos, he holds himself as though he's twice as tall. The vampire lord seems to fill up the space, dwarfing the other man. "The decision of how we progress while awake lies with me and me alone, per how the council decided before sunset of the long night."

"Then the failure of this, and the ultimate demise of our people because of it, rests solely with you." Ventos continues to glare.

"I have known that long before I made the oath with a hunter. I knew it from the first moment I was awoken to this cruel and distant future." Ruvan's words are heavy; they begin to shape the outline of the leaded core he carries within him. The grief I have gleaned sketches of but not the whole picture. "I am ready to accept responsibility for my choices and whatever comes with them. Though I am optimistic the long night ends with us."

Ventos leans in, looking like he's about to say something more. But he ultimately eases away, muttering something about going to an "academy" under his breath as he storms out of the room.

Ruvan and I stand awkwardly, his back to me. His words were bold and strong, but they were a facade for a tired man whose shoulders hunch the second Ventos is gone. I can feel him work to collect himself. To still harbor that foolish hope and passion to protect his people. Passion I never remember Davos showing for us. Passion I've tried to both keep and squelch impossibly at the same time…

My chest aches. My eyes burn. I'm angry, frustrated. I want to scream. I want to weep.

And something, *something* compels me to reach out even when every better sense tells me not to. My hand meets Ruvan's shoulder. His muscles tense and he inhales deeply. I breathe with him. The skin at the base of my throat—where his mark is—tingles slightly.

I try to open my mouth to speak, but I can't find the words. His body is hotter than the forge underneath my palm. He'll burn me if I continue touching him and yet, I can't stop. I want—

"I'm all right," he says, finally.

I quickly pull my hand away. What was I doing? Comforting a vampire? I turn to the forge.

"I'm sorry for what he said." I can feel Ruvan's eyes on me as he speaks.

"I don't want the sympathy of vampires." I don't want sympathy from anyone. I've had my share of hardships, but so have others, far worse than me.

"We don't have to be your enemies." His words are as tired as I am angry.

"That's all you've ever been."

"Once every five—"

"My father died because of you." My hands stop moving; they're limp at my side. I stare blankly at the tools in front of me. I don't know why I'm speaking. I know doing so is foolish. Pointless to seek sympathy I don't want. Yet I speak anyway. I can see my father's face as he tucks me into bed, swearing that he will keep me safe from the vampires that stalk in the night. "Ventos was right; I lost someone important. We all have. My father was a hunter, and a good one, too. Hunter's Hamlet was lesser when a man like him died. That was the nightmare I had this morning. Being in this bloody place reminds me of everything your kind has done to me, to my home, to my family."

"I'm sor—"

"Spare me your apologies."

"Do you want them spared when they would be sincere?"

"Sincerity over the death of a hunter?" I scoff. "I thought you all hated our kind."

"Many do. Many blame all humans for the curse. But I'm capable of hating a circumstance while still pitying the people trapped within it. I know the curse was not your fault and you must see that too." This is the second time he's brought this up—seeing the people of the hamlet as victims of these circumstances. We certainly haven't had the easiest time of it and, *fine*, if I had a choice I would've preferred to live outside walls…

Ruvan continues to linger. Watching me. I wonder if he's waiting for something. Waiting for me to say something else? Waiting for me to do something? For me to conclude that we are more alike than not? His silence wears me down.

"None of us really want that life," I say softly. It sounds like a confession. But I wonder who I'm confessing to. Him, or myself? "We're proud of it, sure. Everyone in Hunter's Hamlet knows why we sacrifice. Why parents give their children to the fortress so that those beyond our walls don't have to make the same choices. We don't like it, but we accept it, and in return we have all our needs taken care of. We have each other—a community. It's more than a lot of people ever get."

I've heard tales of hardship beyond the walls from the people who join the hamlet. Some towns where there's enough wealth for all but it's kept by one. Other places that never see enough food. Places where brutal men and women rule with iron fists and cruelty that is somehow different and worse than the vampire because it's from our own kind.

He listens intently and then finally says, "It's odd."

"What is?"

"That you see yourself as trapped…and yet your people are the ones who hold the curse on us." He takes a step forward, hands open as if pleading. "If it's that bad for humans, too, then why would the hunters not release us?"

"So the vampire could go and attack the rest of the world?" I plunge the sword into the hearth.

"The rest of the world? We want *nothing* to do with your world, that's much the point. We want to be free to live our lives here in Midscape, where we belong." He looks to the still-shuttered windows—looks through them and out to something beyond. "I've never seen outside this city. And unlike your hamlet, I don't have everything I need. I want so much more. I want to see the dances of the fae court or hear the siren duets at new year. I want to see plains so vast that the horizon swallows them." His voice has gone soft with wonder and wistfulness.

I try to ignore the ache at what he said. There's a dull throbbing in me, like a call to all that lies beyond metal and heat—to a world meant for knowing. A world I clearly haven't given half as much thought to as he has.

"You need blood for your magic," I weakly counter.

"We could find blood enough in Midscape if we were not confined by the curse. Sure, human blood is the most potent, but others would suffice. We were doing it during our moon festivals long before the dryads made the humans."

I search his face, wishing he could be lying. But I can feel the truth in him as keenly as the heat of the forge…or the tingle at the base of my neck. This would be so much simpler if I could write it all off as him misleading me. Because if he's not…if he's not…

Then he's just a lonely, desperate man standing before me, begging for tenderness Hunter's Hamlet never allowed me to grow into.

"I need to focus on this work," I say softly, and put my back to him. "I only have a day to make the necessary adjustments."

Ruvan lingers, and for a moment it seems like there's more that he wants to say, but he doesn't. Instead, he says, "I'll tell the others to bring their weapons of choice; prioritize those."

He goes to leave but hesitates halfway through the room. I can feel it. I can feel him. His every movement threatens to prickle my skin into gooseflesh. I had hoped that this keen sense of knowing attached to him would fade the more time that passed following our oath, but it only seems to be growing.

"And Riane, you look tired. You should be sure to get some rest; you're going to need it." He leaves me with that.

The vampire lord is right, I am tired. But it's the sort of tired that sleep will do little for. What I need is that which is already before me.

fourteen

THE HAMMER IS A MEDITATION.

Strike. Pause. Inspect. Straightening blow. Heat. Repeat. Cool.

There is a rhythm to the forge throughout the year—planning in spring, stocking in late summer when the traders arrived, forging hard through fall and winter. Drew always said he hated those late months. That was when we would get ahead for the coming year while the weather was cool and the smithy was all the more lovely to be in as a result.

For the longest time I thought it was because my brother was lazy. How could he not enjoy the smithy when the world outside was piled high with snow? But then he became a hunter, and a lazy man does not hoist the sickle.

So, one Yule, as I stood off to the side of the town square—forbidden to dance, of course—with Drew keeping me company even when he could dance with any eligible lady he desired, I asked him why he hated it outright. He told me that he hated the smithy in those cold, long nights not because he didn't want to work, but because the constant striking of metal rang painfully on the inside of his skull—a relentless noise that lingered even long after he went to sleep and brought an ache in the morning.

I didn't understand his resentment for the noise then.

I still don't.

To me, these sounds are a heartbeat, echoing across my ancestors. We have all shared it, and many more will share it in the years to come. Or perhaps not. Perhaps, as the vampires put it, this long night will finally draw to a close. Hunter's Hamlet will wake from the nightmare it has existed within. We will reemerge into the human world, bleary-eyed and hopeful. We can see the sea, and distant cities, and maybe even grassy plains so vast the horizon swallows them whole.

The vampires come to me, one by one. Everyone but Ventos.

Lavenzia brings Ventos's broadsword—the one thing he was unable to carry earlier. I'm surprised to find I don't mind her company. She's silent as she sits by the window, staring out at the cold mountains turned platinum in the moonlight. Silent companions are the best kind because they don't distract me from my work.

Winny is the next to come, with dozens of little daggers that weren't in the armory when Ventos was collecting things because she "doesn't trust them out of her sight for long." She has a bow for her fiddle now, and she draws it along the strings deftly. I almost think that she is playing to the beat of my strikes because every time I change up my rhythm, Winny's playing changes, too. Light and fast, slow and soulful. The duet has me fighting a smile.

They come and go, silent guardians, or perhaps jailers. I pay them no mind regardless. I have a job to do, one that keeps my hands busy, muscles strained, and brow dotted with sweat. I think I am the closest to happy that I can expect to be here.

But it comes to an end, as it always does.

When dawn breaks, I'm wiping soot and metal from my hands. I admire my handiwork. It's then that I realize just how much I completed. More than should have been possible. I've forged like this before, lost to the world. But even at my most productive, even at my strongest, I couldn't complete this much in the span of a day and still feel this good.

It must be the bloodsworn magic. The vampire power and strength that still surges within me. I touch the hollow between my collarbones. My work feels tainted by—

Him.

It's as if I've summoned Ruvan with a thought.

A hazy dawn shines in beams, cut by the iron of the windows, striking a patchwork on the floor. I opened the shutters long ago to have the light of the moon to work by and now the sun has entered without welcome. The vampire lord stands underneath the archway that leads to the old armory. The thick night that continues to slumber in the castle is wrapped around him like a blanket.

His hair is silvery in the low light, the same color as the metal I've been working with for hours on end. It's a complement, even I must admit, to the golden hue of his eyes. He is a man of pure night and winter's chill, and yet…he does not feel frigid in this moment.

Something about him is scalding.

It's like I've stood here before. Like he's come to me in this smithy many times. This moment, his presence, it's achingly familiar and yet so different that an intense awareness has taken me. I know him in my blood. I feel him there, threatening to overwhelm me if I'm not careful.

"Are you finished?" His low rumble cuts through the smithy, reminding me of just how silent it has been since I stopped working and started cleaning.

"Yes."

He steps forward. I straighten away from the weapons, staring, stunned, as he walks into the gray light of morning. He doesn't burst into flames. His skin is kissed gently by the sun. The only reaction he seems to have to sunlight is blinking a few times.

"Are you prone to staring at men?"

My cheeks burn instantly and I look back at the table of weapons. "I wasn't staring."

"Admiring, then?" He draws out the words with purpose.

"Hardly." I snort. "I thought vampires burn in sunlight."

"When the curse claims us, in life or death, we do. But not before," he says. "The vampir are not a people of the night naturally. Yes, our magic has always been at its strongest around the full moon. But it was the curse of the hunters that caused our people to begin existing only by moonlight."

"I see."

He comes to a stop beside the table. "You don't believe me." I hate how it's not phrased as a question. He seems to know my thoughts.

"I don't know what I can and can't believe when it comes to you," I murmur.

"When will you accept that I can't lie to you, even if I wanted to? And this might come as a surprise, but I *don't* want to." He looks at me through his lashes, face still downcast toward the weapons on the table.

His hair hangs between us like a veil. Like armor protecting us both in the prodding of the other. Old gods forbid what we might find if we probed too deeply with this bond connecting us.

"Can I help you with something?" I motion to the weapons, putting the topic of sunlight to rest. So much for plotting to "accidentally" rip off the curtains.

"I should think it obvious that I'm going to inspect your work." Ruvan checks the leather guards I carefully replaced on each of the hilts—an extra layer of protection between the vampire's flesh and the silver. "I'm not going to allow you to attempt to find a loophole in the words of our bloodsworn. Some kind of way where you do not deal the killing blow but a faulty weapon does."

"I can do that?" I blurt.

"No, so you shouldn't look so hopeful." He chuckles, though it sounds somewhat sad. "Ventos would be after me again if I didn't double-check everything. Not having to deal with his griping is my real motivation."

I purse my lips. "I didn't do anything to sabotage any of you. Your weapons are twice as good as when you brought them here." I brush past him, going to leave.

"I can see that. Thank you, Riane." It's so odd to hear sincere gratitude from a vampire.

I stop, looking back at him. I've never spent this much time alone with any man, save for Drew, and time with my brother is *vastly* different. Every other time I've been in such close quarters with a man they've either been too nervous to speak, eager to get away from me as quickly as possible so they don't get in trouble, or they see me as a conquest, something to aspire to. A forbidden fruit they're eager to pluck. Ruvan doesn't seem to want anything from me. And I don't seem to make him nervous in the slightest.

Maybe this is what it is like to be just a woman, with just a man. Though nothing about either of us is "just" anything.

"If we're going to face danger, it helps me also to make sure you are all at your best," I say finally.

"That is very true. I had hoped you saw it that way."

"I really couldn't have sabotaged the weapons?" I ask without meeting his eyes. "Not that I did, or even tried." Guilt floods me. I was so lost to the forge that I didn't even think about trying to find a way to kill the vampires for the whole night.

"You could've tried. But you would be compelled to tell us what you did before it would harm us. That urge would grow greater and greater, becoming unbearable the moment before we would be harmed by your action."

"Wonderful," I remark dryly.

"Be grateful for the terms of our oath; it means we're both guaranteed safety."

"Vampires and safety, something I still have a hard time even thinking could go together."

"Vampir," he tries to correct yet again. Ruvan takes a step closer and I don't move away. We stand toe-to-toe. He searches me without a touch. I can almost feel the faint caress of magic running down my shoulders and arms. "You really think you could never be safe around me?"

"You are my sworn enemy." My voice has fallen to a whisper without my bidding.

"But what if it didn't have to be that way?"

The question begs an answer, one I don't have. Not because I want to dodge it…but because I've never given how things would look if they were different genuine thought beyond childhood musings. However, since I've been here, the question seems to return relentlessly.

What would I want? A forge, I think. It's in my blood. It's who I am. But what would I make if not sickles and armor? Where would it be if it could be anywhere?

What would Ruvan want beyond his fae courts, songs, and great plains? Do I care to know? Dangerous. Forbidden. I might.

"Why do you care about what I think of you so much?" I can't help but ask. Even though there's a small part of me that wants to ask what *he* thinks of *me*.

I can feel him withdrawing slightly. I've put him on the spot. His hand twitches as though he's about to reach for me, but he doesn't.

"I have lived my life surrounded by creatures that want to kill me." His voice is soft and on the verge of breaking. "Perhaps, in you, is a strange sort of redemption—hope, that if I can turn a hunter into an ally, then ending this curse should be a trivial matter by comparison."

"I will never be your ally."

He moves lightning fast. His fingers are wrapped around my chin, thumb nearly touching my lips. I flinch. I have never been so focused on a touch so delicate. So light it hardly exists at all.

"Because you still fear me? Is that it?" Ruvan's lips split with his smile, placing his fangs on display. But his ferocity lacks the bite it once did, thanks to his haunted eyes. "You'll meet the ones you must truly fear soon enough."

He releases me, leaving without another word. Heart hammering, I sink against the table for support, gripping it tightly. My skin is aflame and I fight for composure.

There is a sickle on each of my hips. I have a large hunting knife made of steel strapped to my left thigh—for use as a tool more than a weapon. Attached to my right is a similar knife but cast in silver. There are four small daggers hidden in other locations on my body. One on my wrist, two on my ribs, and one in my boot. They're all practical spots that are easy for me to access in a moment of dire need. I just hope they're enough. They'll have to be.

Each of the vampires are armed with their own silver weapons. A sight I never could've imagined, even having worked on their respective blades the entire day and night. Ventos has strapped his broadsword to his back. I still catch myself admiring the craftsmanship of it. It must have been forged long ago—when silver must've been cheap and plentiful.

Lavenzia is armed with her rapier. Winny carries a short sword and ten throwing daggers that are strapped to a belt stretched across her chest. Ruvan carries two sickles, much like I do. He's armed with the weapons of hunters. I wonder if he did it to try and provoke me.

No…I don't think he'd do that. He's not…well, I can't call him *kind*. Can I? At the very least, he hasn't been cruel toward me when he easily could've been. He gave me free use of the smithy. He's allowed me peace at night to rest. He's almost been kind, beyond taking me from my home, that is…

The more I think about him, the muddier my thoughts and feelings become.

"You all know the path, right?" Callos asks. He and Quinn are unarmed and unarmored. They stand before the doors that lead into the main hall. They're not coming to see whatever this old castle holds.

"We do." Ruvan nods. "If we're not back in two days, you know what to do."

"Let's hope it doesn't come to that." Quinn wrings his hands. "A year isn't a very long tenure for a vampir lord."

A year? "You've only been the vampire lord for a year?" I blurt. Ruvan's eyes swing to me, along with everyone else's. I would have turned scarlet with embarrassment if not for the somber aura that radiates from all of them—notably Ruvan.

"Yes, only a year," Ruvan says with a note of finality, checking his grips one more time. He looks back to Quinn. "We'll do our best, friend."

"Right then, off we go." Ventos steps forward and lifts the thick iron bar that was bolting the doors opposite the hall's entry closed.

The muscles of Ruvan's back strain as he pulls open the door a fraction.

Winny slips through. "Clear," she calls back.

Lavenzia wordlessly creeps through the door.

"You both have it?" Ventos asks as he hands Callos and Quinn the massive iron bar.

"We're stronger than we look." Callos smiles up at him.

"I hope so, someone has to let us back in." Ventos laughs heartily and squeezes through the door.

"Riane, with me," Ruvan commands.

Right behind him, I pass through to uncharted territory. The door closes behind and I can hear the sound of the bar re-engaging. The same writhing, uncomfortable excitement as the night of the hunt jolts through my body, just underneath my skin even though I haven't drunk any elixirs. It's a desire that doesn't feel entirely my own and whispers with the same surge of power as when I became bloodsworn to Ruvan.

Give me power. Give me blood.

I grip both sickles at my hips, shift my grip, and grip again, trying to shake the urge. I try and inhale slowly, quelling the restlessness growing within me.

"It's quiet," Lavenzia whispers. Her usual levity has vanished. I can tell from her pose that she's ready to draw her rapier at any second. She has the same sharpness to her gaze as Drew right before he would lunge for me during our sparring.

"Good." Ruvan radiates discomfort as well. Perhaps this gut-wrenching feeling is coming from him and the connection that's been forced upon us through the bloodsworn. "It's still early in the day. We'll need to use every minute they're sedated during daylight to get as deep as we're able."

"Callos is certain about this path, right? Because we certainly can't go the same way as last time after we had to blow it up," Ventos says. He clearly struggles with keeping his voice down.

Blow it up? That doesn't sound good.

"He's confident." Ruvan's gaze falls on me. "And we'll make it; after all, we have a hunter with us."

Great, they really want me to be a hunter. Simply marvelous.

"And just what am I hunting?" I ask.

"What you're made to hunt."

"But the blood oath—"

"The blood oath prevents you from harming me, or anyone loyal to me. These vampir are not loyal to me. They're not loyal to anyone. *They* are the monsters your guild made with their curse." Ruvan's eyes narrow slightly.

I ignore his accusatory gaze. "How will I know the difference between those loyal to you and these 'monsters?'"

"It won't be hard to tell the difference," Lavenzia answers.

"They have the withered and sunken faces we originally possessed." The look Ruvan gives me is pointed, as if he is trying to emphasize that how I originally saw him was a result of this curse and not his own monstrosity.

Sounds like the vampire I know. "Simple enough, then."

We continue through the castle. Winny runs point for our group, staying ahead. Her hair, pulled back, is a streak of gold.

It's as she slips into the darkness ahead that I notice everything in this first room is dark. There are no light sources. No candles. No windows.

I stop, turning. Blinking. "What the…"

"What is it?" Ruvan asks. They all halt, taking a step closer.

"I can see." The finer details are diminished. But I can see the stone walls and crumbling tapestries. I can see the condensation that weeps from the sagging beams of the roof and drips like blood to the floor. "How?"

"It's the bloodsworn magic," Ruvan answers as if this should have been obvious and plain when it is very much not to me. "You have powers of the vampir within you."

"But I'm not a—"

"Vampir, yes, we all know." He sighs tiredly. "But our essence has been linked, a pathway opened between us. Some of my abilities and insights have been given to you and in turn, yours to me."

I wonder exactly what those "abilities and insights" are that I gave him. Can he forge? Can he actually steal my face? Or does he know something more intimate? This is not the time or place to ask and I'm happy to avoid the answer for now.

"Useful," is all I say, and we continue forward.

I pause again, briefly, when I first see black blood.

It appears as drips, then smeared handprints on the walls. Then the corridor opens up. I can see the ghosts of combatants dancing, dried blood painting an outline of a battle long since over in this cobwebbed banquet hall. Turned-over tables and smashed chairs litter the floor, a confetti of debris.

"Good, it's still clear," Winny says under her breath, barely audible.

"What do you see, Riane?" Ruvan startles me by asking.

"A fight took place here."

"Obviously. I want you to break it down for me."

"Pardon?" I meet his eyes.

"How many enemies were there?"

"Is that relevant?"

Ruvan's stare becomes more intense, probing. It ignites panic in me. He *is* suspicious. I knew it. I'm suddenly recounting everything I said and did. What was I thinking, forging weapons? Hunters don't forge.

But maybe he doesn't know that? Maybe this is merely a test of my abilities and not stemming from suspicion.

"I want to know what you see," he insists.

"Do we really have time for this?" Ventos grumbles.

"It shouldn't take her very long. Go on," Ruvan urges.

I step off to the side. I can feel their eyes trailing me around the room. Drew told me how to read the signs of battle…but only in an academic way. He told me about tracking by blood drops and how footprints could shape the tides of a fight. We never had a reason to practice it. We never expected me to go into the hunt. After taking a full turn around the hall, I come to a stop before Ruvan.

"You faced many enemies."

"How many?"

"I…I would guess about thirty." I'm honestly not sure. This isn't my forte.

Ruvan smiles thinly. "Closer to twenty."

"We really should keep going," Winny presses.

But Ruvan is relentless. "What else do you see?"

"Ventos fought here." I point to a spot on the floor at the center of a wide arc of blood. "With a blade that large and heavy there's only so many attacks he could make…and the pattern of the blood supports it."

"Go on."

"Lavenzia was here." I point to a different spot. I might not be a hunter, but I know weapons and how combatants will use them. My life's work has been spent focusing on that. Maybe that will be enough to bluff my way through whatever test Ruvan is trying to put me through. "Her rapier requires finesse; a rapier relies on speed and accuracy. However, managing distance is also critical with a weapon like that. Your footwork leaves lines across the ground as you move past the enemies you kill."

"And me?"

"You…" I lose my words for a moment as my eyes return to the vampire lord. He is the only one whose movements I can clearly envision through the room. "You fight like a hunter would." I can almost *feel* where his attacks landed. How he moved. He moves like me in combat—like Drew.

It's no wonder that we were so well matched in those ruins in the

Fade Marshes. He knows all my attacks before I make them. All of my movements before I can think them. Just as I know his. But why? Did he force hunters here to train him? Or does he have some kind of records of how the hunters fight? I suspect the latter given his earlier statements about records on hunters.

He continues to study me, expression unreadable.

"Can we move along now?" Winny asks. "We have a lot of ground to cover."

"Indeed." Ruvan finally relents and strides forward. I fall into place at his right hand.

We continue down into the depths of the castle. The rooms begin to blur together, a collage of darkness and dried blood. Every forgotten battlefield as a portrait of a fight long passed. In every one, there's the footprints of people fighting against shapeless shadow enemies. But who those people are begins to change. No longer am I confident it's Ruvan and his covenant.

There were other people fighting these mysterious enemies throughout the years. I glance at the others, seeing if I can figure out a way to affirm my suspicion, but I'm silenced by their intense and distant stares. These are men and women haunted by battle and blood. They have the same eyes as hunters returning from the marshes after a full moon.

I begin to glean more information from the endless parade of blood splatters and upturned tables. These monstrous vampires we're hunting are no bigger or smaller in build than our own party. Though they seem fast, and strong, based off the deep gouges that look almost like claws. So much blood, so many battles…yet no bodies.

That's the most disconcerting part of it all.

"Why are there no bodies?" I whisper.

It's a long time before Ruvan answers, "They eat the flesh of the dead."

I ask nothing more.

Winny continues darting ahead and back. She makes hand motions and nods in Ruvan's direction. A code that only they seem to understand. Even though I'm not privy to their secret language, I know it's not good when she returns, her usually tanned skin blanched almost a complete white.

Everyone huddles together to hear her whisper.

"Ahead, at least fifteen of them. There's—"

Ruvan clamps his hand over her mouth. I jerk my chin in the direction she came from, eyes narrowing. The hair on my arms stands on end. The air is electrified.

The vampire lord must also hear the slow scraping—like nails on stone. There's a lower noise, too. Heavier. *Breathing*, I realize. It's ragged gasps drawn through a slack jaw. The vampires around me shift their stances. My heart begins to race, pumping the rush of the impending battle through my veins.

From the darkness, the monster I've been waiting for emerges.

fifteen

I REALIZE THAT I HAD BEEN WRONG DURING THE HUNT. The face of the vampire lord was not the beast that occupied my mind whenever I conjured the image of a vampire. *This* creature is.

The monster is even worse than what attacked me that night in Hunter's Hamlet. Its flesh has hardened beyond leather—looking almost like sculpted stone, stretched tight over bone and sinew, causing an almost insect-like appearance. Its jaw hangs limp, mouth wide, oversized yellowed fangs bared among rows of pointed teeth. The monster's eyes are completely black. No iris.

My hands quiver.

A part of me I don't recognize is hungry for the fight. That reckless disregard for self-preservation urges me forward. Pushing me to do that which I have precious little experience in—kill.

But the other part of me, the human instinct, is frozen in place as I stare at what must be the face of Death.

Lavenzia launches into an attack.

The beast is *fast*.

It moves with jerky, unnatural movements. Faster than it should be able to for how weak it appears to be due to lack of muscle. It swings one of its hands at her; long, bone-like nails extend as claws past its fingertips.

She gracefully ducks underneath its arm, jabbing her blade

at its shoulder. The silver punctures the skin easily. The monster barely gives a gasp of surprise before falling to the ground, dead.

Just as I ease my stance, Ruvan speaks, low and harsh into my ear. "Don't relax. One is harmless. It's the numbers that will kill you."

I look back to the edge of my vision.

If Winny was right then there's still fourteen more. I force myself to grip the sickles. The rest of the vampires move around me, away, toward certain danger. But I am frozen in place. Ruvan remains at my side, just behind the rest of them. I wonder if he's staying to protect me as I falter. He's sturdy and reassuring, enough so that I wouldn't dream of pushing him away right now. Not when my nerves are beginning to fray. His breath moves the small hairs at the nape of my neck.

"Are you scared, Riane?"

I'm terrified. Our companions disappear into the complete darkness, past where my magically enhanced vision can see. The sounds of battle breaking out begin to echo back.

"Yes." I can't lie to him if I tried, and I wouldn't try when the truth is so obvious.

He hums. I've given him cause to doubt me. I can feel it. I press my eyes closed.

"How about more power then?" The question alone feels more dangerous than whatever is coming toward me. He tempts me with forbidden magic. "Even if you're unafraid, the fight would be easier with it."

"What?" I meet his eyes, noses almost touching. His gaze is intense and threatens to consume me. I can almost see the umbra around him coming to life as the aforementioned magic radiates off of his shoulders.

He tilts his head slightly. "You should take it, I think. It might be the only way someone like you survives here."

Someone like me… A human? Or were my fears right? Does he know the truth from my forging and clumsy assessment of battle? Perhaps he's known since I hesitated with Quinn at that icy path.

"Well?" There's urgency in the word. *We're running out of time*, it almost seems to say.

Do I want his power? Do I want his *blood*? That's what he's really asking. I'm disgusted by my initial thought.

Yes.

I hadn't wanted it until now. But his magic is already in me, and terror tastes like desperation. I won't die here. Not now. Not after all I've been through and how close I am to getting to this door of his and freeing myself.

But what will Mother, Drew, my town think of me for this?

They don't have to know, a new voice whispers from the back of my mind. A flush rises up my chest. My breath hitches.

They don't have to know.

There's no one here to judge me for what I'm about to do. No hunters. No town. There's only monsters in the darkness and a man made of moonlight offering me salvation. There's a growing need, wrenching, deep within me. Wanting to be set free again. Wanting him to both make and unmake me. Wanting to, for one blessed moment, be my own woman. To be triumphant. To win over death and fear for just once in my life.

"Give me power," I beg and refuse to allow myself to feel ashamed.

He raises his thumb to his mouth and bites it lightly. The small dribble of blood down to the heel of his palm has me salivating. Any disgust at my body's reaction pales in comparison to my need.

I need it. Give it to me. More, a voice within urges louder by the second.

Ruvan's fingertips slide along my cheek, curling around my jaw. His thumb rests on my lower lip. "Just a touch. Just enough to get you through."

My lips part. His thumb slides between them. Slick with blood. I run my tongue along the cut on instinct and swallow.

Magic surges from him to me as though I am a vessel that his essence is eager to fill. I inhale sharply. Ruvan pulls his hand away as my worries begin to dull and my senses heighten. A frown tugs on his lips, but I don't ask why. I don't want to know what causes his displeasure when this feels so…deliciously *good*.

I didn't know what to expect with the elixir Drew gave me. The oath happened in a blur. But now, I've accepted power with both eyes open. I am ready as it crashes upon me and I use its force as momentum. I spin and lunge into the darkness while I have the courage and strength to do so, chasing the noise of battle.

Ventos and the others are a blur. I cut through the first fiend effortlessly with my right sickle as my left catches the wrist of a second. They both fall with a brief cry of agony, dead from the silver that punctured their skin. Another monster swings for me; I duck and dodge around to his back, slicing up his spine as two more lunge.

Surprisingly, Winny is the first to catch up to me. The lithe little creature is a whirlwind of blades and daggers. She throws two. Stabs another as she retrieves the first dagger. Two more fall by her blades as she reaches for the second.

I keep my focus ahead. There's groaning rising from the depths—a stirring of something mighty and fearsome. *More are on their way.* I can sense them. Many, many more. I split my attention between those around me and the ones that are coming, working to the back of the pack and the front of the next wave.

There's a moment to catch my breath between one body hitting the floor and the next five crashing into me. They come all at once, a clawed hand grazing the armor of my shoulder as I eliminate two more. Five, ten, *twenty*, these mindless fiends aren't going to be what takes me down.

If the vampire lord himself was an even match for me, nothing less than him will stop me. Not like this. Not with his power.

Ruvan. I can feel him moving behind me. I know him as well as I know my own flesh and blood. I leech his power shamelessly to continue pushing ahead, springboarding off a body to get leverage over two, using my sickles in their shoulders to vault farther down the hall.

A smirk cuts my lips. This…this fight now *feels*…almost pleasurable. I am too strong for these monsters to stop me. Their blood is warm on my face and hands. I lick my lips, feeling its sting across my tongue. Their blood is sour compared to Ruvan's. But it fuels me nonetheless. A cheaper, dirtier magic. Still powerful, though. It'll do.

More, the voice in me screams, the same voice brought to life by the elixir the night of the Blood Moon, *give me more!*

I spin, swinging, taking four down at once. It barely registers that the rest of my party is behind me. Too slow. They're missing all the fun ahead. But I suppose I will thin out the pack for them. That way they don't have to worry or struggle much.

The hallway ends in a T. My chest heaves. My breaths are so rough and ragged that they hurt. It's almost as if I am inhaling glass and not air. Yet I gulp it down anyway, muscles screaming, lungs aching. I almost want my body to break.

Break so it can be rebuilt stronger with this magic. I want more—to be *more*.

A rumbling to the right heralds enemies uncounted. I can see them in the distance—a whole horde, barely able to fit through the hall. They scramble over each other, gouging the skin of their allies, all in a rush to get to me. I sink low in my legs and am about to lunge when Ruvan calls out, "Left!"I instantly recalibrate. We're headed *left* and this horde is coming from the right. There's a door, halfway between me and the mass. The vampires' talk of securing routes and ensuring safe passage lingers with me, even in my battle haze. I sprint.

"I said left!" Ruvan shouts. It only agitates the beasts more. Wails and cries rise from *within* the walls. It is as if the entire castle was built on a foundation of these monsters. I now understand what they meant when they said that we needed to travel during the day while "they are sedated." If this is sedated, what will the night bring?

I slice through the first three and kick their corpses back down the sloping hallway, toppling four others. One lunges for me and I kill it with a well-placed jab to its temple. I grab the door, pushing it halfway closed as three try to jam through at once. It's a game of slicing and kicking as I slowly try to work the door closed. At least I have the high ground.

A claw sinks deep into the soft spot of my leather armor at my elbow. I bite back a cry of pain. Blood explodes, the scent bright and sharp even to my nose. I've never been so keenly aware of my own blood in my life. The aroma seems to work them deeper into their frenzy.

Angling myself against the door, locking my legs, I push with all my might. It's me against at least eight of them. I clench my jaw, holding back a grunt as I strain. My muscles quiver but I don't have enough strength, not while I keep having to slash and push through any who try to enter.

"Ventos!" I shout. I need that brute of a man. "Ventos!"

The rumbling that heralds his footsteps is a welcome sound. "I'm here." I would've never imagined I'd be relieved to hear him say that. A sturdy hand slams itself into the door and suddenly the effort I was expending to close it completely vanishes.

I leave the brawn to Ventos, focusing on stopping the monsters from getting through. Together, we're able to get the door closed. I assess the lock and hinges and unsheathe three daggers from my chest. Based on how the door is constructed I think I can barricade it for the time being. I slam my steel dagger into the wood of the frame almost to the hilt. It wedges against the door handle, preventing the latch from being undone. I put two more by the hinges, using a strength I didn't know I possessed to render them worthless.

"That won't hold for long." I cover my wound with my hand. "They'll topple it eventually."

"It'll hold long enough for us to get out of here," Ventos says as we rejoin our companions.

Lavenzia has a deep gash down the side of her face that's quickly knitting, and is otherwise unharmed. Ruvan regards me warily. I give him a cautious smile in return. I'm good, great, even. So why does he look so hesitant?

"She's wounded, too. The scent of her blood is going to draw even more out," Ventos says.

"She won't be for long." Ruvan takes my hand in his. The grasp is surprisingly gentle. "Look."

Sure enough, my wound is already mending. I wipe away the blood and there's only a thin red line where it was, a few droplets still beading in two spots that close over.

"Her eyes," Winny says with a scowl.

"What about them?"

Rather than answering me, Winny looks to Ruvan. "You gave her blood."

"She needed it to survive and I'm keeping her alive at all costs. She can handle my power." Ruvan's tone is not to be questioned. He releases me. "Come on, we need to keep moving. We have to get to the loft by nightfall."

"We haven't been there in ages; do you think it's still safe?" Lavenzia asks.

"They generally lack the coordination to climb ladders. So even if it's not, there should be so few that it's easy to remedy." Winny shrugs.

"Or there's the worst kinds there," Lavenzia mutters under her breath.

"It will be fine." Ruvan glances over his shoulder as the thudding on the door behind us grows louder. "Let's not linger."

We move.

My heart pounds with every step. I want more. More fighting. More blood. For the first time, I feel like a hunter…and, now that the rush of battle has faded, I realize I don't like it.

I stare at my palms, splattered with inky blood. I'm not made for death. My hands itch to create. This need within me…it's not my own. Where does it come from? I stare at Ruvan's back. *Him?* No, I felt it in the hamlet before I ever met him. *The elixir*. Is this the hunter's madness? Fear tries to root within me and I nip it in the bud. Perhaps it is the madness, perhaps not. But I have more important things to worry about for the time being.

"I have to admit, you're decent in a scrap, Riane," Ventos says at my side. I must not be able to hide my surprise at his statement, because he tries to smother laughter and, mostly, fails. "Though I suppose vampir blood is the reason for most of it."

"I'm fearsome enough without it," I try to bluff. Ruvan casts me a look that I can't decipher. Or maybe…that I don't *want* to decipher.

He knows, a sinking feeling in my gut assures me. *He knows of your deceit*.

We pass by a mercury glass mirror and I slow to pause before it. Just for a second. Just long enough to see my eyes ringed in gold. Black veins bulge from underneath my tawny skin. I look jarringly similar to how I appeared in the first mirror I was shown here.

"How…" I whisper. But just like the cause of Ruvan's skeptical glances, I know the answer to this, too.

"It's the blood lore attached to the bloodsworn. We have marked each other's blood, we share life and energy, so I can give you a fraction of my power," Ruvan answers. It prompts me to walk at his side once more. I can hear faint groaning in the distance. There are more battles to come before we make it to the aforementioned loft. "And, to that end, I would appreciate it if you kept running headfirst into danger to a minimum."

"I don't know what came over me," I murmur. I pull down on my cheek, inspecting the gold ringing my eye. "I'm like the night of the Blood Moon, aren't I?"

"You are."

"That means—" The words strangle me. But I force myself to speak them anyway. For the first time there's something almost reassuring radiating from Ruvan, pulsing toward me through this bond we share. "It means the Hunter's Guild really is engaging in vampire blood lore, doesn't it?"

"Yes. A human shouldn't be able to become a bloodsworn as easily as you have—your blood already had the imprints of blood lore upon it. My magic should not flow to a human untouched by lore as it has to you. You were marked by the art of the vampir before me and you will be forevermore." He looks at me from the corners of his eyes with disapproval and concern.

"Marked," I repeat, rubbing between my collarbones.

"Everything we do, all we experience, marks our blood. We are shaped by all we have been, could have been, are, and are not. And you had blood lore upon you before you met me." Ruvan turns to face me. "Your precious fellow hunters were slowly turning you into one of us to kill us."

"You're—you're—" I can't say it. The word is gummy in my throat.

"Wrong?" Ruvan tilts his head slightly, lips quirking into a frown. He leans forward slightly. "You can't say it, can you?"

I swallow thickly, silent.

"Do you know why?" His voice drops. "Because you can't lie to me. I'm right, and you know it as much as our bloodsworn oath does."

My eyes widen slightly. But he doesn't gloat. Ruvan eases away, regarding me thoughtfully as a thousand thoughts race through my mind at once.

If the Hunter's Guild is engaging in the blood lore—the magic of the vampires—to create stronger hunters, what does that mean for Drew? Do the ends justify the means? Is it necessary to become a monster to kill one? If they could and would do it to make the Hunter's Elixir, then why would I think they wouldn't do it to curse our enemies, too?

Perhaps there is something more to this curse they speak of. Maybe it even does come from Hunter's Hamlet. Drew would know.

Drew. My chest aches. I press my eyes closed, favoring the darkness behind my lids rather than the darkness of the hall for a second. What if they used the vampire lore on him to heal him? Will that make him that much closer to becoming a vampire? What if he's part of one grand experiment that will go on because I stole his destiny and the vampire lord is alive?

They would never do that! I can hear in my mother's voice. In Davos's at our dinner table.

Yet…the truth is before my eyes. There's more to the hamlet than I have ever known, and even if I don't want to find out because it terrifies me, because it threatens all I've ever found comfort in, I must. No matter the cost.

The sound of monsters in the distance is welcome. I let out a noise of frustration and charge ahead, a blur of silver and power. I want the magic to burn away these thoughts. I want to use it to survive and think nothing of the implications.

I want to ignore everything that is smudging the simple, neat lines that have always divided my world.

sixteen

I'VE LOST COUNT OF HOW MANY I'VE KILLED. My limbs ache and my breath is short. That was the third wave. Fourth? We're deep in the old castle now and I can feel the stone all around me as though it were a living being. Every wall seems to be filled with more and more of these beasts. It's clear what Ruvan meant about the numbers. The risk of these monsters is not facing them one-on-one, but being overwhelmed in the moment, and lacking the stamina to handle them all. It's far worse here than any full moon I've ever heard Drew describe.

Somehow, I've managed to survive. If my brother could see me now he'd be proud. As shocked as I am, but definitely proud. His training was better than either of us realized. I can move on instinct. Though, even I admit, the vampire magic has helped a lot. I'm not sure how much longer until it fades, but, for now, it doesn't seem like it's waning. And even if it were, I know where I could get more.

My eyes drift to Ruvan. He's as weary and worn as we all are. Yet, by some injustice, he almost looks more handsome with a bit of grime on him. It mutes some of his unbearable perfection and makes him…almost human? Less like some divine creature and more a man that could be touched by mortal hands.

"Here." Ruvan hands Winny a large keyring that was previously attached to his belt. She uses it to unlock one of the many doors we've passed. There's a ladder on the other side.

Winny scrambles up and then calls back, "It's clear."

"Oh, bloody good." Lavenzia heaves a sigh of relief and climbs at Ruvan's motion.

"You next," he says to me.

I climb as well. I'm grateful for every one of my years in the smithy. If not for every hour spent hoisting steel and iron, I could not still pull myself up these rungs after all the exertion of the day.

The "loft" is more akin to an attic. Wooden beams support the roof above us. We stand on the ceiling of yet another large room below. I'm nearly blinded by the twilight that streams through a hole in the roof in the distance. After spending so many hours in complete or near-complete darkness, it's almost painful to see natural light.

Ruvan is the last to climb, following the sound of the door closing below.

"You've been hunting those creatures for a while, right? And people before you were as well?" I finally ask to confirm my earlier suspicions. "How are there still so many Succumbed?"

"An entire world was lost." Lavenzia groans as she sits on one of the rafters of the wooden ceiling. The wood is old, but it holds. Especially well, given that the roof overhead has caved in a few places.

"Countless people Succumbed before the slumber was implemented." Ruvan sheathes his blades.

"I always forget how long it's been." Winny sighs. "It feels just like yesterday."

"For us, it practically was," Ventos says solemnly. "Yesterday and a year."

"What a world to lose, and to wake up to…" Lavenzia says sadly.

"It's why I hate being in the lower rungs of the city and the old castle now." Winny sits next to Lavenzia, resting her head on her shoulder. "To think, I once enjoyed it."

"It's certainly no picnic," Ventos agrees.

As they speak I cross to the opening in the roof, trusting most of my weight to the primary support beams, rather than the rotting planks suspended between them. Snow falls in silvery motes in the gray twilight. The opening reveals more sprawling castle, hidden between ridges and peaks around the caldera.

How deep does this place go?

"No one has lived here for thousands of years. Well, no one still sentient, that is." Ruvan stands beside me. I'd heard him coming thanks to the creaking of the floor and the shifting conversation he left behind. Winny, Lavenzia, and Ventos talk amongst themselves in hushed, barely audible words. "From the records left between lords, all the way back to Jontun, I believe we're the first to have laid eyes on this particular stretch of the castle in almost a thousand years."

"How is that possible? Isn't this your castle?" My curiosity is beginning to bubble over. Perhaps it's his calm demeanor finally wearing me down. Perhaps it's something akin to trust forming between us, begrudging, unwanted, and unwelcome…but budding up like determined weeds between cobblestone streets.

"It's no one's castle, not anymore," he says solemnly.

"But you're the vampire lord."

"*Vampir* lord, and yes, a lord, not a king." He stares out over the frozen spires and rooftops. "I'm a glorified attendant. A watcher and protector. I'm keeping this castle and looking after everyone in their slumber while trying to do my part to end the curse."

"Sounds like a lot," I murmur. I wonder if that's how Davos felt. Drew always blamed his off-putting nature on the things he had seen as master hunter. But perhaps some of it was the stress of looking after all of Hunter's Hamlet.

"It is."

"So the curse has caused everyone in the castle to turn into those monsters?" There's a weight to this place that gets heavier the longer I'm here. A deep sorrow that's the same as the bitter and lonely void I wallowed in after my father's death. This castle has known such immense loss.

"Not just the castle," he says solemnly. "It was placed on our people not long after the end of the great magic wars three millennia ago. It's a slow, creeping poison of a magical nature. No vampir escaped it, and, as long as we're awake, it slowly turns us into the monsters we have been fighting."

"Does the curse get worse for you the deeper we go and the closer we get to its anchor?"

He shakes his head. "Thankfully not; the curse affects all vampir evenly, for the most part. It's a curse laid on our blood with magic humans should have never meddled with. There is no escaping it, only slowing it. That is also why the consumption of fresh, untainted blood restores our proper visages and powers—even blood taken by force, the affront to the lore that it is, is better than no blood. It's why we need the Blood Moon to replenish our stores. We're not strong enough to harvest the blood of those here in Midscape—those with magic—in this weakened state. They'd hunt what's left of us if they saw the danger we've become."

Ruvan's eyes drift back to his companions. His brow furrows slightly with worry. I leave him to his thoughts, keeping my own. He said that his true form was not the monstrous sight I first saw him as, but the almost ethereal man standing before me now.

"The curse weakens your magic and turns you into monsters, and the creatures we're fighting have been turned by it?"

He returns his attention to me with a tired nod. "We call them Succumbed. It's the second stage of the curse. We—" he motions to himself and back to the other three "—are still vampir. We are *Accursed*, but have our wits about us.

"The Succumbed have fallen prey to the curse. They are no longer living, thinking beings and cannot return to what they were, no matter how much blood they consume. They are beasts of instinct, hunting to regain what was lost even though they cannot."

"They sound like they should be weak." But I know better.

"If only. The Succumbed are not without magic. In some ways their powers have been heightened by their frenzy. But they are blunt instruments, lacking any strategy or tactics."

"I see…" I look back out over the vast expanse of ice and stone. "That's why whenever they've attacked us it's been without organization. There's no plan. It's always one or two—if any—hunting on instinct alone." There was never a "hive mind" to the vampir. We were wrong all along, about everything, when it came to our enemies.

"Attack you? But the Fade is only weak enough to cross during the Blood Moon." Ruvan sounds genuinely surprised.

"Weak enough for *you*, but those cursed monsters come every full moon from the marshes." I wonder if I should be telling him this. Can he use this information to find his own way across the Fade during the full moon? Though it's not as if Ruvan has the army I once thought he did…

Ruvan strokes his chin and murmurs, "That explains some things the vampire lords have been wondering about the hunters. They have always been trained far better than we expect for encountering vampir only once every five hundred years. When I found out that they were using blood lore, I thought that explained it solely. But this is far more plausible."

"What *is* the blood lore?" I'm finally curious enough to outright ask. "I understand it involves blood and magic. But how does it work?"

"I'm not sure if a human could understand."

"Try me." I shift to face him.

He appraises me and I must, somehow, measure up. "All right. As I told you before, all blood—all life—holds magic within it. Blood tells the story of a person, their strengths and weaknesses, their lineage, the sum of their experiences. Even their future is all marked on the blood."

"You can…see someone's experience?" I ask cautiously. "Their future?"

"Yes. But like all blood lore, it requires talent and the right tools to do." A smirk slides across his lips, mouth tugged slightly open at one corner, his fang wicked and gleaming. "A vampir can steal a form. What makes you think we can't also steal a thought, if we wanted?"

"The blood lore sounds horrific." Invasive. Intrusive. And yet…I'm deeply curious.

"You might feel that way, but thousands in Midscape didn't." Ruvan looks out over the mountaintops, his voice becoming wistful. "They would come from far and wide for our monthly moon festivals. When our power was at its strongest, we could read the futures of kings."

"Only kings?"

"Anyone who offered their blood."

I consider this a moment. "If vampires can see the future, then how didn't they know they would be cursed?"

"Maybe someone did and they misunderstood their vision. Vampir do not get a complete picture. We can only see specifically what the asker demands of us. So it's possible that no one saw it coming—no one thought to ask."

"Did you look into the future before we ventured down here? Is that how Callos knew the way?" I ask.

"No…the curse has obscured and stinted many of our abilities," he says curtly, avoiding my gaze as if in shame.

It makes me wonder just how powerful blood lore is. So I ask, "What else can the blood lore do?"

"Some can identify truth from lie. Others can glean insight into a person's true nature. We were revered and respected for all our insights into things that had not yet come to pass and the true nature of individuals."

"The hunters can do nothing like this."

"How can *you* be so sure?" His gaze begins to harden. "Just how did *you* get the blood lore on the night of the full moon?"

"What?" Insecurity makes the word rattle in my mouth.

He grips my arm, just above my elbow. "If I had not granted you my power earlier, you would've died fighting the Succumbed."

I try and pull away, unable to deny it thanks to the blood lore, but he holds fast.

"It was clever, I grant you. Allowing me to think you're a hunter so you could secure your place here—protect yourself from the withering by becoming my bloodsworn. But I've shown you my true face. I think it's time you showed me yours." He leans forward and my world narrows to him alone.

"How much can you really know?" I boldly ask, dancing with my words. "You didn't even know those monsters were hunting us every full moon."

"*Monsters?*" he echoes with indignation. "Show some respect. Despite what they are now, they were once my kin, my forefathers, the men and women I should have served were it not for your hunter's curse turning them into what they are. Some of them were alive when I went into my slumber and I woke to find them mindless enemies.

"You think I *want* to see my people cut down? Left out to burn in the sun without the decency of a proper burial? You think I would've let them wander into your world like cattle for slaughter if I'd known?"

Heart pounding, I am captive in his hold. Helpless to do anything but stare in fear and awe at the pain overflowing from him. He feels so deeply. Deeper than I've ever even allowed myself to feel.

"Enough, Ruvan," Ventos calls over. "You're wasting your breath.

You'll never get a human, and especially not a hunter, to sympathize with our plight."

Yet that's what he's been trying to do. Keeps trying to do. Ruvan's eyes don't leave mine. I can feel him searching. Begging for something that I can't give. His magic brushes against me with feather-light invisible touches. It envelops me.

"He's right, a hunter would never sympathize with you," I say softly, trying to keep my focus straight with him staying so close. The words lack their usual bite. I can't put force behind them, even if I wanted to. And maybe, terrifyingly, I don't want to anymore. I can't say all the harsh and scathing things I want to because the bond won't let me… which means they're no longer true.

But Ruvan doesn't seem to see it. "And here I thought that perhaps… perhaps because you weren't *really* one of them you might just…" Ruvan curses. "Very well. Lie to yourself. Try to deceive with your half-truths. Further insult my attempts at kindness and generosity. It's all your kind knows how to do anyway."

He releases me with a light push. Enough to give him room to maneuver around me. But I wasn't expecting it. I stumble. My foot lands on a board, rather than a beam. It plunges straight through the soggy, snowy wood. I'm off-balance, trying to catch myself. Despite his anger and his glares, Ruvan lunges for me. Our fingers pass through each other. His eyes widen slightly as I fall, crashing through the floor.

Wind screeches in my ears. I try and twist my body, to fall on my feet. I might shatter my legs, but I can have my knees take the impact and then—

There's shouting above. *Whizzing*. Two strong arms circle me. Ruvan pulls me to him, twisting us at the last second. We crash to the ground, him softening the impact with his body.

We've landed awkwardly. I'm sprawled atop him, legs tangled. Armor pressed together. I groan, prying myself away. Ruvan's arms are still around my waist. His hair is almost as silver as his armor in the fading light. His lips part slightly.

Just as I'm about to stand with a grimace and an apology, he twists.

"Look out!" Ruvan rolls over and atop me. A clang rings out against his armor, accompanied by a high-pitched screeching sound.

A shadow leaps back, clinging unnaturally to the corner where the wall meets the ceiling, like a frog or spider. Its claws are extended nearly to the size of sickles. Its mouth is permanently opened, a crackling noise reverberating between its four fangs.

"What the…" I breathe in shock.

As soon as I make a sound, the creature's head jerks toward us. It lets out another blood-curdling scream. The sound is in my teeth. My eyes water and ears ring, dizziness overtaking me. The world suddenly has a sickening swirl.

"Riane, get a hold of yourself!" Ruvan grabs my shoulders, shaking lightly. "I need you with your wits." He raises his thumb to his lips, as if he intends to bite it again and give me his power. Even with my consciousness tenuous, the hunger rises within me, eager.

But he doesn't have a chance to break his skin before the beast launches itself into the air.

"My lord!" Ventos booms.

"It's a Fallen!" That's the only reply Ruvan has a chance to give before the monster is on him.

The beast is shadow and wind—a roar of claws and death. Ruvan is unflinching as he positions himself between me and the monstrosity. I watch; the world slows. I capture every detail as Ruvan raises his sickle. He goes for the monster's throat, the creature rears back, the silver clips its shoulder. The beast howls and falls. I think it's over.

I'm wrong.

I watch with horror as it slowly rises once more. An unrelenting nightmare.

"It—It—You cut it with silver."

"Silver is a weakness of the vampir." Ruvan glances over his shoulder, golden eyes swirling with anger. I honestly can't tell if it's directed at me or not. "I told you, these beasts are *not* vampir. The deeper the hold of the curse, the less they are one of us. Be ready."

"There's another!" I bounce onto my feet as movement distracts me from the opposite corner.

"What—" Ruvan doesn't have a chance to react. The creature lunging for him sinks all of its fangs into the hand wielding the sickle, puncturing the leather of his glove. The weapon clatters to the ground as Ruvan lets out a horrible scream. Black blood explodes. Before my eyes, it changes color to a sickly green shade.

I want to make sure he's all right. The urge is strange and unwelcome. Fortunately for me, I have a compelling reason not to spend too much time lingering on the thought. I scoop up my sickle and face off against the monster barreling toward me.

Its gait is strange. It shambles on two legs, sprinting, tipping forward to run almost like a wolf on all fours. Its claws dig into the stone floor with every lunge forward, leaving deep gouges behind. It snarls and clicks at me, sniffing the air. It's all limb and bone and sinewy muscle.

This isn't like the vampire I've been fighting with. There is nothing remotely human about this creature—not even the strange and ethereal way that the vampire seem to mirror humanity.

Every instinct of self-preservation is screaming within me. Telling me to run. To flee. I hold fast. Another thing Drew always said was the mark of a good hunter: being able to hold steady even in the face of death.

I wait until I can see the dark pits of the creature's eyes. They look more like husks, scabbed and scarred over, rather than anything that could be used for sight. It lunges for me.

I sidestep and slash, catching the creature underneath the ribs. It howls and rolls off my sickle, clipping my armor. Luckily I'm still unscathed. It's dazed for only a second before it barrels back toward me.

"We're coming down!" Winny shouts. A rope unfurls, drawing my attention and Ruvan's at the same time. We see more movement in unison, because we both react.

"Don't!" he cries, a hand clamping his wounded wrist. I wonder if they've seen the gash. Surely they must smell it. The scent of rot coming from Ruvan's forearm is the only thing my nose can seem to focus on. "It's a nest of Fallen. Keep moving, we'll meet you at the old workshop."

"My lord—" Lavenzia begins to say.

"That's an order," he barks, harsher than I've ever heard before. Ruvan makes another strike at the first monster and then spins, grabbing my hand. "We have to run."

I barely have time to process what he's said before my arm is nearly ripped from its socket by the force of him pulling me along. We sprint to a side door that he throws his shoulder into with a grunt. More blood explodes from his forearm.

"Move aside." I throw my shoulder into him, knocking the vampire lord out of the way.

Ruvan faces off against the incoming monsters. He holds out his wounded arm, blood dripping to the floor, mouth set into a hard line of pain and determination. Blood suddenly pours out of the gash and into the air, hovering, defying convention. It circles and spins, flying toward the monsters, coating them.

They screech and hiss as if hit by acid before going unnaturally still.

With all my remaining strength I push on the door. My muscles scream and strain against my armor. But the grunts of the monsters struggling against Ruvan's control is all the motivation I need. The hefty door cracks open. "Go."

Luckily, he doesn't even attempt to be chivalrous. Ruvan steps around the crack in the door, the trance on the monsters breaking as he lowers his arm. I quickly follow behind him. We both put our back to it. The last thing I see is three monsters charging toward us, a fourth feasting on its fallen counterpart.

seventeen

The wood and metal rattles as the monsters pound into it. Four thuds in total. There were even more than I thought.

"Don't say anything," Ruvan breathes, so soft I almost don't hear it. I couldn't speak if I tried. My heart is hammering in my throat.

After what feels like an hour, the pounding and snarling and scratching slowly subsides. I continue to press my back against the doors; my legs quiver with the exertion of making sure the creatures remain trapped inside. Nothing is even trying to break through anymore. But all I can see is those fiends barreling toward me.

A light touch on my forearm has me peeling open my eyes. I don't even remember shutting them. Ruvan slowly raises a finger to his lips. I get the message loud and clear.

We move in strained silence. Our feet drag with exhaustion. The dark passage is seemingly never-ending. The faintest of whispers of wind in the distance, or creaking of ancient foundations, has me jumping out of my skin.

I hope he knows where he's going, but I can't find the courage to ask. I imagine being lost down here. Left to starve. Forgotten. I've been with the vampire for days now and somehow, after my initial fight with Ruvan, this is the first time that I've truly felt like I'm going to die.

The vampire blood—Ruvan's blood—is finally beginning to wane in my veins. I'm growing tired. No, exhausted. I won't be able to fight another horde like I did earlier and Ruvan doesn't look steady enough on his feet to offer more power.

We're going to die here.

The void in the yawning, endless hall before me is alive, encroaching, compressing—in and around. I can't fight it anymore. It's under my skin, hollowing me out from within. The silver of my sickle isn't enough. It was never enough to protect me from all the evil that lurks in the living shadows. Panic claws its way up my throat and escapes as a whimper.

Ruvan turns on me, pressing me into the wall. He clamps a hand over my mouth. With his other hand he brings a finger to his lips again. Eyes intense, he slowly shakes his head.

Don't speak, don't make a single noise, I can almost hear him say, resonating across the tenuous connection we share. I can feel his magic quivering with nerves that I've never sensed from him before. He's becoming weaker by the second. He's afraid too.

Somehow, that calms me. I think his fear should make me tremble even more. He should be my protector and savior in this labyrinth of monsters. His fear should make me spiral deeper into hopelessness. But, oddly enough, it grounds me. Maybe it's because in his eyes, I see humanity—I see real emotion that is mirrored within me. I can understand him.

Maybe I'm calmer because seeing him afraid ignites an instinct to reassure him. To be stable for him if I can't be for myself. As I worry more about his state, I'm less afraid of the unknown that lingers in the shadows. I worry about him instead of myself and that feels like home.

My breathing slows.

His hand slides away from my mouth, but doesn't leave my person. It lingers on my shoulder. Fingertips trail down my arm. Lightly, tentatively, he takes my hand, as if to say, *We can do this together*.

No. That can't be it. He just doesn't want me tripping in the darkness. Though, he hadn't held my hand until now. I squeeze his fingers lightly. He squeezes back and neither of us break the hold.

After many twists and turns, I hear him exhale a sigh of relief. It's faint, but after straining my ears and hearing nothing for what seems like hours, it's loud to me. Ruvan turns and starts with renewed purpose. Eventually, we come to stop at a door. It leads into a foyer, appointed with furniture similar in style to his room. Even though the adornments are far more decrepit, it looks as though they were once even more opulent than anything I've seen so far. We cross into a sitting area, and then a bedroom. He closes every door behind us, agonizingly slowly so as not to make a sound, and then barricades it with what he can. I assist with the heavier lifting. His feet are beginning to drag and I notice him continually grabbing at his wounded forearm.

He takes a turn around the bedroom we end up in, lifting tapestries off the walls and checking behind them. Most crumble in his hands. There's another door that leads to a dressing room, connected back to the foyer. He barricades these doors as well.

While he does so, I pull back the curtains on the window. I need to see something other than the endless, oppressive walls of the old castle, void of all light. Like the tapestries, the fabric disintegrates under my hands. Moonlight pours into the room and I sigh with relief. I never thought the moon could be so comforting, or seeing the sky so freeing.

"I think this is as safe as we're going to get for tonight." Ruvan sits at the foot of the bed, inspecting his wounded arm. He begins to pull at his gauntlet, fumbling with the straps of his plate.

"Here, let me help you."

"You, a hunter, want to help the fearsome *vampire lord*?" He says vampire like I do to mock me, I'm sure.

"I hate to be the bearer of bad news, but you don't look that fearsome right now."

"Let me try harder." He bares his fangs. It might have terrified me once, maybe even earlier this day. But now I snort softly. The expression almost makes me laugh. A smirk slips across his lips as well.

"Still sub-par," I say lightly.

"Ah, damn." He doesn't sound like he means it. "Are you some kind of secret healer?"

"Unfortunately not. But I've seen my share of wounds." Before he can object further, I have three clasps undone.

"You have quick fingers. You take armor off men often?" He arches his eyebrows.

The question catches me so off guard I can't stop the blurt of laughter. "Something like that."

"Quinn usually helps me." He finishes pulling off the last bit of plate. The cotton clothes he was wearing underneath his armor cling to his skin, molded by the plate. It leaves very little to the imagination and I quickly look away, situating the heavy padding he had.

He sighs with relief. I imagine it would feel good to be out of all that heavy plate. Good enough that I briefly think of removing my armor. But I wouldn't want to be caught vulnerable here… I just can't tell if I'm more afraid of being vulnerable in front of the Succumbed, or Ruvan.

My wandering thoughts halt as he exposes the injury on his arm. Two semi-circles of holes left behind by the beast's fangs line his flesh, still ugly and weeping blood the shade of pond scum.

"Why isn't it healing?" I've always seen vampires heal quickly—so long as they're not cut by a silver blade. But this wound is festering; the flesh around it is bubbled, like it has been burned. "Is it because of that magic you used?" I think of his blood swirling through the air, sinking into the creatures, and then how they went suddenly still.

"No, that was my innate gift of the blood lore. I can use blood to gain control of creatures, briefly." He winces slightly. "Though, it took more effort than it might otherwise, thanks to the curse."

"An innate gift. So only you can do it?" It sounds horrifying and is another reminder of just how deadly the man I'm with is…and an underscoring of just how much he could do to me but hasn't. Stealing faces and thoughts, gaining bodily control…what can't a vampire do?

Ruvan nods. "I can't do much beyond the most basic magics of the blood lore, save for this." The explanation jostles my memory back to what Callos said before. Blood lore is more than stealing life and faces.

"The way you talk makes it sound like it's not terrifyingly incredible," I murmur, glancing away.

"Vampir weren't fighters, Riane. The gifts most revered weren't our abilities to kill, or fight."

"The ones you used during your moon festivals—the ability to see a person's true nature, or their future," I remember.

"You were paying attention." He gives me a slight smile, one that looks proud, that almost brings a flush to my cheeks. We're still achingly close and, for the first time, I'm seeing him more as a man than a vampire.

I focus on his arm. "If it's not the magic you used stopping the wound from healing, then what is it?"

"The curse taints the blood. The Fallen—those monsters—are the next stage of the curse after the Succumbed. But their instinct is the same; they hunt fresher blood to try and replace the rot that is within their veins." Ruvan leans back, tilting his head against the footboard. His eyes are glassy and distant. I've never seen him look so weak or tired. "When Fallen bite, they purge their cursed blood to make room for the new. Think of it like a poison."

As he speaks I begin to notice how sunken his cheeks are, how much luster his skin has already lost. Even the whites of his eyes are beginning to dull and gray. More and more he looks like the monster I first met. Ruvan shifts, arms falling at his sides, one knee bent, the other straight. The mighty vampire lord is sprawled on the ground before me.

But I feel no satisfaction at it as I might have once. Instead, those emotions have been replaced with sympathy.

I tilt my head to meet his eyes. "What do you need?"

"Rest." He blinks slowly; each time his eyes stay closed longer than the last.

"Don't lie to me."

"The irony of you saying that to me." He reminds me of the conversation we were having right before we fell. The disagreement that got us into this mess.

I debate against myself, my better judgment, before I finally say, "You're right. I'm not a hunter, not really."

"And I'm going to owe Quinn a vial of blood for it."

"What?"

Ruvan chuckles, the amusement wispy and as thin as his skin is becoming. "He suspected the truth well before I did. It's why I tried to test you when we first entered the old castle; I needed to know how much I had to protect you."

I purse my lips. "Why didn't you kill me for lying to you?"

"You're still human; you can still get us to the anchor. I just have to work a bit harder to keep you alive on the way."

"I know how to fight."

"Yes, and thank the old gods for it, but you're no hunter." He tips his head to one side. "How *did* you learn to fight though?" Ruvan speaks again before I can answer, clarity lighting up his face. "Your brother, the hunter. The one I was fighting in the ruins."

"His name is Drew." I don't know why I am compelled to tell him the truth. One truth escaped and now I don't know if I can keep the others. I'm tired. The fear that nearly smothered me earlier is still lurking in the corridors we fled from. I press my eyes closed. He's right, I'm not a hunter, I can't do this with the stoic strength hunters possess. I have to forge my own path ahead, one that's as uniquely mine as the metal I pull from the forge.

"And what is your name, your *full* name?"

I slowly open my eyes and bring my gaze back to him. He holds it. Calm. Expectant.

"You knew?"

"Of course I did."

"How?" I ask, though part of me suspects I already know. It's the same way I've known when he's worried or afraid. This deepening connection that lives between us.

"I can feel you." The words are almost sultry in how softly he says them.

"Floriane," is all I say. I don't know if I could manage anything else.

"Floriane," he repeats with that smooth accent of his. It sends a shiver down my spine. "It's a beautiful name."

"Now you're just flattering me."

"What reason do I have to flatter you?" he asks plainly.

I blink several times. "None, I suppose," I say with a laugh. One he joins in on. But his amusement ends with a soft wheeze. "The poison—the curse—it's already getting worse, isn't it?"

"It doesn't feel great, I'll admit that much." He wears a tough expression; I've seen it before on Drew. Some nights, Drew would come to me to teach me but I would end up patching him up with the medical supplies Mother kept stored in the smithy. Now I know why she never asked why those supplies were dwindling, and why I never had to replace any myself.

"Is that why you didn't use the mist to get us away?"

"The castle is warded, remember? Old blood lore. The only way in and out is through the receiving hall."

"Right." Though that still doesn't explain how the Succumbed manage to wander to Hunter's Hamlet during the full moons… There has to be another way out. *The gate I saw when I first arrived, perhaps?* No, that was shut tight. It must be somewhere else…

Ruvan's eyes flutter closed and my thoughts are interrupted. His breaths are becoming shallow. Throughout our conversation his muscles have been relaxing. He needs more than rest to fight the poison trying to claim him at the rate he's deteriorating.

I gather my resolve. "You need to drink more of my blood."

Ruvan's eyes open and stay open; the firm line of his mouth, pressed tight with pain, relaxes. Is he shocked? Excited? There's definitely a new energy thrumming in the air around him, in his magic, in me.

"I can't do that."

"Why? You just said fresh blood can help stave off the curse."

"I *won't* do that."

"Why?" I repeat. "You have no problem taking blood from Hunter's Hamlet."

"We only took what we need to sustain our magic so we can try and find a way to destroy this curse. And any blood we take by force isn't as potent—blood lore, to be truly effective, needs blood that's freely given." He sighs. "We are not strong enough to wage war with your kind and, even in the darkest points of our history with humans, we have never intended to. We just want to survive and end this nightmare."

"Does Ventos know the vampires don't want war?"

"I know my covenant all have their own opinions, but I am their lord, and the ultimate decisions fall with me." He stares into the corner of the room, looking at something I can't see. "I don't care if not killing you and working with you makes us weak. I don't care if future generations of vampir curse my name for not expunging the humans that hunted us and our forefathers relentlessly. I don't care if they see me as a traitor for not pursuing vengeance and retribution for the curse. I want *peace*. I want an end to this long night. I want to make sure no one else has to wake up to a rotted world."

I think about what Ventos said in the smithy—about how all of this, good and bad, all rested on Ruvan's shoulders. For the first time, I genuinely try to listen to Ruvan and what he's saying. I try to believe every word. Not just because he can't lie to me, but because…because I know deep within me that he is telling the truth because he *wants to*.

From the beginning, he pulled his punches. Even when I was striking to kill, he held back. He refrained. Yes, he needed—needs—me...but he could've gagged me and carried me down to this door. He could've tortured me into submission. He's answered my questions. He's been... kind.

I begin to allow the image of the monster I've seen him as to melt away. "You need blood to survive."

"If I rest long enough I will recover," he insists.

"You stubborn man." I laugh bitterly. I never thought I would be trying to convince a vampire to drink my blood. I never thought that I would be someone to offer it. But the truth is—"I need you."

His eyes widen slightly and he promptly breaks eye contact. As if, by taking his gaze away from me, he can ignore me.

"Ruvan, I don't want to die here. I don't want you to die. We have to carry on and see this through to the end. Your covenant is waiting for you. My family is waiting for me. And the fate of both of our people is holding its breath for what we do here."

He slowly brings his eyes back to mine, searching. I can feel him reaching out with his magic. Conscious or not, I don't know. But I don't fight it. I don't push him away.

I hate that I'm here. Yet, this place, this moment, this man—*not a monster*—it feels like the beginning of something consequential and inescapable. He straightens away from the footboard of the bed, shifting forward. I remain where I am, willingly trapped.

"I shouldn't."

"Why not? My blood is freely given." I study his face; the softened edges are becoming harder. He's becoming one of those monsters again.

"You feel as though you don't have a choice."

"*Now* you recognize that truth." I give him a bitter smirk. Guilt softens his expression slightly but I don't twist the proverbial knife. Instead I shake my head. "It's different. This time I genuinely want to. I want you to get better, Ruvan, and I will give my blood for it."

"I still can't." Yet, even as he says that, he's consuming me with his eyes. I wonder what it will feel like when he uses his mouth to consume me and a wriggling excitement worms down my spine. I'm darkly curious about what will happen if he keeps looking at me that way. I want to find out where this new path I'm choosing will lead.

"Why are you hesitating?"

"Because I already know how you taste." He lifts a hand, slowly running his fingertips up my arm, my shoulder, my neck.

"Is it bad?" I fight a blush and know I'm losing. I've never been touched like this before by a man. I've never even really been this close to a man before *at all*…and I like it. My mind might have wandered to the more sensual places in the past. But I never saw myself as something to be desired beyond my status as the forge maiden.

But he doesn't know I'm the forge maiden. Ruvan doesn't know or care about the extra rations the forge maiden and her family will get in times of hardship, the prestige in the community, or the respect within the hunters. He doesn't see me as a conquest.

I'm just Floriane, the woman whose name he's only just learned. Who tried to kill him. And yet he still looks at me as if I am the place where the world begins and ends. He still touches me as if my skin is sacred.

"Not at all." He inhales slowly through his nose, as if overtaken by the memory. "You are…*magnificent*. You taste like fire and woodsmoke, like the rare, red orchid that blooms from old blood."

I swallow thickly. "Then what's the problem?" My voice quivers slightly. His intensity has my heart pounding. Even if he just desires my blood and the magic within it…I want him to keep looking at me, touching me.

"I fear that once I taste you again, I won't be able to stop."

"You will stop when I say." I level my eyes with his, matching his intensity with my own.

He leans closer still, overwhelming all of me. "Are you presuming to order me? The fearsome vampir lord?"

"Yes," I say with pride, lacking all hesitation.

He chuckles darkly, the sound rumbling through me and landing right in my groin, so hot that I have to shift to try and alleviate the tension. Does he know what he's doing to me? I hope so…because I don't want him to stop. In this moment, I want more. I want to cast it all aside and just be Floriane—not the forge maiden, not the hidden hunter. The woman.

"As you command," he murmurs.

The forge maiden commanding the vampire lord. No one back

home will ever believe it. Not that they would ever find out… This will be my secret.

His attention is on my throat. His fingers curl around the back of my neck. With his other hand, he traces the mark on the hollow between my collarbones. The soft caresses send shivers down my spine as sparks fly between his finger and the design. "Are you ready?"

"Will it hurt?" Excitement and nerves render my words barely audible.

"Never." There's so much wrapped in that word. "I will never allow harm to come to you."

I tilt my head to the side, expose my neck to him, and brace myself. "Then do it."

eighteen

HE LEANS FORWARD, LIPS PARTING TO EXPOSE FANGS MADE SILVER IN THE MOONLIGHT.

I don't want to look, and yet I can't avert my gaze. His eyes remain locked with mine until the very last second, when his face disappears from my view. His hot breath primes my skin for his lips as they slide across my flesh. I bite my lower lip and hold my breath.

There's the smoothness of his fangs. He adjusts. Slight pressure that brushes up to the line of pain, yet somehow doesn't cross. And then…

Then…

I exhale slowly, a flush rushing across my body as every bit of tension releases at once. My lids go heavy, the world blurs. Invisible pins prick me; I tingle until my hairs stand on end. I am aware of every inch of me and him—of the need growing in my lower abdomen to the point of insatiability. My hands move on their own, reaching for him. They slide over his forearms, grabbing behind his elbows. He tenses, but only briefly. Ruvan relaxes and allows me to pull him closer.

His hands shift. One sliding down, grazing my breast as he wraps his arm around my waist. His other hand remains at the nape of my neck, guiding me with subtle pressure, keeping me exactly where he wants me.

Why does it feel so…good?

We're on the verge of becoming one. I ache. I pull him closer still. His arm tenses. Every bit of his corded muscle is mine to explore as his hot lips are planted upon me. My own lips are suddenly cold. Gasping in moonlight. Wanting his. Wanting more, even if I don't fully know what "more" is.

His presence, his body, has become a second awareness, like a phantom limb, or my hammer in the forge. Like something that should be my own, but isn't. Or maybe was long, long ago.

A low groan rises in the back of his throat, causing the muscles in my neck to tremble. My core tightens. My eyes dip closed. He holds me so tightly that I swear it will bruise and I do not care.

I want to shift closer, closer still. I want to sit in his lap. To straddle him. To lose my fingers in his moonlit hair as he drinks my blood and delights in my flesh.

The magic within him grows. My power is swelling within him. Life and magic slip from me to fill his form. His grip stops quivering slightly, and he drinks slow and steady, initial fervor gone.

We are two candles, but one flame. We cannot and will not let the other go dark. Not while one of us still burns.

My mind spins and I succumb to the delightful sensations. My grip goes slack. Warm…I am so warm and safe in his arms.

And yet, he begins to release me. He's going to pull away. I'm not ready for it to be over. I want more. I want him to continue touching me, kissing me, with and without fangs. I want to feel everything that I was never allowed or never thought I should. I want everything that was denied me because if I don't take it now, will I ever have it?

A whimper escapes my lips.

"It's too much," he murmurs, voice thick and heavy. It makes my breath catch. "I can't take any more from you."

"Do you have enough?" I whisper, opening my eyes. I hope he'll say no.

He is himself once more, the ethereal being that my blood makes him. Starlight is good to him, outlining him in glowing white. His lips are a bright crimson. He licks them, eyes fluttering closed, as though he is savoring every last taste of me on his tongue.

It almost makes me want to lick myself off of him.

"You gave me more than enough."

"Did I taste all right?" I can't help but ask.

"Floriane, you taste…" He trails off. His eyes are shining brighter than the sun at dawn. He stares at me as if all the words of what he was going to say are written on my face. "You taste like strength, and hope."

Hope. That illustrious thing that I've so rarely permitted myself to even be adjacent to. Maybe that curiosity of if, or how, I'm changing is what prompts me to ask, "Could you see my future?"

He tenses. He doesn't want to tell me. I can almost catch a glimpse of what he doesn't say as I see myself reflected in his eyes.

"Ruvan?"

"Even if I had the skills to do so, I would never look without your blessing."

"And here I hoped you could tell me what destiny had in store for me." I tilt my head but the world sways. I'm dizzy. It's not just the heat of his touch. I wonder how much blood I lost as clarity begins to dawn on me.

Ruvan tightens his arms around me once more, holding me to him. My temple lands on his shoulder. Somehow I'm positioned in his lap. I actually made it there, just like I wanted. His heart thrums in my ear, as steady a rhythm as my hammer in the forge. Somehow, his embrace is all I expected and more. I almost want to cry with how good it is to be held. I've been strong for so long, a pillar of the community, carrying the load of silver and expectation alike… I can't remember the last time I was comforted like this.

"Enough questions for now. You need to rest." He raises his thumb to his mouth, bites it lightly, and smears one drop of black blood on my lower lip as he studies me. The pad of his finger lingers on my lip, his nail grazing my skin before he pulls away.

"But you—"

"We can share the power that flows between us. I took too much; let me give some back."

I lick my lips and feel the rush of him in my veins. Outside of battle, the magic is not as needy. It does not demand blood or battle.

Swirling him on my tongue, I try to think of what he tastes like beyond the heavy, metallic note of blood. There's sweetness there, like an overripe plum. A darkness akin to the depth of fortified wine. I can taste something mineral, like the rocky crags that hold the castle.

Kindness. It's an odd thought, but as my eyes dip closed that's what I settle on. "You taste like kindness," I murmur.

He rasps a chuckle and tucks wayward hair behind my ear. "And here I thought life had made me too bitter for that."

"You're not bitter at all." I yawn. "You're…impossibly sweet."

Ruvan's fingers pause at that, fingertips light on the crest of my ear as he moves to tuck hair away from my face. "I am not."

"You are…though I saw nothing of your future."

He huffs softly. "Good. Now, rest, Floriane. We have to get to the anchor tomorrow."

I oblige, succumbing to exhaustion in the arms of the vampire lord.

I'm back in the halls of the castle. But they are not the dilapidated husks that I saw with my waking eyes. These hallways are illuminated by gilded candelabra and the fractured light of polished chandeliers. The tapestries are new, colors bright. The carpets on the floor are plush underneath my feet.

Except, they are not my *feet.*

I pass by mirrors—uncovered ones—and find myself to be a taller, slimmer woman. My short black hair is replaced by long, dark brown tresses and black eyes with deep amber. I move through the halls with confidence, not fear. This is not a place of danger yet. This is home.

The path I take leads me to a metal door—a rare and custom piece that displays the blacksmith's skill. The metal took years to develop; this was merely a test—an experimentation—but it will all be worth it once the daggers are made. On the center of the door is a marking that looks like a teardrop with a diamond in its center, two daggerlike slashes making a V shape beneath it.

I run my fingertips lightly over the familiar symbol before grabbing the handle. A silver needle punctures my skin on the door-facing side of the handle. Extra precaution. I can't have anyone else knowing what I do here. I can't have my research getting out too soon or, worse, falling into the wrong hands. There are some that would want to weaponize my work. I hardly grimace as my blood fills the grooves within the door and allows me entry.

Inside the workshop, I set about my business with confidence. The smith has the right alloy now. We can test it with new daggers during the next full moon. We need the blood of sentient creatures—those with experience to empower the blood. They'll come willingly and give their blood during the festival.

With the right pacts...we'll strengthen the vampir enough that they must no longer live in seclusion. We'll—

There is someone at the door. I turn, beaming. There's only one person who would come and visit me here.

It is the man I saw in the ruins.

"Solos," I say with a voice not my own. "Come and look at this dagger; it won't be much longer now. We can put an end to the horrors once and for all."

I wake to sunlight, warmed by its rays, and a dull ache that slowly retreats from between my temples. I am sprawled upon the floor and I stretch languidly, almost lazily. I feel like one of the cats that would sleep on the top of the great wall that surrounded Hunter's Hamlet and the fortress, dozing in the sunlight without a care in the world.

The previous day returns to me in a rush. I inhale sharply. My hand flies to my neck. The skin is sensitive and the barest touch sends shivers up my spine. I exhale with a shiver and lick my lips, as though the blood from his thumb was still there. The taste of him returns to me.

Ruvan is still fast asleep. He has curled up against the wall, to the side of the window.

Slowly rolling onto my side, I pull my knees under me and crawl over to him. His hair has fallen over his face. His breaths are slow and even; he looks almost peaceful. Just his visage brings back the memories of last night. His strong arms around me, tightening. The feeling of his growing, insatiable need for me. A need I wanted to fulfill.

I rub my neck thoughtfully. Is it the magic of the bloodsworn or something more? I want to say it is just the vampire magic toying with my mind, that I would never desire such things.

But I know better. I have never been needed before. Not in that way. Though I have wondered what it might be like.

There are few suitors in Hunter's Hamlet. Some girls delight in their own hunt, as best they are able with the options they're given. I would look at them longingly as they dressed for their Yule balls and spring dances. Yes, I envied them. Their freedom. Their ability to look past the life we were given and see it as something that could be…hopeful.

Most saw Hunter's Hamlet as a sanctuary from the outside world. Even though we faced vampires every full moon, that was only one day a month. All the other days had safety, full bellies when there wasn't unexpected drought or downpour, and a community where everyone had a role and each role lifted up another.

For me, Hunter's Hamlet was everything I would ever have in life. I knew what my future was as the forge maiden, what it always would be. I never had a choice before me when it came to suitors or a family of my own. I had obligations.

So no men ever dared to look at me the way Ruvan did last night. At least none that ever allowed me to see. And I daresay, I liked it.

I shake my head and try to banish the notion. *No. I didn't like it.* Well, I did…but not from this vampire, not really. I certainly didn't like the silk of his hair or the curve of his mouth. And I definitely didn't like his fangs at all. Not at all… I bite my lower lip and worry it between my teeth. I can still taste him. I still want more of him.

"If you stare at me any longer, I'm going to request a portrait," he says without opening his eyes.

I nearly fall back in surprise. "How long have you been awake?"

"Long enough to know that I have been your sole focus for some time." Ruvan's eyes flutter open. One look from him now has my breath hitching. "How do you feel?"

"I'm fine."

"Good."

"What about you?" I ask. He still looks luminous. Cheeks strong, lips full—though they're no longer stained crimson. I imagine him slowly licking his lips again, savoring every taste. I quickly try and banish the thought. I have to get my wits about me.

"I'm excellent." He stands and I do as well. "We should get to moving while we still have the advantage of light on our side and the old castle is quieter."

"Of course." I adjust my armor, checking what weapons I have left. One sickle, a few daggers. The rest were lost in the hunt and the fall. As I help him back into his plate, I ask, "Do you know where we are?"

"Luckily, yes. I caught my bearings last night. We're in one of the king's old chambers. Assuming Callos's maps and my memory are both correct." His caveat doesn't sound as confident as I would've liked.

"Are there any other types of monsters I should know about?"

He had been going to remove the barricades from the door when he pauses. I don't like the hesitation at all. "Just one."

"Oh, great, something worse than the Succumbed or Fallen?" I think bitter amusement is the only way I'm going to come to terms with what's happening.

"It's not something you need to worry about." He continues moving things away from the door. I go over to help him, using the opportunity to shoot him a frustrated glare.

"I don't want to be in the dark anymore."

"Unfortunately these hallways are very dark."

"That's not what I meant and you know it." I put my hands on my hips. "If we're working together, then let's work together. Really and truly."

"You're one to talk." The words aren't as biting as they could be.

"I mean it. Let's take this from the start again."

"All right, Floriane." Him using my name still gives me pause. It's strange to see his mouth make those sounds. "There's only one other type of cursed vampir. Not much is known about the curse and how it works. The humans didn't exactly give us a primer on it."

"If one exists, I don't know about it. That's the truth." I push aside the stone dresser we positioned in front of the door.

"Unfortunate." He catches my chin, bringing my face to his. I suck in air, holding it. His intense stare is back, those bright eyes capturing me. "You're lucky you taste so good otherwise I'd be far more frustrated with you."

I try to speak but only get as far as opening my mouth.

Satisfied. Smug. He releases me. He knows exactly what he's doing to me, and as frustrated as that makes me, I also…like it. I want him to keep touching me so badly that I might take matters into my own hands if I'm not careful. Now that I've given myself permission to indulge, I don't have a good answer for why I'm not constantly.

"Whatever the reason, the curse doesn't affect all vampir equally," he continues, as though he hasn't just turned my knees to jelly. "Some only become Succumbed. Other vampir, Fallen. The final kind is the

Lost. I've never even seen one myself, but the records of the vampir lords who came before me speculate that the Lost are the husks of powerful lords lost long ago. So I theorize that the impact of the curse is somehow related to the innate power a vampir had before the curse was laid and not about the length of time someone has been cursed."

"Exceptional." I sigh. "So there is a greater, more powerful enemy to look out for."

"As I said, they're rare. The early lords might have cleared them all. There's not a record of a sighting for centuries."

"What makes them different than the others?"

"As I said, I only have partial records, but other lords who have encountered them and survived have noted that they are large, winged monstrosities. They're fully immune to silver so they have to be cut down. And perhaps the most dangerous is that they are able to hypnotize using sound."

I wait for him to say that he's just joking, that none of this is real, but his expression is deathly serious. "Well, then let's hope we never run into one and find out if those legends are true."

"Agreed."

The old castle is quiet, as quiet as it was when we first set out. The darkness is still inky, thick. I can feel the other entities we share these halls with. We are not safe by any stretch. But the monsters around us slumber. There is no feeling of movement. There are no currents on the still air.

It takes me half the day to realize that the path we're taking is familiar. It is the ghostly outlines of tapestries. The forgotten tables that have crumbled under their own weight underneath chandeliers that I saw glittering in my dreams mere hours ago.

I slow to stop in a large banquet hall.

Ruvan pauses as well when he notices that I'm no longer following. He walks back to me, encroaching on my personal space to whisper, "What is it? What do you hear, or see?"

"I know this place."

"You mean it is similar to something you have seen before?"

I breathe soft laughter. "No, I've seen nothing like this castle in my life. There is nothing this grand in Hunter's Hamlet, not even the fortress."

"Then—"

"I think I saw it…in my dreams." I look to him and hastily add, "I realize it sounds impossible to say aloud. But I promise you, I'm not—"

"You *can't* lie." A frown tugs on his lips.

"What do you think it means?" I whisper.

Ruvan looks around the room. I wish I knew what he was thinking. For all the hints and glimpses the magic we share gives me, I have no real idea what's going on in that head of his.

"We shall see," he answers enigmatically.

I take him by the arm. "Tell me."

"Not yet."

"You don't think I have a right to know?"

"I don't think I want to share something until I'm certain of it, one way or another." He pulls away from me, the knowledge retreating with him. "Now, we need to carry on."

"No." I don't move.

Ruvan slows and looks over his shoulder. "No?"

"I said no," I repeat. "I won't carry on until you tell me."

"This isn't the time or place."

"Then speak quickly."

"You are relentless." He rubs his temples, though I don't feel any genuine agitation across our oath. If anything, I think he's using the motion to hide a smirk.

"I've been told I hammer at something until it submits to my will," I say.

"That much I believe." Ruvan sighs. "I wonder if our bloodsworn has, indeed, given you some power of the vampir."

My hands relax and I let go of whatever I had thought he was going to say. I certainly wasn't expecting this.

"But I'm not a vampire…"

"No, and the rites to make one are complex and involve great power and sacrifice on the part of vampir and human alike—so great that there are only a few writings on it from King Solos, and the process was immediately outlawed."

Solos. I heard that name in my dream. At least, I think I did. "But you've researched it?"

"There are only a few, limited tomes on the art, but I've always been intrigued by forbidden things." He smiles slyly. "In any case, becoming bloodsworn isn't part of the rites to turn a human vampir. But there's not other information on what would happen with a human and vampir bloodsworn, as it's never been done before. I could theorize that, in taking the oath and fortifying it with the ritual I performed, deepening it with more of my blood, I have given you traces of the vampir's power. Perhaps you saw the future us walking through here in your dreams."

Was that what it was? "Maybe," is all I can say. My head is pounding. The dream, though fading, was different...but I can't put my finger on how. It's becoming hazy in my memory and Ruvan is right. This isn't the time or place to discuss these matters and, moreover, I don't want to anymore. There are questions lurking that I don't want to answer. The idea of new magic growing within me has me shaken. "I guess we'll know more as time goes on."

He picks up on the hint and says nothing more.

The rooms blur, one after the next, but I know when we're getting close to our destination. Sure enough, with one or two deviations to account for collapsed passageways and barred rooms, we took almost the same path as the woman in my dream.

It couldn't have been the future. I swallow thickly. What has this bloodsworn awoken within me? I fear I have invited the magic of the vampire—and all that comes with it inside of me...and now it might never leave.

nineteen

THE METAL DOOR IS BEFORE ME. Even if I hadn't recently seen it in my dreams, I would know it's important at a glance. It's at the end of a long hallway that opens up just before it and is different from every other door we've seen. Unlike in my dreams, it's tarnished with age. Cobwebs are thick around it, clinging to the dulled symbol on its front.

"It doesn't look like anyone else's made it yet," Ruvan observes solemnly. There's nowhere for them to hide in this small antechamber and they certainly cannot open the door for reasons I now understand.

"You don't think anything happened to them, do you?" I find I no longer wish to see them die horrible deaths.

"I hope not." The answer isn't as reassuring as I would like. I know how much they mean to him. "But they knew the risks of being awoken during the long night. We all did."

"You keep saying awoken…"

"I'll explain more once we have survived and are back in the upper castle. For now, we keep our focus."

I catch his hand, bolder than I've ever been with anyone, much less a man. "Do you promise you'll tell me?"

The question draws his sole attention to me. The air around him feels…hesitant. Almost scared. But what is he afraid of? Certainly not me. Promising something to me? I think we've already made the ultimate promise to each other by becoming bloodsworn.

"Yes." He faces off against the door again. I can see his

shoulders tense and feel his apprehension. “Now, I want to see what’s inside. I’m ready to find this curse anchor and put an end to all this.” I reach for the handle but he stops me with a touch on my wrist. “I should warn you that—”

“There’s a small, silver blade on the other side of the handle and that’s why a vampir couldn’t open it,” I interject to finish for him.

“How did you…”

“Already told you, I saw this in my dream,” I say somewhat impatiently.

“Have you had any other strange dreams?” He focuses intently on me.

“A few,” I admit.

“And you didn’t think to tell me?”

I arch my brows. “It’s not as if we’ve been on the best of terms this entire time.”

He opens his mouth to object and slowly shuts it, reconsidering. Then says, “Tell me of them when we return to safety. For now, let’s focus on our mission.”

I nod, close my fingers around the handle, and feel the familiar prick on the pad of my hand. There’s a surge of magic that flows to the door. It draws blood and power from me in the same way that Ruvan drew from me last night. The symbol in the center of the door glows a faint crimson, burning away the cobwebs and age. A lock disengages deep within. I pull and shake off the remaining dust to reveal bright silver, as though it is freshly forged. As the metal dulls I’m reaffirmed in my suspicions—it’s not solid silver. The handle is, but the rest is different.

There’s something special about the metal this door was made from. I’ve never seen a metal like this before—it’s smooth with the faintest swirl of red, almost rust-like.

Ruvan doesn’t move. He stands there in silent awe long enough that I shift to face him.

“Is everything all right?” I ask.

“Ever since the discovery of this door in Jontun’s records by the awoken Lady two thousand years ago, it has been a mystery. And every clue any lord or lady has ever found since points to this place as being one of the best possible locations for the anchor of the curse. It’s one of the original blood lore workshops; it was sealed off, a perpetual mystery… Now we're here. And—" A rumbling from up the hall interrupts him.

"That's not good." My words sink with my stomach.

"Get inside." Ruvan grabs my shoulder and pushes me within, following just behind. He positions himself by the door. Holding it from the inside, ready to push it shut. He narrows his eyes at the darkness behind us. I stay close to him, hand on my sickle.

"I don't know what the point of this is!" Winny's high voice cuts over the growing cacophony. "We're about to run into a dead end."

"Close that door!" Lavenzia shouts back. The sound of splintering wood echoes down to us. There's a grunt. Followed by a screech. "Get off him!"

"We're here," Ruvan shouts up the hall. "Keep running!"

Winny is the first to emerge from the thick shadow and into my realm of perception. Her eyes widen as they meet mine. She calls back over her shoulder, "Lavenzia, Ventos, you owe me three of your vials. She is the real hunter deal." *They did suspect me*. I wonder if Winny will resent me when she realizes that I'm going to make her lose those vials.

Lavenzia comes next, helping an ailing Ventos down the hall. "Now is not the time for gloating, Winny!"

There's a thundering behind them. I step to the other side of the door, opposite Ruvan, sickle drawn and ready.

Winny breezes past me first. Lavenzia is slowed by Ventos's weight as she supports him. A horde of Succumbed are hot on their tail. One swipes for them; Lavenzia lets out a cry, grits her teeth, and presses on.

I launch into action. Sprinting to meet them, I dart around and bring up my sickle. I catch three with the motion. Their blood oozes around my blade. The monsters fall and fill me with the same satisfaction as yesterday. I might not be a hunter, but I'm learning to love the hunt. Especially when I'm fighting for a cause.

We're working backward to the door. I'm fending off as many as I can, Winny's daggers *whizzing* by my head. Lavenzia and Ventos clear the door frame.

"Floriane!" Ruvan shouts. I tumble back into the room, dodging a swipe of one of the beast's claws. With Winny's help, Ruvan shuts the door. Lavenzia jabs the few who would try and make it through.

For a second, no one speaks. Our ragged breaths fill the workshop. The screaming of monsters falls silent on the opposite side of the door as they slam into the silver with enough force that the embellishments break their skin. Whatever that silver alloy is, it's still enough pure silver to kill a vampir—or, at least a Succumbed.

Laughter fills the room. It comes in the form of deep wheezing from the ground where Ventos lies. The sound devolves into groaning.

"They got me good." He curses.

"Let me see." Ruvan is at his side.

"You don't need to fret over me." Ventos tries to shoo him away.

"And you don't need to pretend like you don't need help sometimes." Ruvan shakes his head and brings his hand to his lips.

I know what he's about to do and my mouth waters; I want him for myself. I want to taste him again. To feel that rush of power. To have him in my arms. If I opened my mouth right now I couldn't stop myself from begging for it. The need is so mighty it frightens me some, but I refuse to deny it; I've spent my life denying myself things and here I'm no longer forced to.

"Here, drink."

"My lord, I couldn't—"

"It's only a little and I have strength to spare. Drink." Ruvan brings his palm to Ventos's mouth.

The energies within me shift, pulled like tides to the moon as the magic changes in Ruvan. Power leaves Ruvan's body and flows into his vassal's, like a part of me vanishing.

I wonder if Ventos can sense the difference my presence makes in Ruvan. Then a different thought strikes me—if blood is empowered by experience, are Ventos and I connected now in a way that we weren't before? I fight a grimace.

"How do you feel?" Ruvan asks Ventos, helping him up.

"Better than I should, given what we've been through to get here," Ventos says.

"Are you two all right?" Ruvan turns to the other members of his covenant.

"We're fine," Lavenzia answers. "A little scraped and bruised, tired, but fine."

"Really glad to see you, though," Winny adds.

"The feeling is mutual." Ruvan's relief is palpable at the sight of his knights. No, his friends. The way he looks at them has my gaze shifting as well.

"Did you run into any more trouble along the way?" Ventos asks.

"None after the Fallen." Ruvan shakes his head. "Did they go after you?"

"You kept them busy long enough that we managed to give them the slip. Glad the hunter made it, or we would've been in a tight spot just now." Ventos nods in my direction with what seems like genuine respect.

"About that…" I start and lose my words when all of their eyes are on me. I don't *have to* tell them anything. If Ruvan wants them to know, he can tell them. And yet…I'm compelled to say something. I need to—*want* to work with these people. We've made it this far, they continue to protect me, and they're not the vampires I was expecting. I owe them the truth. Like it or not, we do share a bond now of blood and experience. "I'm not actually a hunter."

"Ha! I knew it!" Lavenzia sticks her tongue out at Winny, who crosses her arms with a pout.

"Winny, you should be happy about her lying to us, because it means you weren't actually working with a hunter." Ventos shakes his head like a disappointed father. I'm not sure if it's because things have changed after our journey into the old castle, or if it's because I'm allowing myself to see them in a new light, but these vampires seem different now. Warmer.

"Let me have a moment to be upset, it's been a long day and I have a multitude of reasons to be grumpy," Winny says, deadpan.

Ruvan just continues to stare at me. I can feel his curiosity. The longer that I'm around him the more that I'm beginning to pick up on the subtle shifts of his magic. The more that I'm able to read him.

"My brother was—*is*—a hunter. He's the one who taught me everything I know about fighting, even though he wasn't supposed to. I was the forge maiden of Hunter's Hamlet."

"No wonder you looked like a natural in the smithy." Winny relaxes her pout.

"Are you just tickled over the fact that you were tricked by a human, my lord?" Ventos asks dryly.

"If any human was to trick me, I think I'm glad it was Floriane." Ruvan's words are warm.

"Floriane?" Lavenzia repeats. "Your real name?"

"Yes, my full name. But if you'd like to keep calling me Riane, that's fine, too." No one has ever called me Riane before. It seems fitting to give them that continued permission. I do feel like a different person on this side of the Fade.

"Good to finally meet you, Floriane." She gives me a nod of her head.

"Glad to know the real name of the woman I'm working with. Though I might still stick with Riane from time to time." Winny outstretches her hand.

I consider it for a moment, but finally accept, clasping it tightly. "Riane is fine with me."

"Now, let's find this anchor and end the long night." Ruvan turns to face the room.

"I do wonder how some long-ago human sneaked into our territory right under our noses to lay this curse. Though, perhaps I can see how, now." Ventos side-eyes me. I sigh. As if I had anything to do with that person. Maybe he doesn't realize that humans don't have as long lifespans as vampires do…then again, I realize I don't actually know how long a vampire's lifespan is. The hunters call them eternal beings, but I've learned that's not the case.

I look to Ruvan. What he's said so far has led me to believe that his existence might be as fleeting as mine is. He has spoken of previous vampire lords throughout the ages; it seems like there are many who came before him—another difference from the hunters' stories of a single vampire lord stalking us for millennia.

Leaving the thoughts and questions for later, I turn my attention to the room. Lavenzia lights a few of the sconces, casting a faint, orange light on this forgotten place.

The air has settled since our initial entry. The dust coats the tables, silver vessels, glass jars with various questionable substances and items floating within them. The vampires fan out through the room, careful not to touch anything, disturbing only with their eyes. I wonder if they'll just *know* what the curse anchor is on sight and sense. So I leave finding it to them.

Instead I allow my mind to wander back to what this room might have been used for—back to my dreams. The room has been forgotten for ages. In my dream everything was bright and shining. Everything was new.

It couldn't have been a glimpse into the future… The past, perhaps? Is that even possible? Ruvan said that for a vampire to perform their magic, they must have blood freely given. In which case, would I be seeing Ruvan's past? He's the one whose blood I consumed. Magic is tied to the blood, written by experience. But that isn't a likely explanation, either. I try to force the woman from my dream to sharpen in my memory, but doing so makes my head hurt.

I walk up to one of the tables. Laid out are a number of vials in racks with notes attached to them. I'm not sure if they want me to be looking, but I do anyway; it's hard not to. I'm so curious at this point. I fought and bled to be here. I have as much of a right as they do to know what all the struggle was for.

Plus, it's not like any of them stop me.

They all hover around the notes left out, but I'm drawn to a palm-sized token next to a quill that's weighted down by dust and cobweb. I lift the token and turn it over in my hands. Sure enough, it's made of the same material as the door. It's not pure silver. It's too warm to be silver. And the luster is off. It's not a silver variant I recognize either.

The smith has the right alloy now. We can test it with new daggers during the next full moon. That was what the woman said in my dream.

"Could this be the curse anchor?" I ask no one in particular. All attention is quickly on the disk in my hand.

"No," Ruvan says finally. "But why do you ask?" He approaches.

"It's a strange alloy and is made of the same metal as the door."

"Looks like silver to me," Lavenzia says, also coming for a closer investigation.

"It's not silver," I assure her.

"Of course it is."

"No, it's not," I say, trying to keep my agitation to myself.

"I would know silver." Lavenzia rolls her eyes.

"I think I should know silver better than you, since I smelt it."

"She has you there," Winny chimes in.

Ventos snatches the disk from my hand before I can react. "You think we don't know what silver *feels like*? The subtle burn? The creeping itch?"

I purse my lips and inhale slowly. *Old gods help me from putting this hulking man in his place so viciously he'll be nursing the verbal lashing for weeks.*

"Is it wise to handle silver with your bare hands just to prove a point?" Ruvan arches his brows at Ventos. The latter suddenly realizes what he's done and his hand goes limp.

I catch the token before it falls. "There are two types of silver: pure and steel variant," I try and explain, rotating the coin between my fingers. "Well, now I suppose there might actually be three types of silver. Pure silver is exactly what it sounds like. Fresh from the mines and not mixed with any other metals."

"We know all too well about pure silver," Ventos says with a note of disgust.

"Not quite," I say, but then quickly add, "You might, I can't be sure. But if you're talking about the weapons you wield, that's a steel *variant*. You can see it by the subtle waves in the weapons when you look very closely."

"But if they cut us, we'll die." Lavenzia eyes her rapier. "Not the same can be said for steel."

"Pure steel, yes. Modified steel, also yes," I agree. "But steel variant silver is different. It's…" I trail off as I hunt for my next words.

"It's what?" Ruvan says softly.

I have no reason to be ashamed. In fact, I have every reason to be proud of my family for our ingenuity in the forge; I always have been before now. I am part of a long line of illustrious forge maidens. Without us Hunter's Hamlet wouldn't have survived this long. But… the weapons we made have also killed countless vampire—victims of the curse that I've now seen with my own eyes.

I already wish that I could ignore all that I've seen. I don't know anymore with confidence who is good and who is evil. All I can do is keep going forward with what I do know—that I really believe I can trust these people.

"It's a special alloy invented by my family ages ago. It's what all the weapons are made from. It's a secret trade not written down in any book or ledger, but passed from mother to daughter over centuries.

Pure silver, though effective against vampire—vampir." The correction surprises me. I speak faster, hoping they didn't notice. Judging from the subtle shift in Ruvan's expression, the brief furrow of his brow, the sudden intensity in his gaze that threatens to burn away my attempts at pretending it never happened…he heard it, loud and clear. "Pure silver is too soft to make weapons out of. Anything made of pure silver would bend and dull instantly. You'd get one cut, if you're lucky. It's not suitable for combat."

"So you humans created something with all the effects of silver, but strength of steel." Ventos draws his broadsword, looking down the blade. I wonder what he thinks of wielding weapons made by my family, for hunters, against his own kind. Whatever thoughts he has bring a grimace to his mouth. "Clever, vile creatures."

"Still your tongue," Ruvan snaps before I can even register what Ventos said. The vampir lord has squared his shoulders against one of his most ardent defenders. Ventos goes to speak again, but Ruvan speaks over him before he has the chance. "Floriane is a loyal member of this covenant. I will not have you continuing to insult her."

"I said nothing of her, only her kind." Ventos rolls his shoulders and tilts his head from side to side, as if he's getting ready for a fight.

"The slight is the same."

"And what of all she said about us? About the vampir? No doubt about you?"

"She is learning and moving past the errors of her ways. We can do the same."

I wonder if all of this is because Ruvan caught my correction. His intensity does not seem to match the brief moment of etiquette I afforded his people. Especially since it was purely by accident. I wonder how much comes from the night we spent together.

"You didn't even know her name until a few hours ago," Ventos scoffs. "Don't let the bloodsworn go to your head. She's a tool to get what we need and has already fulfilled her purpose."

"The curse is not yet broken." I surprise myself by being the one to speak up. "Until it is, I am a member of this covenant. That was the promise I made. My purpose is far from fulfilled and I'm on your side until it is…and maybe after, depending on how we all proceed."

Ventos looks like he's just as surprised as I am. He blusters a bit and the incoherent sounds fade into a scoff. He stomps away. "Silver, steel, alloy, it doesn't matter. Whatever that is, it's not the curse anchor and we should get back to looking."

Lavenzia sighs. "Ventos is right." She wanders away as well.

"You never finished your explanation." Winny startles me with an expectant and eager stare. "What type of silver is that? If not pure, and not steellike?"

"I don't know," I admit. "I know it's different, I can tell that much. It has blooms similar to silver variant, but they're reddish instead of a brighter platinum." I let the disk drop to the stone floor. It fills the room with a dull metallic sound. Quickly after, I drop one of my last remaining silver daggers. The sound it makes when it strikes the floor is a high-pitched, clear tone that rings long after I've picked it up. "You heard the difference, didn't you?"

"It all sounded like metal to me." Winny shrugs.

"They definitely sounded different," Ruvan says thoughtfully.

"Pure silver and steel variant both have that sharp-pitched sound. There are other things that I could do to prove that this isn't pure silver, or steel variant, but I would need the smithy."

"I take you at your word." The way Ruvan says so makes it sound like he's speaking for all of them. Judging from Winny's, and even Lavenzia's, expressions, he might actually be speaking for the two of them. But Ventos and I will never be on good terms, that much seems clear by the fact that he doesn't even look back my way. "So then what's special about this new silver?"

"I'm not sure yet," I admit. "But I can tell you the door to the workshop—the majority of it—was made from the same material as this disk. There was some pure silver plating on the handle, but the rest was *this* metal."

"It seemed to channel your blood magic when you opened the door," Ruvan aptly observes.

I nod. "That's what it felt like for me as well, which gives me some theories surrounding what this metal might be." I doubt the reddish lines are by chance…

"Then you shall have time and space to investigate these theories when we return. Anything you need shall be yours," he decrees.

I'm startled to silence, unsure of how to respond. Lavenzia narrows her eyes slightly and returns her focus to her hunt. A grin worms its way across Winny's lips. I don't know what has her looking so smug.

"So I can keep it?"

"You may. Conduct whatever experiments you'd like on it—just keep Callos informed. He's the archivist among us. If we fail in our mission, he's the one who's going to pass on the chronicles of our attempt to the next group to be awoken."

"Thank you." I pocket the disk. "Ventos is right though, you all should keep looking for the actual anchor."

"Don't try and win me over with your agreements, human," Ventos grumbles while keeping his back to me.

"I am perfectly capable of not trying to win you over while still being able to admit when you're right."

"Admitting when someone else is right isn't a strong suit of his," Lavenzia hums, pretending to inspect a shelf. "So it's hard for him to see it as something other people can do."

For a moment Ventos looks like he's about to turn and rise to the bait, but he remains as impenetrable as one of the castle walls and keeps leafing through the various notes. The rest of them return to it as well, hunting for the curse anchor that will set us all free.

twenty

THE RECORDS AND NOTES ARE LAID OUT ACROSS THE TABLES IN CHRONOLOGICAL ORDER AND, BASED ON DATES IN THE TOP RIGHT CORNERS, THEY'RE *ANCIENT*. I want to lift one up to get a closer look, because I can't believe my eyes, but I don't. If the parchment is really three thousand years old, I'm afraid they would disintegrate in my hands if I tried and whatever information they possess would be lost forever.

"How has this parchment survived?" I murmur.

Winny surprises me with an answer. "Blood lore. It's how most of the castle has sustained this long. Craftsmen would infuse what they made with a bit of their own magics."

I eye the ink used on the papers with a little more suspicion. Though the forge maiden in me is wondering just what blood lore meant for the blacksmith of the castle.

"Anyone find anything?" Ruvan asks.

"It's just notes on old blood lore ritual over here. Fascinating stuff. But not really helpful," Lavenzia reports.

"I see no curse anchor underneath the tables." Winny is now crawling around. And then climbing on bookcases.

"What does a curse anchor even look like?" I ask, wanting to be more helpful. *But if it hasn't been found by now…* My chest grows tight.

"Callos says it can be anything—any object magic can tether onto," she answers, coughing up dust as she perches at the top of a bookcase. "You'll know it when you feel it, though. It'll have that *zing* of old, powerful magic."

"My lord, what if it's not—" Ventos doesn't even have a chance to finish.

"No. I won't entertain it. It *must* be here," Ruvan says, his voice stretched a bit with annoyance.

Must be? Or you don't know what you'll do if it's not? I want to ask, but keep my mouth shut.

"Look again," he commands.

So we do.

And again.

As the vampir hunt, I begin to read. I don't understand the blood lore in great detail, yet. But I'm gleaning more information by the moment.

I'm not a scholar so my reading is slow; there is no time for such things in Hunter's Hamlet. We learn practical skills and share practical information. Much of even our own history has been lost over the years—deemed unworthy of passing down through stories around the hearth. If it isn't directly related to keeping us alive, what's the point of exerting energy on it? The only history books I know of are kept in the fortress, reserved for the eyes of the master hunter.

I'm curious enough to keep slowly trudging along the lines of text, and various records begin to paint a picture. But even if I understand the words, half the meaning is nonsensical to me because I don't know the finer points of blood lore. Still, there are a few things I can gather. One is that two people were keeping record. And the second…

"There was a human here," I announce, pausing their search. I can glean as much from what I've read. And from my dream… The woman I saw last night didn't have the gold eyes of the vampir. "A woman."

"Of course there was," Ventos grumbles. Every footstep he takes is heavier than the last, frustration at the lack of curse anchor weighing him down. "A human infiltrated us long ago, lurked within our walls, made a place only humans could get to with that blasted door that would kill any vampir that tried to open it, and cursed us. And I'd bet anything she was in cahoots with the first hunters."

I just stare at him for a long second, waiting to see if the idiocy of what he just said dawns on him. When it doesn't, I speak slowly to emphasize the point that's been sticking with me ever since I first heard of this room. "A human infiltrated the vampir enough that they were able to…build a room in the castle?"

"Well—"

I point to the door. "That door is *not* easy to make. It's solid metal and massive. And there's a magic locking mechanism. That took ample time and resources to forge, much less install. And you think some human did that without your Vampir King noticing? Either the human had more power than the vampir or your king was extraordinarily inept."

"How dare—"

"Don't, Ventos, she has a point," Ruvan steps in. "What else did you find?"

"She was looking for some kind of protective spell. Something that could be used to fortify and strengthen."

"More like she was being used by a vampir who was the one doing the researching." Lavenzia looks back at the table, poring over the notes.

"Well, whoever wrote these notes was working directly with the king of the vampir."

"Which was three thousand years ago." Ruvan frowns at the notes, as if they have somehow betrayed him. He crosses to me, standing a little closer than what I think was normal for us a mere day ago. "What does it say, specifically, about the king of the vampir?"

I bite my lip lightly, staring at a name. I recognize it. From Ruvan mentioning it, and from my dream last night.

"She was working with a king named Solos—"

They all go deathly still. Their change in demeanor is sudden enough that I'm silenced.

"You know him?"

"Know him?" Winny scoffs. "He's a legend."

"He was the last king before the long night." Ruvan shifts, definitely closer than would be generally considered "appropriate" for two people in our circumstances. Oddly, I find his presence comforting. A line was crossed the moment he drank from me, a barrier between us removed. He squints with focus as he looks at the paper, as if trying to read it.

"There's no way a human was working *with* King Solos." Ventos crosses his arms with a huff. "The king of the vampir would never lower himself to such a thing."

"Lower himself?" I repeat softly. No one seems to hear but Ruvan.

His silence is deafening. I try to pass it off as the conversation moving too quickly.

"He could've been using the human for her blood," Winny says. "Made the door so only a human could open it—and he was the only one in control of them."

"Unless this human was the one who betrayed him? Solos made this place to cage her in, conduct his experimentations, and she gleaned knowledge of the blood lore because of it." Lavenzia frowns at one of the sets of vials before her.

Control? Cage her in? I'm liking this King Solos and the early vampir less and less by the minute.

"You don't think a human would actually try to go against him, do you?" Winny murmurs. "Solos was a true king of the vampir; he had all the might of our people. He was the inventor of blood lore and knew it better than any. No human would dare cross him. And, given how humans were used in those early days…"

"How were they used?" I finally ask.

None of them seem to be able to look at me.

"Callos could tell you more, he knows the histories," Winny says, more weakly than usual.

"They were used roughly," Ruvan says flatly and then shifts the topic before I can inquire further, no doubt intentionally. "You mentioned some kind of protective spell? If she was working on such a thing, could it be the start of the curse?"

"A protection against vampir for humans, that's where my mind went," Ventos agrees.

"I don't think that's it." I run my fingertip along the edge of the notes thoughtfully. They ignore me. Winny even wanders away.

"We'll have to ask Callos when we return. Lavenzia, will you use your blood to mark these notes for preservation so we can bring them back?" Ruvan says.

"Absolutely." But Lavenzia's eyes drift to Winny before she can bite into her thumb. The latter is crouched in the corner of the room, scratching at something. "Winny? What is it?"

Everyone else's attention pivots to her.

"I think there's a trapdoor here."

"And you're trying to open it?" Lavenzia shakes her head. "Is it a good idea to open secret trapdoors in strange places?"

"We've come this far…and I certainly don't want to go back the way we came. Not after *someone* disturbed a whole horde of Succumbed." She looks pointedly at Ventos.

"It wasn't my fault," he huffs.

"It certainly wasn't ours." Lavenzia grins.

Ruvan sighs, drawing all eyes to him once more. "Let's scour the room one more time. If nothing, we'll take everything else we can." His eyes are distant and his voice softens. "Too many past lords thought this was it. We must honor them by making their sacrifices to learn of this room, to secure routes with their lives, count."

As the rest of them debate what's best to bring back to Callos, Ruvan makes a few extra laps under the guise of "looking for anything else important." But I know he's still searching for the anchor—still hoping it might be hidden somewhere. His gaze is unfocused, haunted.

I can't believe it but…my heart is aching for the vampir lord.

"Ruvan?" I say softly, just loud enough for him to hear, as the other three are organizing the journals and vials into a box for Ventos to carry. "Ruvan," I repeat when he continues to stare at a now empty bookshelf.

"I thought it was here," he whispers, voice quivering softly. "I really, truly, thought it was here."

"I'm sorry it wasn't." Sorrow rises from the soles of his feet. I stand in it next to him, as though we are adrift in an ocean of his making. The backs of my knuckles brush lightly against his. That prompts him to face me, but I am somehow pain to him, because his expression crumples and he shakes his head, avoiding my eyes.

"I should have known it was too much to hope for."

"Perhaps something in here will help find it," I try and offer optimistically. The hurt he's exuding is too great to ignore. It's in the pit of my stomach, as if this is my pain.

The bloodsworn magic is a dangerous thing. I need to begin actively fighting it, or else it might completely overwrite my feelings with his. I might find myself in too deep with the lord of the vampir. Deeper than I'll be able to escape from when the time comes.

"Hopefully." His expression is contorted and pulled by the weight of disappointment. "I had just thought that perhaps I might be the one to break it." He scoffs. "Foolish. Lords far better than I have been awoken and they couldn't."

"You made it farther than they did."

"And what good did any of it do?"

I grab his hand, jerking his face back to me. "Every step is progress, even if we can't see it in the moment."

He sighs, face relaxing. Ruvan reaches up and tucks a strand of hair behind my ear. "You wouldn't understand what it's like to go to sleep with hope and wake up to find your world in shambles."

"I know what it's like to be born into a hopeless situation though," I counter. "And I know what it's like to work on something, to dedicate your life to it, and know it might never be enough. To be all right with merely being a vessel for generations of knowledge—one link in the chain. Nothing more."

His fingers linger on the swell of my cheek before his hand falls back to his side. "Maybe you're right."

"Of course I am." I nudge him.

He dares a smile. It's small. But I think it's the sincerest thing I've seen from him. There's no pretense, no hate, none of the mess that brought us together and still lies around us, piled like twisted steel of false starts and half-hearted attempts.

"I think we're ready to go," Winny calls over.

Ruvan angles himself away from me to ask, "Do we have everything we might need?"

"Hopefully. We have as much as we can carry," Lavenzia answers.

"I can carry more." Ventos seems offended at the implication otherwise.

"As much as we can carry without being *too* encumbered." Lavenzia rolls her eyes. "So, will it be the trapdoor? Or the way we came?"

"My vote is for the trapdoor." Winny raises her hand.

"I'm not sure if I can fit." Ventos adjusts his pack on his back. There are a few rations—obsidian blood vials—left behind on the tables to make room for even more notebooks.

"Suck it in, big guy." Lavenzia pats his belly.

"You're lucky I like you." Ventos shoots her a glare.

"What does our illustrious lord, and hunter but not a hunter, think?" Winny asks us.

To my surprise, Ruvan turns to me. I quickly weigh the options and decide on, "The trapdoor."

"Really? We don't have a clear path forward that way," Ruvan cautions. "It's uncharted territory."

"We've made up half of all this as we went." I shrug. "Perhaps, if this room is so abandoned and so hard to get to, we won't find any more who have Succumbed to the curse."

"You're too optimistic." Lavenzia adjusts the blade on her hip.

"At least someone else is." Winny opens the trapdoor. "I'll be everyone's meat shield again and scout ahead. If I come back, everything's fine. If you hear screaming, assume it's not." She grins slightly and slips into the darkness, disappearing.

I continue turning over the disk in my pocket as we wait in tense silence. It's such a unique metal. I'm trying to guess what it might be made from by weight and feel alone. I scratch it lightly. I need to be back in the smithy again to make any headway on discerning it.

"It's clear." Winny reemerges. "I've no idea where it goes yet, but it's clear."

"In that case, we move quickly and silently," Ruvan decrees.

A ladder descends into the darkness of the trapdoor, bringing us to a narrow hallway. Ventos has to take off his pack and sword to sidestep through. Lavenzia carries the box for him. The passageway opens to a spiral staircase.

My enhanced vision cuts through the inkiness enough to make out the shapes of the others. But I follow more on sounds than sight. Ventos is hardly silent with his massive sword clanging against the wall periodically. Winny's short breaths huff ahead as she bounces forward and back.

But my focus is on Ruvan, how he's moving behind me, every step closer to me than the last. His hands glide over the stone walls on either side of me for support until I'm positioned between them, my back nearly brushing against his chest.

Without warning, his lips graze the shell of my ear. "Don't be afraid. I'll keep you safe," he whispers so softly that I think I've imagined it.

I'm instantly transported back to last night. To the feeling of him grabbing me. Pulling me closer. His fangs as they penetrated me.

My breath hitches and I miss a step. Ruvan is there in an instant. His arm glides around my middle. My back is flush against his front and I can't find my breath.

"Careful," he whispers before letting me go; I can almost feel him grin. As if he wasn't the one who made me trip in the first place.

I continue as if nothing happened and hope none of the others noticed. But my mind is elsewhere. Thinking of being alone with him again. Of his strong body pressed against mine. Him consuming me. I shiver and try to get my racing mind under control.

We emerge into a study. More books and records are wedged in every location. Lavenzia lets out a low whistle.

"Callos would have the best day of his life with this," she says.

"This is all really old… Think it was Jontun's?" Winny asks.

"Maybe," Lavenzia says.

"Callos already has enough that we're bringing back to keep him busy; I am *not* carrying any more books." Ventos trudges toward the opposite door. Winny follows, Ruvan and Lavenzia behind. But I linger.

"What is it?" Ruvan halts when he notices I'm not with the rest of them.

Rather than answering, I take the medallion from my pocket and place it into a mirrored divot on the drawer of the desk. It fits perfectly. I press and a small hatch pops open in the middle of the desk.

"What the—" Lavenzia murmurs.

"What's inside?" Ruvan asks as I open the latch all the way.

"Some kind of letters." I delicately take a small bundle from the hidden compartment.

"We'll open them when we're back. We've already been gone too long. Quinn and Callos will be worried." Ruvan holds out his hand expectantly. I cross and hand him the letters. "Callos will work through everything and discern if anything is useful here at all."

The remark gives me pause. *If*. If there's anything useful. What if there isn't? What if we don't find a way to break the curse? Will I be bloodsworn to the vampir lord until the end of my natural days? There was nothing in our initial vow that gives me reason to think this oath can be broken for something as simple as not finding the curse anchor as expected.

I want to ask, but I don't—I can't.

Down a series of connected rooms, up a stairwell, and through a locked door that Ventos breaks down with his broadsword, we emerge back into the western wing of the castle—where I first arrived. Just like that, I'm back at the beginning, and yet everything is changed.

twenty-one

CALLOS AND QUINN ARE SHOCKED TO SEE US. Delighted, but very surprised. They don't even bother hiding that they had already begun to write us off for dead—something that the others don't seem to find nearly as unnerving as I do. Apparently it's quite normal to go into the old castle and never be seen or heard from again.

Our return quickly becomes a small celebration. Quinn announces that he will gladly dip into the stores of blood to replenish everyone's strength. It's still odd to see people dropping blood from obsidian vials into water goblets, but it doesn't unnerve me as it once did. Moreover, I know now how much they need it.

Their faces had been looking a little gaunt, a little more monstrous, the longer we spent in the castle depths. I wonder if it is a function of being so far from the sun, being so close to others who had Succumbed to the curse, or how much power and energy they all exerted. Likely all these things combined.

Just like back in Hunter's Hamlet, I use the smithy as an escape when the festivities start up. Because just like in Hunter's Hamlet, these celebrations aren't meant for me. I might be on better terms with them all, but I'm still not "one of them." I can't expect to ever be. So I carry their weapons through the main hall, past their chambers, and into my quiet solitude of creation.

But, when I'm here, my hands don't move. The forge is cold. Sad. No matter how hard I try, I can't seem to spark it.

Where do I belong? Moreover, *what* am I meant to be? Perhaps Ruvan can tell me by looking into my blood. Maybe I'm not "meant" to be anything. I'm as malleable as hot metal, waiting to be shaped. But what shape will I become? The metaphorical hammer has always been in other people's hands—be the forge maiden, keep Hunter's Hamlet protected by outfitting the hunters. Allow the master hunter to decide my husband. Have a child. Pass on the vital information and trade of my lineage.

Stay in line and do everything you're told. Never think about anything else because if you do you might realize just how suffocating all the demands and expectations are. My breath is ragged. My feet pace across the floor as fast as my heart pounds in my chest.

For the first time, I have control and I…I don't know what I want.

I try to smother the thoughts by holding on to the disk and thinking of the dream. There's more to that than Ruvan or I know. Something is different within me. Something is changing and I'm helpless to stop it.

I feel him before I hear him—his sturdy, unyielding, blistering presence.

The world parts for Ruvan, as if he's the one standing still, and the rest of us are moving around him, pulled by his undeniable power. Ventos's earlier remark about the bloodsworn confirmed my suspicions. This pact must be what's changing me. The longer I'm in this arrangement, the less I'm who I was, and the more I'm someone new. Someone I don't know yet. Someone I couldn't have imagined myself becoming even in my wildest dreams.

"Shouldn't you be celebrating with the rest of them?" I ask, staring at the cold forge rather than looking at him. If I look at him, I'll give in to his hands, his mouth, again…and I won't feel the slightest bit guilty for it.

"They need their victories where they can find them. Ending the long night isn't on their heads, it's on mine. I'm not sure what *I'm* supposed to be celebrating," he answers with a solemn note that pulls his voice into a lower register. I grip the disk tightly to prevent my arms from breaking out in goosebumps at the richer, fuller sound. "We don't even know yet if we're any closer to breaking the curse. We certainly didn't find the anchor and for that I feel more like a failure than any triumphant hero."

"I wanted to ask you something about that." I still haven't turned to face him. I don't have to face him to see him with my eyes that can now see even the thickest of nights. Instead, I'm building him in my mind's eye. The way he holds himself, out of his plated armor, back in his velvets and silks. Trousers that graze against his thighs, tucked into leather boots. Soft, yet sharp. And his snowy hair that constantly falls into his eyes.

Snowy hair like the man who has been occupying my dreams... I try to keep my focus on the present. I've been needing to ask this question and I can't get distracted now. And Ruvan is nothing if not very good at distracting me.

"Yes?" he asks as if he is somehow completely oblivious to the effect his presence has on me—that my bones have gone white hot and are searing me from the inside out. I wonder if mine has the same on him. If every minute that passes this channel between us grows deeper and deeper, until it's large enough to swallow both of us whole.

"If we don't break the curse, what happens to me? Do I stay here forever?"

"Ah," he breathes softly, the sound becoming a low, rumbling chuckle. "We didn't really plan for that contingency, did we?"

"I realized we didn't."

The sound of the heels of his boots hitting the stone floor reverberates against the ceiling as he slowly approaches. Each step echoes like thunder on a distant horizon. He is the lightning, making my hair stand on edge.

"What do you *want* to have happen?"

I inhale slowly in time with his hands as they rise. They hover over my shoulders, a breath away from touching me. If I moved in the slightest I could bolt away, or topple into him. I still don't know which I want more and that terrifies me. I think of him holding me last night, but thoughts of him crushing me against him morph into when he stole me away—when he kidnapped me from my home and attacked my family.

"I want to be able to think clearly," I whisper.

"Why can't you?"

"You know why I can't."

"I suppose I do, if you're half as ensnared as I am." He has yet to touch me. *Why won't he touch me?* The memories of that room return with aggressive clarity. Pale moonlight, just like what shines through the window of the smithy now, casting him in a silver purer than any I have ever worked with.

With an exhale, I'm back in his arms on that forgotten floor. His fangs are in me. I stop existing; he stops existing. We're one.

I shake my head and do what I should have done already. I lurch forward. I stumble away. Wrapping my arms around myself, I rub my biceps and I try and shake the phantom feeling of his hands on me. Of him underneath the pads of my fingers.

I can't allow myself to have him. I can't…

The hot tension that was swiftly growing between us begins to evaporate in the cool night. Yes, he's lightning, and I'm tinder. One spark too close and I'll be done for. I'll burn away, and all that will be left is this insatiable need to collapse the space between us into nothing.

"Well?" I demand, not allowing myself to lose focus. "What happens to us and our arrangement if we can't break the curse?"

"I don't know," he admits.

"You don't know because you don't want to? Or because you don't understand the magic that binds us?" I finally turn to face him and I wish I hadn't. If I hadn't, I wouldn't have seen the brief flash of pain across his face. I wouldn't have seen him swallow thickly. But I still would've felt the uncertainty, and that would've been enough. "You wouldn't release me," I whisper.

He is silent for a painfully long time. "Having a forge maiden here could prove useful."

"I would never make anything for you again," I swear.

"Keeping you from Hunter's Hamlet, disrupting your family line, it could save generations of awakenings to come." The words are uncharacteristically cruel. I can see from his expression that he doesn't mean them. Yet, they still deal a glancing blow.

"You wouldn't make a difference, keeping me here. My mother would teach someone else. My family line runs long. But we're not so proud as to let the one thing keeping Hunter's Hamlet from being overrun by vampir die with us. We're too determined to survive for that."

"Determined to survive," he repeats with purpose, approaching. "Yes, you are a stubborn one, aren't you?"

"You like me that way." I speak before I can second-guess myself.

"I do." He speaks so quickly that I know he hasn't given much thought to the words, much less the sentiment behind them. My heart begins to race. The world narrows once more, focused only on him. On the vampir leisurely stalking toward me. As if he intends to devour me whole.

"Y-You do?" I take a step back and bump into a table; he has me cornered. The side of his mouth quirks up slightly. "Why?"

He tilts his head, assessing me, as if he's still trying to find the answer to this question himself. "You…" The word hovers.

"Me?"

"I find you…intriguing."

I can't stop a burst of laughter. "Intriguing?" I repeat. "I *intrigue* you?"

"Yes, and I want to know you better. I want to see all the bits and parts of you."

"I'm not a *tool* that you can inspect and use however you want." I use Ventos's word from earlier. That's one thing I do know, I realize. Despite all my uncertainty surrounding my future, I know I never want to be seen as a tool or a trophy ever again. No matter what happens here, or back at Hunter's Hamlet, I refuse to allow it to happen.

"I don't see you as a tool."

"Just an amusement, then." I stick out my chin, glaring up at him and fighting to ignore the stirring within me as he comes to a halt, toe-to-toe. I grip the stone table for support.

"'Intriguing,' I said," he forces out of a tense jaw.

"Hardly a compliment."

"The best compliment I could pay," he counters. That silences me long enough for him to continue. "My world has been monotony. It has been torture, day after day. My family, gone. Everyone I ever knew, dead or lost." He laughs with such bitterness that I can almost taste it on my tongue, drying out my mouth. "Even something as simple as eating…what I wouldn't give for decent food. Not rations. *Food.* To sit and savor. The smallest things are torture. A torture I hoped I would never wake to see, and yet knew I would. Torture I hoped—still hope—to end. Your presence here has been the first thing to break the endlessness of this unyielding pain that I have known for my entire life. To bring a glimmer of warmth, of optimism. I've already accomplished the impossible with you at my side. Maybe I wouldn't release this bloodsworn oath because I want to see what else we can do together. I'd want you to want that, too."

As he speaks, small tingles rush across my body, like I'm sinking into a too-hot bath. It envelops me, rushing to my head. He doesn't remove his eyes from mine and the world narrows on us together. There's more to what he's saying than the bloodsworn. I know it. This—all he is saying, this pain, it's all real.

I open my mouth, but words don't come. It sounds like he resents me and yet also pays me a compliment in the same breath. It sounds as if I am the last thing he really needs, but he desires me anyway. And I know he is all the same for me. He is nothing I needed, or expected, or even asked for. And yet…

He's all I could've ever wanted. As loyal as I am to his cause. A fierce protector. A deeply flawed, skilled, beautiful creature.

"Please, tell me you're lying." It's the only thing I can think of to say. The only thing that I want to beg to be true.

"I can't lie to you; and I never would."

"I wish you were," I whisper.

A stress fracture rips through the tension between us at my words. His arms are freed. His hands slam against the table next to mine. I'm pinned between them, leaned back over the stone.

"I assure you the feeling is mutual," he nearly snarls. He is burning, not with rage, but with desire.

"I should hate you." Panic is rising in me alongside a growing need that mirrors his. I can't need him. I can't want him. *I won't.* And I remind myself of all the reasons why. "You killed the master hunter. You killed—might have killed—would have killed—my brother!"

There's fire in his eyes as he glares at me. I jut my chin out and glare right back. Our noses almost touch. I think of him the first night we met, calling me a monster, ripping me from my home. I think of him last night, his mouth on my body, filling me with a pleasure that shouldn't be possible. How has this become so complicated?

"Just as I know I should hate you," he growls, fangs shining. The sight of them should fill me with fear but instead…it's excitement that surges through me. I've given him so much blood and yet my body is ready to give him more. *Give him everything.* "You were born to kill me. You have forged countless weapons that slay my kin."

"They were Succumbed; you kill them too."

He briefly considers this, but his verdict is to be only more frustrated. "You would use those weapons against me. You tried to. Even when you swore yourself to me you thought about placing a silver dagger between my ribs."

"You wanted to use me to get what you wanted. You saw me as nothing more than a tool," I counter.

"I wanted to be good to you but you made it very hard in those initial hours." The very corners of his lips have a slight curl to them. There's a thrill in this anger. A relief that's just as good as his fangs in me.

Why do we thrive on hating each other?

No…this isn't hate. This is denial. A *want* to hate. And that's our permission and our forgiveness. There's a part of us that thinks, if we can still hate each other, then it excuses the rest. It excuses last night. It excuses the growing desires that are going to tear us in two and stitch us back together as one.

All can be forgiven—this need and how we are about to act upon it—so long as we continue to fulfill our roles as enemies. Even if we're not. Even if we've long stopped fitting neatly into them.

"I never wanted you to be good to me," I hiss through clenched teeth. "I wanted you to hate me. I still want you to hate me."

"But I don't." His nose brushes against mine. Our lips are almost touching. I'm burning at his touch. "And that makes me want to—*want you*—even more."

"Then let's hate each other until we can't stand it." I meet his eyes. This is the moment before we break. The last breath we take on our own. "Let's hate each other so we can forgive ourselves for wanting each other."

"Every instinct tells me yes. But I could never hate my intriguing forge maiden," he whispers, eyes dropping to my lips. "I don't want to. I've acknowledged every reason why I should and now I will let them go. I forfeit them for you."

There's the truth of it. We thrive on our hate because it is our survival.

And yet…yet…what if there was another way? What if I could find it, forge it? I am strong enough, capable enough…maybe, just maybe…

"I wish I could ignore all of this," I breathe.

"I wish I had never taken you here."

"I wish I had never become bloodsworn to you."

"I wish I had never tasted you." He licks his lips.

"Is it consuming you, too?" I don't have to say what "it" is. We both know. I'm certain the memory of the night we shared has been on his mind almost as endlessly as mine.

"With every waking minute. I didn't head to our chambers to even attempt sleep because I knew you would haunt me there too. *You* haunt me every moment I'm not touching you."

I hadn't even thought of sleep. The idea was the furthest thing from my mind and I wonder if that's because of him. Did he plant the thought without realizing? Or did his energy alone drive me to the conclusion?

"How do we free ourselves from this torment?"

"I don't know if I want to be free." His gaze drops farther, to my neck. "You might be torture and temptation incarnate. But you are strength and power. You are damnation and salvation trapped in curves that should be forbidden."

A tickle of pleasure slips down my spine like an invisible fingertip. I swallow. He's looking at me again with those ravenous eyes. And, once again, I don't want him to stop.

I give in. "Do you want to?"

He lets out a low groan, pulling me closer. Our hips are flush. One arm wraps around my shoulders; the other hand is in my hair. I am pulled taut with delicious tension. More. *More*. Then release.

"I want to more than I've ever wanted anything. So much it terrifies me." His fangs are little crescent moons determined to dig into me. I quiver. I want them to, even though there's no reason for it. He's not wounded anymore. I can't use the excuse of survival to explain this away.

"Did you drink the blood with the rest of them?" The mere idea of another's blood touching his lips ignites an ugly streak within me.

"I couldn't, all I could think of was you. I don't want anyone else—in blood or body. Nothing will ever taste as sweet as you."

"Well, you need to keep up your magic to fight off the curse." I don't recognize my voice. It's deeper, almost sultry.

"Floriane…" he murmurs, eyelids growing heavy.

"One condition." I rise to my toes to murmur in his ear. My hands splay across his strong chest for support. "I taste you after. Give me your power. Keep me drunk on it." *Give me that sweet haze of magic.* I'll need it for what I want to do in the smithy. I need it for my own satiation.

"I will until your body gives out and you can no longer handle me," he repeats his words from the night of our vow and descends on me. His hard body presses against mine, pinning me to him. Ensnaring me with muscle and velvet.

I bite my lower lip in pain as his fangs pierce my flesh; I exhale delight as all sensations fade away. There are no aches in my muscles, no bruises or scratches from our long journey into the depths of the castle. My corporal form is gone, locked in his arms for safekeeping, as my consciousness dives into the well of power between us.

This magic, blood magic, is fed by us both. By the exchanging of power—his and mine. My fingers creep up the firm plane of the front of his shirt, seeking out the mark at the base of his throat. He growls, biting harder as my nails outline my blood mark on him.

A moan escapes me.

He grips my rear, hoisting me up onto the table. My legs are around him on instinct. Ruvan tips me back, better exposing my neck and chest to his mouth and hands.

It should hurt. I should be screaming. But heat drips down my torso like blood, and pools in the pit of my stomach. All the racing thoughts I had from before are stilled. *This* is exactly what I wanted.

The gift of his bite and body is over too soon. He pulls away. I try and hold on, but he won't let me and I slip off the table. Ruvan locks his eyes with mine. His hair has fallen into his face, a moonlit mess. His golden eyes shine from the shadows his furrowed brow casts, contrasting with the sharpness of a painter's brush against his pale flesh—as striking as his bloody lips. Ruvan moves his hands to my face. One of his thumbs glides over the swell of my cheek a little too easily. Lubricated by blood.

He drags his tongue slowly across his fangs, carving a line into the muscle and filling his mouth with his own blood. I realize what he is about to do a mere second before he does it. A whimper escapes my lips. Needy. Shameless.

I love it. *Make me beg for you, Ruvan.* My insides have turned molten. *Give me power, give me life.*

His lips crash onto mine.

I grip him tighter, pulling him closer as I taste both of us on his tongue. He tips my head, I release my jaw, the kiss deepens. His fangs graze against my lower lip. More blood. More power. More of the purest pleasure that should have never existed for me, and now I can't get enough. This is everything that was denied to me in the hamlet and now everything that I want. That I might have always wanted if I'd ever let myself even try to imagine.

And yet, even as I indulge in him, a scrap of common sense—of my dignity as a human of Hunter's Hamlet—returns to me. The heat in my lower stomach begins to boil with conflict. *What am I doing?* the woman who was raised in the hamlet asks from the corner of my mind. *This is the vampir lord!*

I release him, shoving him away. The world tilts slightly; I wonder how much blood I've lost. But thanks to his blood surging through me I can stand tall. We've intertwined ourselves deeper still. I can almost *hear* his thoughts now.

"You…" He can't form words while he licks his lips.

"I can't—We can't—I don't but I also—I can't think clearly right now—You should go." I stumble over my words and adjust my clothes, wondering when they became so skewed. I was certainly very aware of his hands moving…but I didn't think he was touching me that much. Everything is a pleasurable blur. "I have work to do."

Ruvan steps forward; his fingertips graze my arm. "The work will keep. Come back with me to my quarters. Stay with me tonight." His eyes are still drunken. I hate how deeply his lust still stirs me. Even when I have just satiated that need it threatens to return again. Maybe this is why I was always denied carnal pleasure. It's a distraction. A delicious, decadent distraction.

"We have what we needed. I need some time alone to my thoughts. Please, go." I say the last word with the edge of a command. Hurt has him retreating. He's confused by my demeanor.

Good, so am I. I'm a walking contradiction right now and his presence is a reminder of all the reasons why. I can't just erase, or ignore, a lifetime of training for a few moonlight kisses, however good they are.

Ruvan leaves without another word. But I can feel him—his restless, toe-curling, fiery energy—up until the moment that I presume he falls asleep. Because then the world is still, and I'm finally able to get work done.

twenty-two

The sky is already turning a hazy amber; the sun will be up within the hour. I imagine that they'll all sleep through the day after the festivities tonight, which means I have anywhere between eight and ten hours of uninterrupted solitude.

It's time to get to work.

With Ruvan's magic still burning within me I ignite the forge, turning it from red, to orange, to yellow in tandem with the sky. The power within me is as bright and hot as the flames that dance in my hearth. Taking the disk from my pocket, I place it in the center of one of the tables and simply stare at it. What books are to scholars, metal is to me. I scan and search it for whatever information it will yield from a glance alone.

When I'm done, I pick it up. I bite, taste, scratch at, drop, and scuff it. I tap it lightly with a hammer. I do everything I can to feel and inspect it without materially damaging the disk. As curious as I am about its secrets, it's still more precious to me intact—at least until I can confidently recreate it. So, for now, I can't risk smelting it or any other more intensive investigations.

My inspections reaffirm my existing suspicion that it's certainly unlike any other silver I've come across thus far. Excitement tingles through me. A new metal to explore. To try and recreate.

I roll up my sleeves and don one of the heavy leather aprons that hang on one of the pegs in the smithy. I then begin to scrounge for supplies. Fortunately for me, this smithy was left well-stocked when it was abandoned. There are ingots of iron, copper, brass, steel, even some gold.

Pure silver is missing, however. *Of course it would be.* If they had pure silver then they wouldn't need to steal the weapons from hunters during the Blood Moon.

An idea strikes me.

I speed back up the hall to the upper armory, grateful I don't run into anyone along the way. There, I pick through the oldest of the weapons that have been collected from the hunters across the centuries. Given what Ruvan said, the Succumbed are the only ones to wander to our world regularly. Vampir like him have only come once every five hundred years. But if there's a broadsword here, there must be—

My fingers land on a small, needlelike dagger. Silver. *Pure* silver. I can tell by sight, touch, and sound. There are four of them in total. I cradle the weapons in my hands. They were made by one of my ancestors, easily over two thousand years ago, when we didn't know yet how to make silver steel.

"Thank you," I whisper to whatever great-*great*-grandmother made this for me to find and return to the forge.

I place the four daggers inside the crucible. It's going to take every try I have to get this right, if I'm able to at all, and it's best not to waste more than I need to. Once I have the daggers melted down, I pour the majority of the metal into a channel. When the silver has almost cooled completely, I break it into pieces while it's still malleable.

My resources secured, I go back to the crucible. What I'm about to do isn't like any sort of forging I've ever done. I don't know anything about magic, or blood lore…not really. But I'm learning. And what I do know is that blood—my blood—holds power. And that power might just be what I need.

I dig the point of one of the sickles I sharpened before we left into my forearm near the elbow. It's a small cut, enough to drip five droplets into the crucible. The blood bubbles and hisses the second it meets the hot metal, turning it black. I let my body decide how much to start with. Using as much as I bled before my wound healed over.

Magic in my blood… It's still hard to wrap my mind around the truth but I believe it at this point. However, it uncomfortably blurs the line between human and vampir. Vampir were always the ones with magic in the stories and they hunted us purely for the sake of food. Humans had no innate power.

It was a lie. Humans carry our own magic. Was the deceit among the people of Hunter's Hamlet intentional? Or merely a forgotten part of our history? What will either case mean for our future?

I briefly wonder what my own innate ability of blood lore is. If it's anything, it must be forging.

The metal has cooled to the point I was waiting for and I banish the worrying thoughts from my mind as I carefully lift the vessel with tongs and pour the liquid into a second, small, rectangular mold.

I work quickly and confidently up until when the metal has cooled into the shape of a new ingot. I hold the tiny bar in one hand, the disk in the other, and close my eyes. I test their weight, temperature, smoothness. As expected, it's not right. Not even close. But there's still more to try.

The door in the depths of the old castle was able to channel magic through it. That was how the lock was disengaged. The pure silver of the handle was made to ward off vampir—curious on its own, but a topic to muse over another time—but this metal was what the power within the blood moved through.

There has to be some special property to it. Something I'm not seeing. My knuckles turn white and my brow furrows as I stare at the two pieces of metal in my hand. They do nothing.

I either have no idea what I'm doing, or my theory is totally wrong. Either is possible. I purse my lips and think back to the door. A piece that large… I drop the ingot I just made. It rings out with the pitch of pure silver and dents just as easily. I didn't change the properties of it at all with my blood.

The door had some other alloy in the metal to strengthen it. It must've. This time I put the bar back into the crucible along with iron, carbon, and limestone. More blood. And back on the heat.

As I'm waiting for the metal to rise to temp and meld together, I walk the perimeter of the smithy, repeating the thoughts of the woman from my dream.

"The smith has the right alloy now. We can test it with new daggers during the next full moon."

Folding my arms, I lean against one of the walls in the back corner, tapping against my biceps.

"All right, Floriane, accept that your blood holds magic as much as theirs does." I hammer the kinks of my doubt away with forceful words. "Good. Now, what do you know about magic in the blood?"

Two things—that all vampir can see the future using it, and that some vampir have unique abilities beyond that.

"But you are not a vampir," I continue over the crackling of the hearth. Drew told me once about the record keepers in the fortress, using their quills to record and sort their thoughts. For me, the sound of my own voice is far better than any pen and parchment. "You cannot see the future…but you might still have some innate ability?" I'm not sure, but the logic seems sound since I am bloodsworn to Ruvan. That might have awoken some power within me.

"If that dream wasn't the future…then perhaps it was the past?" I push away from the wall.

The smith has the right alloy now. Was that person referencing the smith who worked this smithy? I begin walking again, running my fingertips lightly along the walls, feeling for any changes in the stone.

A few stones jut out awkwardly, but result in nothing. I need to run back to my metal work before I can continue searching.

Trial and error. I spend the day bouncing between tending to the forge and scanning the walls as my silver supply dwindles. As the sun begins to set, I wipe sweat from my brow. I'm close, I can hear the whispers of my ancestors saying so. I'm on the cusp of something great.

When I run out of silver, I only have a small back corner of the room left to inspect. I don't expect much when my fingers fall into a lock set deep in the stone—hidden by shadow. Heart racing, I inspect it and quickly set about breaking it. It's nothing compared to my grandmother's lock in my family's smithy.

A concealed door swings open, revealing a narrow space lit amber by the day's last rays filtering through a dusty window high up in the back of the room. I had been hunting for a storeroom like my family's—somewhere that might be holding extra silver—but this is even better. It's an office.

Unlike my family, which passed down all our techniques and recipes orally, this past smith seemed to be as much of a record keeper as the woman in the workshop. Dusty tomes are stacked on shelves above an orderly desk. Two leather books slumber side by side underneath a heavy blanket of dust.

"And what are you?" I whisper.

The ledger to the right is a record of all the metals heading in and out of the smithy.

But, to the left… "A record book."

I slowly leaf through the pages. My chest grows tight. I shift my weight restlessly from foot to foot. *This is it, this is it!* I scream inside.

Sure enough, laid out neatly is a series of notes on how to make the blood silver—a metal designed to both channel and store magic in the blood. I wasn't too far off in my attempts, all things considered. Only one or two adjustments. I would've been able to make it on my own, but this saves so much time.

I bite my lip and scan the office, though there's not much to be found other than the books. No silver. Each experiment took only a little of the metal, but I've been working as though I'm possessed. I worry the ring around my pinky. Sliding it off feels like I'm removing a piece of myself. Like I am betraying my family.

"You'd understand, right?" I whisper to the piece, wondering if Drew can somehow hear me. "You would," I reassure myself before I head back to the forge to place the ring into the crucible, and put the crucible on the fire before I can second-guess myself.

My chest is tight as I watch the ring melt—the first piece I ever made, a gift for my brother and me to share. Emotion fills me and pours out with the blood from my arm. As I work, I weep for my family. Every strike of my hammer is a worry. Again and again they repeat.

Will Drew forgive me for all I've done? Will Mother? Will they recognize me when I return? *If* I return…

I'm not even striking the metal anymore. I'm hitting the anvil. Vision blurry. I wipe my eyes and nose, sniffling heavily.

I don't even remember making the blood steel dagger when I'm done. It's not my best work, but it doesn't need to be. I'm not going to spend time honing a weapon made purely for experimentation.

I drop the dagger first. It doesn't dent; it holds its shape. The resonance it makes is delightfully similar to the disk. I try not to allow myself to get too excited, but it's hard not to when the fruits of my labors are taking shape right before my eyes.

The color is off, slightly. The disk is a brighter silver—slightly duller than a pure silver ingot, and the lines in it are subtle. But my dagger is boldly swirled with what looks almost like rust. I hold up my left arm, dagger in my right hand. I've cut myself more times tonight than a bad night sparring with Drew. But every wound has been worth it, even if my healing has slowed as the hours ticked by and Ruvan's blood has begun to fade from my veins.

But even without his blood in me, there is still magic. I just need the right tool to harness it. I draw the blade against my forearm. I gasp sharply, but not with pain.

Ruvan's essence. It's drawn from me with the blood. His magic, his power. Invisible hands, the same size and shape as his, run over my body. Across my shoulders, down my arms. Up from my ankles to my thighs. I shudder.

After that initial sensation passes, the air feels colder. I exhale and my breath clouds, as if the temperature of the room—or my body—has actually dropped. My breaths collect into the hazy figure of a woman. She stares at the forge. But I blink and she's gone, replaced by red.

Blood coats the weapon's edge, collecting on the rusty lines I hammered into place. It's as if the dagger is made of soapstone rather than metal, eagerly drinking up the liquid I've provided it. The dull color of the dagger turns ruddy. I slowly slash it through the air, making sure what I'm seeing isn't just a trick of the light.

It's not.

The dagger is actually glowing faintly.

A squeal escapes me and I give a small hop, letting loose my delight. Mother and Drew will have to forgive me now. Just wait until I tell them what I've done. Which… I'm not entirely sure what that is. I've no idea what this faint glow *means*, of course. For all I know, this is an obvious phenomenon to a vampir. But for me…

I forged magic.

Power is coursing through the weapon. I can see it lingering in the air with every twist of the blade. Restless. As if begging for release. But I've no idea how to release the magic I've stored within it. So I'm left doing nothing as it slowly fades and the blade dulls back to how it was fresh off the anvil.

I want to slice my arm again and see it glow. But I refrain. Those strange sensations hold me back. I don't know what to do with this weapon, yet. But I will figure it out. Perhaps it is in the notes—or in the journal I've uncovered in the office.

Later. Figuring out the implications will have to wait. The rest of them will be waking soon. I tidy the smithy of all the evidence of my experimentation, returning the remaining ingots to the office and shutting it tightly. I keep the forge hot, however, and set about to sharpening the covenant's blades as I told them I would when we first returned.

It'll be suspicious if I'm seen having worked all night with nothing to show for it. Luckily for me, sharpening the weapons takes a negligible amount of time since they were so recently honed. I have them laid out on the table and my dagger hidden when I hear footsteps approaching.

I'll tell them of the dagger, of course…but I want to tell Ruvan first. It will be like a peace offering given how we last parted. I shiver, recalling the feeling of his presence in and around me. I can't wait to see his reaction. He'll be proud. He'll be—

I'm disappointed the moment I can tell the footsteps don't belong to him. I know that he has yet to wake—I can sense him still asleep from how calm I am. There's not the restless energy permeating my world that feels like it's wound up like unleashed lightning whenever he's around.

The footsteps are too light for Ventos but too heavy for Winny. Too noisy for Lavenzia. I make a game of trying to guess who it is and settle on Callos. I'm wrong.

"You're up early," Quinn says.

"I never slept." I ease away from the table of tools. It's not my finest work, but anything done in haste will be lacking. And they won't be able to tell the difference. I hope. "I got a bit sidetracked."

"I see." Quinn inspects the weapons. Boldly, he runs his thumb parallel to one of the blades.

"Careful, they're freshly sharpened. I would hate to have to explain to Ruvan what happened to his faithful attendant."

"If I wanted to kill myself on a silver blade, I would've done it long ago." Quinn eases his hand away.

"Quinn, may I ask you something?"

"Only if I may ask you something in return. One for one." He brings those haunted eyes to me.

"Deal. What exactly is the 'long night?'" The way they speak of it makes me think it's more than the curse.

"The long night began after the curse was laid." He crosses over to the window and looks out over the setting sun. I can see him wince slightly, but he stands in the sunlight anyway. As if in defiance. "The curse took hold quickly in our blood. Vampir abandoned the other townships and cities across the mountains for Tempost. They came looking for a cure, but only found more death in our main stronghold."

I cross to the window as well, standing next to him. But he continues to look past his reflection and into the city beyond. He seems to be staring at a specific point in the distance—a large building with an arched roof and four bell towers on every corner.

"So many lives were lost during the proverbial sunset on our people. The lykin to the north, northwest of us, hunted our kind mercilessly when they became the Succumbed. As the curse worsened, the lykin became more…proactive in their culling of our people, claiming it in the defense of all of Midscape.

"It all happened so quickly that there wasn't even time to send out request for aid…even if we had, I doubt the packs of wolf-beasts would have allowed any goodwill and supplies to pass. They had seen what we had become and were determined not to allow any of us to escape."

"So the long night is a metaphor for this dark time the vampir face?"

"I believe that's two questions."

I side-eye him. "It's still just one. It doesn't count as additional questions if you're being cryptic and I'm seeking clarity. They're follow-ups."

He chuckles softly, but the levity doesn't reach his eyes. "The long night earned its name from how we postponed the curse." He has my undivided attention now. "The vampir conducted a blood ritual unlike any the world had seen. The high lords and ladies, advisers, right and left hands of the last of the king's bloodline, entered into a final pact.

They gave their lives to create the long night, the great slumber, a chrysalis that the remaining vampir could hide within."

"Chrysalis…like a butterfly's cocoon?"

He nods. "You have the idea of it."

I think of vampir by the hundreds, slumbering upside down like caterpillars. Waiting to awaken once the curse on them had been lifted.

"The stasis halts the progression of the curse. It keeps us from becoming Succumbed or worse. But it doesn't cure us. The moment we're awoken from our slumber, the curse spreads once more." There's a long pause. I'm not aware of just how long until he turns to face me.

I'm pulled back to reality from my thoughts. I can feel the expression on my face. My lips are tugged into a frown. My brow is furrowed. I try and force my expression to relax, but it only makes the lump in my throat worse.

"It's all so…sad."

Quinn's eyes dart to me, widening slightly, brow furrowing. He clears his throat. "The plight of the vampir is a tragedy. We suffer quietly, alone. Our people were never a far-reaching one like the elves or fae. We never possessed the inherent, bodily strength of our closest brethren, the lykin, or the deep magics of the sirens far to the north. We were weak before the blood lore—only confident in interacting safely with those beyond our mountains around the full moon. And just when we found strength, it was stolen from us." He stops his musings with a confounded expression. "I know what I want my question to be."

"Yes?" I'm startled by his sudden shift. The increase in intensity.

"What you just said about the vampir, that our suffering brought you sorrow, did you mean it?"

My mouth immediately begins to form the word "no." But I stop myself short. Do I feel sympathy for the vampir? Instinct tells me not to. My mind says I could never.

But my heart…

"I did; I do. I know what it's like to live feeling like there's no hope, no way out, no future other than a grim one paved by others' hands. And it's a fate no one should endure. At this point, the vampir are as much victims as we are," I echo Ruvan's words.

Quinn inhales slowly and exhales something that sounds like relief. He runs a hand through his dusty brown hair, turned full rust in the sunlight. He shakes his head as if in disbelief. I suppose we can share that sentiment.

"I never thought I'd see the day a human would take pity on our kind. But then again, I never thought I'd see the day where my lord, any vampir, would become bloodsworn to one such human." He drops his hand, holding it out as though it is a peace offering. "I suppose, if any human is to walk among us, I'm glad it's you, forge maiden."

I chuckle softly. I suppose Ruvan must have shared the truth with Quinn and Callos. Not that I mind. I can't deny that I've begun trusting them all. Clasping hands with Quinn, I say, "I suppose, if I am to walk among vampir, I'm glad it's with your lord and his covenant as well."

Quinn releases my hand, placing both of his in his pockets, as if to physically prevent himself from ever even thinking of extending such a peace offering to me again. I turn back to the window, thinking of what my next question to him will be. But we're interrupted.

Winny's hasty footsteps grow close and she bursts into the smithy. "Quinn, Riane—Floriane, come quick. It's Ruvan."

My heart sinks to the pit of my stomach. Her wide eyes, her frantic tone…

"What is it? What's happened?" Quinn asks, rushing to meet her. I follow, determined not to be left behind, pulled by an irrational fear threatening to consume me.

"It's the curse. He's on the edge of becoming Succumbed."

twenty-three

THE WORLD HAD BEEN TOO QUIET. Everything was too still. Ruvan wasn't merely sleeping…he was in trouble.

He came to the smithy, hungry and needing, because he could feel the curse ravaging him, brought on by the Fallen's bite. He was ailing, and I didn't notice. I pushed him away at the end. What if the sensation I felt with the dagger was drawing strength from him? Could this be my fault?

Guilt clings to me tighter than my sweat-slicked clothing.

But *should* I feel guilty? Or is this just the bloodsworn oath playing tricks on me? My thoughts are losing shape, turning liquid, unable to keep form in the fires of my rising panic. I can't discern what's real and what's not. What feelings are my own and what's been forced upon me by this magic bond with a vampir?

All I know is I must get to him. Once I can see him, once he's within reach, everything will begin to make sense again.

I think.

I hope.

We race up and through the banquet hall. We're into Ruvan's chambers in a breath. The rest of them are in the main room. Ventos paces before the window. Lavenzia is seated on the settee where I should have been last night, hands worrying between her knees. I hear Callos's voice coming from Ruvan's room.

Quinn brushes around me, heading right for the bedroom. I follow behind but Ventos steps in my way, glowering down at me.

"And just what do you think you're doing?"

"I'm going to see Ruvan." I glare up at the mountain of a man.

"You're not needed."

"I might be able to help," I say quickly. "With my blood."

He snorts. "As if a human would ever freely give their blood to the vampir lord."

They don't know, I realize. Ruvan never told them what happened—how we survived the Fallen that attacked us. Why? Did he keep it a secret as an honest mistake? It slipped his mind? Though, it's not as if he's had much time to casually speak with them. Perhaps the opportunity never arose.

Or perhaps he is ashamed of you; you heard how they spoke of the mere idea of their former king working with a human.

I push away the thought. It's a silly notion because to be ashamed he would need to think that something significant happened between us. We were surviving, nothing more, nothing less. I also ignore that petty whisper in the back of my mind because…*I don't care what he—they think of me*. Of us. Of this. Of whatever is or isn't happening between us. Because nothing was—is—happening. I don't care at all. Not in the slightest.

I shake my head and scatter the frantic thoughts. None of it matters when Ruvan is in there, just out of arm's reach, hurting with an affliction that I might be able to help ease.

"I gave up my blood freely to become his bloodsworn. I did it again—believe me or not—" I add hastily at the sight of Ventos's expression "—after we escaped the Fallen. And I will now if you let me pass."

Ventos doesn't move. He continues to scowl.

"Ventos, please."

"Let her go, Ventos," Lavenzia says without rising. "It's not as if she's going to hurt him now of all times."

"But he's in a weakened state," Ventos protests. "The bloodsworn oath could falter."

"The oath is strong," I insist. "And, even if it weren't, I swear to you

I will not harm him." I surprise myself with my own conviction, and given his shift in expression, Ventos as well.

Ventos relents. "Fine, go."

Wasting no time, I enter Ruvan's bedroom for the first time.

It's exactly what I would expect based on the rest of the castle: old and crumbling. The back left corner has collapsed. The ceiling barely supported by a few beams that landed in a convenient way. Though, perhaps it's sturdier than I initially assume since the rubble looks old, as though it all fell in years ago and hasn't moved since. The window is missing two small panes of glass and wind whispers through. The temperature plummets as I cross the threshold of the door.

Luxury—if it can be called that—clings to the places it can. The marble carvings of orchids around the hearth have been polished. The candelabras placed on the perimeter of the room are oiled to a shine, glinting in the candlelight. A tray is set out on one of the nightstands, holding glistening bottles of amber-colored perfumes and empty bejeweled goblets. The curtains on his bed look almost new. His duvet is embroidered with gold and gems, either new or preserved with some kind of magic.

My assessment of his bedroom halts as Ruvan consumes my attention. His skin is gnarled once more, gone from full with a healthy flush to almost stony. I can see it now, *this* isn't his natural form. When I first arrived here I only saw the monster I expected—no, the monster that I *wanted* to see. But the way he is meant to be is not weak and fading. It's not drawing shallow wheezes through barely parted lips. He's meant to be strong, and sturdy. As ever-present as the moon itself.

I rush to his bedside, drawn with an urge I've not felt since the night of the Blood Moon. *He* was the one that elixir was pulling me to that night. I had sensed him…perhaps in the same way the Succumbed vampir in Hunter's Hamlet had sensed me in my home despite the salt that lined the doorjamb.

I table the revelation as I take up Ruvan's clammy hand, wrapping it with my fingers. His eyes are mostly closed, but his lids flutter, as if he's afflicted by nightmares. Callos is seated next to me on the bed, Quinn on the other side.

"Why is it so bad?" I ask. I want them to have a reason other than me and my dagger. "He was fine mere hours ago." *He even had my blood*, I think but don't say.

"It's the Fallen's bite," Callos says solemnly. "It's eating him away. Honestly, it's a testament to his strength that he hasn't given in yet. But it's too much… He'll continue to fade like this until the man he is dies. After that, when his eyes open next, it will be as one of the monsters you saw in the old castle."

"I gave him my blood to stave it off," I say. Callos looks surprised, but seems to believe me. "He was fine after."

"Even if he was…his connection with the curse was deepened greatly with that bite. The curse is increasing its hold on him faster than the rest of us now and every day will become worse than the last," Quinn says gravely.

"Can I give him more blood?" I ask, my grip tightening on Ruvan. He hardly even moves when I touch him or speak. He's somewhere else, far away. Somewhere none of us can get to. His magic has never been so thin and frail and it causes panic to rise in me.

"Fresh blood will help, for a time. More than preserved blood will," Callos admits.

"Then take it." I thrust out my arm.

"It's not a permanent fix." Callos turns to face me, rather than Ruvan. He looks up at me over the frames of his spectacles.

"The only permanent fix is breaking the curse, I know," I say softly. "But we have to try; we have to do something to stave off the curse for now. We can't leave him like this." I won't allow him to become one of those monsters.

He sighs. "I can't guarantee how long the strength you give him will last. It might become a futile effort after a time."

I know how fleeting it was from last night. But now I'll give him as much as he needs.

"We could supplement with the blood we collected on the night of the Blood Moon," Quinn suggests.

Callos shakes his head. "The blood of the bloodsworn will be better. It's fresher, not merely preserved through ritual and vial. Plus, we need to save the blood from the night of the hunt for the next group that awakens."

The way he says it makes me think this "next group" will be coming soon. Though I don't dare ask why. I suspect I don't want the answer.

"I'm happy to give it." A chill rips through me at the sentiment. Was I just speaking? Or was it the bloodsworn magic taking over my mind? *Help him survive*, a voice in me screams, *see this through*. But where is that voice coming from and can I trust it?

"Very well, we'll do it now. I'll perform a ritual to strengthen and fortify the blood. Hopefully give it some extra impact." Callos stands. "Wait here."

He departs, leaving Quinn and me in silence at Ruvan's bedside. We're both left staring at the frail form of the lord of the vampir. To think, *I once feared this man…* Now he looks like nothing more than a sickly, monstrous grandfather.

I bite back laughter that burns like tears. I'm torn apart in ways I never wanted. Never asked for. I need a forge that burns as hot as he does and a hammer as swift and sure as everything I knew in Hunter's Hamlet to put me back together. I need both…and can only ever have one. And I know what I must choose when all this is over.

I'm not meant for the world of the vampir.

But perhaps I can help him while I'm here and we'll see this through to its end. Not just for the bloodsworn magic that's pushing me. But for all our sakes.

"Are you sure?" Quinn whispers, as if he can read my thoughts.

I catch him glancing at me from the corners of his eyes. "I am."

"You're keeping the vampir lord alive."

"I know, and I wouldn't have it any other way," I say resolutely.

Callos returns with a golden chalice. The sequences of the moon have been etched around its lip along with swirls and symbols that mean nothing to me. No one bothers explaining what's happening. So I'm left to watching and assuming.

One by one, they approach the chalice and utter the words, "Blood of the covenant." They take an obsidian dagger, no longer than Callos's palm, and pierce their flesh, each in a different location. Winny rolls up her sleeve and slices down by her elbow; Lavenzia pulls back her hair, slicing just behind her ear; Ventos cuts beneath his kneecap; Callos's slice is by his knee; Quinn half unbuttons his shirt to dig the dagger point into his left breast.

Every cut is shallow. No more than a few drops of blood are added to the chalice, carried on a divot in the fuller of the obsidian dagger. Every slice is made over the symbol of a diamond with a long slender teardrop underneath, two stylized wings arcing around either side.

Ruvan's mark.

So when the dagger is finally passed to me, I know what to do. All five of them hold out the chalice before me. Each of them supporting the base with two fingers.

I unbutton the top button of my shirt and run my fingers over the hollow of my throat where I know Ruvan's blood mark is on me. Gently, carefully, I pierce my skin. Blood flows freely in rivulets over the dagger, down my fingers, and spills off my knuckles into the cup. I give more than the rest of them. I pour my power out until the wound closes over. The last of the strength Ruvan imparted to me with his kiss leaves my body with the crimson liquid.

"Blood of the bloodsworn," I intone.

The liquid in the chalice deepens in color, giving off its own natural light briefly. The glow is similar to the shade of the dagger in the smithy. I wonder now if, or how, it could be used in these rituals. I have so much to learn about the blood lore. There's so much more I can do for them if I'm bold enough to learn and brave enough to try.

The light fades, leaving nothing but a thick and inky paste in the goblet.

"Give it to him," Callos says reverently.

I take the stem of the chalice and the rest of their grasps fall away. Alone, I move closer to Ruvan. The group hovers a few steps away at the bedside. Gently, I slip my hand underneath Ruvan's neck, right at the nape, lifting slightly so the weight of his head tips back and his mouth parts slightly.

"Drink, please," I whisper. His eyes flutter, as if he hears me. The skin of mine that touches his warms slightly. He knows I'm here. I'm sure of it.

Placing the chalice at his lips, I tip slowly. The thick liquid oozes into his mouth. His throat works to swallow.

"That's it," I murmur, continuing to pour. I want to dump the whole thing at once so he's better instantly. Watching him imbibe, sip by sip, is agony.

The chalice is empty and I hand it back to Callos. On instinct, I press my fingertips into the base of his throat, where my mark is on him. I try and pour something of me into him—something more than the blood I gave.

I'm already suffering the absence of my brother and distance from my home, don't make me suffer your loss too.

Ruvan's eyes flutter open and I breathe relief. His skin begins to fill out once more. The gray seeps away. His usual pallor returns. Even the rosy hue of his cheeks and dusk of his lips is back. His eyes are lustrous pools of molten gold once more and yet his expression is one of heartbreak and sorrow.

Our worlds narrow onto each other and, for a second, we breathe in tandem. He has returned to me and I to him. My fingers twitch and I fight the suddenly insatiable urge to pull him to me. To crash my mouth against his. To hold him until we fall into a deep and dreamless slumber.

"How long was I out for?" He sits, rubbing his temples lightly. I ease away to give him space, trying to exhale the tension as I do.

"Only a few hours," Quinn answers. "At least, that would be my assumption based on how you were last night and when I found you."

"A few hours and I feel like death."

"Looked like it, too," Winny chirps, but her voice is void of its usual songlike levity. She's trying to lighten the mood, but misses the mark slightly. Worry has taken root in all our hearts.

"It's getting worse." Ruvan voices what we've all just seen. What we already knew.

I open my mouth to object, but Quinn cuts me off.

"It is," he says gravely. None of the others are able to look at Ruvan.

"I won't succumb yet; I still have work to do," Ruvan says, determined. "We haven't even had time to go through all the records. The curse anchor wasn't in the workshop, but I'm sure those records will lead us to it."

"And what will you do if they don't?" Ventos demands to know.

"I'll keep hunting."

"Until you become a Fallen or, worse, a Lost?"

"I will work until the last moment if that's what it takes to free our people from this long night!" Even though Ruvan is seated in bed, he suddenly seems to consume all empty space in the room. The very foundations of the castle seem to tremble at his voice.

"I don't want to kill you." Lavenzia is the one who finds the bravery to speak in the wake of Ruvan's rage and frustration.

"What?" I whisper. None of them hear, even though I'm searching each of them for a truth other than the one being presented before me.

"No other lord or lady has expected it of their covenant," Ventos says solemnly.

Ruvan avoids their pointed stares and murmurs, "We're so close, I can feel it… I must keep working."

"If you push to the point of the curse taking over, you're likely to become a Lost, and we're not strong enough to kill you," Callos says, matter-of-fact as he cleans his spectacles. "You have to know your limits, for all of us, awake and still slumbering."

Exactly what they're talking about finally hits me—he's expected to go off to die, to end himself before the curse can end him. I think of the needles in the collars of the hunters. The expectation to take one's life before they could become a monster exists here, too, and my heart crumples at the realization.

Ruvan says nothing. He stares at his hands, curling and relaxing his fingers. He's like a mirror to how I was when I first arrived. I never imagined that between us I would be the strong one.

And I'm going to need every bit of strength I ever had.

I see his frustration, uncertainty, the need to do something when all seems hopeless. I know the pain and frustration he feels all too well and I wouldn't wish it on anyone. But Callos is right: Ruvan is limited right now, he must take things easier.

I, however, have no such limits.

"There might be a way to prolong Ruvan's strength in fighting the curse," I say. All eyes are on me. What I'm about to suggest is a long shot, I know it is. But it might be our only choice—if blood is strength, and blood lore is blood made even more potent, then Ruvan needs strength through blood lore. And there's none stronger than, "The Hunter's Elixir."

Ventos is at my throat, fist balled in my shirt. "You would have him drink something the hunters made?"

He barely manages to speak before Ruvan's hand is on his wrist.

Ruvan's knuckles go white as he grabs and twists with an immense strength his body doesn't show. Ventos winces, and his grip goes limp. I breathe freely again. Ruvan pulls Ventos's hand away from me, but holds it and the man in place as he says almost too calmly, "You touch her again and there will be consequences."

The room is stunned to silence, myself included.

Ruvan relaxes the hard stare he was giving Ventos and releases the large man. Ventos steps away, rubbing his wrist, looking more confused than hurt. Ruvan turns to me with a small smile, as though he hadn't just threatened one of his own. "You were saying?"

I try and find my thoughts again after that outburst. "I know, it's not ideal. But…what we just did, what we just made in the chalice, it looked almost *exactly* like the Hunter's Elixir."

Winny raises her hand. "What *is* the Hunter's Elixir?"

"No one knows but the master hunter. He's the one responsible for preparing and administering it. The recipe is more closely guarded than the substance itself—which is saying something—to steal either is punishable by death." I rub the back of my neck, remembering the night before the Blood Moon, Drew pressing the obsidian vial into my hand. "The hunters store the elixir in obsidian vials. Just like you store blood here to keep it fresh."

"Curious," Callos murmurs, stroking his chin.

"It's what I drank the night of the Blood Moon—the thing that made you say I had the blood lore performed on me." I look to Ruvan again. "My brother gave his elixir to me and told me only to drink it if I needed to. A Succumbed had made it into town…and when I drank, the vampir could sense me even across a salted threshold."

"Just like I could sense you in the marshes," Ruvan says softly, affirming my theory.

"I might not know how they make the elixir, but I think you're right, it's some kind of blood lore." I'm finally ready to admit it aloud. "And it's *powerful*. It can make humans strong enough to fight against the vampir. The draught my brother gave me was special, so he said. But it did make me—someone who's not a hunter—able to go toe-to-toe with the vampir lord himself. This also means Drew should know where to get more of it." *If he's still alive*. But I still refuse to believe otherwise.

"If we can steal some, maybe it could help give you the strength to ward off the curse for as long as you need?"

Everyone is silent, chewing on this information. I wait on pins for their verdict.

"It might work." Ruvan is the first to speak. Then the rest of them do, as if they'd been waiting for his permission and assessment.

"This might be a way for her to run back across the Fade and tell her human companions all she knows about us." Ventos is ever confident in me.

"I won't run and I won't betray your trust," I say.

"How can we know that?"

"I'm sworn to him—to help all of you. I can't do anything that would hurt any of you *at least* until the curse is broken. And I—" I stop short.

"You what?" Ventos demands.

"I wouldn't even after the curse and oath are broken," I finish softly.

He snorts. "How can we believe her?"

"I do," Winny offers. Lavenzia still looks unsure, but she doesn't say she disagrees, which I take as a good sign.

"I do too. And at the very least, this elixir will be worth studying," Callos adds. "Knowing what the hunters have will only help us—or future lords and ladies—in our fight."

What have I done? I'm giving people who would kill everyone and everything I've ever loved access and insight into one of the few defenses we have.

Doubt vanishes when I look at Ruvan. I must help him. And if this means we succeed in breaking the curse then it doesn't matter what the vampir know. Vampir will never cross the Fade again. Ruvan would uphold our deal even if there wasn't a bloodsworn oath holding him to it.

This is worth it. It has to be…or I've damned Hunter's Hamlet, and no one will survive the next Blood Moon in five hundred years and whatever vampir lord or lady that comes for us then.

"Let me go back across the Fade," I say. "I'll bring you the elixir."

"How do we know we can trust you to return?" Ventos asks.

Ruvan announces, "Because she won't be going alone."

twenty-four

"BUT YOU—YOU CAN'T CROSS THE FADE IF IT'S NOT THE BLOOD MOON," I SAY HASTILY. The idea of bringing a vampir back to Hunter's Hamlet is as uncomfortable as a hammer hitting too-cool metal and ricocheting off with a deafening clang and a vibration that runs up your whole arm.

"*I* can't," Ruvan agrees. "As a distant descendant of one of the first kings, my powers are too deeply entrenched in Midscape to slip by the keystones that mark the Fade unnoticed. But one of my covenant might be able to."

"Can we?" Lavenzia seems surprised by this information.

"The Succumbed can do it on the full moon," Ruvan says.

"They can?" Quinn is startled alongside the rest of them.

"Hunter's Hamlet is attacked most full moons," I say, remembering Ruvan's and my conversation before we fell through the ceiling. Ruvan had been surprised by the information; it seems sensible the rest of them are as well.

"How are they getting out of the castle?" Winny asks.

"There's the old portcullis." Lavenzia's mind goes right to where mine first went. "By the sea."

Callos considers this and arrives at the same conclusion I did. "It always seemed shut tight. Though, I'm not sure where else they could be getting out from. The full moon strengthens even the Succumbed. Perhaps they can sense the blood on the other side of the Fade? Or perhaps it's some old habits that draw them across; maybe they're old vampir going back to the summer castle before the land was torn up. Either way, if they can do it, we should be able to find a way while our powers are heightened as well."

"It'll take a lot of magic, which means a lot of blood." Lavenzia puts her hands on her hips.

"We have rations," Ruvan says.

"Which we don't want to dip too deeply into. It's a long time until the next Blood Moon," Quinn cautions.

"It'll be enough if all the rations go to one person." The rest of them still at Ruvan's words. "Worse comes to worst, we'll leave finding the curse's anchor to the next lord or lady and their covenant. We'll sustain only one of us, until the time comes to wake the next group. It wouldn't be the first time it's come to that in our history."

Only one of us… That means only one of them would be awake, and the rest would go off and end themselves before the curse could. That person would wait, alone, counting the days until they wake the next lord or lady and their covenant. Locked away in some safe corner of the castle, no doubt. Not daring to venture too far.

Their lives are hard and lonely enough as they are. But they at least have each other. What Ruvan is suggesting sounds almost too heartbreaking to bear. And yet, they all seem convinced it's the right path. They're all willing to make that sacrifice.

"It won't come to that." I stand as well. "We will break the curse. While I'm off getting the elixir, you and Callos can look through the information we got from the workshop. I'm certain there will be something useful there," I say to Ruvan.

His lips quirk upward slightly in a grin. "When did the human find the bravery to give orders to the vampir lord?"

I roll my eyes and ignore the remark. Though it lingers with me even as I ask, "Who's coming with me to Hunter's Hamlet?"

"Ventos will go," Ruvan decrees.

"*What?*" Ventos and I say in almost perfect unison. He's the absolute last person I would want to join me.

"You were worried about her not coming back," Ruvan says to Ventos. "What better way to ensure that she does than going yourself? Besides, I don't want to deal with your griping and grumbling if you're left here. Having you here disparaging her the entire time would wear my patience very, *very* thin." There's a whisper of murder in Ruvan's voice. A not-so-subtle threat that even I can hear.

"So you'd rather him disparage me to my face?" I fold my arms and look pointedly at Ruvan.

"If he does, tell me so when you return and it will be dealt with," Ruvan says casually. As if I'm not going to be putting up with him in the meantime. But his movements have a grace to them that promises violence should his clear wishes be denied or ignored.

"*If* I return." I glance at Ventos from the corner of my eye. He looks less and less happy by the minute. I'm not sure I like my odds of going off with him. For all I know he'd find the first opportunity or excuse to leave me helpless, trapped in the Fade.

"Ventos wouldn't dare return without you." Ruvan clasps my shoulder, bringing my attention solely back to him. "I would go with you if I could. But I can't. So we must divide and conquer. While you go on this excursion, we'll continue searching for any useful information on the anchor here. I know you won't let me down."

I want to object further, but not with everyone present. The last thing I want to do is say or do something that would offend Ventos and make my travels worse.

"The next full moon isn't for two weeks yet," Callos observes. "We have time to prepare."

"Good, we'll use every moment of it." Ruvan sounds so sure, so confident, but my stomach is knotting with worry and apprehension. I know I suggested this plan of attack…but I'm already having second thoughts. "Callos, go and collect all the information we presently have on Hunter's Hamlet. The rest of you go and help him. We'll begin our planning promptly."

"You should rest," I say, placing a hand on Ruvan's shoulder. I notice how Lavenzia focuses intensely on the gesture and I resist the urge to pull away. I don't want to retreat from Ruvan. I am not simply the forge maiden any longer—I'm not forbidden to touch and be touched—and I will not allow myself to feel guilty.

"I'm inclined to agree," Quinn says.

"It doesn't need to be tonight, my lord. We can have these discussions in the coming weeks," Callos says.

"The idea is fresh and we are committed to it—there is no time like the present." Ruvan is insistent. There's a sturdy resoluteness to his shoulders and jaw. No one is going to be shaking him from this decision. "Moreover, I want to have time to sleep on, challenge, and debate our plans before finalizing them. We will not let this lie."

"Very well. I will do as you bid." Callos bows his head and starts from the room.

The rest of them exchange wary glances, but all reluctantly agree. Quinn is the last one out. I can feel his questions about my lingering presence—my hand still on his lord's person—but he doesn't voice them. I wonder what the rest of them will say. My ears burn with everything I can't hear…

She's staying with him. Alone. She touched him.

Forbidden. All of this is so forbidden.

I pull my hand from his shoulder, balling it into a fist. I hold it to me as though it's wounded. My other fingers wrap around it, massaging my skin. My flesh is my own and yet—

"Floriane?" Ruvan says softly. His fingertips land lightly on my chin, guiding my eyes back to his. "What is it?"

"I'm afraid."

"Afraid of what?"

"Everything." I shake my head and voice all the conflicting feelings that have sunk their thorny barbs into me for days. "What's happening to me?"

"What do you mean?"

"Am I just a puppet now?"

"Why would you think that?"

"I need you. I want to push you away. I've always been told I cannot allow myself to be touched and yet all I want are your hands on me." My words become hasty. "I saw you lying, dying, becoming one of those monsters, and all I could think about was saving you. I had to see you—save you—be with you."

"Floriane, breathe," he says softly.

The suggestion only heightens my frustration, making my breath hitch further. "I *am* breathing."

"You're panicking."

"Of course I am!" I reach for him. My hands smooth up the broad plane of his chest like a lover's before balling into fists in his clothing like an enemy's. They tremble as the idea of strangling him passes through my mind for the first time in days. Desire is quickly thwarted by instant nausea at the mere notion of hurting him. "All my thoughts feel controlled by you. They keep coming back to you."

His hands lightly land on mine. I want to slap them away, but I'm consumed by his calm, stable gaze. Ruvan is as sturdy as iron. "I promise, you are still your own woman."

"Then why do my thoughts no longer feel like my own? Why can I think of nothing but helping you?" I beg him for answers that I don't know if he can give me. But I need them. I need them more than I need every shuddering breath I'm struggling to draw. "Do I really want to help you? Or is this need just the magic of the bloodsworn taking over my mind and infiltrating my thoughts? Do I actually, genuinely care about you, Ruvan? Or do I want you to die as fiercely as I was always told I should? As I always thought I did?"

He says nothing. The silence is worse than anything else he might have come up with. It makes me want to scream.

Yet I whisper, "Tell me, please."

"I can't." The words are soft and somehow all the more grating because of it. "I can't tell you because I don't know your heart; that's something only you can know." His hands grip mine. "But I can tell you what my heart is saying. It's saying you're not alone in this confusion, or this unbearable need to explore all that's happening between us—all we could be despite all odds."

I grow still as his eyes become even more intense. I'm drawn to him, pulled by invisible hands and unyielding needs. "You feel it too?"

"Of course I do." He shakes his head. "I see you and I don't know if I see the monster hunter that I always pictured—the bloodthirsty woman who came for my throat with a silver sickle on the night of the Blood Moon—or if I see Floriane…" His voice grows softer, more tender. "The forge maiden who has brought a heartbeat back into the castle of my forefathers, one I can hear echoing up softly to me with the sharp clang of metal. A woman who has hands that can kill or create. A woman who enthralls me more by the hour with every layer of pain and hurt, knowledge and power, goodness and darkness that there is to her."

I let out a huff of laughter and shake my head. *He* saw me as the monster. Just as I saw him. We both looked at each other and saw what we wanted and what the world had told us to see, not what was actually there. And now that we're confronted with the truth…

"I don't know what to do," I confess. My heart is slowing and thoughts clearing thanks to his firm, steady grasp. "I don't know what to believe. Do I trust in my training and the instincts it gave me? My sense, logic, or reason? Or do I trust in my heart?"

"What do you *want* to trust in?"

"I don't know," I repeat, painfully honest. "My training—everything Hunter's Hamlet gave me—is who I've always been, it's what I've always known. When times were tough, I never had to question. All I needed was blind faith to make it through. I've never had to worry about what I want, what I need, because I've never had any kind of option. Now I feel like I'm drowning in a sea of them."

"I see you, Floriane. I know *exactly* how you feel." The words are deep and purposeful.

My hands relax, and I hunch over him. My forehead is drawn to his before I can think about it. I shut out the world by closing my eyes and I simply breathe.

In the wake of my silence, he speaks. "I was born into a cursed and dying people. From the first moment I drew breath, I was already in a distant line of succession that charted the course of my life. I should have never even thought of leading the vampir but here I am. My covenant looks to me for help and guidance but I'm not the lord they need. I'm no one, really."

I laugh softly and lean away. "The lord of the vampir, calling himself no one."

"It's true, though." Ruvan gives me a tired smile. "I'm only the vampir lord because my people had to plan out thousands of years of leaders when the long night began. I am far, far from their first choice. And the next person will be even less so. That's why I *must* end this curse. I can't trust that the next person, or the one after, will." He pauses, head dipping back into his pillow. His eyes are glassy, gaze soft and distant. Ruvan turns his head, looking to the window. "No… it's more than that. I want to end the curse selfishly, too. To prove that I was worth something—that my life has meaning. That I wasn't some throwaway lord at the end of the list."

"I don't think anything about anyone is 'throwaway.'"

"Even about a vampir?" He brings his eyes back to mine.

"Perhaps," I say. But then force myself to say what I really mean. "Yes."

Ruvan smiles gently. "Now, I've told you of the inner workings of my heart. Tell me, Floriane, what are yours? What does your *heart* say about us? Not the instincts brought on by your training. Your heart."

The one thing I've never listened to. The one thing I've hardly ever heeded. I've always known what's right for me because I've been told and directed.

What does my heart say?

"That…I feel for you," I confess. "That I want to keep learning who you are and knowing you."

"And I feel for you." He pulls me a bit closer, his hands still around mine. "I ache for you. I burn for you. *I want you.*"

He wants me. Heat pools in my lower stomach. My throat is dry, mouth wet. I swallow thickly.

"There might still be a part of me though that sees you as my enemy," I confess.

"I know."

"And sometimes, that part that tells me I should hate you, all the voices of my family and ancestors, might win out over my want to be gentle to you, to know you. I might not always be the person I want to be toward you, for you."

"And that's all right." Those words are among the sweetest I've ever heard. It feels as though he has accepted me for all I am and yet also all I'm not. It's as though he is the first person to look at me and really, truly begin to know me. My mother sees me as her daughter. My brother as his sister. The hamlet knows me as the forge maiden. They all see and know parts of me, but has anyone ever, truly tried to see the whole picture? "Neither of us will win against our entire upbringing in days, or weeks, or even years. We will have to work to learn something new day after day. But…" Ruvan leans up to brush his nose against mine as he tempts me with an almost kiss. "I dare think learning you will be a delight."

I shiver as his warm breath runs over my cheeks. I consciously force all doubt aside. All second-guessing. And, for a moment, it works. Long enough for me to say…

"Kiss me."

"There you are, commanding the vampir lord again."

"What are you going to do about it?" The words are coy, sensual, said on the back of my tongue with the edge of a grin.

"I'm going to kiss you, just as you command." His lips press gently against mine. Ruvan doesn't go for my neck, he doesn't go for my blood at all, only my lips. The kiss is relief and more tension. It's everything I needed to free my brain of this constantly burning desire. To heat myself to the point that I'm malleable enough that everything will go back into place.

Instinct tells me to loathe everything about this man. I *should* resent these circumstances. The way he makes me feel…

I should hate it. I don't want to hate it. I *can't* hate it…

I love it.

twenty-five

I'M LOST IN THE KISS FOR WHAT MUST BE A SHAMEFUL AMOUNT OF TIME. His tongue slips into my mouth, grazing against mine. It begs permission. He sings to me without words and my body rises in harmony, soaring high above the rafters and the castle spires overhead.

His hands frame my face, holding me in place against him. They provide me structure so my world doesn't rattle apart with how *good* this moment feels. Hunter's Hamlet, the title of forge maiden, they fall away like shackles I didn't know were wrapped around me so tightly that I hadn't been able to take a full breath in my entire life.

Be with him, Floriane.

Just *be*, Floriane.

I push him back and his hands slide down, skimming over the curves of my chest. The touch is barely there and yet every muscle in my core shudders with delight. *Take me, make me, break me,* my body silently demands of him as he collects my thighs in his palms. I move to his whim, straddling him as he kneads the muscle of my rear.

We slip apart and come together, again and again, until he finally pulls away as breathless as I am.

"We should go," he whispers across my lips.

"But—"

"They're waiting for us," he reminds me.

I straighten away, reality slowly filling in the gaps that pleasure had created. "They're going to suspect something."

"They already have."

"What have they said?" I ease away so he can stand. Never have I been so focused on the way a man rises to his feet, the long, strong line of his back. The pert roundness of his rear that I focus on for far, far too long.

"Nothing, yet. But they will."

"How do you know they suspect something then?"

"They're my covenant, they are all bound to me as I am to them." He pauses briefly, hands on his nightshirt. His eyes dart to mine and I can sense a brief moment of hesitation. One that ends with him pulling it over his head. "See."

"Oh." That's all I can muster.

I know what he's trying to show me—the markings that are similar to mine across his body. There's one by his elbow. One underneath his left pectoral. One indented into the V shape that disappears into the front of his trousers, leaving me jealous of some black ink. But, if I'm honest, my focus only grazes on the markings and, instead, lingers on the indents of his lean muscles—the deep shadows hammered by struggle and famine. Scars accent his flesh, white and deep, crisscrossing over his perfect form.

"The other marks." I manage to find words despite the sight of him leaving me nearly breathless. "Are you bloodsworn with all the others, too?" I saw similar marks on his covenant.

"They have sworn their oaths to me, marking our blood…but it is not quite the same as a bloodsworn. The bond of a bloodsworn is different, deeper." Ruvan pauses midway to collecting his shirt, instead standing before me. I lean back slightly, trying to take him all in. I don't know what I've done to earn such a display but I don't want to risk doing anything that could end it. "This scar is from the first time I went to the old castle. This one is from before the long night, when Tempost was a city of desperate people."

"And desperation breeds stupidity," I echo my mother's words softly.

"Too true." He wears a bitter smile. "This one is from when I first awoke. And this is from when I was clumsier with weapons…" He lists off all his scars, one by one, until he reaches his forearm. Unlike the other scars, the skin is still gnarled and greenish. Festering. "You know this one."

"It still looks so poorly."

"It might always." He pauses. "Does it disgust you?"

"I don't think anything on you could disgust me."

He's as surprised as I am. Ruvan's lips part slightly before smirking. "You're certain of that? Your eyes held a lot of disgust for me when you first arrived."

I shake my head and huff. "What do my eyes hold now?"

"They hold…" He trails off, pausing, thinking. My breath grows shallow as I wait for what he's about to say—what I can feel but have yet to put words to myself. "Not disgust."

"Will you be all right?" I ask, slightly shifting the conversation away from that place of breathless tension.

"I have no choice."

"I'll help you," I say with conviction.

"Because you are my bloodsworn?" he asks with guarded eyes.

"Because *I* want to."

"Good." He squeezes my hand and resumes getting dressed.

I slip out of the room, giving him privacy, and take the moment to collect myself. The skyline of Tempost catches my eye out the window and I pause before it, inhaling deeply and letting the air out slowly. My breath fogs the glass, turning it into a more mirrored surface.

Dark, short hair. Dark eyes. Tanned skin mottled with my own scars. It's still me. Just as much as Ruvan's mark is between my collarbones. The bloodsworn and the vampir are now a part of me, as much as the smithy is, as much as my mother's words, or my brother's training, or the hamlet's old stories are… They all are me. Yet not one *defines* me.

I won't let it. I want to choose every moment, one after the next. I want to be my own woman.

I *will* be, for the first time ever.

"Are you ready?" Ruvan emerges, adjusting one of the worn, velvet coats I've seen him in before. The high collars suit him, I decide. As achingly handsome as ever.

"Yes."

We've been seated around one of the tables in the main hall for hours now. A large, slate tablet that almost fills the entire tabletop is covered with the chalky outlines of my clumsy scribbles of Hunter's Hamlet.

"And what's this again?" Ventos points to a shaded swath of earth.

I'd be more frustrated at having to explain myself over and over if my drawings weren't so terrible and this wasn't so important. "That's the salted earth. It shouldn't pose any trouble…but there isn't anywhere to hide in that stretch so we'll have to move swiftly to avoid someone seeing us coming from the marshes."

"Salt will prevent mist stepping across. You'll have to run to the next cover." Winny points to one of the square farmhouses. "To here, and then here…"

We repeat a plan, second-guess it, and change our approach. Everything is carefully debated. It's exhausting, but necessary if we want to succeed in getting a vampir into Hunter's Hamlet and all the way to the fortress.

"Let's break, for now," Ruvan says with a yawn. His eyes have already lost some of their luster. I don't know if the others have noticed yet, but it's enough to worry me. "It's getting late, and we're still catching up our strength from our venture into the old castle."

"I thought you'd never suggest it." Winny stretches her hands over her head, rising to her toes. "Good sleep, everyone. See you in the morning to do this all yet again, I'm sure." She yawns and promptly heads to her room.

The rest of them trickle out. But Callos remains hunched over the table, long enough that it's clear he's waiting for something.

"What is it?" I ask.

A frown crosses Callos's lips. "I'm not sure…"

"I know that look." Ruvan places his elbows on the table, careful not to scuff my drawings with his forearms. "You see something."

"I'm not sure," Callos repeats, firmer than the last. "But I think *something* is familiar. I need to research a few things first." He rolls his shoulders back, tipping his head from side to side and massaging his neck. He's been hunched for hours staring at my drawings and hanging on every word with an intensity I've never seen someone possess for knowledge before. "I'll let you know, my lord, whenever—if ever—I find something."

"Make sure I'm the first to know." Ruvan squeezes Callos's forearm and stands. I can't help but notice that Ruvan has been favoring his unwounded arm more and more.

"I always do."

"Thank you for all your hard work, dear friend."

"It's my pleasure." Callos's words are only half true. He does enjoy knowledge and its pursuits. That much I can tell. But the circumstances under which he's forced to gain the knowledge…it saps any joy he could glean from it. His golden eyes turn to me. "Do you mind if I record everything you've written here so we don't lose it?"

I didn't realize I had a choice. I look to Ruvan, deferring to the vampir lord.

He gives me a tired smile. "Don't look at me, he asked you. It's your knowledge that you're sharing with us."

I stare at the map I've drawn. Even as bad as my attempts at cartography are…it's still a detailed rendering of Hunter's Hamlet—*of home*. It will be the home of forge maidens, hunters, tanners, farmers, cobblers, and humans standing against the vampir for years to come. I run my fingertips lightly, longingly, over the frame of the slate tablet.

Or, maybe not for years to come. If we succeed, it will be a town like any other.

"You may," I say softly, surprising myself. I expect Callos to be giddy with this permission, but he's not. He knows what I'm allowing him to do. Out of everyone…I dare think he understands. Perhaps because he's the most well-read and he knows the long and bloody history of this conflict. "But I have one request—a condition."

"Yes?"

"If I ask it of you, you'll destroy the records."

He winces at my ultimatum.

But I continue regardless, "I know, or have gathered, you're not the sort who would want to destroy any kind of history or record. But I have no guarantees, should we fail in breaking the curse, that the next vampir lord or lady would be as understanding to humans as Ruvan has been."

"If it comes to that, I will leave the next vampir lord word and make it clear all we have accomplished and things will be different. They will try to work with the hamlet after all I will tell them," Ruvan says, far too optimistically.

"*If* they heed those words," I counter gently. "And even if they do… it's unlikely they'll find a human to help them further. You only have me on your side with luck that you didn't kill me and I didn't end up killing myself. The chances of circumstances aligning for another lord or lady is slim." And if what Ruvan said earlier is true, those future lords and ladies are likely not to be nearly the same caliber of person Ruvan is.

"We saw the hunters' collars on the night of the Blood Moon," Callos murmurs. "I saw one used."

I nod. "The people of Hunter's Hamlet are trained to die before we help a vampir, or let one take our blood. I'm amazed you managed to collect any blood at all for your stores."

The more I speak, the more I think about how impossible it is that I'm here. That I'm still willing to work with Ruvan. More than willing to work with him… I massage my neck, thinking of the feeling of his arms around me. The heat of our bodies pressed flush together. The need that rises within me to a melting point the moment his hands and fangs are upon me.

Ruvan sees the motion and I quickly drop my hand. The thoughts have sparked the kindling that is constantly in wait between us. I can feel the start of that push and pull beginning. A need that will drive me mad if not satiated.

"So if this doesn't work—if it doesn't look like we'll be successful…" I force myself to stay focused, for now. I might indulge myself later. "Then I want this information destroyed. Because, if it's not, the next vampir lord or lady will use it to annihilate everything I've ever loved and I can't carry on with that weighing on me. It'll be too unbearable."

Callos sighs and then, to my surprise, says, "Very well."

"Truly?"

"I give you my word. Sorry, but that will have to be good enough, as you cannot be bloodsworn with two people." He chuckles. "And I would not dare to enter into any kind of oath with another's bloodsworn."

Ruvan takes a half step toward me at the mere mention of another oath. A protective aura envelops me. He's put off by the mere idea of

Callos doing *anything* with me. The sensation causes heat to rise up my chest, threatening to reach my cheeks.

I've been guarded and protected my whole life. But Ruvan's defensiveness feels different. Delightful, even. It's because this is the protection I choose and for that reason, unlike the protection the title of forge maiden offered, I can remove it with a request.

"I believe you," I say, and offer Callos an encouraging smile.

"I appreciate your trust." Callos dips his chin. "I shall extend the same faith to you."

"Oh?"

His eyes dart between me and Ruvan. "To keep our lord at his best." He has the makings of a coy grin. I'm too stunned to say anything else before he bows his head and departs down the stairs.

Ruvan's hand slips into mine, drawing my attention to him.

"You're right, they know," I whisper.

"Let them know." He shrugs. "This world is dark and the night is unyielding; the least we can do is fill it with sweet, forbidden dreams."

Once more, I'm stunned to silence. Ruvan takes advantage of the moment, leaning forward to hoist me into his arms. I grab his shoulders for stability.

"Where are you taking me?" I ask, somewhat playfully. I already know where—his bedroom—and, for the first time, I am ready to be there.

"I am stealing you away, of course." He has a grin that promises all those aforementioned, forbidden dreams. The sort of grin that I've only ever seen men give to women before they slip into the night together—the sort that makes my head spin and heat swell from my toes all the way to the tops of my ears. "As vampir lords do."

"Ah, yes, and I am a hunter, so I should put up a fight." It strikes me, briefly, that I can call myself a hunter now. I still can't lie to Ruvan, so it must be true. The revelation fills me, thrills me, as much as he does.

"I welcome it. I like your fangs."

"Careful, or you'll find out just how hard I can bite." I extend upward and take the muscle of his neck between my teeth, biting just hard enough to leave a mark.

Ruvan lets out a low growl and takes the stairs two at a time. He can't get there fast enough.

twenty-six

We move wordlessly, seamlessly, flowing together from the moment he sets me down and opens the first door, to me opening the second. Our bodies slide against each other, mirroring our mouths. One moment I'm in the main room, the next my back is pinned against the door to his bedroom. His hands pulling at me, hoisting me. My legs wrap around his waist.

I feel him. Every inch of glorious, perfect muscle. Every hard-earned scar. Every strand of silken hair. I run my hands over him as though I am inspecting him.

Ruvan's breath is hot on my throat. His lips drag up to my chin, sending shivers down my spine. He draws a ragged breath against my flesh before kissing me again with a hunger I didn't know one could possess—one I share.

"What do you need?" I whisper against his mouth, eyes half closed. I can see him through the curtain of my lashes—his sharp jaw and the shadows that cling to his face as tightly as moonlight.

"I need you," he rasps.

"My blood?"

"Your body."

Holding me in place against him, my legs locked around his waist, he spins from the door. Before I know it, my back is on the bed. The mattress sags under me and I'm pleasantly surprised to find it doesn't smell of dust and age, but of honeysuckle and sandalwood.

He rounds to the foot of the bed, staring down at me. The moonlight strikes against the flawless line of his jaw. It illuminates his silver hair. He looks like a god on this mortal plane and I am his offering, ready to be devoured.

Ruvan raises a knee onto the bed. Slowly, like a beast on the prowl, he crawls atop me. His knees work their way between my thighs until my back arches, our hips meet, my breath hitches. At the same time, his hand glides up my side to end at my breast.

A moan escapes me, deep and throaty. Followed instantly by a blush. I raise a hand and bite my knuckles. Between my teeth I say, “I’m sorry. It’s that, I’ve never been touched like this before.”

He pauses, assessing me thoughtfully. Cupping my face, his thumb grazing my cheek. I await the verdict of whatever it is he is debating. But time drags on and he says nothing.

“Is that all right?” I finally ask.

“You are perfect,” Ruvan whispers, placing a gentle kiss on my lips.

“I’m sorry I don’t have much experience.” It never bothered me much until this moment. I never had a reason to feel insecure about never having lovers, or never kissing or touching, because that was what was expected of me. Everyone in my whole world knew it.

But Ruvan isn’t from my world. He’s a whole world unto himself. Where do I fit into it? Can I?

“I said you were perfect,” he says firmly. “The sorrow of other men will be my blessing and delight.” Ruvan bites my neck gently. He doesn’t break the skin. A tender kiss. A lick. A whimper escapes me in place of a moan. “Don’t hide it, Floriane. Don’t be ashamed. Moan, scream, weep so long as it is from pleasure. Let me hear you.”

“But the others—”

“They won’t hear. But I’d hardly care if they did.” He pulls away, hovering over me. One arm on either side of my face. His body pressed against mine. My world is him and him alone. “Tonight, forget about everything else, Floriane. All you should do is feel. Put all other thoughts aside and savor it.”

It’s easy to have my mind go blank when he slides back down my body, taking one of my breasts into his mouth over my shirt. Another moan flies from my lips, and another. His hands, his mouth. I am on fire.

I now see why finding a suitor was all some young women thought of. When this toe-curling pleasure is something that one can simply have at will when they have a partner… He shifts again and his palm lands at the crux of my desire. I inhale sharply and he almost purrs with delight.

His fingers move, generating delightful friction. Lightning races through me, arcing out into tiny tingles that pucker my skin into gooseflesh straining against the cool night air. My back arches, my chest tightens.

Ruvan seems to know exactly how much is too much, and when it is not enough. My eyes flutter closed, blocking out light and sound and thought. There's only him, seemingly everywhere at once. Every sense is overwhelmed. My toes curl as the pressure builds, and builds, and builds.

I am about to break. This man will shatter me into a thousand pieces with his tongue and fingers alone. My breath catches as I try to give him warning but the crash is upon me before I can find words.

Shudders wrack my body and cries escape my lips. It's over in moments that felt like glorious millennia. I seize from the waist down, muscles contracting, sending new waves of pleasure with every bit of pressure. Ruvan slows his movements, pulling me to him and removing his hand from between my thighs at the last moment. My face is pressed against the crook of his neck and I am both vulnerable and protected at once.

He presses his lips to my forehead. "Breathe, Floriane."

"I…what…I…" Words have failed me. They're gone, floating along the blissful sea that all other thoughts are scattered and adrift in.

"How do you feel?" he asks.

"Good." It's not enough. That one word isn't enough to encompass the happy buzzing that has taken residence in my muscles. It's not nearly enough to contain something so raw and real as what I am experiencing right now. But it will have to suffice.

He chuckles softly, as if he knows all those things. As though he can hear them in that one, not quite good enough, word. "Good," Ruvan echoes.

Despite myself, I yawn. The tremors are settling and the bed is far more comfortable than I expected. My body grows heavy.

"You should rest, you've had a long day."

"Here?" I murmur.

"Where else?"

Rather than arguing, I close my eyes. The settee in the main room is the furthest thing from my mind right now. Leaving is far too much effort.

Two strong arms around me. A heavy duvet. Winter outside the window, trying to find its way in but the fire keeps it at bay.

I shift, tilting my head to look up at him. Two, bright eyes shine back at me in the moonlight. His lips take on a thin, crescent shape.

"You're awake," I say.

"How could I sleep when I am in so much wonder at the stunning creature in my bed?" he almost purrs.

I can't help but laugh. "You're incorrigible." I'm hardly a new presence in his bed, his life. I almost exist exclusively here, now. His comfort has become my home...so much so that I no longer even think of leaving the mountains.

"How much longer will this persist?" I ask. He knows the heart of my question, his slight frown tells me as much.

"Soon...my love. They will know the truth soon enough. When our work is done."

Dawn breaks and I don't move. The comforter and furs must be made of lead, because I've never felt anything so heavy in my life. The afterglow of last night is as settled on me as Ruvan's arm is around my midsection. His heavy breathing tells me he still slumbers and I slowly twist to avoid disturbing him.

Not for the first time, I admire him in the early morning. But this time I'm much closer than the last. I can see the gentle curve of his lips and every long lash that rests on his cheek as he slumbers. I have the odd sense that this isn't the first time I've woken like this… A dream?

My attempts to remember the details are met with a flash of pain through my body. It is an agony not brought on by any physical trauma, but my mind wreaking cruelty upon me. I'm clammy, cold. Shame tries to grab hold of me.

What have I done? I can't be here. I can't be with any man, but especially not him. I see my mother's disappointed eyes and my brother's horror behind my shut-tight lids. I can hear Drew now: *Out of everyone you could've picked, Floriane…*

I can't be here. My breath is quickening. I'm going to disturb him if I stay, either with weeping or screaming.

Somehow, I manage to escape without waking him and I retreat into the main room. But it's still too close to him. I can smell him on my skin.

I flee to the one place I've always had stability: the forge.

Fortunately it's early enough that no one stops me along the way. Within minutes, the hearth is hot and metal is in it. I can move without thought here, and I allow my mind to go blank.

But my reprieve from facing my choices is short-lived when Ruvan appears. I can sense his presence and don't turn from the anvil. He slowly approaches as I strike the metal with my hammer, waiting to speak until I've put it back into the forge.

"What are you making?"

"I don't know yet." The words are a little curter than I intended. *You made your own choices last night, Floriane, don't blame or take it out on him*, I scold myself.

He hesitates a moment. "Are you all right?"

I finally look at him and immediately wish I hadn't. I'd hoped he'd be indifferent. That, somehow, we'd manage to not talk about what's transpired between us. Or, better yet, he'd also be wracked with misplaced guilt, etched upon his soul by everything we've always been taught to be.

"Floriane?" He takes a step forward.

I want to tell him to go away. I want to tell him I'm fine and that last night meant nothing to me and will never happen again. But I know neither is true. My heart has never soared beyond my chest, or fallen from my body like it does when it's around him. Even if I want to ignore it, even if I harbor guilt for it, this isn't something I can brush aside…and doing so wouldn't be fair to him either.

"I… I'm not all right," I admit. His lips part and his eyes fill with panic as his brows knit in sorrow. I shake my head quickly, my work forgotten as I step toward him. "It's not you. Not really. I wanted last night. But I…" I stare at a crack in the floor. "I'm still struggling with this, *us*, you and I as more than enemies. Every time I'm near you, my heart races and I want to touch you. But I hear them—my mother, brother, father, the whole town—judging me for every breath I take and don't use to curse your name."

"It was too much too fast," he says softly.

"I knew what I was doing and I'm trying not to—I *won't* allow myself to feel ashamed," I say firmly.

"Good." He takes both my hands in his. "But we both already acknowledged, this will take time. Neither of us can ignore all we have been." I give a small nod. "We'll go slower."

"I'm sorry."

Ruvan catches my chin and brings my eyes to his. I can still faintly smell myself on his fingers and that has me fighting a flush. It reminds me of the passion he filled me with.

"You have nothing to apologize for." He smiles, eyes shining in the early sunlight. "Are you hungry?"

I blink at the change in conversation, though it's not unwelcome. "I'm actually not. Which is odd." I glance back to the forge. I've been hammering away for the better part of an hour now and didn't eat much last night.

"Not really."

"Oh?"

"When King Solos made the blood lore, he sought to strengthen the bodies of the vampir. By adding onto our blood time and again with the power of others, until we could subsist completely off what few things we could grow, hunt, and forage in the mountains of our lands."

"But I'm not—"

He interrupts me with a knowing smile. I don't even have to say, *a vampir*. "Your blood has been marked with mine; some of the fortifications I have extend now to you."

Marked.

I am marked by him. Even long after our bloodsworn comes to an end and the curse is broken, all experiences—all we are—remains on our blood. But what will it mean when we end the curse… *When*. I will it into the world.

What happens *after* for Ruvan and me?

I don't know. That's a question I'm not ready to search for the answer to. I have enough I'm trying to sort through as it is.

Ruvan releases my hands. "Your metal is glowing white. I'll give you some space and leave you to it."

"You don't have to," I say before he can leave.

"Are you sure? If you need time—"

"I'll tell you what I need." I try and offer him a reassuring smile. "Assuming I know it."

"We're both figuring this out as we go," he agrees.

"Oh, speaking of figuring things out as I go, I have something I want to share with you. I found it yesterday—two days ago? Before you fell ill." Time is blurring together with all that's happened and how little sleep I seem to need now. "It's back here…" As I move, opening the door to the blacksmith's office and retrieving the ledger and my dagger, I tell him of my discovery and experimentations. When I finish, the dagger and ledger are on one of the tables between us.

"Incredible," Ruvan whispers.

"You really think so?" I ask uncertainly. "Even though it might have drawn power from me and put you in that state?"

"I'm fine, and this discovery is more than worth any pain I must experience." With a few words, he alleviates all my guilt.

"What do you think it does?" I ask.

"I don't know…but I know someone who might." Ruvan straightens away from the table and starts out of the forge. I already know who he's going to retrieve, so rather than calling after him, I seize the opportunity to appreciate him walking away. Then, wearing a smile I don't bother fighting, I turn back to the forge with renewed purpose.

twenty-seven

CALLOS ASKS JUST SHY OF A THOUSAND QUESTIONS. Even after I tell him the entire story of how I found the office, and all my work, he still probes. When he does finally fall silent, he stares intently at the dagger and the ledger for several long minutes. Long enough that I return to striking while I wait.

"A moment," is all Callos says before he runs from the room in a blur.

"How often does he get like this?" My throat is sore from answering all of Callos's questions.

Ruvan chuckles. "Often. At least when something has captured his imagination. He's our resident scholar and archivist. What Jontun was to Solos, Callos is to me."

"I see." I check on the metal melting in the forge.

"And what is our smith working on now?"

It's odd to hear myself called a plain smith and not a forge maiden. I don't dislike it. It further eases the pressure that was always pushing down on my shoulders.

"I'm seeing if I can smelt another silver variant."

"Yet another metallic breakthrough in the span of two days?" Ruvan folds his arms and leans against one of the tables. He sounds impressed and pride swells in my chest.

"We'll see." This is the first time in my life I've had access to nearly unlimited resources. "It's for Ventos."

"Ventos is rather partial to his broadsword."

"He's too useful with it to dream of replacing it," I say. "But he's not going to be able to take it back to my world."

"Why not?"

"Broadswords haven't been smithed for the hunters in generations." I hoist the rod-shaped mold I'll be pouring the liquid metal into onto the table. "The form used up too much silver and quickly depleted stock. The silver mines are far to the northwest and traders come rarely; the seas are infested with monsters up north, they say. Thus we have to preserve our resources as best we're able. Broadswords were smelted down to make smaller weapons in my great-grandmother's time."

Ruvan listens intently, eyes shining as if I am the most fascinating thing to ever exist. "So you're making him a new weapon?"

I nod and pick up my tongs, getting ready to take the crucible from the heat. "And for myself, too. In Hunter's Hamlet, if there's any suspicion about a person they're often forced to be nicked by a silver blade—just to ensure it's not a vampire who stole someone's face. Obviously we don't want that happening to Ventos."

"Obviously."

"So, I'm trying to make something that can pass for silver but isn't pure. Or is modified enough that it won't harm Ventos."

Ruvan is momentarily distracted by the flames that spontaneously combust when the river of golden heat meets the cooler mold. I return the crucible to the side of the forge to cool, changing out my tongs and picking up my hammer.

"Your process is fascinating," he murmurs. He doesn't know it, but being wide-eyed and enthralled with the endless mysteries and possibilities of heat and metal is the most attractive thing he could've ever done.

"I agree that the process is fascinating, but I'm biased."

"Biased, maybe. But that doesn't make you wrong." He shifts his weight and clears his throat. "Do you think you could teach me how to do it?"

"Usually smithy apprenticeships are about a decade, and that's just to make the more basic things. Another five to ten years before I'd let you hold a hammer and even look at silver work or anything else complex." This isn't my smithy, not really, but the instincts of my family are too ingrained in me to ignore. There is a procedure to someone learning the way of the forge and every step is there for a reason.

"Fifteen years to work with silver? Did you begin smithing when you were born?"

I snort. "Felt like it, but no. I began working in the smithy when I was five."

"That's so young," Ruvan says thoughtfully.

"Not for Hunter's Hamlet." I watch the metal as it slowly cools, gold changing to amber. "None of us *expect* to live long lives, though many of us do. At least, those of us that aren't hunters. The promise of Hunter's Hamlet is that you'll only ever have to fear one thing—the vampire. Everyone takes care of everyone else otherwise." I glance his way. "So even though most people are comfortable, if you can ignore the constant fear, we all know our days could be numbered. We know we're only ever one full moon away from death. It's common for young folk to be treated like full men and women by the age of thirteen. That's the youngest a hunter can go out.

"But, yes, I began working the smithy when I was five. Sweeping, fetching water and other things for Mother, all small tasks that a young one could do safely. The jobs that would strengthen my body and help me grow accustomed to the sights and sounds of the smithy. That way, when I did begin doing more, I was ready."

"And how old are you now?" Ruvan asks. I'm startled that he doesn't know. And I almost drop my tongs when I realize I still have no idea how old he is either. I long ago figured out that Ruvan isn't the ancient being I once thought of the vampir lord as. But how old is he in actuality?

"Nineteen." Using tongs, I take the freshly smelted bar of metal from its mold and carry it to the anvil. The residual heat still radiating as red throughout the metal has it slowly curling around the head of the anvil, beginning to form what will be the base of my sickle shape. "And you?"

"Counting the slumber, or not?" Ruvan asks coyly.

"Let's say both."

"Not counting the long night, I'm twenty-four," he says. "Counting the long night, around three thousand, one hundred and twenty-four."

"What..."

"The long night has been the past three thousand years while we slumbered in stasis to avoid succumbing to the curse. But for me, it was mere moments." There's a heaviness to his words that lingers as I return the iron to the forge. I remember Quinn's mention of the chrysalis slumber.

Callos returns before we can speak further on ages, or long nights.

"There was mention of something like this in the notes you brought back." He opens one of the books he carried in and I find it filled with loose papers I recognize from the workshop in the old castle. Two books he lays out also have the same script as some of those papers. He arranges them next to the blacksmith's ledger. "There's word here of encasing blood magic within metal—using it to preserve and carry power."

Wiping my hands, I approach and scan the page he's pointing to. On one side is a rough sketch of the door I opened down in the old castle. It's not exact. But it's close enough that I can tell it's an early concept. On the opposite side are some notes, almost like messages passed back and forth between two different people. There's the same hand that I recognize from the workshop alongside a penmanship that matches the forge master's ledger. They're focused on the specifications and details surrounding the actual *how* of building something like a magic door that channels blood magic.

"Like the disk and the door."

"Exactly. There was a public missive on behalf of King Solos, written by Jontun, that outlined an idea for how the vampir might be able to collect, preserve, and use the blood that was freely given by patrons from all over Midscape during our full moon festivals throughout the month as strength. I'd forgotten about it entirely until I saw these notes. This metal, and daggers made from it, could be what they had intended." Callos points to one of his books. "Look, here, this is a record in Jontun's hand. And here, these notes, you can see the script is the same. I'm confident we've uncovered a tool our predecessors were planning on using to fortify the vampir."

Leaning over, I look at the notes. I see the similar handwriting Callos is pointing out. But I also notice something else. "If the vampir could gather blood that way, then they had no use for humans. That would make a human want to work with them to uncover this power." I point. Just like I suspected in the workshop, there were two people keeping record. "See? If that's Jontun's handwriting, then this is someone else's.

It's here in the notes from the workshop and in the margins of the blacksmith's ledger. It must be her."

"Winny told me of your theory on the human woman," Callos says delicately, cleaning his glasses. "But I think this is far more likely to be King Solos's writing. Which is an extraordinary find! The man was notorious for writing nothing down; Jontun did everything for him." He speaks like he's trying to console me.

"I know it was the woman." I look to Ruvan for assistance. He knows of my dreams. *Dreams*… I had one last night, I realize. Didn't I? Or was it nothing more than a wishful fantasy?

Ruvan frowns. "We still believe that human was more of an… *experimentation* for Solos than a partner."

"I don't think that—"

"Solos wouldn't work with a human." Callos is convicted.

I bite my tongue and resist correcting him, continuing to share an intense stare with Ruvan. I wonder if he's remembering the dream from the old castle. But he says nothing and my heart sinks.

Callos speaks, oblivious to our tension. "These discoveries are truly incredible," he whispers. "To think all this time there was even more to the blood lore hiding in King Solos's old workshops. It might take weeks to really go through everything, but this is a treasure trove of information. I wonder if some of this is the makings of the first blood lore tomes. Perhaps we could piece together Jontun's lost records of Solos's early work since the original ledgers were lost."

I run my fingers over the journal, remembering the dream I had while in the old castle with vivid detail. "But the human—"

"There's no way King Solos would've been truly working with a human." Callos is clearly very sure of himself. "This mastery of the blood lore could only be King Solos."

"Why?"

"He was the *inventor* of blood lore," Ruvan says matter-of-factly. "It came from his work on the first humans to come to Tempost."

"I thought vampir could always use the magic of the blood?"

"Vampir could, but it was only during the full moon when our powers were strongest. Blood lore strengthened us at other times. But the cost…" Callos pauses, chewing on his words.

"Are you finished here?" Ruvan says suddenly.

I glance over my shoulder. The forge is still hot. My metal waiting for me. If this were back in Hunter's Hamlet, Mother would chastise me until I was red in the face for what I'm about to do. But…I'm curious what he has to say next.

"I'm at a stopping point," I say. "I can pull out the metal and let it cool and come back later. It'll keep."

"Good, come with me, then." Ruvan holds out his hand.

"Wait, where are you going?" Callos jumps from his seat as Ruvan is already pulling me from the smithy.

I leave out all my tools where I left them. Another thing Mother would be aghast at if she saw. The little bit of rebellion brings a smirk to my face. *This is my smithy now, no one will dare interfere*, I think, *I can do with it as I please.*

"Where are we going?" I ask as we ascend the hallway past the others' rooms.

"The museum. It'll explain more about how we know Solos couldn't have been working with a human."

"Museum?" I sound out. The word is new and strange in my mouth.

"Yes, it's out in the city, and since we can't mist step on castle grounds, we have to go to the receiving hall."

This is a greater excursion than I thought if he's talking about mist stepping.

"The museum?" Callos catches up. "Do you think that's wise?"

I don't know what this "museum" is, but given Ruvan's current state, I assumed it was something that I didn't need to be too worried about. But now I'm wondering if it's dangerous.

Callos is of the same mind. "We haven't cleared out that section of the city in months."

"It's early morning, we'll be back well before the sun sets," Ruvan says. "Not to mention, last time we went, it was mostly empty."

"Where are we going?" Winny is up.

"Great, now it's a party." Callos takes off his glasses and frustratedly wipes them on his shirt. I can't help but notice how he makes it a point not to look at Winny. Perhaps removing his glasses was the excuse not to.

"I like parties." Winny stops at the bottom of the stairs.

"Get your daggers, Winny. We're headed into the city."

"Ooh! I'll get Lavenzia, she'll—"

"The last time Lavenzia escorted me to the museum she broke a sculpture when she thought it was a Succumbed," Callos says deadpan.

"You're right...let's leave the brutes behind." Winny laughs and rushes off.

They are preparing for battle against the Succumbed and wish to protect these, no doubt magic, sculptures in the process. "Should I get a sickle?"

"It can't hurt," Ruvan says. "Put on your armor, too."

We ready ourselves for battle with a brief stop in the armory. Then, Ruvan leads us up the stairs and back through the door that connects with the chapel. As we cross through the cavernous room, I get another glimpse of the statue of the king hovering above the altar. Holding his book and looking skyward.

"Is that King Solos?" I ask as we begin rounding up the stairs. His visage is familiar to me.

"It is," Ruvan answers. "That is the chapel where blood lore was first used."

"The book he's holding is said to be the first record of blood lore—a spellbook, humans might call it," Callos says. "It's what I hoped you might find down in the workshop, if not the curse anchor. But alas on both counts."

"The first record of blood lore is missing?"

"The first *three* are," Callos says sadly. "No one knows what happened to them, but their loss certainly stunted our ability to fight against the effects of the curse. If we'd had them..." He trails off as we reach the opening in the castle. Callos leans slightly, looking over the city. "Perhaps things might have been different."

"No point in dwelling on the past." Winny hops onto the buttress I walked across on my first day here, strolling like it's nothing. Callos follows her into the blustery cold with a sigh.

I stare at the gap, gathering my courage.

Ruvan extends a hand. "Would you like me to take you across?"

I look up at him, unaware of just when he came so close.

"Quinn told me of your first trip... It might be safest." He gives a weary smile. "I don't want to have to jump after you a second time."

The memory of him leaping after me in the old castle returns. The safety of his arms. The deafening sound of his plate clanging against the hard floor, the wind knocked from him as he shielded me from the brunt of the impact.

"I don't want the others to think I'm weak."

"Knowing when to accept help is a sign of strength, not weakness."

They already know I'm not a hunter. What would it hurt? "It won't exhaust you too much?"

"Careful, Floriane." His voice is low and thick. "You'll make me think you actually care for a vampire, speaking like that."

"I thought it was vamp*ir*?" I arch my eyebrows, not willing to be caught off guard.

He chuckles. "You, my bloodsworn, may call me whatever you please. May I?"

I can only manage a nod. Ruvan leans forward and scoops me into his arms. My arms wrap around his neck on instinct and I hold him tightly for support. Our eyes meet. My breath hitches. I'm drawn to his lips constantly now. But the sun shines light on my better sense.

I can't kiss him in front of them. I can barely handle my own judgment. The judgment of others would be too much.

His eyes trail down my face, landing on my mouth, then dropping to my neck. Ruvan's muscles tense slightly. His strength ripples around me. My thoughts wander and I imagine him carrying me back to our chambers. In my fantasy, we make it as far as the chapel. For the vampir gods to see, he lays me on the stone, velvet coat beneath me. He kisses down my neck, slowly, sensually, ripping through my shirt with forceful and controlled movements. Then he—

"We should get going," I force myself to say as my cheeks grow hot. "They're almost across." Somehow time seems to have slowed from the moment he scooped me up until now. What was only a minute, seconds perhaps, felt like a small eternity he and I shared.

"We should," he agrees, sounding somewhat…forlorn? Before I can linger on it, Ruvan leaps onto the beam. I tighten my grip slightly. He chuckles and the sound is inside of me as much as I hear it. "Don't you trust me?"

"Obviously I do. But I don't like how helpless I feel like this." The ground is very far away, and while his steps are confident, it's hard not feeling the snow or ice, not knowing if I am one second from plummeting.

"Shall I put you down?"

"Don't you dare." I glare up at him.

He smirks, but keeps his focus ahead. The expression slowly fades when we're about halfway across. "I must apologize for making you do this on your own the first time."

"You thought I was a hunter."

"Even if you were a hunter, this was too risky for a human."

"It was. But I'm fine. All's well that ends well."

"All's well that ends well," he repeats. "I like that expression."

"Haven't you heard it before?" I ask. He shakes his head. "It's a fairly common one."

"In your world, perhaps."

I hum. "I wonder just how much there is we don't know about each other's worlds, still."

"A good many, wonderful things, I think." He smiles slightly.

Our conversation is cut short by our arrival at the far end, where Winny and Callos are waiting. Ruvan puts me down gently and we head inside. We roam back through the hallways and rooms, back up to the first hall I arrived at. The sword I brandished against Ruvan is still on the floor, discarded. I can't help but smile at it now.

"We'll go first and scout it out. Take the attention of any Succumbed," Winny says, walking toward the far end of the room. I notice a small circle of stones I hadn't before. She stands in the center and disappears with a smoky cloud.

"That's the opening in the castle's barriers?" I surmise.

"It is," Ruvan affirms as Callos steps away. "Are you ready?" Ruvan extends a hand to me.

"I am." My fingers slide against his and he guides me to the circle.

In a moment, I breathe shadow and darkness, bracing myself for whatever this mysterious "museum" holds.

twenty-eight

I STAND IN A CITY OF STONE AND ICE. Frost lines doorways and sills; ancient stalagmites hold fast to balconies, making idle threats with their dangerously sharp points. City buildings I saw from the castle are more massive than I could've imagined. They tower over me, several stories tall. The fortress in Hunter's Hamlet is only four stories at its tallest point and for all my life I thought it was the highest building that could be made.

Turning, I take it all in. The silence. The snowfall glittering in the sunlight, dancing on my lashes and swirling in my clouded breaths.

"Welcome to the city proper. Tempost, the cradle of the vampir." Ruvan releases my hand.

"It's…" The shining spires, the glistening cobblestones, the ironwork that scrolls down the building's sides…the beauty of it steals my breath.

"It's not much, not now. But before—"

"It's stunning." I find my voice again.

Ruvan's surprised silence relaxes into an easy smile. He seems lighter outside the castle, stands a little taller. "I'm glad you like it."

"What was it like before the long night?" I ask.

Ruvan's gaze grows soft and distant. He stares down the silent streets. "The truth is, not even I really know."

"You don't?" I glance over my shoulder, making sure Winny and Callos aren't nearby, before I lightly touch his elbow.

"No…I was born after the curse was laid. Even as a boy, I only saw a shade of Tempost's former glory. People were already becoming Succumbed, killing each other to survive. But in the city's heyday, it was a place of splendor." His words are full of yearning, of nostalgia for something he's never even known. "The elders would say that things were quiet during the month, but the festivals around the full moon would pack the streets with people of all shapes. They would—"

"It looks all clear." Winny jogs over from a large, nearby building, interrupting Ruvan's musings unbeknown to her; Callos strolls behind. I quickly drop my hand, hoping they didn't notice.

"That's good." Ruvan smooths his palm over the buttons of his coat. I've never been so enthralled with iron buttons before. But the way they slip underneath his long, elegant fingers before popping free is entrancing. It almost makes me lick my lips. It makes me want to slowly drag my tongue across the tips of my teeth. Feeling if I have—

My mind gutters.

Fangs.

That was what I had been thinking.

I suddenly become very focused on the architecture of the buildings, the layouts of the streets, *anything else but him.*

"Are you ready?" Callos says in a way that makes me think it's not the first time he's asked.

"Yes, of course." I settle my hand on the sickle as we approach a hulking structure ahead.

Columns line its front. Its entry is an archway so massive that a horse and cart could fit through. Overhead is a crest and engraving coated with thick frost and snow, rendering it illegible.

"Are you all right?" Ruvan asks softly as we approach. Winny and Callos are leading the way. Winny I expect, but Callos taking the charge into battle is something I didn't think the man did.

"I'm ready." I nod swiftly, keeping my hand on the hilt of my sickle.

Ruvan gives a soft huff of what sounds like amusement. He's underestimating me again, just like he did when we first descended into the old castle. I'll show him. I'll—

My thoughts stop for a second time, my feet mirroring, halting in my tracks.

I stand in a two-story atrium. Snow falls through the cracked glass of a dome above. There's a stone desk, framed with marble, directly ahead of me. Its chair has long since been turned to dust.

But what is suspended from the dome consumes my focus. Overhead is a massive skeleton of a winged monstrosity. Fangs larger than Ventos's broadsword point toward me as if it were about to swoop down and consume me in one bite. Claws sharper than my sickle extend from four legs. It's held together and suspended by wire some smith must've spent hours making.

"What…what is this place?" I murmur, my hand relaxing at my side. As fearsome as the skeleton is, it's not about to come to life and attack me.

"A museum," Callos repeats, somewhat dumbfounded. The way he's looking at me causes the heat of embarrassment to crash down on me, competing with the chill in the air and winning.

"Well that much is obvious," I say forcefully. Too forcefully. Ruvan arches a silvery eyebrow.

"Yes, well, we're headed this way." Callos arcs around the desk, heading for a secondary atrium where statues stand sentry.

We round a side stair to a mezzanine. I'm focused on the statues the entire time. One is crowned, similar to the chapel in the castle. But two others are gracefully frozen mid-dance—a butterfly-winged fae and what looks like a human, laughing, arms wrapped around each other. Another tells the tale of a man and his mountain lion foe. A fourth is the horrific image of a vampir I imagined long before arriving in Midscape; it is a woman hunched over a limp body, stony blood dribbling down her chin in frozen rivulets.

Everything we pass has the thin sheen of frost and dust. Timelessness and immeasurable age, frozen together and suspended in eternity. I don't want to touch anything. I hardly want to breathe.

These halls feel forbidden to me. They're something unlike anything I've ever seen, ever even dared to contemplate. I'm not meant to be here. And yet, yet…

My heart is racing.

With every corner we round, every hall we descend, is a thrill.

Weeping paintings have me putting their colors back together, imagining what they might have been, could have been. Statues stare at me with silent eyes. None of it is magic, as I originally suspected, but it has all captured me—grabbed my imagination by the teeth.

I've barely scratched the surface of this wondrous place when Ruvan says, "Here we are."

We've stopped at a long, narrow corridor. There are more skeletons here, but they're not like the large monster in the entry. These are held upright by solid metal rods through their core, rather than suspended by the ceiling. Between them are statues, rough at first, but slowly becoming more refined as the hall progresses. There are paintings and tapestries coloring the walls around them.

"Over this way," Callos says, starting for one of the closest statues. He uses the side of his hand to scrape off frost and grime from a placard before it. As he does, I focus on the statue itself. It shows two men clasping hands underneath a full moon. "The first moon pact."

I read the placard. "Vampir and…lykin?"

"Our celestial brethren. The lykin's ancestors, too, found strength in the moon. But our paths diverged greatly when their leaders made a pact with the ancient spirits in the deep woods for their strength. The vampir made no such pacts and retreated into our mountains instead." Callos points to a skull on a pedestal. "See, here, vampir weren't so different from humans originally. We didn't know the blood lore, yet, so we had no reason for fangs."

I stare at the skull of the fangless vampir. Callos is right. It is almost the same as a human's. Except, even their skulls are more lovely, delicate. The bone is perfectly smooth, as though it were sculpted from a single piece of marble.

"The vampir were physically changed by the blood lore?"

"Yes, it was the only way we could survive," Ruvan says solemnly.

"Vampir were weak by nature," Callos says, moving us down the hall. There's a faded portrait of rows of beds, men and women occupying them. Attendants were frozen among the rows.

"We had our own strength," Winny objects to being called weak.

"We did. We could use the power of the turning moon to dredge up deep magics that we could use to perform wonderful feats of magic, of reading the stars, or creating great works of art," Callos agrees. "But only during that time. It made the early lords and ladies fearful of the outside world—compared to the rest of Midscape and all their magics, we were weak. So we fortified ourselves in our mountains and only welcomed others in when the moon was full."

"And then, the blood lore began," Ruvan murmurs as we come to a stop before another statue of King Solos. He wears the same crown as in the chapel—though this crown is made of stone, not iron and ruby. "With the infusion of blood magic, we were able to strengthen our people beyond just the full moon. New blood and all its power and experience was added to the vampir."

"We became faster and stronger with every addition. We could fully open our borders to trade and travel as every other kingdom had. Tempost became a bastion for art and culture and music. We read the stars and the fae sang of our abilities to see into a person's soul through their blood," Callos says proudly.

"And just look at us now..." Winny murmurs, trailing her fingers along railings and statue bases. "How far we've fallen. How short-lived it all was. How easy it was for the same magic that made us, to undo us."

Callos stares after her, forlorn. His eyes shine with a longing that makes my heart ache.

Ruvan must see it, too, because he says, "Why don't you take Winny to see the tapestries? I know how she enjoys sewing."

"Are you certain? As the archivist, it's my duty to keep record of history," Callos objects, shifting awkwardly. "There's more to discuss about King Solos and the early humans in Tempost."

"As the current lord of the vampir, I think I am well qualified to assume that responsibility." Ruvan dips his head in Winny's direction; she's inspecting what looks to be a replica of the city of Tempost in its caldera.

"Very well, shout if there's trouble," Callos says, dashing over to where Winny has wandered. They exchange a few words before disappearing together down a side hall.

"I hope you don't mind." Ruvan turns to me. "His time alone with Winny is rare. I figured it would be nice for them."

"Are Callos and Winny courting?" I'm slow on the uptake with these things. Knowing that my courtship would always be formal, brief, and mostly arranged for me by family, fortress, and town, I've never paid the ways of it any mind. Maybe I wouldn't be feeling perpetually hot and cold around Ruvan now if things had been different for me and I'd been more experienced.

"Not yet. Maybe not ever."

"Ever?"

Ruvan shrugs slightly. "Nothing is guaranteed."

"Nothing is," I agree, my fingers lacing with his. "Perhaps that's why they should."

He huffs softly, looking down as if to hide his small smile. Is that the ghost of a blush on his cheeks? "Perhaps you're right. They likely would've never met if not for the curse."

"Why so?"

"Winny was training to be a member of the castle guard. Callos had just earned his position as a head teacher in the academy."

"Academy?" Yet another unfamiliar word.

"Don't act so surprised. The vampir were among the first to record written history. We took it as our responsibility to record the present and past, as well as the futures we saw through blood magics. Our annals dated almost all the way to the formation of the Veil—the barrier that separates this world from the Beyond."

"How long ago was that?" I follow him as he approaches the miniature town Winny had just been inspecting.

"About six thousand years ago."

Six thousand years… I rest my hands on the edge of the stone table the miniature town has been built upon. I need something sturdy. *Six thousand.* It's such a long time. Longer than Hunter's Hamlet has been standing. Longer than anything I've ever known.

"I wonder if there is anything from my world that old," I whisper.

"I'm sure there is. The Natural World and Midscape were once one world of the living. Before it was given to the humans, much of the land was occupied by elf, fae, vampir, mer, lykin, and who knows what other magical monster and beast roamed the early lands that we could only dream of now—like dryads or dragons." Ruvan rounds to the opposite side of the table. He points at a tall building. I recognize it as the one Quinn had been staring at from my smithy window. "The academy is here. The museum is here. And of course you know the castle up on the mountain. My favorite place, though, in all the city is the tower of stars, over here on this ridge line. The Succumbed had overtaken it before my birth. But I saw pictures of it in books and I heard the stories of glass disks there that brought the stars right before your eyes, so close that no bit of the future could escape you."

As Ruvan speaks, he points. I follow along, drifting through the museum at his side, absorbing as much of the vampir's history as I can possibly fit between my ears. I learn more of the important things—I learn about how the vampir and lykin eventually split territories as a result of the lykin disagreeing with how the vampir approached the blood lore. The former believed that blood should only be drawn from animals, if ever, but the vampir needed blood deepened by experience to truly gain power from it. I learn of how half the city was built after the lore began, the speed and strength it afforded the vampir enabling them to build twice as sturdy, twice as fast.

I learn of important notes on history. His. Mine. *Ours*. That my home was once in the territory of the vampir. That the fortress the hunters have made their home was actually the far southwest gate of the castle and that is why the wall extends all the way to the sea, back through the Fade and toward the castle it was once a part of.

I have questions, of course. In the hamlet they say that the fortress and walls were made by the first hunter. But I don't contradict Ruvan. I don't want to do anything that would make him stop talking. His voice is delightful.

Moreover, the last time I was this curious about something was when my mother was first showing me how to make silver steel. But that was knowledge I had some inkling of. Everything Ruvan is telling me is new. I want to know it all. I've embraced him with open arms and now I want to try to also embrace the truth of our worlds as well—whatever that might be.

"What's that way?" I ask, pointing to the right as we reach the T at the end of the hall we've been strolling through.

"That way…" He hums. "I think it's armors from antiquity."

I inhale sharply. *Old. Vampir. Armor*. I have to see it.

"Would you like to see it?" Ruvan reads my mind and holds out a hand with a warm smile. My heart does a skip.

"I thought you'd never ask!" I take his hand and yank him down the hallway.

He erupts with a laughter brighter than any I've ever heard from him. It matches the shimmering gold of his eyes and flawless platinum of his hair. "Do you even know where you're going?"

"No, but I intend to find everything I can along the way!"

"I've unleashed a monster." He keeps laughing the entire way as I tug him along, taking him from room to room.

"You're wrong," I say.

"What?"

I give him a small grin over my shoulder, taking in his ethereal face. The warmth of his hand around mine. *How wrong I've been…* "We've never been monsters."

The sun is hanging low in the sky and my stomach is roaring by the time we've finished scouring every bit of the museum. Ruvan and I have ended up in a rooftop sculpture garden turned winter wonderland. The silent statues peer with blank eyes through ice so old it's turned blue.

Ruvan has gone ahead and now leans against the railing, giving me time and space until I'm finally ready to join him.

"You seem to have enjoyed yourself." He smiles, but it doesn't quite reach his eyes.

"I've never been to a place like this before. I didn't know they existed," I finally admit. I had expected him to laugh at me for the confession, but he looks confused instead. He's really going to make me spell this out. "There's nothing like this in Hunter's Hamlet. Even though we're still a functional, living town, we have no museums, no academies, no concert halls or—what did you call it? That place Tempost had long ago, the one of many cages containing curious beasts of different shapes and colors?"

"A zoo?"

"Certainly no zoos *ever* in the hamlet." I laugh softly and rest my elbows on the railing. The frosty stone is biting cold and, oddly, it feels good. The sharpness is welcome. Between the cold and the fresh air, my head feels clearer than it has in years. "If we had many different types of beasts, we'd probably eat them."

The wind becomes a third companion as it picks up, sweeping down the peaks to batter my face, as if the world itself is reaching out to cup my cheeks and whisper, *It will be all right, don't cry.*

I'm not crying, I want to reply. But don't for the lump that's suddenly appeared in my throat.

His hand rests lightly on mine. "Tell me more about the hamlet."

"Well, the master hunter is in control of everything. Underneath him is a small town council that helps manage day-to-day matters outside the fortress. They—"

"No, Floriane, tell me about the hamlet through *your* eyes. What was it like there for you?"

I meet his gaze, the lump in my throat only getting worse. I struggle for words. Croak. And loosen my vocal pipes with a bitter laugh.

"I was taken care of. I was." I'm not quite sure why I have the need to emphasize that so much. "I grew up with the love of my family… but that's the only love I ever knew. To the town I was always the forge maiden, the girl who would be married off shortly after she reached womanhood. I had all I wanted, but could never ask for more. Could never dream of it." I look out over the decaying city. "There would be noise and life of the forge, but even there I was an outsider. My hammer moved for others.

"I never had art. Music, but rarely, only on special occasions, and it was never for me to simply enjoy. I didn't have histories to read, mathematics, or an education beyond the smithy. All I've ever known is survival. My bodily needs were met while my soul starved." I have never hated my home more than in this moment. And, yet, despite it all I still love it. It's still home. "I wonder if the first hunters laid the curse out of spite," I softly wonder aloud. "After the Fade was formed, our world became so small and we were so cut off from all the wonder here. We had nothing."

Ruvan is silent for long enough that I end up looking his way. He stares beyond the horizon, brows knitted slightly.

"Or they laid the curse out of hatred for what King Solos might have done to those early humans during the discovery of blood lore.

The museum paints the creation of blood lore in rosy colors because it is our history. It helped *us*. But it glosses over the human cost of it at the time." Ruvan shakes his head. "Am I any better than them? I killed your master hunter in cold blood."

"You thought he was the curse anchor."

"I would've killed your brother if you hadn't intervened." His solemn words draw my eyes to him. The wind whispers between us but it sounds like a howling chasm. For the first time in weeks, I feel far from him. "I would've been no better than Solos, spilling human blood because I could—because in that moment I was the one with the power."

"Speaking of Solos," I begin and then pause, searching for words. I know what I must ask, and yet, am apprehensive to. Everything they've said about this king, the clipped words, the mention of humans…it doesn't bode well for what I need to know. "You brought me here under the pretense of explaining to me why Solos would never work with a human."

"I suppose I did." He hesitates. I can feel discomfort oozing from every inch of him. I can see it in how he shifts his weight, hunching his shoulders slightly.

"Tell me; I'd rather know the whole truth than the rosy one." I meet his eyes and hold his attention, removing any doubt for him that I am about to let the matter rest.

He sighs heavily and is silent for an abnormally long stretch of time. I shift my weight on the railing before my skin turns numb and blue. Finally, when Ruvan does speak, it's slow and pained. "According to Jontun's histories, the first humans that came to Tempost were a small group of travelers who arrived for the full moon festivals. They wanted to research the magic of the vampir. And they got more than they bargained for.

"Solos discovered that human blood was more potent and powerful for us than others. Perhaps because of their connection to the dryads who first made them. Perhaps from the fae rituals they were taught. A combination, likely. But they were too valuable to the vampir to simply let go after the festival. They came to us, expecting warmth and hospitality like the fae…then never saw their homes again."

"They became captives?"

Ruvan gives a slight nod. "The majority of the vampir didn't know what was happening at the time. Even Jontun's writings from the castle on Solos's actions are brief. He sheltered his people from the brunt of his crimes."

"What do those writings say?" My stomach is already churning, but I ask anyway. I have to know. I can't let the matter rest.

"The human's blood was used to uncover the blood lore and strengthen the vampir. Toward the end, a few were lost to the experimentation of strengthening the body." He hangs his head. "Those notes were only found much later...but, even if most vampir didn't know the full scope of what was happening, it doesn't excuse it. Our strength was paid for with the lives of innocents."

I stare back out over the city, letting the words sink into me. All these towering buildings and their splendor were built with the power of the blood lore fueling the vampir. Their beauty is tarnished some by an unforgiveable history.

"When did it end?" I ask.

"Just before the curse was laid. After the deaths, the remaining humans were led away by one of their own...ultimately cut off on the other side of the Fade. Solos couldn't cross with his armies to retrieve them. When he tried to send a search party over, the humans fought."

"The first hunters," I realize. That group of humans, fleeing horrors, were the founders of Hunter's Hamlet. Our history from the beginning has been steeped in blood and hatred for the vampir. "That's why you thought the curse anchor was across the Fade, and why the hunters were the ones to lay it."

"I can't say we didn't deserve the curse." His admission startles me. The curse has always been talked about as the most horrible thing to happen to the vampir. But the true history is far more complicated. "I don't expect you to forgive me for the actions of my forefathers, but I am sorry for them. And once the curse is lifted and the power of the vampir is restored in full I *will* make every attempt at amends to the people of Hunter's Hamlet."

I'm silent. The wintry air of Tempost puts my thoughts on ice. I search, deep within me, for the red-hot rage I once felt toward the vampir and find nothing. It's cooled and hardened into a firmer resolve—into the woman I'm working on becoming. Even in the face of these revelations, I still don't hate these people. The curse was laid three thousand years ago. One hundred years before Ruvan himself was even born.

Ruvan goes to move away. I grab his hand and his cheek, guiding his eyes back to mine.

"I'm going to hold you to it, you know," I say softly, firmly.

"Do you hate me?" he whispers, eyes shining.

"Hate you *again*?" I grin faintly. He huffs in amusement. It's the closest we can get to levity right now. "You weren't the one to lay the curse. I don't blame you for it and I don't blame you for wanting to save your people. This curse, justified or not when it was made, is hurting all of us now. I believe the founders of the hamlet would've wanted it to end if they'd known their own people would be harmed and forever linked to the vampir. We have to move forward."

Ruvan stares at me as if I am the source of the moon and stars. His lips part slightly, his face relaxing, and for a brief second, I think he is about to weep. But then, laughter.

"May I kiss you?" he asks. Given our actions around each other, I'm surprised he feels the need to ask. And yet, after our current discussion, I appreciate it—and him for it—all the more.

"You may."

He pulls me to him, kissing me firmly but gently and, for a brief moment, the world pauses.

There's nothing particularly sensual about the kiss. Perhaps it's the lack of lust that makes it all the sweeter. This expression of pure joy and acceptance with someone I've come to know and care for. Exploring the museum today was possibly one of the best days of my life and this man—not the vampir lord or his forefathers—was the one to give it to me.

I intend to tell him so as we lean away, but the clouds shift in the distance. A beam of sunlight strikes us, turning everything golden. It would be picturesque, if not for Ruvan's wince.

"Do you want to go inside?" I ask softly. I wonder if the sun is becoming more biting with the curse's progression on him. It's yet another reminder that he's fading from this world. Not meant for much longer with us.

"No, I want to see the sunset. I don't know how many I have left to see." It's somehow worse hearing him voice my thoughts aloud.

"Do you need my blood?" I ask.

"Not here," he murmurs, suddenly oozing discomfort. Does he not want Winny or Callos to see? They certainly are aware of us by now. "I shouldn't—I've asked too much of you, Floriane. Today truly put everything into perspective."

"Everything?" I echo.

"My history. What my forefathers did for their own sakes, ignorant or uncaring to the cost it carried. I wanted to be better than them. Even when I was a brute and took you, I vowed I wouldn't be the monster you thought I was."

"What are you talking about?"

"I had no intention of using you for your blood. My only goal was to get you to open the door."

"*Never?*" Is he honestly trying to say the thought never once crossed his mind?

"Well, perhaps if you became a problem," he confesses with a somewhat sheepish smile that's quickly abandoned. "But never like what's happened."

So much has happened in so little time. It's hard to decide what, exactly, he's primarily focused on. "What's happened" between us hardly seems bad. But this could be him needing his own space to process. Our discussion has no doubt dredged up the voices of his past, just like I had mine surface this morning.

"Sorry for not becoming a problem." I try and keep the levity. I enjoyed myself today, despite all odds, I truly did. I don't want things to turn sour at its end.

"I think you definitely did," he murmurs.

"Then it's mutual," I agree softly. *You should be trying to kill him!* a part of me still nags. *Keep your hand on his*, another voice, soft, strong, and foreign to everything I thought I was whispers from the pit of my chest. It echoes up from a previously smothered and mostly ignored place.

Footsteps crunch in the snow and ice behind us. I slowly, subtly shift my hand off his.

"Are you two about ready to head back?" Callos asks. "It's getting late."

Ruvan pushes away from the railing. I expect him to say yes, but he surprises me instead when he says, "Not just yet."

"Oh?" Winny tilts her head slightly.

"I've decided to take Floriane to the academy."

Winny and Callos exchange a look, one that holds an unspoken conversation that only they seem to be able to discern. Callos finally speaks. "I think that's a good idea."

"Me too." Winny sounds more reluctant, but her agreement seems sincere.

"You do? Both of you?" Ruvan is surprised.

"Floriane should keep learning about us. And beyond the blood lore, there's nothing more important in our history than the long night," Callos says.

"Shall we go ahead again?" Winny asks.

"I think I'd like to take Floriane alone."

"It's getting late, my lord." She looks to the setting sun.

"We'll only be a short while, back long before true nightfall." Ruvan's tone makes it clear he doesn't want to be questioned again.

Callos seems to pick up on it. He rests a hand on Winny's shoulder. "Our lord can take care of himself, however I could certainly use an escort back."

"All right," Winny relents. "Ventos keeps the academy well patrolled anyway. But if you're not back within the hour, we're all coming to look for you."

"I would expect nothing less from my loyal vassals." Ruvan smiles and holds his hand out to me. "Shall we?"

I take it, and we are whisked away into the darkness.

When the world rematerializes, we stand before what I know without doubt is the academy. Even if Ruvan hadn't pointed it out to me in the miniature of the city, I would know its architecture anywhere. From the pointed archway over the entry, to the four bell towers, it has been embossed onto the landscape of my dreams, tied to this impossible circumstance I've been woven into.

"This way." Ruvan's movements have a solemn reverence as we head inside. I try and follow his lead, not quite sure what to expect as we ascend the stairs. He halts without warning. “This place… You won’t pass a word on it to those of Hunter’s Hamlet?”

“I swear it.”

“No matter what happens?” Ruvan’s golden eyes are piercing. Intense. Probing.

“No matter what happens,” I echo with a nod. “Callos promised to destroy the information I gave him about Hunter’s Hamlet if we fail in breaking the curse. I promise the same with whatever you’re about to show me.”

The intensity melts from his face and he reaches for my hand, giving it a squeeze. The motion is familiar and reassuring. It’s friendly, but also somehow more intimate.

We trust each other, deeply and truly. When did that happen?

He leads me under the main archway.

The immediate entry of the academy is a small room. There’s a stone desk, with a symbol emblazoned on the wall behind that I’ve never seen before. I can tell it’s another blood mark, but I have no idea whose it is. We continue through the halls of the academy, heading straight back toward where the mountains are, and then descending.

At first, the hallway is well formed, but after two more rooms, and through another door, it becomes rough and misshapen. This is not a well-planned passage; its construction reeks of haste. Desperation. Inexplicable worry worms its way up my throat. I swallow hard and try to banish the sensation to mild success.

We come to a stop before an iron door. I know something is wrong from how Ruvan comes to an abrupt halt, an arm outstretched to hold me back. Protect me. He inhales deeply and his demeanor changes. His muscles are tense. The air around him seems to vibrate with power.

He’s readying himself for battle.

I grab my sickle and slowly creep alongside him. Ruvan swings the door open and I’m ready to pounce. Motion almost has me swinging but I stop at the last second.

A snarled question cuts through the silence. “What’re *you* doing here?”

twenty-nine

I SHOULD HAVE SWUNG WHEN I HAD THE CHANCE. I should have sunk my sickle right into Ventos's smart mouth. I ease out of my stance; Ruvan does as well.

"I wanted to show her the cavern," Ruvan answers, even though I'm the one Ventos is staring down.

"She has no business here."

"She does if I say so."

"I don't mind leaving," I interject. Both of their attention is on me. "Despite what you might think, Ventos, my goal isn't to make you uncomfortable."

"No, your goal is to kill us."

"I'm not trying to kill any of you." *Not anymore, at least.* Though Ventos keeps testing my resolve.

"No more." Ruvan rests a firm palm on Ventos's shoulder, giving the hulking man a shake. "She is not your enemy."

Ventos looks from Ruvan to me. "If you step out of line in here, even just a toe, I *will* kill you. I don't care if you're the bloodsworn of the current lord. I wouldn't care if you were the queen of the vampir herself. I will kill you." This isn't an idle threat. He's not trying to make me feel strong or bolster himself. This is a firm and resolute promise. Calm and assured in its deadliness.

"Vento—"

Before Ruvan can finish, Ventos has already stomped away, his form becoming hazy among the chill that curls in the air almost like frost, illuminated unnaturally by the jagged points of crystal. The vampir lord turns to me. "I'm sorry."

"For what? I don't begrudge him his skepticism."

"You don't?"

I shrug. "I had been planning on finding a way to kill you the second the oath was over."

Ruvan blinks, shock passing across his face quickly before he releases the tension with a low chuckle. "The thought crossed my mind, too."

"Good to know we had so much in common from the start."

"Ah, yes, both contemplating murder, a smart match made right there." Ruvan holds out his elbow. "If you're still willing to see, I'd like to show you my people."

I take his elbow and enter a cavern colder than death.

Everything is awash in a faint red glow. But the light is so faint that it cannot reach the cavernous ceiling overhead, nor the walls on either side. The space is so vast it seems as if it goes on for infinity. I blink, forcing my eyes to adjust, leveraging the magic Ruvan gave me to see. But even I can't see to the farthest reaches.

The glow is emitted by jagged points of what look like rubies the size of people. I nearly trip down the short stairs to the floor of the room as I realize—there *are* people. Hundreds of them.

I cross over to one of the vampir, frozen in time. It's a man with his arms folded over his chest. He's suspended just off the ground, the crystal built up slightly underneath his heels and toes. Small orchids bud up around the base of the crystal, also glowing, and emitting a faint, floral aroma. He seems peaceful, as if he's sleeping. I tilt my head this way and that, getting a better look through the jagged edges and smooth planes of the chrysalis.

Ruvan allows me my inspection and then continues to lead me through the rows of sleeping people of all shapes, sizes, and colors. I've never imagined a place of so many people. But it would take a mighty population to fill the streets above. "This is…everyone?"

"This is only a third of what we were. And these are just the people we could save. The people who could be rounded up fast enough and who could manage the blood rites to slumber through the long night." He comes to a stop before a book positioned on a pedestal at the center of the room. People are missing in rungs out from the tome—jagged crystals on the floor, no longer glowing and as dark as old blood, are the only remnants of hundreds.

"Did the magic fail at one point?" I ask.

"No, these are the ones who were awoken. The lords and ladies and their covenants who came before us." Ruvan sighs. "About every eighty to a hundred years, assuming everything goes right, the guardians and leaders are turned over. There's a new vampir lord or lady awoken and seven are woken with him or her as their assistants and sworn protectors. At the end of their life, however quickly it comes, if the curse has still not been broken, they awaken the next round." He rests a palm on the book. "The original founders planned five thousand years of lords and ladies. Who would've thought that might not be enough?"

Every jagged crystal base, dull without the magic of the vampire within to sustain it, represents a person. Someone with a dream. Someone who had a life that they left behind as they closed their eyes for the long night.

"It must be jarring," I whisper, kneeling to run my fingers over the crystal points. "To go to sleep and wake up thousands of years later."

"It's certainly not easy. It can take us months to acclimate… Callos wandered the academy for days on end when we first were restored and Lavenzia sat in the shell of her favorite bakery, silent," Ruvan says, guarded. His gaze is distant and haunted. "The guardians are little more than ghosts. And from the moment we're awoken, we know our chances of ever seeing our loved ones again are next to none."

He turns away from the pedestal and book, starting down the rows. I follow silently. I can imagine the eyes of the vampir staring at me as I pass from behind their lids. Accusatory.

Did the early hunters really do this? Even if they did…and even if Ruvan is right and King Solos treated a group of early humans as little more than animals to be experimented on and killed for our blood… those were the actions of one man. How much longer must these people wait until their dues have been paid? How much suffering should be inflicted upon them until it is enough?

Who were the real monsters thousands of years ago? Who are they now? I was once so sure of that answer and now I have no idea.

"Here," Ruvan says softly, stopping before a broken husk of dark ruby. I stand next to him. Something compels me to wrap my arm around his. Our sides are flush. I examine his face in profile as I wait for him to be ready to say whatever he clearly has locked away. "This was where I was."

"How long ago were you awoken?" I stare at the empty shell. The broken stone, dull without his magic to fuel it. This was mentioned at some point, I think, but it feels like years ago that I first arrived. I wasn't the same woman then as I am now and heard things—or didn't hear them—differently. My world was still simple.

"Only about a year ago. The last lord held on a long time to wake us just before the Blood Moon so we would be at our peak strength. Enough time to acclimate, read the records of the previous covenants, hone our skills, and shake off the dust; but not long enough that we'd languish or, worse, succumb to the curse."

I see Ruvan in yet another new way. He was born in a different time. He, all of them, grew up in a Tempost that was in the midst of its fall. They encased themselves in ruby as their world was crumbling, not knowing when, *or if*, they would ever wake up…or what they would wake up to.

"The first thing I did when I awoke…was kill the last lord." Ruvan's arm trembles slightly. He stares at nothing, no doubt looking straight back to that night a year ago. "He was succumbing to the curse but holding on because the rest of his vassals had already fallen. He had to be the one to wake us. He pushed himself to the brink to do it. And I had to be the one to kill him." Ruvan covers his face with his hand, looking away. "Yet every night, I still think of him. His dark eyes. Covered in his blood. And I—I—"

"It's all right." I tighten my grip and shift my weight from foot to foot. Without thought or hesitation, I rest my fingertips on his chin and guide his face back to mine. His hand falls away and he looks at me with those eyes of his—haunted and bright. "You did what you had to."

"I know. But it… I was the one to carve out his chest and yet mine is the one with the hole in it."

My hand drops to rest on the center of his breast. "There's no hole here," I reassure him. "Just the strong heartbeat of a good man."

His hand wraps around mine, holding me to him. Without looking around for where Ventos might be, Ruvan tilts his head down and presses his forehead against mine. His eyes dip closed and mine do as well. For a moment, we breathe together. We lean on each other and my thoughts melt away.

"Thank you," he whispers.

"For what?"

"For not being the hunter I thought you were." I can hear the smile on his lips without opening my eyes. "For giving me—all of us—a chance."

I laugh softly. "Even the strongest steel can bend…with enough patience, time, and force."

Ruvan pulls away with a small grin. The moment slowly dissipates. It's not a breaking or snapping feeling. It's not abruptly undone. But it fades. Settles. There is a new feeling between us now. Every emotion deepens the more I understand him and the more he understands me.

"We should go back." He eases away. I release him, but it's harder than it has ever been. And not as a result of some deep desire. But a quiet yearning. A want to be near. "It's getting late."

"We don't want the others to come searching," I agree. I'm ready to crawl back in bed with him and, hopefully, tomorrow morning I don't need to escape.

Ruvan scans the room, squints, and starts in a direction other than the door. Ventos stands before another encapsulated vampir. His hand rests lightly on the crystal.

"Is that a future guardian? Or lady of the vampir?" I lean in to ask Ruvan under my breath.

He slows his step. "No. She's not one of the leaders, and didn't sign up to be a guardian. She wanted to, but Ventos wouldn't let her…"

"Who is she, then?"

"His bloodsworn. His wife."

I blink. Several times.

Bloodsworn…*wife?*

thirty

WIFE?

Wife?

My mind repeats the word time and again. Are bloodsworn and wife the same in vampir society? "Ruvan—" I don't get a chance to ask.

"Ventos, we're heading back to the castle."

"Go on ahead," Ventos says.

"It's getting late and Lavenzia will grump if she has to come hunting for you while the Succumbed are more active."

Ventos sighs. "All right, all right."

He leaves his wife's side and falls in line with us as we weave through the other slumbering vampir. I try and focus on anything other than bloodsworn and wife being used in the same sentence—as possibly having the same meaning. My desperation has me asking for more personal information from Ventos than I ever have…or wanted.

"Do you visit her often?"

He side-eyes me. "What's it to you?"

"I'm just curious. Ruvan said she's your—" I choke slightly on the word and clear my throat, quickly recovering. "—wife."

Ventos glares at Ruvan, but quickly abandons the emotion with a heavy sigh. "Yes, she is. And I used to come much more. It'd been too long."

"Do you still come before you do something that could get you killed?" Ruvan asks.

"Every time." Ventos folds his arms, as if he's trying to shield himself from these personal questions.

"Do you ever think of waking her?" I've never seen Ventos this vulnerable, or tender before. I can't help but wonder what sort of woman would end up with him. For the first time, I think of him as having a part of him that could be considered soft.

"Every day. But more than I want her as a companion, I want to build a world she can return to. I want to help end this so she can wake up and help rebuild." He smiles weakly, arms falling limp at his sides. "She's a brilliant healer and one of the last. The generation of vampir that returns to the world is going to need her. She's too precious to waste on us now."

"We'll make a good world for her," I say.

He seems startled by my confidence. Ventos pauses and I do as well. He sizes me up and down. For the first time, I think I'm close to measuring up.

"See that you do, Floriane." Ventos charges ahead.

"I think that's the first time he's used my name," I murmur.

"Careful," Ruvan whispers in my ear. "Before you know it, he'll call you 'friend.'"

I mull this over the short way back to the castle. We don't mist step until we're out of the academy, so I assume that it has some kind of similar warding as the castle. The momentary silence gives me an opportunity to try and untangle my thoughts...less about Ventos and more about what Ruvan said.

Wife.

The word returns in full force to the forefront of my mind as he hoists me into his arms to carry me back across the buttress that leads to the winding stair and chapel. All I can think of is the recently wed in Hunter's Hamlet. Partners hoisting their spouses to carry them across the threshold of their home. I'm transported back to my town. Ruvan is there with me.

I'm fighting crazed laughter at the thought of the fanged vampir lord in Hunter's Hamlet, carrying me into the smithy in a compromise so that I may carry him into the home. My thoughts spiral until I'm seeing him sitting at my table across from Drew and Mother. I'm imagining domestic, nightly habits and going to bed next to him—imagining more, much more than we've done so far. Our clothes are off. The marriage is consummated.

"Is everything all right?" Ruvan asks as he sets me down. Ventos has paused at the top of the stairs.

"No," I answer point blank. Ruvan's eyes widen a fraction. "I think you and I should talk." I give Ventos a pointed glance.

He's quick on the uptake. "I'll let everyone know you're back safe." Ventos wastes no time in fleeing from the rising tension.

"What's wrong?" Ruvan has picked up on it, too.

"I'm going to ask a simple question, and I need a simple answer…" I trail off as I meet his eyes. *You don't have to ask*, a small voice whispers from the back of my mind. *You don't have to know*. Because what Ruvan says next might change everything. This fragile peace. This affection. It will be different if—if— "Are bloodsworn and wife the same thing to the vampir?"

Shock relaxes the muscles in Ruvan's face, one by one. His lips part slightly. They try to form a word and fail. I want to run, to flee from what's happening. I regret this choice I've made.

"It's complicated," he says finally. The bond between us seems to hum uncomfortably. He's dodging my question. A half-lie.

"It's not, really; it's a simple question. Yes or no?"

"The vampir existed long before the blood lore—long before becoming bloodsworn with someone was even possible…" Ruvan trails off, breaking his eyes from mine. I take a small step forward and re-summon his attention. I dip my chin slightly and muster all the intensity I can manage. Ruvan sighs before continuing. "But after the blood lore was created by King Solos, it became common to become bloodsworn in place of other ceremonies, as it is a deeper binding than any other vow."

Blood rushes through my ears, propelled by my hammering heart, and renders me deaf. My fingertips tingle; my arms have gone numb at my sides. They're heavy. My whole body has become cumbersome. My spirit wants to fly away, to leave this place, to unhear what he said.

As the words settle on me, Ruvan's expression shifts slightly as well. His eyes flash with pain that he quickly buries. His face goes blank, passive. The insurmountable wall of the vampir lord I first met returns.

"So we're…you and I are…we're married?" I finally manage.

"Believe what you will." He tries to move past me.

I catch his wrist, holding him fast. We face different directions, arms barely touching, unable to see eye-to-eye at this exact second. "What do *you* believe?"

"It doesn't matter."

"It does to me." It's the only thing that might matter.

"Floriane—"

"Stop dodging around our bond and just tell me the truth, please."

"I didn't have a choice. I went out in the night of the Blood Moon, knowing I might die, knowing that the people I cared about might die, because I thought that the curse anchor lay in the heart of the master hunter."

Davos, dead on the ground. Wide-eyed and bloody. Ruvan's words from that night echo back to me. *Tell me where it is*. Words I didn't yet understand. Drew flashes across my mind, searing pain across my chest. *He's still alive, he has to be*, I refuse to believe otherwise. But if he isn't…what will that mean for Ruvan and me? Another question surrounding us that I don't have a good answer to.

"I was foolish, going against my adviser. Callos told me the curse anchor couldn't be in a human but I didn't believe him. And then, *you…* In you I saw the only chance we had. The Blood Moon is one night, and if I was wrong and Callos was right, we needed a human. I took you because I didn't have a choice. Because"—the arm I'm holding goes limp—"every vampir is hoping, waiting, for someone to end this long night. And we're running out of time. We only have so much blood to sustain the enchantment on all my slumbering kin. Every five hundred years between Blood Moons thins our resources more and more to the point of nearly breaking."

His voice has gone ragged. Hair falls over his shadowed eyes as he hunches over. My grip slackens on him.

"I had to keep you alive. You know I did. You understand, don't you?" Ruvan says softly. "It didn't matter if keeping you alive meant making you my bloodsworn or how my people would view our bond—the lord of the vampir taking a human hunter for his bloodsworn. It didn't matter how I felt and, in that moment, Floriane, I didn't care how you felt. I'd decided that if it meant the curse would end it would all be worth it."

"But then the curse didn't end," I whisper what we both know. I push us toward the here and now. Toward what we've both been ignoring without being fully conscious of the fact. "The anchor wasn't in Davos, or in the workshop. So where—*what*—does that leave us?"

He straightens, looking back at me, eyes darting all over my face. His lips are parted again and he drags his trembling thumb lightly over mine. I wonder if he even realizes it…or if he's moving on his own. On instinct. On the needs we've been both indulging and suppressing, night after night and day after day.

"Still trying to break the curse," he whispers.

"That's not what I meant." I shake my head slowly. I hear the voices of the people of the hamlet. Their disapproving stares become too much for me. Suddenly, I'm just the forge maiden again. Carrying the weight of their expectations. "I can't… I can't be married to a vampir." My voice has gone small. "I'm the forge maiden; I'm to be wed to a man of the master hunter's choosing."

His grip slackens. His hand falls from my grasp as he studies my expression. "Even if you don't want to be?"

"It's never been my choice," I whisper. "The one dream that I would indulge, rarely, would be to dream of choosing my life and my partner. If I were to wed, I'd do it for love." Every word is harder to say than the last. "I thought I had a choice here. I was telling myself that here I could be the woman I wanted—do what I wanted. But I couldn't, could I? You took that from me as much as they did."

His eyes widen slightly. Ruvan speaks with haste. "It's not as if your kind recognize our bloodsworn. They don't even need to know."

"But *I* know." I touch the mark at the base of my throat. It's hot, as hot as this need—this frustration—that burns within me whenever I look at this exquisite sculpture of a man. "I know that I am…" I shake my head and muster the courage. My eyes meet his. "That I am your wife!"

Ruvan's expression is still utterly unreadable. He approaches one slow step at a time, closing the entirety of the space between us. I inhale sharply and all I breathe is him—the smell of the fire that crackles in his room, the moss that grows on the castle walls, old leather and wood and the spirit of this very castle itself manifests in the air around him. It's intoxicating. It's agonizing. I'm dizzy.

"If you want, you can be *nothing* to me," he whispers roughly.

"But the bloodsworn—"

"Will be nothing the moment we break the curse."

"And if we cannot break it?"

A sickle-sharp smile curls across his lips. It's bitter. Almost sinister. It's something I haven't seen from him since I first arrived in Midscape.

"If you hate being bloodsworn to me so much then you'd better fight with all your might to break it." He eases away.

"It's not that I hate—I—I—" *I just wanted a choice.*

"You don't need to placate me." His shoulder brushes mine as he walks past. I'm left standing in his wake. Stunned. Dazed.

By the time I'm able to form words again, he's long gone.

Snowfall is heavy in Tempost, stacking high on the eaves and street sides. Hundreds of people stamp it down, push it out of the way, as they bustle about. I make my way through in awe.

Hot candy bubbles in a cauldron. The night is streaked orange by sparkling sticks, carried by eager children. A woman leans over a street stall, attempting to pass out pendants with constellations into them.

"With the stars at your neck, fate is yours!" she calls.

I pause.

"You aren't honestly thinking of buying one, are you?" A man is at my side with a similar shade of brown hair as mine and familiar green eyes. "It's not real, you know."

"I know what I came here for." I pat the pouch at my hip. A few coins jingle within.

Came here for...

There's a man before me now. Different than the one at my side earlier. A man with all too familiar gold eyes and long, white hair pulled underneath his hood.

A man still unknown yet.

A man who smiles with the weight of destiny.

"Give me your hand," he says, "I have time for one more."

I kneel before him, holding out my palm. The vampir cups it with both his hands pulling it toward him. He leans down, slowly parting his lips. Fangs sink into the meat at the base of my thumb. Just enough to break the skin. When the tip of his tongue runs over my flesh, I shiver.

His eyes dart up to mine. I inhale sharply.

"You..." he whispers, "are our destiny."

It's been days and we've hardly spoken a word to each other since our—*I don't even know what to call it.* Argument? Disagreement? Intense conversation? Debate?

I drop my hammer with a heavy clang that's in perfect harmony to the frustration simmering within me. He hasn't even drunk from me during this time. I can see the hollows of his cheeks growing deeper. Shadows cling to them. I shake my head. I still can't believe that I *want* him to drink from me. But he needs his strength.

How did I get here?

The question lingers in the back of my mind. Persistent. Clear. But the answers are hazier than the dreams that try to flee from me with each dawn.

Of course I know how I got *here*, in that I know the events that led me to this particular place and time. I remember every step that was taken. Every decision that was made. But there's a disconnect in my mind somewhere between those choices and where I've ended up. How...*how* a forge maiden could end up in the vampir castle. How could *I* end up working by moonlight and sleeping by sunlight?

The only time I can escape the questions is when I'm in the smithy. Here things are still consistent. I know how metal reacts to heat. I know the sound of the hammer. My hands move on their own without the necessity of thought. I can shut off my restless mind and simply focus on creating whatever it is I please. And I'm mostly left alone... Mostly.

I turn from my work at the sound of footsteps.

Callos enters the smithy. "Sorry to interrupt."

"You're not, but it's fine." I pull the metal from the forge and begin hammering. Callos and Winny have been visiting me more since the museum. They seem to take turns.

"Are you still working on the sickle for Ventos?" he asks over the clang of my hammer.

I nod and keep my focus. There's only about thirty to forty strikes I can get in before the metal is too cool to work with. Callos waits to speak again until I have returned it to the forge.

"I saw the new needle daggers you made for Winny. She was quite delighted to have replaced what was lost in the old castle." His tone betrays nothing of his thoughts on my showing her some favoritism.

"Delighted is putting it mildly. She cracked my back in several places with her embrace." I don't think I've ever been hugged so hard. Vampir strength makes them good huggers.

"I could use a good back crack." Callos stretches.

"Then Winny is your girl." I turn back to my metal. I hadn't intended for anyone else to know I'd made her something, lest they all come calling. I'd been too restless one night to sleep. So I got to work. Having a forge perpetually at my disposal—one where Mother isn't overseeing the management of resources and timing—is turning out to be delightful. At least there's something delightful here, right now.

"That she is," Callos says softly, so soft I almost miss it. The tender note to his voice makes my heart ache in a way I pointedly ignore. But before I can, he asks, "Do you want to tell me what happened yet?"

At first I wasn't keen about his presence, but we've found a peaceful rapport. We're cordial, but not *overly* friendly. The interactions have the same air of professionalism about them as when the tanner would come to speak with Mother about new designs for the hunter's leather armor. Though, now he's pushing his luck.

"I've told you that nothing happened."

"And I do not believe that in the slightest." Callos is too smart for his own good. The way he's able to read so quickly and synthesize information is its own form of magic. He's possibly the smartest person I've ever met. But I find I much prefer when he's directing that focus toward topics other than me. "You and Ruvan are completely different around each other this past week."

"We are not." I pick up my hammer again.

"You indeed are." Callos settles into his usual chair, notes and records sprawled around him. "You hardly occupy the same space for very long. You avoid looking each other in the eye. And you barely manage a word to each other."

"And all that makes sense, because we're sworn enemies."

Callos snorts. I brandish my hammer. He rolls his eyes. "None of us have been sworn enemies since your first night here."

I huff and begin smithing again, trying to hammer out my thoughts. "Shouldn't you be focusing on the mysteries of the blood silver?"

He's been determined to learn more of its history. I suspect it's a temporary diversion from searching for the curse anchor. Given the recent failure, I can't blame him.

"Lucky for you, I'm exceptional at multitasking."

"*So* lucky." I shake my head and use the banging of my hammer to discourage any further conversation. He shouldn't care what's happening between Ruvan and me. None of them should. And, in fact, our distance should make them happier.

It should make me happier.

So why am I so miserable?

"In here again?" Winny is never long to arrive after Callos. I wonder if Winny is reading too much into his and my temporary companionship. I hope not.

Now that Ruvan has pointed out Callos and Winny's simmering relationship to me, I can't *not* see it. The way Callos looks at her from over his spectacles. The way she decides to sit a little too close to him.

"My work is in here," Callos says.

"You can take your work anywhere." Winny lays out her daggers by the whetstone. They were honed beyond the point of perfection days ago. But she keeps at them. I must bite my tongue to stop myself from scolding her whenever she loses focus to stare at Callos while he's not looking.

She's going to take off the tip of a finger if she's not careful. Though I guess it'll heal quickly if she does. Everyone must learn somehow, and if all you lose is the tip of a finger in the process then it's not too bad, all things considered.

"But I don't have the expertise of our resident forge maiden anywhere else."

"Do you know what the blood silver *does* yet?" Winny asks.

"We're still working on it." Callos runs his finger along the hilt of the dagger. "It might be faster if we had fresh blood that wasn't of the vampir." He glances my way.

I give him a slight glare, all exasperation. After the first time cutting myself with the blade, I have no interest in doing so again. I won't find Ruvan prone in bed again, halfway to succumbing to the curse. Especially not when we're hardly on speaking terms following the revelation of our marriage…

"We should know more what the blood silver does—or what they intended for it to do—before we experiment too far with it," I say.

Callos leans back in his chair, folding his arms. "Sometimes, the only way to learn magic is to take a risk and get a bit bloody."

"Speaking of getting bloody"—I leverage the opening to shift the topic—"I need both of your help."

"With what?" Winny asks.

I hoist one of the sickles I've been working on. It's far from perfect. Far from passing as a hunter's sickle. But I want to make sure my base premise is correct before I spend my remaining days honing it. The moon is growing full and time is running out.

"We're going to the old castle," I announce.

thirty-one

"THE OLD CASTLE?" they say in unison, sharing a look.

"Time to put all your hard work sharpening your daggers to good use, Winny." I start out of the smithy.

She's the first to catch up. I'm glad to see her bringing her daggers. "*Why* are we going to the old castle?"

"This isn't a sanctioned trip, the vampir lord—"

"We're not going far," I interrupt Callos. I've no interest in getting Ruvan's approval. Since he seems to have no interest in speaking to me these days, either. "We just need one Succumbed."

"For what?" Callos balks.

"I need to see if this silver will kill it. If I'm right, it won't. And that's where you'll come in," I say with a nod to Winny.

"Why do you want your silver to *not* kill the Succumbed?" she asks.

"I need something that has all the properties of a silver steel—at least to the naked eye. But not enough silver to be deadly to a vampir. When Ventos and I return to Hunter's Hamlet, he'll raise suspicion if he's not wielding a silver blade. But we can't give him an actual silver one in case they force him to cut himself on it." It won't fool my mother. But hopefully we won't run into her…as much as it hurts my heart to think.

"Smart." Callos sounds impressed.

"I have my moments," I say over my shoulder with a grin as we reach the top of the stairs.

"Moments of what?" Ruvan asks, halting me in my tracks.

I stare up at him, nearly having run into him. We're a breath apart. His expression the last time we were this close is seared on my memory. His frustration. Hurt.

If you want, you can be nothing to me.

I don't want that. I know I don't. But I haven't found the words, or the courage, to say so yet. I'm still wounded from all he didn't say, or tell me sooner. All he did, and his forefathers did, that I didn't know I needed to forgive him for—all that I find myself struggling with during quiet moments even if I seem completely fine when I'm busy. He was right, we came together so quickly and now I'm ricocheting backward, away from him, like a hammer striking an anvil directly.

Maybe I will find words for him again before I leave for the hamlet. But the fuller the moon grows, the closer I am to returning to all I've known, the more a sense of shame creeps upon me, unbidden. Unwanted. Yet undeniable.

"Moments of brilliance," Callos says, pushing past the tension as if he doesn't sense it when I know he does.

"That hardly is surprising," Ruvan murmurs, as if the compliment is hard for him to say.

"Why thank you." My shoulder brushes his arm as I step around.

"We're going to the old castle," Winny reports. I freeze, shoulders rising to my ears. I was hoping to avoid this.

"The old castle? Why?" Ruvan's footsteps pick up behind me.

"I need to test something."

He grabs my elbow. "You can't go to the old castle."

"Why not?" I whirl.

"What if something happens to you?"

"Winny and Callos are coming."

Ruvan's frown deepens. "Callos is hardly of help in a fight."

"Thank you for all your confidence, my lord," Callos says dryly.

His eyes dart to his knight. "Sorry."

"We'll only be a moment." I try and pull my arm from Ruvan's grasp. He holds firm. "Let me go."

"I'm coming with you," he insists.

"I can protect myself."

"Riane can look after herself. And, either way, I don't think you coming is a good idea, my lord." Winny comes to my aid. "You're too close to the curse. You're in no position to be fighting Succumbed. One bite from them might do you in."

"It's a risk I'm willing to take," he insists.

"For what?" I ask.

"For you." His attention rests solely on me and I swallow thickly.

"I don't want you to." I'm imagining him in bed again, withering away, but this time we can't bring him back from the brink.

Ruvan's resolute expression evaporates. His shoulders slump slightly. Without another word, he releases me and pulls away.

An urge rises within me to follow him. To hold him fiercely and reassure him that I will be all right. Maybe there's still something for us, an ember still smoldering, determined. We just need to protect that flame, however small.

I catch his hand. "Ruvan."

His eyes meet mine again, summoned by his name.

"I couldn't stand by while you gave in to the curse."

Yet again, he hears me, but he doesn't seem to understand. He withdraws. "I know. You'd have to kill me, hunter."

"That's not…" I try to say, but he's gone, retreating back to his chambers.

"Not what you meant?" Winny finishes for me with a sad smile.

"You're speaking the same language, but neither of you are hearing each other," Callos aptly observes.

"And what do I do about it?" I look between them, hoping one of them have an answer for my problem.

"Give it time," Callos says, finally. "Ruvan isn't a man to be rushed. I think you're similar in that way. You'll both be ready when the time is right."

Callos and Winny head for the giant doors that lead to the old castle, working to get them open. He's right; I'm not ready yet.

But what happens if I never am?

That question haunts me as we descend into the void of the old castle. It lingers with me as we come upon a Succumbed and my sickle does nothing to it. The silver as harmless as plain steel.

You wouldn't understand, *he'd said. The words ring through my ears. I can still see his back to me, walking away. Fists clenched with determination as he's always done since we were children whenever a task vexed him.*

I sprint through the hallways and secret passages, heart pounding in my throat. Let me be wrong, *I plead with myself. But I'm not, I know I'm not. I know him better than anyone and all the pieces have fallen into place.*

I know what he's done before I hear the screams rising to a quick crescendo and then, silenced.

Staggering, I grab the wall, clutching my shirt over my chest. Nausea fights for control of my body but I refuse to allow it. I have to see with my own eyes. Maybe, possibly, I'm wrong. I could be wrong, *I repeat it over and over until I arrive at the first workshop we established—his workshop.*

Bursting in, I come to another abrupt halt as the scent of blood assaults my nose. So much blood…so many bodies… They'd come here with me, because of me. They'd stayed because of me. I raise a hand to my mouth, keeping in a scream of my own as a pair of gold-touched eyes turn toward me.

A monster.

I run.

Every day and night, I try to sort through my feelings.

Hammer. Hammer. Hammer.

My thoughts are as relentless as my work. If I attack this problem with enough force, I can bend it to my will. I can make something useful out of it. Or the very least something I can *understand*, something I could explain when I'm inevitably confronted with Drew or Mother. Oh, old gods, how will I ever even manage to look them in the eyes after all that's happened?

I don't have an answer. For any of it. And I feel all the further from clarity as Ventos and I stand together in the receiving hall of the castle. It feels like I was just here with Ruvan, Callos, and Winny; it's hard to believe the moon is already full overhead.

At least I have *something* to show for all my struggles. Even if my mental state is worse for wear from my relentless hammering at my situation, Ventos has a new sickle on his hip—perfect in every way. No leather guards the silver of the hilt from his grasp.

"How long will you be gone?" Quinn asks.

"Only a few hours, I hope." I readjust my leather armor. It's been cleaned, but it shows signs of wear from the trials that I've been through to get to this moment.

"A few *hours*?" Ventos is startled. I can already hear the rumbling working its way up his chest that comes out as a grumble. "I don't want to risk being in the human world that long."

"I said *at most*." I give him a small glare and hold firm on my original time estimation. "I hope we can move faster than that as well. The longer I'm there, the more time there is for someone to recognize me. And if someone recognizes me, they will ask questions that I don't have good answers for." I've already begun debating what I might say if I am caught and cornered, but none of the rationales or excuses sounds good enough in my mind. At this point I'll be making up a lie on the spot and that is guaranteed to end badly. I am many things, but a good liar is not one of them.

"Be safe, both of you." It's a wish and a command from Ruvan. He truly wants us to be safe, me included. That much I'm certain of. Somehow the sincerity makes the sentiment all the worse. If he cared—cares about me, then why would he pull away as he has? If I truly care, how did I let him?

I'll talk to him when we return, I vow. I don't like how unfinished things feel. And if I'm his wife now—as hard as that still is to think—then we need to sort things between us.

But far more troubling than our still evolving relationship is how he *looks* now. Ruvan is becoming haggard and thin. As the moon has grown, he has withered. His cheeks are gaunt and eyes sunken. I know he's subsisting off of *some* blood, and perhaps the strength of the moon. I worry how much they're depleting their stores to sustain him. And that makes his determination not to touch me—to drink from me—all the more confounding. He's putting all of them at risk to not draw from me.

I know the rest of them can see his ailments. They've done more and more for him each night. His covenant works to help him as best they're able by cleaning the table from our meager dinners, or bringing books and papers to him to read rather than he going himself to collect them.

I'm the one who could help him the most, and yet he *still* refuses me. Though…I haven't exactly gone and offered. Much like the hunters and the vampir, I don't know who's at fault anymore and all I want is for the situation to be resolved.

"We'll do our best," I say to him. "Don't worry; I'll be sure to keep Ventos safe," I add with a touch of arrogance, attempting to inject the slightest bit of levity into this heavy moment. I surprise myself in how successful I am. The rest of them chuckle at Ventos's shift in expression.

"We'll see who looks after who." Ventos huffs. "Let's get this over with." He holds out his hand.

I meet Ruvan's eyes one final time, hoping to convey my thoughts. When I'm back, we'll talk. We'll fix this. But I still don't have the courage to say those words. So, instead, I take Ventos's hand and hold my breath as we make our way back to the hamlet.

Shadow. Sharp on the lungs. Harsh on the eyes.

I gulp in salty sea air as we're paused on a rock. Ventos doesn't wait for me to catch my breath. I don't ask him to. I won't slow us down.

Darkness collapses on us once more with a *pop*.

We stand in a glade of night. Living shadow curls around us, taking the shapes of ghostly trees and plumage of the same shade. At our right is a large slab, overgrown with ivy and moss. The foliage is so thick that it's nearly impossible to make out whatever words were once etched on it.

We move again.

And again.

And again.

Finally I rip my hand from Ventos's to place both palms on my knees. I'm doubled over, breathless. I hold up my hand. "A minute, *please*."

"Sorry," he mumbles. "I wouldn't want to jump so much but it's hard to sense anything in the Fade, which makes it nearly impossible to catch my bearings."

"It's all right. I know you're doing your best, but it's hard on my body."

"I can imagine." Ventos looks warily out into the darkness. "We should keep moving though. I don't like this place. It reeks of elf magic."

"Was it this hard to get through on the night of the Blood Moon?" I straighten. "Ventos?"

"No," he reluctantly admits, wiping his forearm across his brow. He's exhausted, too, and we haven't even made it yet to Hunter's Hamlet. "The Fade was thinner and our power was stronger. It almost felt like walking through, then."

"You do know where you're going, right?"

"I think so. This place is so different from that night. As though the land itself has been shuffled… But I think we're almost through." He holds out his hand. I take it and brace myself.

Every muscle and joint in my body screams. Mist stepping is utter agony. I'm being ripped apart and stitched back together, time and again. But I grit my teeth and bear it because every burst of pain is one step closer to home.

The moon is low in the sky when we finally emerge to somewhere that looks familiar. I heave a sigh of relief and collapse into the marshy earth. The squishing and squelching of the mud doesn't disturb me as it might have once. It's real. We've crossed through that world of living shadow and are now back in the realm I've always known. I gulp deep breaths of the wet air of the marshes and stand with renewed vigor.

I'm home.

thirty-two

"I CAN'T TAKE US MUCH FARTHER," VENTOS SAYS, AS OUT OF BREATH AS I AM. "I can only mist step to somewhere I've been before—or I can see—and this is my limit."

"This is fine." I look to the moon to be my guide. "I know the approximate way from here."

I lead Ventos through the marshes, heading south, southeast, until we come across the main road that snakes through the swamp. We move faster after that. Even though the road is slowly being reclaimed by nature, it offers sure footing.

Both of us are silent. The hunters will be out tonight, looking for Succumbed. I know if we run into a hunter, Ventos will be forced to kill them; no amount of pleading would prevent it. The hunter will have seen a vampir with a human and they couldn't be allowed to live. So the only alternative is to avoid any confrontation at all costs. Luckily, most of the hunters patrol the deeper marshes. Succumbed tend not to walk on the main road, so we're left alone.

I didn't realize just how much power I had gained from the bloodsworn—and no doubt also from consuming Ruvan's blood as well—until I was back in the Natural World. In Midscape I'm weak compared to the vampir. But here I can see in the darkness and not slip once on slick stone; my movements are easy and confident. I'm fairly certain that I can even smell the hunters out in the swamps and know when to slow or speed up my pace.

The small hairs on the back of my neck stand on end as we

pass the ruins Ruvan and I fought in. I can still smell the blood that was spilled there.

I pause.

"We need to keep going," Ventos whispers.

"I know." The dream I had on the first night in the vampir castle returns to me along with a dull ache in the back of my mind. I see the outline of the white-haired figure in the ruins, even though he's not actually there.

"Floriane."

"I know," I repeat and start forward again.

About three hours before dawn, the great archway is visible in the distance.

"That's it?" He hums his question, staring across the salted earth to the fields that are dotted with farmers' homes. Those are the brave few who put their lives on the line by living closest to the marshes to grow food and keep livestock for the whole town. His eyes settle on the slow rise that ends with the wall that envelops the town proper and the silhouette of the moonlight-washed fortress.

"Yes. Home."

"I never made it this far on the night of the Blood Moon," he admits. "I've spent the past year wondering just what the home of the people who've turned our lives into an eternal nightmare looked like."

"Is it everything you imagined?" I ask dryly.

"Not in the slightest," he admits. Ventos rubs the back of his neck. "It's almost as pathetic as Tempost is these days."

I should take offense, but I laugh softly. "I don't disagree. We're both living sad half lives in constant fear of the other…and for what? It's part of the reason why I'm so convinced the curse needs to end. No matter who started it, or how justified they were or weren't, it's not helping anyone, anymore." I scan the farmhouses for signs of life as we speak. We must make it past the salted earth quickly, so someone doesn't see us, since Ventos can't mist step across.

"The bloody curse never helped anyone to begin with," he mumbles. I still feel like I don't have enough information about those early days of the curse to agree or disagree. Even though Ruvan has told me some of the horrors Solos committed, something still isn't sitting right with me. There are too many gaps in the history Jontun recorded when I begin to think about it too closely.

"The best thing we can do is end it. And then, hopefully, both vampir and human can go about their lives. We can reclaim a world we thought was lost to us forever." A cloud slowly creeps over the moon, casting the world in shade. "We should move."

"One second." Ventos raises a small vial to his lips and drinks. His eyes are luminescent in the darkness as power flushes them. They fade, but not to their usual yellow hue. They're stony—a hard and misty gray. Ventos's flesh ripples out from the center of his face as though it has become liquid and is being blown around. His lips extend. His beard falls to the ground. His body shudders.

I watch as his bones crack and snap. His muscles melt away, deflating to become lean and thin. Wispy strands of dark brown hair grow from his bald scalp. The groaning of tendons stretching and tightening and the popping of joints fades. Ventos is gone, and another hunter stands before me in his place. Even his clothes were transformed into leather armor.

A shudder rips through me, creeping horror chasing its heels. This was what the Succumbed did with my father's blood. The vampir had enough sense and wit—no, just instinct—to steal his shape and face. It feasted from his body and then hunched over him and performed this grotesque ritual to steal his skin, leaving his body a forgotten husk.

"Floriane." Ventos shakes me lightly. "What is it?" Even his voice has changed. Everything about him has been reshaped, down to his vocal cords.

"It…this…" I push him away and stagger to the wall that barricades the marshes from the salted earth and Hunter's Hamlet, upending the mostly empty contents of my stomach.

"Is it a side effect of so much mist stepping?"

I don't look at him while I speak, nails digging into the stone. One bends back. One breaks. The pain is sharp and keeps me in the present and focused. It keeps me from falling deeper into the void my father left. "No. I'm fine."

"You don't look fine."

"I said I'm fine," I snap. Ventos's currently human eyes are surprised. I sigh. This isn't his fault, but where do I begin? "My father…had his face stolen. It was a Succumbed who did it. But… I—I… Just now was the first time I've seen a vampir transform into someone else and I wondered if that was how it looked when it happened to my father. I thought about the Succumbed eating him in the marshes to try and infiltrate us. Or maybe to reclaim a part of itself that it lost."

Ventos rests a hand on my shoulder. But he doesn't pull me toward him. He doesn't demand I turn. "For whatever it's worth… The vampir don't steal faces to be wicked or deceitful. Honestly, we don't even enjoy it. I certainly don't. It's painful and uncomfortable to be squeezed into another body. If I could spend the rest of my days without ever doing it, I would be content."

I never expected Ventos to be a comfort…but he is. I glance over my shoulder. The strange face is less alarming now that I'm expecting it. I'm glad, however, that I don't recognize whatever hunter it belonged to. This would be harder if I knew the man whose blood had been taken for it.

"I'm better now," I insist to myself more than him. "We should keep going. We have to get back to Midscape tonight." The thought of how haggard Ruvan looked when we were leaving makes me want to do this within an hour. If I'm wrong, and the Hunter's Elixir fails to keep Ruvan strong, we need to start immediately planning what we can do next for him. I will not let him go off somewhere to die. As long as I draw breath, so shall he.

"You're not going to hear me arguing," Ventos says. "I hate the way this world feels; I want to leave as quickly as possible."

"How this world *feels*?"

"It's… I'm not quite sure how to put it. Callos would have a better description for it. But this world is quiet. It feels dead. The hum of magic that exists within living creatures is here, too, but it's fainter. There's not a whisper of greater power everywhere like what's in Midscape."

I try and think if I can feel a difference between this world and Midscape, reaching outward with my mind, my heart, and searching as I walk. I *can* feel a difference, but I can't be sure if it has anything to do with magic. It might feel different because this is my home.

I'm finally home.

Our steps are silent along the cobblestones of the main road. Even though we make haste, we don't sacrifice stealth for speed. By the time the moon emerges from the clouds we look like two hunters returning to the fortress early from patrol. Not that anyone sees us. The houses are shut tight for the full moon.

I wonder how much of the uneasy silence is due to the invisible scars left by the Blood Moon. People are still mourning losses, made all the harder by survivor's guilt.

The road takes us into town. Ventos pauses in the main square, looking up at the bell tower.

"It's of our make. There is no question about that," he murmurs.

I can see it, too. There's no way I could've before I went to Midscape. But now that I've spent time in Tempost, the vampir's architecture is undeniable. It's eerily similar to the bell towers of the academy. "This really was once all your land."

"The far southeast reaches," he agrees. "I swear, the Elf King that carved the Fade had no sense of geography. I hear the fae lost a lot of land in the cleaving, too."

"I wonder if humans are fighting the fae too," I murmur. The silver mines we source from are far to the north, right past where the fae lands would've once been according to the maps I saw at the museum. Perhaps that's why the silver supply stopped. I think of another town just like Hunter's Hamlet, battling fae instead of vampir. "Do fae hate silver, too?"

"Not that I know of. But Tempost was shut to the rest of the world before I was born in an effort to contain the curse so I never met a fae." Ventos shrugs. "That's a better question for Callos."

"Right. Anyway, let's keep going." But the thought of silver has me swinging wide through town. Before I know it, I'm really back.

"Where are we?" Ventos looks at me curiously, no doubt because I've inexplicably stopped in my tracks.

Home.

I stand in the spot the Succumbed stood a month ago when it turned my way, when I drank the elixir and changed my life forever. The silver bells have been taken down from the eaves over the door, and the salt is gone from the doorstep. Tied around the knocker is a black ribbon—a symbol of mourning, of death. They've been on the other doors of Hunter's Hamlet, more than I have ever seen, but this one is different.

This one steals my breath. Is that ribbon for my brother? For me? Or both of us?

But everything, save for that black ribbon, is the same as I've always known it. The curtains are pulled tight over the swirling glass of the windows. My mother's window on the second floor, right next to mine, is dark. I'm certain if I went inside, I would hear her snores.

"Floriane?" Ventos whispers.

"My family's home," I finally answer, tearing my eyes from the ribbon on the door.

"We don't have time for—"

"I know," I admit. "I'm sorry…just one thing." He grabs my wrist as I start toward the side of the house. "One thing, Ventos, I promise. That's all. *Please*."

Our eyes lock. Disapproval radiates off him. He doesn't want to allow this to happen, but he already knows he has no choice but to let me. He knows I won't leave without being allowed this; I can see it in his expression. His fingers slowly uncurl.

"A minute, no more, and no one sees."

"Don't worry, I know how to sneak around my home." I maneuver back and around the house. Set apart from all the other dense buildings of Hunter's Hamlet is the smithy. Too noisy. Too hot. Too much of a fire hazard to be placed too close to anything else. Under cover of darkness, I slip inside and head right for the hearth.

It's warm.

I cover my mouth to prevent the sigh of relief from escaping as a whimper of emotion. Mother has continued the forging. I'm not really surprised. This is what we were meant to do, what we were raised for, all we've known. The women of the Runil family hammer metal. We are the mothers of sword and shield for Hunter's Hamlet.

But the relief of knowing she carried on, even without me, staggers me for a moment.

I head back to the hidden door behind the smithy, overwhelmed with nostalgia. It feels as though I just locked this door, bidding the silver within to stay safe over the night of the Blood Moon. I'm half expecting Drew to walk in for our training as I spin the tumblers on the puzzle lock. The code hasn't changed and the lock comes undone.

I wouldn't dare to leave a written message. I don't even think I know how to write enough words to tell Mother all that's happened. But I can't leave without putting her worries to rest. I take a small bar of silver and turn it perpendicular to the others, resting it right at the top of the stack.

You must keep the silver tidy, Floriane, Mother would instruct. *It is rare. Sacred. We keep it safe. We respect it and pay honor to it at every step of our process.*

She hammered those lessons into me, time and again, until the silver was always lined up just so. But once she finds this bar so out of place, she'll know. It's a message only she can read behind a door that only I could unlock. "I'm alive, Mother," I whisper. "I'll come home as soon as I can."

I lock up and leave.

"You get what you needed?" Ventos has taken to standing just off the street under a doorway, out of the moonlight.

I nod. "Thank you."

"I won't tell Ruvan about this detour." He pushes away from the wall. "He'll worry needlessly."

"Thank you." He and I share a conspiratorial look. One that feels… respectful. Almost friendly.

We come to a stop before the great fortress. I tilt my head back, admiring its mighty silhouette. I never fully appreciated its beauty. And I never asked enough questions as to how we built such incredible structures and then lost all knowledge of it for our own homes.

Ventos asks the all-important question. "How do we get in?" The thing I've been racking my brain over since this course of action was decided.

"The fortress only has one entrance and exit." I point to the silver-plated door to the left of the heavy portcullis.

"The other side?" He's scanning the walls even as he asks. He knows just as well as I do that getting over the sheer walls that wrap in Hunter's Hamlet is next to impossible.

"While, yes, the only access to the outside world from Hunter's Hamlet is on the other side, it's even more fortified since hardly anyone ever goes in or out. Less silver, though, likely." Drew hasn't told me much about the outside. Then again, beyond wondering about the silver traders, I haven't asked. No one goes out of Hunter's Hamlet. People come in, joining the community from time to time. But they only ever have harsh words to say of the outside world—a place where there is hardly ever enough food to go around and the few lord over the many. Even locked in with the vampir, they prefer the hamlet.

I wonder if people will leave once the threat of the vampir has been ended. There are harsh places out there, certainly. Places like Tempost is now. But there also must be places of beauty—like Tempost was in its glory days. Perhaps people will be brave enough to explore, to find those hidden corners of the world. I think I would like to.

"How are we getting in, then?" Ventos asks.

"Only one way." I stand a little taller. "We're going to have to walk in."

"Won't they question us?"

"The guard changes at midnight. That's going to be our best chance to avoid too many inquiries." I glance up at the moon. "Get ready and keep your head down."

"All right, I'll follow your lead."

To my surprise, Ventos does. There's no further questioning or doubting. As a cloud passes over the moon, there's movement on the other side of the portcullis. I take our chance.

Hand on my hip and repeating everything Drew ever told me about his life, I yank open the door to the fortress. In the back of my mind, I hear the cautions of the elders of Hunter's Hamlet—of my mother.

Never try to follow your brother into the fortress, Floriane. He is a hunter now and belongs to a world you are not made for. The punishment for sneaking into the fortress, even for just a look, is death.

thirty-three

As expected, the guards who were on duty in the small passageway that leads to the inner courtyard of the fortress are leaving. They glance over their shoulders with tired, bored eyes and see two hunters, wet with marsh mist, mud up to their knees, with hung heads. One of the two night guards pauses but doesn't ask anything. He, no doubt, just wants to go to bed.

I lower my hand and rub my thumb along my blade. A red droplet falls to the ground. Ventos does the same. The light is dim enough that his blood looks identical to mine.

Not one word is exchanged.

We emerge into the dusty courtyard of the fortress. The stink of blood and sweat has soaked into the hard-packed earth. I pause, thinking of the time Drew has spent here, the hours training with Davos. Is this where he bled and fought? Or were those special sessions spent elsewhere?

As much as I want to stop and muse, to take it all in, I don't. I'm a hunter who has seen this place dozens—hundreds—of times. I follow the night shift guards into the main hall.

The room of tables and benches is more crowded than I expected for this late at night. Though Drew did mention once that many kept the hours of their prey, I had been hoping for quiet, dark halls to slink through. Some hunters sit in quiet reverence, praying to the old gods whose names have long been lost to time. Most eat and converse. Others polish their silver sickles, alone and silent. *At least they take good care of the blades*, I think.

At the far end of the hall is an altar lit by a hundred candles perched on narrow shelves, now made more from candle wax than stone. On the altar is a wooden cask, locked in a steel cage. *The elixir*. Drew said that only Davos holds the key to the cage and can administer the draught. He pours out just enough to fill the golden chalice—barely larger than a thimble—positioned under its tap.

I'm beginning to figure out how I might be able to procure a key when our plan suddenly goes sideways.

"M—Mardios?" someone stammers behind me. I glance over my shoulder. Ventos remains calm despite a hunter rushing over to him. Even though I didn't recognize the hunter whose face Ventos stole, someone else clearly did. "Mardios, it is—" He draws his sickle. "Cut yourself, fiend."

"I'm no fiend. Just a hunter who finally found his way back," Ventos answers with an exhausted sigh for emphasis. More hunters are beginning to gather. I allow Ventos to have the focus, slipping off to the side. No one pays me any mind.

"Then prove it with a slice of your hand."

"I already sliced my thumb to get in." Ventos folds his arms. "Which would you like next? Me to chop an ear up?"

"Stop stalling." The hunter thrusts forward his sickle. That silver is real. And if it nicks Ventos's chin, the ruse is up.

Ventos slices the side of his wrist against the sickle still on his hip, immediately smearing the blood away. "There. Proof enough?"

To my relief, the other hunter lowers his sickle. Luckily, the hunters don't pay attention to the shade of Ventos's blood, or notice that his wounds have already closed underneath the smear of blood. All they looked for was the initial cut. "We can never be too careful and you didn't quite sound like yourself."

"It's been a long month wandering the marshes." Ventos remembers the stories I told him earlier today, just before we left.

"How did you survive?" another hunter asks.

Ventos spins a tale of head trauma combined with a memory thicker than the fogs. He's far more clever and eloquent than I would've given him credit for. It's a huge relief. I keep half an eye on him as I slowly edge around the perimeter of the room, trying not to look too suspicious.

If he can keep the attention on himself for long enough then maybe I can get the elixir. The cage certainly isn't *that* strong, and it looks old. There must be a weak point in the forging that I can exploit. Then I'll—

"What is this commotion?"

I freeze in place. My heart is in my throat. For the second time tonight, I'm strangling a noise of raw emotion. Of pain and relief.

"Mardios made it back," the first hunter reports.

"Did he?"

I slowly turn to face the speaker. The voice is different. Deeper. Rougher. And yet I'd know it anywhere.

Standing at the base of the stairway that feeds into the hall from the upper levels is a man in full hunter's attire. He has no sickles, but walks with a cane I've only ever seen Davos hold. His eyes are sunken and ringed with shadow. But his gaze is as sharp as that of the raven perched on his shoulder.

Drew. My brother.

He has been chosen as the master hunter.

I fight sickness. Something about seeing that infernal, unnatural bird perched on his shoulder makes me want to scream at it to get away from my brother. *He is not for you*, I wish I could say, *you can't have him*.

The vampir have changed me more than I realized. Because I look at my brother being bestowed one of the highest honors of Hunter's Hamlet with resentment and horror. The vestments he wears with pride are what will make him see me as his enemy now.

Will he be obliged to hunt me for what I've done? I rub the hollow at the base of my neck where Ruvan's mark is hidden. Even if Ruvan undid the bloodsworn, do I have a place to return to?

"No one survives the Blood Moon."

"I did," Ventos insists.

"So I see. And now you must tell me how." Drew continues to speak with that unnatural lilt to his voice, one I've never heard from him before, not even in jest. It's eerily similar to how Davos always sounded. He smiles Davos's same, haunted smile. "Come, we will discuss privately."

I sink farther back behind the crowd, hoping Drew doesn't look my way. I know if I focus on him too much I risk drawing his attention. We always knew when the other was seeking us out. But I can't *not* stare.

My brother is alive. He might be the master hunter. He might resent me for all I've done and what I'm trying to do. But the feeling of him still existing on the other side of the tether that unites us wasn't a lie.

Just like I hope the similar feeling of Ruvan still drawing breath is equally true.

Drew leads Ventos to the back of the room, to a pointed doorway at the left of the altar, almost completely hidden. They disappear and the rest of the hunters go about their business. As the gathered, chattering masses begin to retreat, I make my way to one of the benches lined before the altar with the cask of elixir. I sit with my sickle on my lap, pretending to polish it.

Do I get the elixir now? I glance over my shoulder. *No, still too many.*

Time becomes hard to follow. Minutes are slipping away, falling into hours. I can feel the night thinning like a man's hairline.

Ventos still isn't back.

I look over my shoulder again. There are only three left, all in the back of the hall. Their heads are bowed in some kind of prayer. Perhaps for the hunters still out tonight. This will be the best chance I have. I should go for the elixir.

But instead, I slip through the door on the other side of the altar, readying some kind of excuse or explanation for when my brother undoubtedly recognizes me, and an excuse for why I'll need him to get me elixir. I need neither. The room is empty.

There is a rack of casks similar to the one on the altar on the other side of the wall that's now at my back. Wheat is so precious in Hunter's Hamlet that only a rare bit is saved for the brew master—to ferment for the old gods on high holidays. These casks look the same as those in the brewer's barn, but the smell is vaguely metallic. Familiar. I realize where I recognize it from and am suddenly wondering if this is how the Hunter's Elixir is made. If these casks are full of elixir, then we have what we need. But where is Ventos?

My musings are stilled as I discover a passageway in the far corner of the room. The racks have been slid to the side, revealing a doorway. I hear hushed whispers and distant wheezing. The passage smells of must and something…ripe. Almost sweet? But in a horrible way.

Rot.

Carrion rot. That's what the smell is. My stomach turns as I stand on the precipice, knowing I must descend into those depths and meet the horrors that await me.

I'm not ready. But I have no choice not to be. Ventos and Drew must be down there.

The passage becomes icier the deeper I go. The weeping on the walls turns to frost. Eventually, I end up in a room that is a duplicate to the main hall in almost every way—from its vaulted ceiling, supported by beam and buttress, to the ghostly outline of an altar at the far end. But unlike the hall above, this room is lined with even more rows of casks. There must be hundreds.

My focus is not on the fermenting elixir, however. Rather, I can't take my eyes from the altar at the far end. Candles support a latticework of heavy cobwebs rather than flames. The altar itself is carved from stone, done with such extreme skill that the ruffles of a sculpted altar cloth look like they could flutter at the faintest breeze. The stone stitching looks as if it would feel warm to the touch, like real fabric.

The fabric parts at the front of the altar for a crest I have seen before. Two diamonds are stacked on each other, the top smaller than the bottom. Arcing around them is a sickle shape. It is the same symbol as what was on the silver door in the old castle of the vampir.

That's not the only similarity to the vampir's home. A stone figure stands above the altar, much like King Solos in the chapel Ruvan and I became bloodsworn within. The man wields the weapon of the hunters—a silver sickle—in one hand, and three leather-bound tomes are balanced on his other palm. A raven's feather is pinned by a black brooch to his wide-brimmed hat. Sleek leather armor is carved to his body, a cowl lowered around his shoulders. His face is hard to see from my vantage, but I don't need to in order to identify him.

Just like in the hall above, a cask is on the center of the altar. But this one is not bound in a cage. It sits out in the open, held together by plates of iron added over what appears to have been a very long time as some are thick with patina.

As incredible as it all is, my focus narrows on the two men positioned in the center of the room. I quickly dash behind a row of casks, peeking between them. Ventos kneels before the altar, his face bloodied. Not the face he'd stolen. *His* face. The ruse is up.

"How long have you been hiding?" Ventos snarls up at Drew, who's looming over him. "You really thought you could undo the long night in a way that serves you?"

"You *will* tell me how you infiltrated my stronghold," Drew says ominously. "One way or another." He raises the cane. Its handle is a silver raven's head with a wicked-sharp beak. "I grow tired of your dodging. This is your last chance."

"I'll gladly die for a true vampir lord. Not some coward who abandoned his people for the chance of stealing a crown," Ventos wheezes. How did he become so bloodied? Drew couldn't defeat Ruvan on the night of the Blood Moon. To trounce one of the vampir lord's right-hand men without so much as a scratch…

The whistling of the silver-topped cane ripping through the air startles me from my thoughts. I leap from my hiding spot. "Drew, no!"

The cane freezes in place. He slowly turns. Our eyes meet and—my heart stops.

I don't recognize him.

That harsh expression. Those cold and distant eyes. The tilted hunch to his shoulders, weighed further down by the glare of the raven still perched there so intently that its claws have pierced the leather vestments my brother wears. Dots of blood ring its black talons.

Drew is like my father was when he returned to us on that cold morning. He has the face of a man I know, I love, my family, but it is not the man I know occupying the flesh. Drew has been taken over by something evil. Something far more sinister than even Ventos's stolen visage.

"Drew?" I say softly, hoping to see a glimmer of someone I recognize within him. I reach for my pinky ring to spin it and its absence sends a pang of longing through me. "Drew, it's me."

He slowly lowers the cane and, for a brief second, I see my brother. He blinks several times. "Flor?"

"Drew, I—" I don't get to finish.

The cane clatters to the ground as he grips his head, screaming and writhing. Drew stumbles back. Ventos rises, lunging for him.

“Don’t hurt him!” I race forward. But I’m not fast enough. Ventos reaches him before I do, but he doesn’t grab for my brother. He grabs at the raven perched on my brother’s shoulder at the same time as Drew.

“I will not…hurt…her…” Drew grinds out, ripping the bird from his shoulder. Ventos holds it with his strong hands as the bird tries to fly away.

“Let’s see if you’ll show your real self before I pop your bird brain right off,” Ventos growls. I don’t pay attention to him. My brother needs me.

I’m at Drew’s side as his knees collapse. I brace myself, allowing him to fall into me, easing him all the way onto the floor.

“Drew!” I don’t know what’s happening to him, but I didn’t come all this way, we didn’t fight and struggle for our lives, just to have him die now on me.

A flurry of feathers slaps my cheeks. Talons rip at my skin. The raven has escaped Ventos’s grasp and tries to gouge my eyes out.

Ventos slashes for the bird with his sickle, catching right where its wing meets its body. But the sickle I made him was for show. It’s too dull to cleave wing from body in a single strike and the bird can still fly.

The raven soars into the rafters, raining bloody plumage. It tilts its head back as if it’s going to speak. As though it would wake the whole fortress with one mighty caw. But instead a sharp voice strikes me right between the temples, causing my head to throb.

You will pay in blood, like the rest of your forsaken kind. I will have the throne I earned, and my vengeance for Loretta.

Its cryptic message given, the bird flies into a far corner—a vent shaft, as far as I can tell—and disappears.

thirty-four

Pay in blood. Throne. Vengeance.

Loretta.

The words echo in my mind, felt more than heard. Their sound fills me with raw hatred that bubbles up like a scream waiting to be unleashed. It fills me with a craze like the one from the elixir I drank on the night of the Blood Moon. An endless need for more. More hurt. More blood. More…

Power.

"Floriane, Floriane." Ventos shakes me. I blink several times and return to reality, retreating from the daze that infernal winged beast put me in. "We have to leave, *now*."

"What happened?" I ask, looking from Ventos to Drew. He is as still as death. My heart seizes. "What—"

"There's no time now, but we're not safe here. We have to—"

"Of course we're not safe here!" We continue interrupting each other, taking turns. "We knew that from the moment we—"

"We are not safe because there is another vampir here!" Ventos finally gets in the last word.

"What?" The world has tilted and I'm flooded with the same sensation as when I first arrived at the world of the vampir. None of this is real. It can't be.

"That bird was a vampir taking the shape of an animal."

"Vampir can do that?"

"Of course we can. We don't because we have a bit of

respect for ourselves. Stealing the face of humans is one thing, but beasts? We're not lykin." He scoffs a bit. But his expression quickly turns serious once more. "Now that it knows we're here, we have to go." Ventos thrusts out his hand.

I look between it, my brother, and the cask on the altar.

"Not yet."

"Flori—"

"We came all this way for the elixir, we're not leaving without it." Leaving my brother is like physically ripping off a limb. I can almost hear a tearing noise as I leave him on the ground and move for the altar. But his heart is strong under my fingertips, and work must be done. To the right of the cask on the altar is a rack of obsidian vials, the same as what I've seen the vampir use, and identical to what Drew gave me on the night of the Blood Moon—too close to be chance.

Sliding the opening of the vial to the side, I place it underneath the tap. A thick, inky liquid drips into the vial with large, wet *plops*. Five drops is all it takes to fill one to the brim. I hand it out to Ventos. "Here."

"We should go." He takes it despite his objection and doesn't stop me from filling a second vial.

"We need to get as much as we can." I hand the second vial to him, going for a third. I'd take the whole cask if it weren't bolted and chained down. Freeing it, at this point, would take far too long and risk the integrity of the overall cask.

The echo of a door slamming open far above rumbles through my chest. There's shouting and the stomping of many footsteps. I'm only on my third vial. Ruvan is going to need more. The elixir wore off on me so fast. He'll need much more than three to sustain himself and this is our only chance. Callos asked for some too, maybe he can make more if I take enough?

The racing of my mind is interrupted by Ventos grabbing me. The blood continues to plop onto the floor from the open tap of the cask. I shut the third vial, pocketing it.

"We're leaving."

I rip my arm from his grasp as magic ripples around him. "Not without my brother."

"What?"

"We can't go back with—"

"I'm not leaving him!" My voice echoes. I don't care who hears. If I leave Drew here, they're going to kill him. I know it. There's no precedent for what's happened and the raven has abandoned him. The hunters will assume vampir involvement at this point. "They will kill Drew in an overabundance of caution." I give sound to my thoughts. "I left him dying once. I won't do it again. I refuse. Can you move both of us?"

"You—" Ventos is cut off by light appearing. I kneel down, grab my brother, and thrust a hand up toward Ventos. He looks between it and the onslaught of hunters that spill from the stairwell.

We're gone in a blink.

The main gate of town materializes around us. I'm clutching Ventos and Drew each with a death grip. But the vampir staggers and stumbles. He coughs inky blood, resting his hands on his knees.

"Ventos?"

"The bastard." His crazed grin is stained black. "He thought those meager barriers could stop me?"

I hate to pressure him when he's so obviously struggling but… "We can't stay here. We have to keep moving."

Ventos nods and takes my hand once more. He looks toward the fog of the marshes and the world spins then collapses into shadow.

Only to re-materialize with a *pop*.

Again and again, he moves us. On the fourth time, Ventos staggers. Magic flares and shadows unfurl from him, but they dissipate on the wind. He drops to his knees, sinking into the soft earth of the marshes. Blood coats the front of his armor from his coughing and sputtering.

"Why is this happening? Is it because you're moving two people?" I rest a hand on his shoulder.

"That's hard enough…but no…the fortress had a barrier not unlike the castle's. Even poorly made…it—" He coughs up more blood. "It was enough to wound me as I forced us through."

"The vampir that has taken the form of the raven made a barrier?" I ask to clarify.

Ventos nods weakly, eyes still focused ahead, as though he's gathering the strength to move us once more. But no magic curls into existence. The air is still. I wonder if he's taking the brunt of the wounds onto himself, sparing Drew and me.

"That must have been its den. Whoever the bastard is, he had the sense to try and keep away other vampir who'd want to kill him for turning against our kind. I should have known better."

I take the vial from my pocket and stretch out my hand. "Here."

"No, that's for—"

"It won't matter to Ruvan if we die here. Take it and get us back to safety," I say firmly. Ventos searches my steely expression. "Listen, I know the hunters. They are going to canvas these marshes and the sun is almost up. Your powers are weakening as the moon sets. You won't be able to get us back to Midscape soon, and I'm afraid of what will happen if we try and stay here."

"But—"

"Your wife needs you alive. What good is making her a new world if you die here?" I thrust the vial into his chest and he stares at me, stunned. Maybe it's cruel of me to bring her up. But we all have people we're living and fighting for. "Take it."

"Half." He snatches the vial with a grumble. It's so small that Ventos must pinch it between his thumb and index finger. How daintily he raises it to his lips is juxtaposed by the exhaustion of the massive man, the black blood that has oozed down his chin. He takes a single sip and his eyes go wide.

I know that feeling. Something in me, awoken by the elixir, sustained by Ruvan, still yearns for it. But I don't give in to those urges. Not even now, when Ventos hands me back the half-empty vial. Even though part of me wants to drink from it, I close the container tightly and return it to my pocket.

Ventos stands, stronger than before. His muscles bulge, engorged. I take his hand and we continue our flight to the safety of Midscape.

The sun has just crested the horizon as we land in the receiving hall of Castle Tempost. I collapse on the ground with a heavy sigh. Ventos, of course, is no worse for wear thanks to the elixir still surging through him.

"Stay here, I'll get the others," he says. Before I can reply, he's gone, moving with vampir speed that I can barely keep up with using my human eyes.

I finally, slowly, release Drew's arm. The steady rise and fall of his chest floods me with relief. He's still unconscious, but it looks like the wound left by that wretched bird has finally stopped oozing blood.

"You're lucky you were unaware for all that," I mutter. "It's not something you would've wanted to deal with." I draw my knees to my chest, wrap my arms around them, and rest my cheek atop. "You're going to be so cross with me when you wake up and you see where I've brought you."

But he *will* wake up. I've saved him from certain death by bringing him into the halls of the vampir. It seems so backward I bite back a laugh.

"Floriane." My name on Ruvan's tongue startles me from my thoughts. He stands in the door, flanked by Quinn and Callos Much to my relief, he looks no worse for wear than when I left. Ventos is nowhere to be seen. Ruvan's expression bounces between relieved, joyful, and agitated. Unfortunately for me, it ends on the last as his eyes dart to Drew. "Have you lost all of your better senses?"

I stand. "If I had left him there the hunters would've killed him."

He storms over. "Now the withering will kill him."

"We can return him to the other side of the Fade," I say calmly.

"We're not strong enough to cross the Fade when it isn't the full moon."

"You said vampir were strong the three days *around* the full moon. We can bring him back tomorrow after the search parties have died down."

"You want to take that chance?" Ruvan arches his brows. "What if we can't cross?"

"We also have the Hunter's Elixir to help."

"An elixir that *I* need to survive." Hurt flashes through Ruvan's bright eyes. He searches my face and the insatiable urge to touch him nearly overtakes me. "An elixir you, and Ventos, risked your lives to get for me." His voice has gone softer with gratitude.

"Callos will learn how to make more." I shift my gaze. "Won't you?"

The bespectacled man looks uncomfortable with being put on the spot. "I'll certainly try."

"And you'll succeed." I shift back to look up at Ruvan looming over me. "Drew will be here one day at the absolute most. The moon will be mostly full tomorrow; we'll bring him back then." I'm not sure what Drew will be returning to…but I have twenty-four hours to figure out that solution.

Ruvan purses his lips.

"Plus, he will have useful information for us—information that might help Callos with how to make the elixir. And about the other vampir that was in the hunter's fortress."

Judging from the fact that Ruvan isn't utterly shocked at the mention of another vampir, Ventos filled him in on that discovery. The muscles in his cheeks bulge as he clenches his jaw. They must be locked up, because he can't get out a single word for a few long seconds, even though I can feel displeasure radiating off him. Displeasure I doubt is entirely aimed at me given the recent revelation of an unforeseen enemy.

"Quinn, take the hunter to the same room Floriane first resided in. Callos, go back and tell Ventos, Winny, and Lavenzia to figure out a guard rotation. Then, Callos, immediately get to work on figuring out this elixir." As Ruvan barks his orders, the men jump into action. Quinn lifts Drew as though he weighs next to nothing, even though I know my brother is quite a few stones.

The two regard me warily for the first time in weeks. I suppose I can't blame them. I've brought a hunter back—a real one. Whatever trust I was building with them has been damaged. I just hope it's not irrevocably. It won't be once I can speak to Drew and hopefully glean useful information for us all.

At the very least, my brother is alive. That's more than enough for me.

"Thank you," I say softly as the other two leave.

"You *should* be thanking me." Ruvan gathers his height. He's so painfully close, and yet he doesn't touch me. In fact, he spins away. "I've let you bring a genuinely deadly hunter here. I've given you enough deference that my men are listening to your insane orders." He runs a hand through his hair, strands falling between his fingers like platinum. Ruvan looks at me between them. It's as though he's torn between wanting to touch me, and needing to be away. "I might have just damned the fate of my people, for you."

"You didn't," I try and reassure him.

"But I could've. I could've and I did anyway." Ruvan approaches with purpose once more. "What I've done, *am doing*, with you could be the end of everything I loved."

"We have hardly done anything." I insist to myself its true.

"If we've 'hardly done anything' then how have you become my everything?"

I stagger back a step, clutching my stomach and the heat that has pooled there with the question alone. What do I say to that?

"We could stop." My voice has dropped to a whisper as well. I don't know why I'm saying this. I don't mean it.

"Neither of us want that."

"Don't we? Haven't we been trying to avoid each other since your admission of your forefathers' crimes and our marital status?"

"I was never avoiding you."

I roll my eyes. "Of course you were. And why wouldn't you? How much could you really care when you said I could be nothing to you?" It isn't until I'm speaking that I fully admit just how deeply those words cut me. If he could shut off all affection he felt for me that easily, then how real was it to begin with?

"Did you honestly believe me?" He raises his hand slowly, extending his pointer finger. He runs his knuckle down my cheek, the pad of his finger down my neck. "When have we ever been 'nothing?' From the first moment I sensed you…I had to have you. From that second on, I knew I would never be satisfied again until I knew you."

"Killed me."

"Tasted you. Spoke to you. Had you."

My lids are going heavy. His touch, simple and slow, is a force I can't ignore. All I can focus on is his mouth. Heat is bubbling up within me, making the world turn slowly. I can almost taste him on my lips as I lick them—the phantom memory of his taste tiding me over until this second.

"I still know that I should hate you for what you've had me do. I should hate you for being a distraction. I should hate you for everything you are. All those voices—the voices of everyone I knew and all who taught me—still live in me."

"And yet?" I give sound to the words left hovering after his sentiment.

"And yet…" he echoes, so faint that I wonder if I imagine it. "Yet, I find myself more ensnared by you each day. I find my upbringing easier to fight, ignore, or outright forget. I find that even being frustrated with you is a thorny bramble that only pulls me closer to you." His one arm snakes around my waist, jerking me toward him. Our bodies are completely flush. His front melts into mine. "Floriane, you are fire, and chaos, and infinite possibility. You've brought not just a heat and heartbeat to these halls but to my bones. I don't want to move forward without you at my side, so long as you will have me, so long as you want to explore *us*."

"Us?" I manage to ask. The words are slowing the world. The time between each beat of his heart, strong under my fingers, grows longer. This is what I've been wanting and missing: him. His closeness. Nearness.

"Despite all odds, despite my wants and fears and every scrap of better judgment, despite knowing that I do not deserve you after all I've done to you and your loved ones, I fear I might be falling in love with you."

Love.

How I wanted to be loved. I spent years imagining this moment—where a man swept me into his arms and claimed he wanted me. Not for the prestige of the forge maiden. Not for the clout my family brought in Hunter's Hamlet, or the safety of being surrounded by silver. But for me.

Me.

And here it is. That dream realized. In the shape of the man who's both taken and given me everything.

"What about your people?" I manage to say, thinking of where we last left things. Of the hurtful words we still need to sort through.

"The world will say I *shouldn't*. But I care less and less for what the world thinks. I choose you." He continues to stare down at me with that same intensity as before. The same that I know he's turning inward.

"What will happen to us after this is over?" I come back to that question that hangs around us like an uncomfortable chaperone.

His grip tightens as if someone has already told him to let me go. "If this curse can be broken, then we could find a way to live as any two lovers would. So long as you *want* to remain with me."

Lovers. Living. Life after the curse and the long night that I've been trapped in alongside him since my birth.

There was never an end to it outside of my wildest dreams. In my waking hours, there has only ever been sustaining and persevering despite all odds. What would I even want my life to look like on the other side?

"I fell asleep in a different time, dreaming of a future. I woke disheartened and forlorn. But the future I dared hope for is you," he murmurs, the tip of his nose touching mine. His eyes are aflame as he tries to strike me down with his gaze alone. "Tell me what you want, Floriane. I'm sorry I took the choice from you once; I never will ever again, I swear it. Say the word and I am gone, say the word and I am yours. Do you choose me?"

My heart is hammering so hard that my ribs rattle. My head aches. "I want—"

Lavenzia interrupts me as she rounds the corner, hastily announcing, "He's awake."

thirty-five

I FLY THROUGH THE HALLS, MY FEET LIGHT, MY HEART RACING NOW FOR AN ALTOGETHER DIFFERENT REASON. I hear thumping and grunting. It makes me move even faster.

"Unhand me, monster!" Drew shouts. "You will not take me again!"

There's a heavy thud. I round the door and find Drew and Quinn on the floor. Drew is fighting to gain the upper hand. Quinn is stronger, but far less trained. Drew raises his knee; I can see him about to pivot to throw Quinn.

"Drew!" I step in.

My brother freezes the moment he hears my voice. His head tips back and eyes meet mine. "Floriane… Floriane!" He moves almost as fast as a vampir, catching Quinn off guard and throwing Ruvan's manservant nearly halfway across the room with his vigor. Drew jumps to his feet, races over to me, and immediately crushes me with his embrace. "You weren't a dream! You were real."

Moisture streaks my cheek. I pry myself away from him and look on in shock. He's crying, too. My stoic, tough, fierce brother…is crying. I've never seen him cry before, not even when Father died. He followed me into that dark void of emotionless nothing and smothered any tears he might have cried there. When he emerged…he was void of anything he felt deeply enough to make him cry.

Until now.

"You're alive," he chokes out, looking me from head to toe

and back. "How? How are you—what did they do to you? Don't worry, you're safe now. I'll get you out of here." He positions himself between me and Quinn, who just rolls his eyes and sighs.

"What did we do to her?" Ruvan slides into the door frame as smoothly as his voice. "We kept her alive. Shielded her. Clothed and fed her."

"You—you're—" Drew looks between us all, searching for an answer. His confusion peaks when he sees I'm not distressed in the slightest. I rest a hand gently on his shoulder. It's smaller than I remember. He's still strong, of that there's no doubt. But he's not hammered steel as I once saw him. He's been withering away, even without being in Midscape. "I don't know what they told you, Flor, but they're—"

"Vampir," I finish for him.

Nearly at the same time, Ruvan says, "Flor?" with a touch of amusement that I determinedly ignore. I hadn't told him that nickname of mine yet.

"Vampir?" Drew repeats. "Vampire?"

"No, vampir," I correct. "That's the proper way to say it. We've had it wrong for thousands of years."

"They got to you. They're in your head like they were in mine." Drew grips me with both his hands and shakes so violently that if my head wasn't aching before, it certainly is now. "Break free! You're stronger than them!"

There's a light breeze at my back that heralds Ruvan's arrival. The vampir speed to cross such a small gap definitely wasn't necessary. But it had the effect he no doubt sought as Drew gapes up at him.

Ruvan's hands curl around my shoulders. "I know you are Floriane's brother, and that alone is the reason why you still draw breath. But I care less and less for your relationship the more you manhandle her."

There's a rough, protective edge to Ruvan's voice that almost brings a flush to my cheeks. Combined with what he said earlier about developing genuine affections... A wave of heat crashes over me, quickly passing when my brother yanks me from Ruvan, standing between him and me.

"Don't you dare touch her, vampire."

"Vampir," I correct again. "Brother, it's me. Just look at me and you shouldn't have any doubt that my mind and body are still well and truly my own." He slowly eases away from Ruvan. Still glancing between the two vampir, he finally brings his eyes to me. I can feel his probing stare. I meet it.

"There's no way…" he whispers.

"How can I prove to you it's really me?" I never imagined I'd have to prove that I wasn't under some kind of control. But I was foolish for thinking otherwise. Drew still believes the vampir are a hive mind. All mindless slaves to the vampire lord. I slowly raise my hand.

Drew mirrors the motion. Instinct, really. We've never tried to put what *this* is into words. Others have asked, but we've been hopeless at explaining. It's something we've always done. Something we always will do. Mother said she'd find us sleeping in the crib, palm to palm. As if that tether was the sole and key reminder to the other that we were still there. It's why we wore our rings.

My twin's hand is flush against mine. He closes his eyes and breathes a sigh. His shoulders relax. And when he looks at me again it's with a clarity I hadn't yet seen.

Welcome back, I want to say.

"It really is you." He eases his hand away and I do the same.

"It is."

"What…" Drew trails off with a shake of his head. Warily, he looks back at Ruvan and Quinn.

"Ruvan, Quinn, might I have a bit of time alone with my brother?" It's a demand phrased as a question. If those vampir don't want to be hit with my hammer the next time they visit me in the smithy, they're going to give me some space.

Quinn looks to Ruvan, who continues to regard Drew warily. But even the vampir lord relents to my request. "Very well. But we'll be just outside. So don't try anything," he says more to Drew than me.

With that, the two vampir depart, leaving us alone.

I cross to the bed. The sheets are still bloodstained from my recovery. The covers are thrown back, no doubt from Drew's awakening. I sit on the edge and motion for Drew to join me. He does reluctantly.

"I know, you have a lot of questions."

"Are you all right?" That's the first one that flies from his mouth and it brings a tired smile to mine.

"I am." I take both his hands.

He turns mine over. "What happened to your ring?"

"I…" I swallow thickly. "I had to use the silver. I'm so sorry—"

"It's just a ring. You can make another in your sleep." Drew shakes his head with a small smile. My stoic, steadfast brother, always focused on the bigger picture. And here I had been fretting he'd be upset. "I know if you forged with it, you really needed the protection, and I'm glad you were kept safe."

"Thank you for understanding." I don't tell him I used it for experimentation and silently vow I'll make us both new ones—better ones—as soon as I'm able. "Now, we don't have much time and I have so much to tell you and so much I need you to tell me. I'll start from the beginning and go quickly…"

I tell Drew everything—of the Succumbed making it to Hunter's Hamlet, being taken by Ruvan, and the vampir's curse. His expression darkens as I mention becoming bloodsworn. His grip tightens on mine as I detail the horrors of the curse realized in the old castle.

As hard as it is, I tell him the parts I don't want to say. I admit to sharing with the vampir some of our silver processes. I explain the new fake silver steel I've created with Callos's help deciphering records of long-ago vampir smiths.

I fill in every gap between now and the last time we saw each other. The only thing I leave out is the dagger I made with my silver ring—I don't know how he'd feel about my forging with blood magic—and the details of my relationship with Ruvan. There are some things I'm still not brave enough to push.

When I finally finish, he stares at nothing. I wait patiently, though that patience is tested when he wanders toward the window. He stands, just like I did when I first woke up in Midscape, and looks out over their world. Except, unlike me, he's been told all the secrets of this place within an hour. I've given him the information I've had weeks to process in a matter of minutes.

He rests his forearm against the glass, then his forehead. "How is it possible we've all been wrong for so long?"

"You believe me, then?" I stand, too eager to sit. But I don't move from the bed in case disappointment makes me fold like flimsy metal.

"I would *always* believe you, Flor."

"You didn't at first."

He chuckles and shakes his head. "You're right. But that was fearing your mind was not your own. Now that I know it is, I've no reason not to believe you."

"Other than it goes against everything we've been taught." I stand next to him, admiring Tempost and its frosted spires. It looks almost like the cookie house the baker would make and display in his window during Yule. The prize confection of the hamlet. Everyone always had a small piece at the end of the celebrations.

"I know you'd never lie to me and, moreover…" He trails off, straightening away from the window. Drew's eyes are distant and unrecognizable. "I have every reason to believe you now."

"Why?"

"Because that creature—that monster—was in my mind." Hatred mars my brother's features, twisting them in a way I've never seen before. It curdles my stomach a little. "The raven is no bird. And it is not a new raven with every master hunter. It is the same one, time and again, controlling the hunters for who knows how long."

I tap the windowsill, quickly tallying the pros and cons of what I know I need to ask him. Even if he believes everything I've said and knows these vampir can be trusted…it's hard to have your world turned over in an instant. I should know. Still, I must keep pushing him. We don't have much time before we need to return him to the Natural World.

"Drew, I want to hear what you have to say, but I think the vampir should listen, too."

He regards the door warily, as though they might come bursting in at any second. "Can't you just relay what I say?"

I rest my hand on his forearm. "I know how hard this is, must be. I'm sorry for everything I've thrust on you, Drew. But if I thought there was another way or a better way I would've already pursued it." His eyes meet mine and I dip my chin in what I hope is a reassuring way. I answer his unspoken question, "I trust them, I do. And they're going to know a lot more than me. We'll all benefit from you being able to tell them directly what you know; I don't want to risk forgetting a single detail."

He sighs. I know he's going to agree before he does. I know what resignation sounds like in his voice. "All right, let's have a chat with the vampi—" He catches himself. "Vampir."

I offer a small smile of encouragement. "You know, you're handling all this better than I did," I say as I start for the door.

"Like I told you, I had that man—monster in my head for weeks." He rubs his temples, eyes temporarily distant. "I know there's a lot more going on here. Just like I know that he would've had me killed by the next man he chose as a master hunter if you'd left me in the fortress. So thank you for not doing that."

My instincts were right. I'm both relieved and horrified. Our adversary is deadly and cunning in ways I know I don't yet understand. But I'm ready to. The more I know, the more clever I can be. I'm not going to lose now when everything I love is in the balance.

"Gather everyone else in the receiving hall," I declare as I open the door, much to Ruvan, Lavenzia, and Quinn's startled expressions. "We need to talk."

"About what?" Lavenzia asks.

"Time is precious; let's keep the questions to a minimum for now. You'll find out soon." I start down the passage.

Lavenzia looks to Ruvan, clearly unsure if I'm allowed to make orders like this. When he says nothing, she sweeps into a dramatic bow. "Very well, if the lady of the vampir lord commands it."

Ruvan's gaze turns harsh and cold. Lavenzia merely shoots him a smug grin as she heads back toward our stronghold. Whatever undertones were just exchanged, I don't linger on them. But…*lady of the vampir lord*, it doesn't have a bad ring to it.

Within minutes, we're all gathered in the receiving hall. Lavenzia has returned with Ventos, Callos, and Winny, and they join us at the table we've claimed. Not much has been said. Drew is intensely focused on Ruvan, no doubt because he now knows that the man sitting across from him is the one who nearly killed him, the vampir who was Drew's mark on the night of the Blood Moon, and the one who now wears mine.

"I've filled my brother, Drew, in on everything that has transpired here." I rise from my seat, resting my fingertips on the table in a pose that I imagine—hope—to be imposing and somewhat intimidating. No one says anything, which must be a good sign. “He knows about the curse and that we’re working to try and break it.”

Ventos radiates disapproval but says nothing. I’m certain that a few weeks ago he would’ve. Do I dare read into his silence as the foundation of real trust?

“I’ve gathered us all because Drew has information of his own to share. As Ventos and I discovered, there was a vampir hiding in the form of a raven. And that vampir seemed to be controlling the minds of the master hunters and thus Hunter’s Hamlet across generations, Drew most recently.”

“That’s possible?” Winny whispers. She looks to Ruvan, whose face betrays nothing, and then to Callos.

“There’s writing from Jontun’s personal records of the blood lore being used in such a way, long ago. Though it’s brief and was never published at large due to how dangerous it was deemed,” Callos admits hesitantly. “Some archivists have theorized that was how King Solos could control the initial humans kept for their blood. That he had tapped into their minds and made them his willing servants. They knew nothing beyond pleasing the vampir.”

The information is heavy and I slowly ease back into my seat. Ruvan had said that he wouldn’t blame the initial humans for resenting the vampir’s treatment so much that they would lay a curse. But I hadn’t considered it possible that the Vampir King had stripped complete autonomy from them to the point that not even their minds were their own. If that’s true, how did one escape? How did the one who led the group from the castle break the blood lore?

The more I learn, the more questions I have.

“If they were rare, and private records of Solos and Jontun, how does a rogue vampir know how to perform this feat?” Ruvan asks the question on all of our minds. His tone is rough, angry.

“Could this other vampir have been a lord?” Ventos wonders. “He knew *powerful* blood lore to disarm me. It wasn’t unlike your blood control, my lord. He might have once had access to these old tomes.”

Ruvan’s focus remains on Drew. “Tell us everything you know about the vampir that controlled you.”

Drew swallows thickly. I can tell how hard this is for him to talk about. I know as a hunter he’s sworn to keep his ways a secret from all who would seek them. But that was before we both knew the hunters have long been a front for a vampir, seeking…

Vengeance. Blood. Loretta.

"When Davos was killed, the bird took flight," Drew begins finally. His eyes drift to Ruvan. "We fought." Ruvan shifts slightly in his seat next to me but says nothing. "Everything went hazy, blurry. I was fading in and out of consciousness… I could feel my life slipping away. But then the bird came to me and it *spoke*. I thought I was hallucinating from blood loss. But it asked if I wished to live, and of course I told it yes. It said the price would be my blood."

"A bloodsworn?" I direct the question at Ruvan and Callos.

Callos considers this and asks Drew, "Do you have a mark somewhere on your body? One like this?" Callos grabs Winny's hand and holds up her arm, pulling down her sleeve to expose Ruvan's mark on her body.

"No, I don't think so." Drew shakes his head. "Not that I've found."

Ruvan hums. "A bloodsworn would leave a mark that could be seen and questioned. It would make sense for this vampir to not arouse suspicion." He looks to me. "Plus, I told you that becoming bloodsworn doesn't grant any kind of control over the other. This is blood lore, no doubt, but not a sworn oath."

"It didn't matter what it was to me in that moment," Drew continues. "I told the creature to take my blood. I had promised it to my family, to the hunters, had spilled it in the marshes—it had long since stopped being my own, anyway. I had to keep living to serve."

The urge to touch my brother is overwhelming. I think of all his smiles. The joy he'd project from being a hunter and serving Hunter's Hamlet. All a lie. All a farce. He'd been living for everyone but himself.

And I never saw it.

Me—the one who's supposed to know him better than anyone, who should know what he's thinking with a mere glance. I didn't see past his front. Maybe I didn't want to. Maybe I couldn't. No wonder he never gave up on those childhood dreams of escaping the hamlet. He was still dreaming them.

The idea shakes me to my core, rattling a cornerstone of my world much more important than the hunters themselves ever were.

"Then, the raven drank from my wounds. I felt its beak pierce my flesh. Its talons sank into me, and I drifted away, lost and trapped within my own body." Drew rests his head in his hands, staring at the grains of the table. No, looking past them, back to that horrific place he describes. "I would see the world and could feel myself moving within it. When I looked in a mirror, I would see my own eyes. But I would not see the bird on my shoulder. Hovering behind me was a man."

"Mirrors show the truth in all things; even the most powerful blood magic can't obscure it." It now occurs to me why the vampir covered all their mirrors. I can't imagine the pain it would be to know you were cursed but only ever see yourself as you once were. "Describe this man," Ruvan commands.

"He had bulging veins and paper-thin skin. The whites of his eyes had turned black. His hair was a mottled brown and his protruding fangs were gnarled. He looked like Death itself."

"It sounds like the curse," I say.

"It does." Callos taps his fingers. "A vampir would be afflicted by it, just as we are, even in the Natural World…but perhaps he's been able to subsist off human blood and whatever other strength he can derive from this blood lore he's woven. That's how he's made it for so long outside of stasis."

"What did he have you do?" Ruvan remains focused on Drew.

"Normal things for the master hunter. Or, I thought them normal. Tasks Davos always performed. But I suppose it would all seem normal…that bird was in his brain, too. That vampire—vampir—*is* the master hunter."

"When you say this man was in your brain…" Winny leaves her question hanging.

"He commanded me. He had control of my body. It was as if my mind had been removed entirely. And if I tried to break too close to the surface he would push me back. He would tell me that my sacrifice was for the greater good. That I had failed in killing the lord of the vampires but I could still serve the hunters with my submission and begin our preparations for the next Blood Moon."

"Why would a vampir be trying to kill the lord of the vampir?" I sweep my gaze across the table. None of them seem to want to answer. Their silence and stewing anxiousness only further spurs me. My mind begins to follow the logical progression of what's laid before me.

"He had mentioned a throne... What if he's trying to take power for himself?"

"To be the lord of a crumbling castle and a cursed, slumbering people. Truly something to kill for," Ruvan says dryly.

I purse my lips. "No...it's not that. You said a human could be given the blood rites and turned into a vampir."

"That blood lore hasn't been done since King Solos, and there's only record of one human being turned. Human blood was too valuable unturned and the cost was too high."

They're thinking like vampir, that's why they don't see it. That's how the Raven Man stayed two steps ahead. But I'm catching up.

"Unless this vampir wants to make his own kingdom." My hands are almost trembling. Though I'm not sure why. Anxiousness? Excitement stemming from the sense of figuring out this puzzle? Fear? "What if the Raven Man is the one who laid the curse?"

"What?" Lavenzia gasps.

"No, think about it," I say hastily before anyone else can object. "This vampir flees across the Fade and cements his control in Hunter's Hamlet, where he knows he has a steady supply of blood, of power, and willing servants. You had said there was record of a human group escaping after those experimentations and subsequent losses—what if this vampir is the one who helped them escape? Then he earns their trust by laying the curse, *knowing* that it will affect him, but he has a whole stockpile of resources to see himself through. He was going to let the rest of the vampir die off and then turn the people of Hunter's Hamlet into his new followers without them even realizing it.

"But he didn't account for the long night and deep slumber. So now he's been waiting, trying to hunt the vampir—knowing the lord would come to try and beat the curse. And once the lord and his covenant were dead—"

"There would be no one left to wake the next watch," Quinn whispers in horror. "The rest of the vampir would be locked in an eternal slumber and he could deal with us at his leisure."

"He wants more than just the lord of the vampir," Drew says. "He would whisper to me at night and tell me that the vampir were just the start. When he had full control of the blood lore, he would use it to rally the lykin, and then he would kill the Elf King."

“He wants to rule all of Midscape.” Ruvan scowls, folding his arms. Murder is in his eyes.

I lean forward, over the table, and tap my finger into the center. “*This* is the man who laid the curse. This is the man we’re after. We get this Raven Man and we don’t just free the vampir, but the hunters as well.”

“Flor, we’ll be in the debt of the vampir, then,” Drew murmurs in disbelief. It’s hard to imagine. But I also think it’s true, even if it’d be the last thing the hunters will want to admit.

“Enough, at least, that the hunters might be willing to agree to the ceasefire we spoke of. Because the vampir will be in our debt, as well.” I turn to Ruvan. “That’s your answer. That’s how we win. Kill the Raven Man, end the curse, and give a reason for all of us to make peace.”

thirty-six

THEY'RE ALL SILENT FOR AN ANNOYING AMOUNT OF TIME. I expected them to be as excited as I am. As full of energy, ready to go conquer our foe.

But none of them move.

Until Ventos explodes.

He bolts upright from his chair, sending it toppling. With a roar, he grabs the table edge, hoisting it with every bit of strength in those bulging muscles. Winny is halfway across the room, but Lavenzia, who's closest to Ventos, seems unsurprised and unbothered. The table falls back to the ground with a thud that seems to rattle the whole floor. I wonder, if he carries on, if we could end up plunging through the floor and back into the old castle beneath us.

"No!" Ventos roars. "No. I will not hear another word of this treachery." He thrusts a finger in my direction. "You—You were alone with him. You had an opportunity to commiserate. You're trying to make us turn on our own. To confuse us and—"

"That's quite enough." Ruvan slowly rises.

"You're not going to let her spew this nonsense on your watch, are you?" Ventos balks. So much for whatever trust we'd been building. I sigh. No, Ventos is a hothead. I knew that from the start. He'll be back to normal in no time if I give him enough time and space.

At least, I hope.

"You saw and heard what I did, Ventos," I say calmly.

He stills.

"Do you think what she's said is wrong?" Ruvan demands.

"There is no possible way one of our own would hatch a plan so nefarious." Ventos shakes his head.

"There were a hundred years of power squabbling as the curse ate away at our people," Ruvan says gravely. "Men and women who squandered precious time in pursuit of a throne. It is not so hard to believe that one of them might have turned their sights elsewhere. And Solos was not without enemies."

"You only believe her because you're bloodsworn. You told us it wouldn't change you. That you saw her not as a *true* bloodsworn but as a means to an end. A necessity and nothing more."

The words sting more than I want them to. They echo what Ventos called me long ago—a tool. There's no reason for me to hurt this much. Ruvan owes me nothing.

No, I am his wife. The word still sticks strangely in my mind. But I find myself using it more and more to reassure myself.

"I believe her because what she's saying makes the most sense." Ruvan's voice has dropped, becoming dangerously quiet. I see the shadow of the vampir lord that took me and became my bloodsworn. But now that ferocity is turned toward one of his own in my defense. It's almost unthinkable.

"Could it be another vampir who crossed the Fade and got stuck there? Maybe it's nothing nefarious and he's just been surviving?" Lavenzia asks optimistically.

"If that were the case, wouldn't he treat Ventos as a savior arrived and not torture him?" I volley back.

"Maybe he was worried after working with the humans for so long we'd see him as an enemy?" The question is weak and betrays how unsure Lavenzia herself is about the possibility.

"What about what he said?" Ventos stops his furious pacing, deciding to stay rather than storm from the room.

"What he said?" Callos asks.

"Before he escaped us, he spoke: *You will pay in blood, like the rest of your forsaken kind. I will have the throne I earned, and my vengeance for Loretta,*" Ventos repeats. I remember the words just as sharply.

"Who's Loretta?" Lavenzia wonders aloud after the words have sunk into everyone.

"Pretty name, songlike, but I've never heard it." Winny must deem Ventos calm enough, because she returns to the table.

"I've never read about any Loretta." Callos shakes his head.

"Pay in blood, pay like the rest of *your* forsaken kind," Ruvan repeats softly. Then, louder, "Why forsaken? Why 'your kind?' Does he not see himself as one of us?"

"Glad he doesn't if he's trying to kill us," Ventos declares.

"It could be one of those earlier rifts you mentioned," Callos says with a small nod toward Ruvan. "Perhaps he's the leader of one of those early factions that fought for power following, or even before King Solos's death but before order was restored in desperation. It could explain why he sees the throne as his."

"But what Drew said…he might mean the throne of the Elf King." Winny scratches her head. "All this guessing is horrible." I can't disagree with her.

"Or maybe he was once human." Drew sees the final piece to this puzzle, what I overlooked. All eyes are on him and my heart sinks. Perhaps things aren't as simple as I once thought. It's possible that Ruvan and I were both right, in our ways. "You said that humans can be transformed into vampir *and* that a group of early humans escaped Midscape to found Hunter's Hamlet shortly after the first human was. What if this man was that experimentation?"

"It would explain his appearance being slightly different from the vampir, even one afflicted with the curse." Ruvan strokes his chin thoughtfully.

"And he would be even more motivated to curse the vampir if he was the man Jontun wrote about when speaking of the experimentation." Callos stands, beginning to pace on the opposite end of the room where Ventos was previously. "A human turned. Loretta was likely a lost love, equally brutalized by the vampir. He's one of us, but doesn't see himself as such because he was forced to take those rites. He wants revenge and our kingdom as recompense. It all makes sense."

"Great, now is all this talking going to lead to stabbing?" Lavenzia folds her arms. "We know where the bastard is, why not get him?"

"Getting him back is going to be hard enough." Ventos motions to

Drew. "We can't risk launching any kind of attack until the next full moon."

"You can't honestly think that now that we know where he is, we're going to sit here peacefully," Winny protests. "A month is *forever*."

"You were asleep for three thousand years. What's a month?" Quinn rolls his eyes.

"I'm also of the opinion that we should go and get the bastard before he can find another form to take and give us the slip," Lavenzia says.

The five of them argue. Ruvan and Drew are both silent. My brother stares at his palms. Ruvan's mind is somewhere far away.

"This is what we're going to do." I slam my palm on the table. That combined with the volume and tone of my voice stuns them all to silence. "Drew, before you leave, you're going to tell Callos everything you know about how the Hunter's Elixir is made as well as anything else you can think of about this man. Callos, you're going to get some elixir brewing as quickly as possible for Ruvan. Quinn can assist. Winny, Lavenzia, Ventos, you're going to begin planning our attack in conjunction with Drew—however much time he has left with us at that point. If the elixir does give us enough power to get back, Drew will be our eyes on the Natural World's side of the Fade. After Drew leaves, we continue to plan and prepare for the attack by searching for any other history we can find on who might be the Raven Man."

"I won't be able to go back," Drew says warily. "Not now that the Raven Man knows I'm free."

"Not all the way to Hunter's Hamlet. You can stay hidden in the marshes." I reach for his hand and squeeze it. "I know what I'm asking is hard, but it's only a month." The rest of them have made their sacrifices to help end this curse. It's time I make mine. For all I want Drew to stay here with me, I know he can't. And I can't go back with him. Not yet.

"The Raven Man always seemed wary of the marshes. I should be safe." I can sense Drew's bravery is a front. It cracks a bit when he adds, "For a month, at least."

"And you—" I turn to face Ruvan but am stilled by his expression. There's a shine to his eyes, a shimmer of amusement and good spirits that I haven't seen about him in weeks. I believe that look is reserved only for me, as I've never seen him give it to anyone else.

"You're relentless," he says softly, thoughtfully. The words should be angry or agitated but he almost sounds…happy? My stomach clenches for reasons I can't quite describe.

"When she's set her sights on something, she charges at it with all the ferocity of a wild animal," Drew says with a chuckle. He's wearing a smile now too.

"I am not a wild animal," I protest, giving my brother a glare.

"No, no, that seems about right." Lavenzia smirks.

"Excuse me, I am *not* an animal," I repeat for emphasis. "I am a forge maiden. And, yes, that means I am quite accustomed to hammering at things until I get my way."

"She's always like this?" Ruvan asks Drew.

"Worse, usually."

"And to think I was lamenting I couldn't keep you around longer." I tilt my head to the side and narrow my eyes at my brother.

"You'll miss me and you know it." The jest goes soft, genuine emotion creeping in.

"Terribly," I admit. The mood sags slightly at my tone.

Ruvan clears his throat. "Well, now that we have our plan of attack, more or less, Drew, would you care to see the smithy of the vampir?"

"Depends on how much of a mess my sister has made of it."

"*Excuse me?*" I exclaim.

Ruvan stands with a laugh. "I can't tell if she makes more of a mess of the smithy or herself after a day of smithing."

"Goodbye, I'm leaving, I shall take my chances with the walkway alone," I declare, starting for the door. I never thought having Ruvan and Drew together would be dangerous for me. Dangerous to each other, but not *me*. Yet the two of them seem to be ready to tease me endlessly. How has my brother allied with my accidental husband before he even knows of the truth of the arrangement?

"Oh, has the new lady of the vampir given her orders and decreed we may now return to our business?" Lavenzia asks dramatically. I ignore her. But the words stick to me much like they did the first time she spoke them.

Lady of the vampir. Except I could never be, not really. I'm human through and through, of the soil of Hunter's Hamlet. Daughter to a hunter.

My feet slow to a stop. I hear them behind me, but it hardly registers.

Drew is right, I've never been very good at handling problems I couldn't hit with a hammer. I've always known it, and I've never had to change. But this situation I'm in can't be fixed with brute force and determination.

I am who I am. Ruvan is who he is. We're meant for different worlds. Drew's presence is fracturing whatever illusion I had been trying to craft. No amount of sheer willpower or bloodsworn oaths will ever change who we are in our hearts.

Someone bumps into me. I look over my shoulder and see Ruvan there, hovering too close. He leans down as the others pass us. Drew is talking with Lavenzia. The two seem to be arguing about how best to get him across the gap. Drew is insisting he will not be carried.

"Your thoughts are loud," Ruvan whispers.

"Oh?" What does someone say to that?

"Usually you're a quiet pulsing on the other side of my conscious—a gentle, but firm reminder of your presence. But your thoughts are pounding now."

Like my heart when he stands that close to me. "I'm relieved to see my brother. Nervous about what must be done. Excited to end the curse."

Before I can say anything else, Ruvan sweeps me into his arms. His movements are smooth, easy. He hoists me once more like I'm nothing. My hands go around his neck and in a breath, his face is terribly close to mine. I can feel his heart pounding, the blood in the veins of his throat. I'm reminded of how close we were earlier and how much we didn't say, or do. I can't stop myself from licking my lips. From wishing we might have been afforded just a bit more time alone.

"And here I thought it might have something to do with me."

I arch my eyebrows. "Why would you ever think that?"

"Because that pounding gets worse whenever I draw near." He stretches his neck slightly; our noses almost touch.

My worst fears incarnate. I have entangled myself with a man that I can seemingly hide nothing from.

"We're being left behind," I force myself to say. Just like last time, everyone else has moved ahead, and we're frozen in place.

"So we are." Ruvan moves, leaping into the open air and landing lightly on the beam that supports the other wing of the castle.

At first, I had been afraid of these heights. But now in his arms, I feel safe. Sturdy. Ruvan won't let any harm come to me and that certainty allows me to enjoy the stunning vistas—the archways and pillars of the castle in all their crumbling glory.

"This place truly must have been amazing," I murmur, mostly to myself. But the wind carries my words right into Ruvan's ears.

"It was. But even when I was born, it was long enough after King Solos's death that the castle was falling into disrepair during all the infighting and weakening of the curse. Then we went into our slumber and, when we awoke…everything had changed. It was worse than I could have ever imagined."

I can hear the sorrow in his voice. Not for the first time I try and imagine how it might have been for these vampir—my friends—when they had encased themselves in magic and woke up three thousand years later to the decrepit shell of a world they once knew. The places that were fresh and bright in their memories now in ruins.

"When the curse is broken, will the vampir rebuild or will they move on from this place?"

"We will reclaim our home and it will be better than it has ever been. Of that, I'm sure."

"I hope I can see it," I say softly.

"If it's something you desire, I will make sure of it."

Our discussion ends once we reenter the castle. The rest of the group is already down in the chapel. Drew stands before the altar, looking up at the statue.

"It looks so much like the hall underneath the fortress." Even though his words are soft, they echo in the cavernous space to be much louder.

"That fortress was also built by the king of the vampir," Callos says. "It stands to reason they would have built a hall dedicated to more advanced blood arts."

"And who would've thought it would continue to be used three thousand years after the formation of the Fade," Winny murmurs.

"Except the statue of King Solos was ripped down there and replaced with that abomination."

"The statue of the first hunter, Tersius. The statue that looks like the Raven Man," Drew says solemnly.

"It was ancient there, too," Ventos adds. "Looked as old as this one."

"So, the Raven Man really could be from the time of Solos," Winny murmurs.

Her musings bring up a question I hadn't considered earlier. "I was under the impression that vampir couldn't live forever?"

"Naturally, no. But the blood lore was designed to strengthen the vampir's body. An early goal of the experimentations was to elongate one's life. However, much like turning a human to vampir, the cost was too great," Callos says.

"Was anyone ever successful?"

"No, and it was forbidden after the test group escaped." Callos shakes his head. "It required vast amounts of blood…taken by force. And blood taken by force is the antithesis to the true lore. It's not nearly as effective and can only be used for particular rituals without intense purification."

Blood taken by force is the antithesis of the true lore… I've heard them say it before. If Solos was the founder of the blood lore, then why was Solos keeping humans as test subjects? Was he actually mind controlling them and that was his way around getting them to give their blood freely? It doesn't make sense. I stare up at the statue, willing it to come to life and tell me the secrets of the man it was modeled after.

"Let's move along. The smithy is this way," Ruvan says before I can voice my wonderings aloud, starting for the door that heads to the halls we've been occupying.

The rest of the group lingers in the main hall, beginning to set about their work. Ruvan excuses himself, remarking that he's tired, and heads upstairs. I wonder if I should follow, but Drew is waiting on me to show him the smithy and I only have until sundown with my brother.

Alone together, I guide him down to the armory. He marvels, much like I did, at the collection of antique hunter's tools. And then gazes in wonder at the forge itself.

As a child, he always seemed to resent the smithy. It was work. It was a job he never had to do. But now, his eyes glisten as he runs his fingertips over the anvil. He inspects the billows with care, as though he's going to begin work himself. Much like I did at our family's smithy, he ends up at the hearth, holding a hand over it, feeling its residual warmth with more than his palm.

There will always be the smell of hot metal, smoke, and soot on our souls. Even if his path was different. We are both of the same initial casting.

Drew's inspection comes to an end when his eyes finally land on me. "You look at home here." The words sound sad, and somewhat filled with longing.

"It's a smithy. I will always be at home near a forge." I push myself up onto one of the tables, swinging my feet.

"No, it's more than that, you're comfortable among them. You move and act like them now. You're stronger, faster. Your face is fuller and brow more relaxed." After a quick inspection of my work, Drew leans against the table opposite, arms folded. "If anything, you look more at home because you got *out* of our smithy for a bit."

"You say that like I was supposed to leave Hunter's Hamlet earlier."

"It would've been good for you."

"I didn't have a choice in being there—the hamlet or the smithy." I'm trying to figure out what my brother is hoping to achieve with this line of thought. "You know my circumstances as well as I do."

"And I wished they were different for you and me at every turn." He shakes his head. "You have to know that was one of my reasons for teaching you how to fight."

"You were teaching me so I could protect Mother and myself."

"True. But there was a part of me that hoped you would see how much more you could be. There's more to you, Floriane, than a talented blacksmith. Maybe I wanted you to have the strength to fight back against your circumstances when you were ready."

This line of thought, his words…it all feels like I've swallowed live worms. They squirm uncomfortably within me and make me feel sick. What he's saying isn't wrong. I know it's not. In fact, it's how close it is to the conclusions I ultimately drew that makes me all the more discomfited.

"That was my destiny. I couldn't change it. Until…" My voice trails off. I look to the giant maw of the forge. I can see Ruvan leaning against one of the tables by it, my quiet and steady companion while I work. "Until I finally did realize that destiny is like metal—seemingly unbendable until you put it under heat and pressure. You can forge it into the shape you want."

Drew smiles, genuine and sad. I know his sorrow. For the first time, our paths aren't perfectly aligned. We're not enemies, but we're no longer at each other's sides. Shoulder to shoulder, marching forth. We're each working toward the same thing, but now truly in our own ways.

"And I see in reshaping your destiny you've found yourself more willing to attract the eye of a suitor."

I swallow thickly. The uncomfortable sensation in my gut gets worse. "I don't have a suitor."

"Are you sure?" Drew arches his eyebrows. I manage a nod. "Does the vampir lord know that?"

"We're not—I'm not—It's not like—The bloodsworn is—" How do I explain something I've barely managed to come to terms with? No matter how much I've been able to silence the insecurities that have been engrained in me within my own mind, I'm not ready to face Drew's assessment.

"You were always an awful liar, Flor." Drew pushes away from the table. He crosses to look up at me, right in the eye. There's no escaping his disapproval.

Suddenly, I'm a girl again. "Don't tell Mother," I squeak.

Drew erupts with laughter so hard he has to step away. A scarlet flush races across my cheeks. I'm certain I'm redder than embers right now.

"Oh, Flor, out of all the things—you think I'd tell Mother?" He shakes his head. "Why would I tell her when there's nothing to say."

"Nothing to say?" I repeat softly.

"It's not as if this infatuation will go anywhere." Drew wounds me more deeply than he realizes. "Once the curse is broken, you'll come back to Hunter's Hamlet. Maybe we can go on one of those trips to the sea we always talked about as children. We'll finally be able to leave."

The writhing of my innards has stopped and now everything is painfully still. It hurts to breathe. My fingers are numb.

The coast... We'll go to the coast someday. The promises we made as children when we didn't understand the world. But they could soon be a reality. I would be free of Hunter's Hamlet and the vampir, once and for all. I could go anywhere I wanted. I should be happy. Why am I sinking deeper into the void within me?

"What is it?" He senses my displeasure.

"I thought you'd be more disappointed in me with all I've done." I can't outright lie to Drew, so I focus on a half-truth instead. I don't know why I hurt both at the idea of being something to Ruvan *and* of being nothing to Ruvan.

"I think I *should* be." He sighs and puts his hands on his hips. The movement is awkward. He was expecting the holsters of sickles when there are none. I'll be sure to fix that before he goes back to the Natural World. "I think I should feel and have opinions on a lot of things I can't seem to make heads or tails of right now. Everything is happening so quickly. Perhaps that's in your favor, Flor. I'm going along with things as they come." He shrugs. "We'll sort it out when all this is over, and the Raven Man is dead."

I wonder if he's also sinking into the abyss, allowing everything else to be carried away from him to a distant place where it won't hurt so much. I don't voice my suspicions. Some things are better left unsaid.

"I won't bite into gifted gold," I say.

"Just promise me one thing." Drew grabs my hand. "Be careful."

I nod. "I've been trying, as much as I can be."

"These vampir might be on our side for now. But they're still vampir and you are still human. When this is over, have your silver ready. Have your fun experimenting with your new freedoms here, learn all you can from them, but never forget that there may come a time where, yours or theirs, a throat will be cut."

thirty-seven

THANKFULLY, THE CONVERSATIONS DREW AND I HAVE THE REST OF THE DAY ARE ON LIGHTER, EASIER TOPICS. I never figure out a good response to what he said. How do I tell my brother he's wrong when it took me weeks to accept the vampir weren't what we thought? What will his reaction be when he finds out the truth of my connection with Ruvan?

I swear, I will never harm you. Ruvan's words linger in the back of my mind, as present as the hum of magic that reverberates from him to me through the ether between us. He meant those words, and not just because of the bloodsworn. No matter what happens, even if he and I aren't bonded forever, he will not bring harm to me.

Drew and Callos work together and that gives me time to hammer away in the smithy. Drew needs sickles and armor—things to protect himself with if the Raven Man comes after him in the marshes. The task gives me something to focus on and I pour myself into it until the moon rises and we're back in the receiving hall.

Lavenzia has offered to take Drew across the Fade. Ventos is still recovering from our last jaunt. It's just Ruvan and me to see them off.

"Travel safely," Ruvan says to them both.

"I'll do my best." Lavenzia opens the obsidian vial. It's the half-full one Ventos drank from. One full vial has been given to Callos and the other to Ruvan.

"With any luck, we might be able to come to you again." I

know it's foolish to say, or even hope, but letting go of my brother again is already proving too painful to bear. "Callos will make the Hunter's Elixir before we know it, I'm sure."

"It'll be far from the full moon by the time he accomplishes the feat," Lavenzia says uncertainly. "Traversing the Fade is going to be hard enough as it is."

"Don't worry, I'll be all right," Drew says to me. "We'll be at the ocean soon enough."

"Right." I laugh weakly, resisting the urge to glance at Ruvan. Did he hear? What does he think? "Until then, stay safe."

"I will." Drew pats the two silver sickles at his hips. "I have the best smithery in all of Hunter's Hamlet to see it so."

"The moon is nearly at its crest. We should go so we're at the wall of the Fade when my powers are at their strongest."

I pull Drew to me. My arms won't come undone. I don't want to let him go. I can't. My brother, my twin, I thought he might be dead once before. I can't handle not knowing a second time. This next month will break me.

"I have something I want you to do," I whisper quickly. His leaving has reminded me… "Go to the ruins you fought Ruvan in. Take a look there."

"What am I looking for?" he whispers back.

"Whatever you can find." I don't know what I want him to look for, I just know there's *something* there. I've been trying to recover that first dream I had in Castle Tempost all day to much aching in the back of my skull. That feeling as Ventos and I passed through the Fade Marshes lingers with me. The dreams… There's something to it all, and I've been too distracted and—if I'm being honest—too cowardly to confront it. But I'm wasting time avoiding it.

Drew is the one who ultimately pushes me away. "Be well, sister, and you stay safe also." *Remember what I said*, is left unspoken.

"I will."

Lavenzia takes Drew by the hand.

"Hold your—" They disappear in a puff of black smoke. "Breath," I end weakly. I forgot to warn him about the tricks to make mist stepping better. He'll have to figure it out along the way.

I stare at the spot they left from, the circle of stones on the floor that marks the break in the castle's barriers. I'm not sure how long Ruvan lets us stand there, but I think it's a significant stretch of time because when I move, my legs ache slightly. Drifting from the receiving hall, I head up to the room Drew was in. The bed is still indented with his outline. I can still see the ghosts of us at its edge, at the window, talking about how the world was nothing like we were promised.

In some ways, it's better.

"So why does it feel so much worse?" I whisper.

"What does?" Ruvan reminds me of his presence. I turn, looking up at him. He's remained at my side dutifully enough that it hurts.

"Everything."

Slowly, as if he's afraid of startling me, Ruvan takes my hand. His touch is searing hot. It races up my arm and sets my eyes to burning.

"Talk to me, Floriane," he gently urges. "Tell me everything that's been going through your mind. We've been silent to each other for too long."

I sigh softly. He's asking for more than just today—than our earlier, interrupted conversation. He's asking for all the things I haven't said—that I've been meaning to. All the things I promised myself I'd muster the courage to speak about when I returned from the hamlet.

"My thoughts about our bloodsworn—about being married to you—are still murky and confusing at best. Sometimes I find comfort in it. Other times it eats at me," I admit. Ruvan shifts, as if he's settling in to patiently listen. "I always knew I would be married off, just as I knew I would never have a choice in who or when it would be." I laugh softly. "When I put it that way, it's really not so different than what happened. I didn't have my choice of husband in the end. The world has a twisted sense of humor, doesn't it? You can be completely right about what's ahead of you, and completely wrong at the same time. Maybe I can't actually forge my own path in this world."

"That's not true. You can be and do whatever your heart desires," Ruvan says, soft and firm. "Even the vampir who can see the future in someone's blood will always say that the choice still lies in the beating heart of the person."

I glance away. "I wish you could look into my future. The reassurance would be easier."

"I don't need to taste your blood to see your future." His thumb begins to caress mine. "I don't need magic to see a woman in the process of learning what she wants. I see a woman whose world is so much more than she thought it was, and that threatens her rigid structure. And, as that structure continues to fall away, she'll have to make more and more of her own choices for the first time in her life about what she wants and who she wants to be."

"How do you know me so well?" I'm somewhere between amazed and frustrated. But, in all, pleased. It's comforting for someone to truly see me.

"Don't I though?" He has the audacity to wear a lazy grin. But his eyes are still distant. Somewhere in those golden depths is an emotion that looks almost like sorrow, tinged with longing. "Your future will be what you make of it. If that is with me, then I will help you fight, every step of the way, for all your dreams. If you decide you are meant for someone else then, despite how painful it will be, I will step aside."

"Every time I think I know what I want, I second-guess myself." I can be or do anything. And I can't shake the terror that infinite possibility instills in me. "All these options overwhelm me, and I'm scared of making the wrong choice."

"You won't."

"How can you be so certain?"

"Because you've always had this power; it's in your blood, after all." His hands are on my hips, thumbs stroking. He holds me a breath away from him. Our noses nearly touch. His hair tickles my temples as he peers into my eyes like a scholar pores over a tome. "You're just learning how to use it. So let's try a little experiment. Close your eyes, look within yourself, and tell me what you want."

"I told you I don't know. I'm still sorting through the mess Hunter's Hamlet made me."

"Not in the future. Not tomorrow. Right *now*, Floriane."

"Right now?"

"Yes, decide what you want in this moment, then the next. You don't have to dictate your whole future at once."

"What I want…" *I want you.* I want him to push me against the wall. I want him to bite my neck. I want to taste his lips again. I want to forget everything else and slip into that place of warmth and comfort that only he can seem to provide me. I want the connection we share and to ignore all doubts. I don't want just lust, but genuine companionship.

The mere idea of our magic mingling once more, our essence, sends gooseflesh up my arms. It has me suppressing a shiver rippling down my spine. I can feel him and me so clearly.

There is a carnal need he's awoken in me. Things I've known about, but never thought of. Acts that have never been for me are suddenly made accessible by his existence.

Shed the skin of the forge maiden. If the curse is broken, I'll never be that woman again. I will be able to leave and go wherever I want. Beyond the walls and to the sea. Who knows, maybe farther? Maybe, I'll get on a ship and sail all the way to the silver mines in the north.

Maybe I'll stay here, with him, and choose to be his wife.

"You want?" He brings me back to the present.

"I want to know what you're feeling first." I grab him behind his elbows. I need to know we're on mutual footing.

"I told you earlier, but I will say it time and again, as often as you need," Ruvan says slowly. I hang on his words. "When I first woke into this world and realized that we were still cursed, that everything I ever knew—ever loved—was gone, I vowed I would dedicate my life to saving the vampir. That would be my solitary focus. Every breath. Every step. For my people. I swore away joy. I swore away goodness. I was a mission given a man's flesh.

"But then…then…" His voice trails off. He chuckles. "A hunter nearly killed me on the night of the Blood Moon. And, *oh*, I wanted to slay her for it." I bite my lip; his eyes flick toward the movement. "I could've that night. My mission was the only thing keeping me from doing so. I thought, *Even if she is a monster, she is worth more to me alive*."

We both looked at each other and saw a monster in those early nights. In some ways we were right. In many we were so wrong.

"Then she forced me to learn that my prey were not monsters. *She* was not a monster, but a woman of flesh and blood and *heat*. A woman who tastes of fire and cinnamon. Whose blood whispers of great purpose." Ruvan pulls me slightly closer. "A woman whom I grew to know enough that love could take root."

"And now what?" I whisper.

"Now, I wait to learn if the feelings are mutual—what face she thinks is my true one. Am I the monster or the man to her?"

I had accused his accursed face of being his actual one. No… I raise a hand and cup his cheek. "This, this is your true face."

Relief cracks across his expression. His brow knits, turning up in the center, his eyes press closed, and Ruvan leans his forehead against mine. Through our bond, through the magic and blood of his that lives in me, I can feel his joy. So much happiness over something so simple.

Over being seen.

When we part I stare up at him and wonder if I am the first human—the first person, vampir, human, or anyone—to see him for who he truly is. To know him so deeply. Maybe I'm not the first. Maybe I'm not the last. But I'm here now. I see him…and he sees me.

Not the forge maiden. Not the hunter. Not my blood.

Floriane.

"Right now I want you," I confess. "Kiss me," I demand.

"Yes, my lady." He obliges without a second thought.

The kiss is slow. He brushes his lips against mine lightly once, twice. Then, presses them firmly. He kisses me for me and I kiss him for him. I kiss him because I want him. Because I am falling in love with him, too.

Ruvan pulls away and my eyes flutter open.

"I want you to touch me," I admit.

"How?"

"Like our first night, and in ways I don't entirely yet know," I admit. I grab onto him so he doesn't pull away, so he knows I'm serious in this need. "I want to explore you. I want you to *show* me new things, better than what you already have."

Ruvan licks his lips. "What do you think I could show you?"

"How men and women fit together." A flush rises to my cheeks. I struggle to keep it at bay. I want him to take me seriously. To know that even though I might be a maiden, I'm not ashamed of this need.

His lips brush over mine a third time in the faintest of kisses. I shake my head.

"I shall oblige you, my bloodsworn. But not here." He spins me, lifts me.

We move through the night. His silent steps are wide and sure. This is like a dream. The sky open above me, a million stars illuminating the ghostly path stretched across a frigid abyss. We're back in the castle, through the chapel. I hear the faint voices of Callos and Quinn below, but if they hear us, they don't call up.

Inside his chambers, past the settee I doubt I'll be sleeping on again, and into his room. The night's chill has beat us here through the broken glass of his window. It nips at me as my armor falls away, sharpening my senses and heightening my awareness of what I'm doing. But I don't put a stop to his hands as they move over me. I allow him to help me out of my armor. I unbutton his coat.

We're still fully clothed. I've seen him in just a shirt and trousers before. He's seen me in the same. But this moment feels different. Perhaps because I'm already peeling away the rest with my mind. I know we will be bare before each other soon enough and that has me shivering.

"Are you cold?" He wraps his arms around my shoulders. My hands are pinned between us, splayed on his chest.

I can feel his heart racing. Perhaps that's what prompts me to admit, "A little nervous, I think."

"If it's too much, we can stop. Anytime. You say the word."

I think of when he first drank from me, warning me he might not be able to stop. It brings a smile to my lips now. From the beginning we existed with crossing the boundaries the world placed on us, but honoring our own.

"It's not too much."

"You're sure?"

"Since when are vampir lords so gentle?"

"It's in the process of blood lore—we should only take what is freely given." He picks me up once more for the sole purpose of laying me on the bed. I'm immediately reminded of the first time he was atop me. Heat swells between my thighs, tingling and unbearable. I need him to touch me again and he wastes no time. Ruvan spares no inch of my body with his kisses. My clothes are patched with wet spots from his affections.

His hands are on the hem of my shirt, slowly lifting. "Let me see you."

I nod and he peels away my clothes from my flesh, dotted with chilled bumps. He devours me not with his fangs, but with his stare.

It's as though I am a feast in famine and he possesses a hunger I have never seen before.

Bravery possesses me. I am not going to be the only one exposed. I sit, tugging his shirt over his head. I see the constellation of scars and marks he dutifully pointed out to me before, painting a picture across his flesh of his life until now. The moment we're bare together, he pulls me to him. Our skin is flush up the length of our chests. He bites at my shoulder and I let out a gasp, my nails digging into his back.

Ruvan pulls away quickly. I can see the faintest streak of red on his lips. "I didn't mean to."

"Ruvan…" I cup his cheek, my thumb parting his lips, running down his fangs to the point. "It's all right."

"You know I am not my forefathers?"

"I do." I meet his eyes. "You've never lied to me. I know you don't want to hurt me." I shift. My hips grind against his and a moan escapes me. He holds me tighter. "Just like I know how good you can make me feel."

He chuckles, lids heavy, eyes almost sinister but in the most delightful way. "You still have no idea how good I can make you feel… but I have every intention of showing you."

Our kisses are warm, wet, and breathy. Each is more eager than the last, deeper. Sensual.

His arms tighten around me. All space between us is gone. Bodies tense, hot, and yearning.

I twist, pushing him down onto the bed. My legs are still on either side of him, hands on his chest for support. I study him underneath me in all his glorious perfection. Ruvan knows he is the subject of my inspection and practically preens. He places his hands behind his head, the muscles of his back stretching on either side of his chest in a quite glorious V shape.

"Do you like what you see?" He cocks his head slightly.

"Very much." I roll my hips, the sensation of pulsing heat delicious. I want to replicate it a thousand times over.

"Careful with that." His hands move to my hips, fingers curling around my backside. "You're going to make me want more."

There's a touch of darkness to his words that I relish. I'm torturing and teasing him—us—and, *old gods*, I love it. I lean down to whisper in his ear.

"What if I told you that's my goal?" A sexual creature within me has been awakened by him. I have never met this Floriane before, and now I want to spend *hours* meeting her.

Ruvan opens his mouth to speak, but I silence him as I move my hands down his chest, farther down, still, over his lower abdomen. My body moves with them, shifting back. I kiss his face and move to bite his neck, as hard as I dare. Then I follow my hands with my mouth, biting and licking, all the way down to the point that I have slid between his legs.

His muscles tense. I explore at my leisure. I learn. With hands and mouth I have him right where I want him. The vampir lord is my willing prisoner and I move with agonizing slowness. I listen to his throaty breaths, his gasps. I am victorious when I elicit a moan. What I lack in experience I make up for in eagerness and attentiveness. I remember how good he made me feel when he stroked me between my thighs and I wish to do the same for him.

Right as his breaths are becoming ragged, he sits upright. With a growl he twists us; we tumble back. He moves down my body, ending between my thighs. He explores me with his fingers and tongue in places I have never even ventured myself.

Heat builds within me. It's too much. This is far beyond anything I've ever known. It's everything and not enough. It's building and building until I break with a cry.

Ruvan moves to hold me, just as he did the first time I shattered against him.

When I've caught my breath, I dare to speak. "That was amazing."

"Oh, my dear bloodsworn," he whispers against my lips as my chest is still heaving, my mind still swimming in a euphoric haze. "*That* was only the beginning. I cannot wait to see what madness I will push you to with the rest of me."

I don't have a chance to respond before he's on top of me in a blur of movement, his hips between my legs. We shift, finding positioning on instinct and the guidance of his firm hands. He leans over me, eyes locked, searching. Tilting his head, he dips down and penetrates me with body and fang.

Momentary pain. He bites harder. An explosion of pleasure. We are joined in body and blood and spirit.

The sounds of our passion fill the room. My fingers dig into his back, the duvet, the pillow. I can't find anything solid to hold onto; I'm floating away. My eyes roll back and I shudder. I'm drowning in his pleasure and power. These are new depths I never want to emerge from.

I lean forward, slightly. My lips close around the flesh of his neck where it meets his shoulder. And I bite. *Hard.* He hisses as I draw blood.

Yes, give it to me, I think. The voice from battle is back, but different. It is my own now. I am that voice calling for more, *more! Give me everything.*

Give me pleasure. Give me pain. Break me. Make me.

Ruvan, I am yours.

thirty-eight

We lie in bliss. Our flesh is mended but raw from biting. We have engorged ourselves on the other. Bodies slick and souls full.

I stare at the ceiling and listen to his breathing. We haven't said a word yet. The last sounds to fill the room were moans and movement.

"Floriane." He finally breaks the silence. "That was a lot… are you all right?"

I turn to face him. I find I don't mind seeing him on the pillow next to me in the slightest anymore. The voices that told me to feel shame for what I have done have finally been silenced, once and for all. "Why wouldn't I be?"

"A woman's first time can be painful and I worry I should have gone easier on you."

"Blasphemy." I smirk slightly. "If I needed more breaks, or more tenderness, I would've asked. I wanted exactly what you gave."

"Good." He shifts onto his side and runs a fingertip down my arm. Even still, it leaves tingling in its wake. "Are you satisfied?"

I am. But I ask anyway, "What would you do if I said no?"

"Work until you were." He licks his lips.

"I can appreciate a hard worker."

"As can I." The movement of Ruvan's hand stops at mine. Our fingers lace together. "May I ask you something?"

"Anything," I say, and mean it.

"You've said you would never have a choice in who you married in Hunter's Hamlet. Was that true?"

"You know I can't lie to you."

He chuckles. "Very true." His expression grows more serious as our bodies cool and our heads clear. "*Why* did you never have a choice?"

"Everything in Hunter's Hamlet is kept in order and we all put our faith in that. For that reason, there's almost no crime in the hamlet. No one goes hungry outside of extreme circumstances. People are clothed and sheltered. The security is our reward for the sacrifices we make in keeping the world safe from the vampir."

"It sounds like a lot of sacrifices." He runs his fang along his lower lip in thought. I allow him to stew on his next words. "If your mate would be decided for you, who made that decision?"

"For regular people in the hamlet, it would be themselves. They'd need the approval of their parents, or maybe the town council, of course, but matches were rarely refused. The master hunter has that honor for the forge maiden, since it is a position of great esteem. Usually one of the strongest hunters is selected as the husband of the forge maiden, to help protect the line and solidify the union of forge and fortress."

Ruvan watches me as I speak, lips pressing into a hard line that I don't understand.

"What is it?"

"Did you ever think of running away?"

"Not once. I had accepted my destiny."

"And what will that destiny be once you are free?" He shifts closer, caressing my cheek and neck. His hands on me are a familiar, welcome feeling. "Once the curse is broken and the vampir have sworn never to attack again, what will you do?"

I roll onto my back and stare up at the ceiling. His fingertips draw lazy circles all over my body. But the touch doesn't pull me from my thoughts. I exist in a place that is still only hypothetical. Not quite real. Not *yet*.

"It'll take you a while to completely get rid of all the Succumbed. I'm sure there will be a need for Hunter's Hamlet and a hot forge for a bit longer to keep the Succumbed from wandering into the Natural World."

"But is that what you want?"

"I love the smithy." I look up at him. "I love the heat, the possibilities. It is home for me and always will be."

"My forge maiden—though not so maiden any longer, I suppose."

I laugh and Ruvan leans forward, planting a firm kiss on my lips before pulling away with a sigh. He lies back as well and his side looks so empty that I am compelled to roll over and curl against him. His arm is around my shoulders, my head on his chest.

"Is that all?" he asks. "Just the smithy for you?"

"I'm not sure… Perhaps some travels, perhaps a family… I think I want to figure it out as I go." I yawn. "What will you do when you are free of the curse?"

"The council agreed three thousand years ago when the long night began that the vampir lord or lady to break the curse would be our ruler. All the lords and ladies chosen in the line of succession were selected based on how close they were in title or bloodline to the throne when the night began. So, if—when—we break the curse, I will be king."

I try and imagine it. My thoughts are becoming murky and dreamlike. I imagine a throne room, somewhere in this castle that I have yet to see. The throne is iron, like the crown resting on the statue of Solos in the chapel. He is swathed in a cape of crimson velvet and everything shines. The world is bright. Tempost is warm.

"You'll be a good king," I murmur, lids heavy and slowly closing.

"I will try. For the vampir…and for the humans of Hunter's Hamlet."

"Do you promise?" I ask, vaguely realizing that in none of our plans was a mention of what the future was for him and me.

"I swear it to you. As long as I draw breath, I will protect you and your home."

Dawn breaks through the window. I've only slept a short while. Most of my nights these days are spent awake, tumbling between the sheets with him, my love, my king, my bloodsworn.

Long, elegant fingers rake through my hair, stroking it from my face. As I stir, he places a kiss on my forehead.

"Good morning, Loretta."

Loretta? That's not my name... *Awareness overcomes me, enough that it pulls me away from the bed. No longer do I feel the man's nails lightly on my scalp.*

A man and woman lie together underneath silken duvets, furs piled atop their feet. White hair frames him, splayed out on the pillow behind him. I see his face sharp and clear for the first time. A brunette is curled at his side, covers up to her chin. They share a smile and it's then that I notice their eyes—his gold, hers green. He's a vampir and she's human.

Light glitters off crystal-cut chandeliers, casting rainbows on the fine upholstery of the walls. The castle is as glamorous as I imagined; I vaguely recognize the carvings of the bed. I turn to face bookshelves, full of trinkets, framing a familiar fireplace.

I wake with a start, throwing the covers off me. The sunlight is blinding. I shiver in a cold sweat, my head splitting with pain.

"Floriane?" Ruvan groans, turning over.

I stare at him, wide-eyed. His snowy hair is splayed on the pillow. Shorter, but just as silken as that of the man in my dreams. The man who has been haunting me at every turn has a possible identity now. Given Ruvan's distant lineage, it would make sense...but it seems too impossible to be real.

"We have to go back to the room you first took me to." I stand, scrambling for my clothes.

"What... What's happened?"

"My dreams. I think I know who they're about."

"They're still persisting?" He props himself up, eyes clearer and more focused.

"They never really stopped," I admit.

"And you didn't tell me?" Ruvan frowns slightly.

"We've been busy." Tugging my shirt on, I give him a pointed look.

"Fair... But I still want to know." He sighs.

"Moreover, whenever I try to think about them my head hurts." I rub the back of my skull. The ache is present, but I'm not going to let it deter me. Not this time. I fight to recall the details of my dreams, wincing slightly. "I think I might know who Loretta was."

"How? Who?"

"All of my dreams have had two things in common: a human woman and a man with long, white hair. This was the first time he used her name—he called her Loretta and they were in that room at the edge of the old castle. I know how it sounds but I keep feeling as though there's something—someone—calling out to me."

"What else do you remember of your dreams?" He pulls himself upright.

"I'm trying to remember." I massage my temples. "But it hurts to try."

Ruvan stands, taking both my hands in his and pulling them from my face. He gently massages in my stead. "Harnessing one's innate blood lore is difficult. The struggle is normal."

"How can I stop struggling?"

"It's different for everyone." He gives me an encouraging smile. "But I'm sure you'll get it when you're ready."

"But you believe me?"

"Of course I do." I only manage a nod; I'm suspended in dumb awe at the amount of trust he's placed in me. "Now, let's go inspect this room and see if we can unlock what your blood is trying to tell us."

Together, we dress and speed from our quarters, across the mezzanine. Lavenzia, Callos, and Winny are in a fierce debate over our plan of attack, but none of them call up to us. Through the door and into the stairwell we round upward, but I stop the moment we enter the chapel. Ruvan goes to leave, tugging my arm. But I hold firm.

"What is it?"

"The man from my dreams… I think I know who he is, too." I walk across the chapel, my footsteps echoing. I come to a stop before the altar and the statue of the crown-wearing man holding the book. "King Solos."

"What?"

"They met during a festival…he read her future… Ruvan, I think Loretta was King Solos's lover."

"King Solos took no lovers and fathered no children." Ruvan crosses to me with a shake of his head. "It's what led to such upheaval following his death. There wasn't any clear, irrefutable line of succession—cousins, nieces, and nephews all fought for the throne."

"No," I say firmly. "He had a lover, Loretta. I saw them together. She was working closely with him—helping him." Everything is slowly falling into place. "The workshop in the old castle was hers, not Solos's. Solos didn't enslave the first humans, he was working *with* them."

Ruvan rests his hands lightly on my shoulders, cupping them. Looking me square in the eyes, he says, "What you are suggesting goes against the entire history of the vampir."

"History can be wrong," I say firmly. "Haven't we both learned that by now?"

"But this is…this is King Solos." Ruvan looks up to the statue of the man and his book. "Jontun's writings were explicit."

"Don't you want Jontun to be wrong?" I ask.

"But why would he lie?" Ruvan's eyes are glazed over and distant.

"Maybe because the vampir weren't ready to accept that help came from people they had seen as having 'lesser' magic." I remember how Ruvan described the early humans. "Or, maybe to protect them?" I shake my head. "I don't know. But I believe history has been changed, intentionally or not. Maybe we don't know the full story—the *real* story. Everything we know of Solos was through Jontun. We don't have the whole picture of the man, and never in his words." I place my hands on his hips and draw him close. The contact pulls him from his haze. "I know how hard it is to have your world shaken. But the only way we're going to figure this out is if we open ourselves to looking at everything around us not as we want it to be, or think, or have been told, but as it is."

Ruvan's arms tighten around me. Last night, we embraced as lovers. But I think this might be the first time we're embracing purely as friends. There's no boiling tension. No insatiable need. That's all been *finally* satiated. And what's left is support.

"All right." He finally pulls away, looking determined. "So, King Solos had a lover and her name was Loretta. And if the Raven Man is seeking vengeance for her then—"

"Perhaps he was another would-be suitor?"

"A human who fell in love with a vampir," Ruvan says softly, almost sadly. "And a king's mistress at that. He was jilted and used. Perhaps he even tried to become a vampir to be worthy of her." *Worthy*. The word sticks with me and I try to ignore it.

"She wasn't a vampir," I insist. I know what I saw in my dream.

Loretta didn't have the golden eyes of a vampir. I hope Ruvan is ready to finally accept that truth. "Ruvan, if the workshop was hers—a workshop with a door that could only be opened by a human, with records indicating a human was working with Solos—then Loretta was a human."

"Why would a human be working with the king of the vampir?" He's still stuck in his disbelief. I know, viscerally, how hard what he's enduring is, but that doesn't make me want to shout at him any less.

"Maybe she saw an opportunity to help her people, too. One we don't know about or has been lost to time. Or…maybe she loved him." Her eyes, his, the way they looked at each other in my dream. How I wish I could just show Ruvan what I saw. "Perhaps she was Solos's bloodsworn."

"Vampir have never bloodsworn themselves to humans."

"But you—"

"I was the first." He releases me, pacing the hall.

"You *think* you were. But you don't *know*." I reiterate, "If I've learned anything these past weeks, it's been that we don't know nearly as much as we think we do. If the general vampir population in Solos's time saw the humans as little more than livestock to be used for blood, what would they do if they discovered their king was not only working with a human but bloodsworn to one?"

"They'd never accept it," he whispers.

"Exactly! Jontun must've omitted Loretta from his records to protect both his king and her." I take a step forward. He's on the cusp of admitting it. I can feel it. But then Ruvan shakes his head slowly and a cold sweat covers my body at his expression. Dread has come to keep us company.

"King Solos could've had *any* woman he desired from the elite of Tempost. There's no possible way he would select a human."

I still. "What do you mean by that?"

Ruvan brings his eyes to me; they're conflicted. The muscles in his neck tense as he swallows hard. He doesn't answer.

"What do you mean when you say there's 'no possible way King Solos would select a human?'"

"Even if Jontun's writings weren't the whole picture, there's truth in them. There must be… Everything we've ever known… King Solos would've never chosen a human." Ruvan is interested in looking anywhere else but me.

"Because a human isn't *good enough*?"

"Floriane, I didn't mean—"

"Then tell me what you meant." I close the gap between us. All the anger, frustration, and hurt I felt when I first arrived at this place is returning. Except, now it's worse. Because now I *care* about him. Now I want him to want me because I want him—because of all this hope he's insisted on filling me with.

Ruvan squares off against me. "Solos was a different time. Humans were young in the world, only recently made by the dryads."

"So?"

"Their magics were seen as less than ours."

"So you've hinted. Which I find odd since the vampir were the weak ones who were only confident going out around the full moon."

Ruvan scowls slightly at my jab. "I never claimed it was fair or right. The opposite, if you have any interest in my opinion at all. Really, you should be grateful Solos didn't make one a bloodsworn. Who knows what he might have done to her to uncover the truth of the blood lore."

"Unless Solos wasn't the man you thought," I insist.

"Not every piece of our history is a lie."

"Well a lot of it hasn't been true. A lot of it doesn't even make sense! Why can't you see the gaping holes in it?" I point to the altar. "You say blood lore—true blood lore—relies on blood that is freely given. Does that seem like a magic craft that would be created by a man who kept humans like cattle?"

There's a flash of genuine doubt in Ruvan's eyes, but he quickly smothers it. "Just because the humans have been telling you lies since birth and embracing them doesn't mean we have done that to our own. You might be three thousand years away from the death of Solos and the Fade. But I was born only one hundred years after Solos died. I grew up with tales of the great king from people who knew him. The man was brilliant, extraordinary," Ruvan snaps.

"A great, *extraordinary* man who, according to you and the precious, perfect history that you refuse to question, used and abused humans," I snap.

"I didn't mean—extraordinary as in—" He fumbles over his words.

"I don't know what you mean right now, but it's not reason." I shake my head and start for the stairs.

"Floriane." He tries for my hand but I pull it away.

"Don't follow me."

"Don't be like this." Ruvan's eyes are wounded. I imagine mine are, too.

I stop at the stairs and sigh. *One last chance*. "Ruvan, if we end the curse and you become king, will you still have me as your bloodsworn?"

"What?" He staggers. "Would you even want to be?"

"That's not what I asked."

"But what you want matters."

"Fine, assume I do." I look him dead in the eyes, pinning him to the spot. "If all the vampir were awake. If you would face all their judgment for keeping me—a human—at your side, would you still be bloodsworn with me?"

"But your wants matter." He's using my wishes to hide and it infuriates me. He's being evasive and he knows it. He knows what I'm trying to ask and his dodging is really all the answer I need.

"You keep telling me to choose my future, now I want you to choose yours. If I wanted to remain your bloodsworn, even after you were king of the vampir, would you do it because you loved me? You said you would defend me, and the hamlet, from your people, but will you defend our love?"

He opens his mouth, letting out the start of a word that just hangs there. Silence sinks in as fast as my heart is sinking in my chest. Drew was right…none of this means anything. It never did.

What a fool I was for working to take this seriously. To think I might have entertained remaining his wife. To honor and love him.

"All right then." I head up the stairs.

"Floriane, it's not that simple!" He races after me.

"It *is* that simple! You either believe me, or you don't. You're open to helping me find the truth about our history, or you're not." I spin on the stair, looming over him. "You love me—truly love me and want me by your side—or you don't."

"Do you even want me to love you?" He raises a hand to his chest. "Because I can never tell with you!"

"You know how hard this is," I snap.

"Hard for us both!" He throws his hands in the air. "I was born to hate you."

"As was I."

"But do you love me despite that? Do you love me as I love you? You're demanding all this of me and yet you still have not told me how you truly feel."

I purse my lips and inhale slowly. I'm too mad to think rationally. Because all I can think of is him pushing me aside. Him revering a king who he believes looked at humans as little more than test subjects. Him saying he believes in my dreams and then his actions directly contradicting it.

"Is that my answer, then?" He chuckles darkly and shakes his head.

"Ruvan—"

He speaks over me, words bitter and harsh. "What does it matter? Fine, then, your answer is no and mine is as well. You wouldn't be my bloodsworn because the vampir would *never* accept a human as their queen. Especially not one that is a descendant of those who cursed us."

We stare at each other, words ringing in our ears. I can still feel his magic in me from the night before, filling the hollow left behind by his body. A void that will never be filled again. Who knew there were so many ways to sink into darkness?

"All right, then. Glad we could clear that up before I convinced myself this was real." I turn to leave.

He curses under his breath. "Floriane, where are you going?"

"Anywhere but here."

"Don't leave. We should talk—"

"*Don't*," I hiss as he starts up the stairs. "Don't follow me. I want to be alone."

"We should talk this out," he finishes his sentence with purpose. "We're both…" He rubs his temples. "A lot has happened, emotions are high, and we're both being foolish."

"You don't think I know that?" I glare at him. But my anger softens some. I sigh. Why is this all so difficult? How can I care for someone so deeply and yet they wound me in equal measure? "You're right, we need to talk. But first, I need some time alone, please. We'll talk when I'm not so cross and can think clearly."

"We should talk now."

"I don't want to talk to you now," I say firmly. "Give me some space, let me clear my head, and we'll sort this out later."

As I leave this final time, no footsteps follow.

thirty-nine

I STAND AT THE PRECIPICE OF THE TOWER, AT THE TOP OF THE STAIRS, BEFORE THE BROKEN WALL THAT LEADS TO THE BEAM TO TRAVERSE BACK TO THE WESTERN WING OF THE CASTLE. Wind and snow batter my face, freezing my tears to my eyelashes.

He didn't mean it. I didn't mean it. We *didn't mean any of it*. That's what my heart tells me. We're both navigating something new and complex, something neither of us have a primer on how to handle.

Moreover, I know how hard it is to have truths you hold so dearly they're sacred be questioned. It's hard. Scary, even. Ruvan is a good man and he'll come to his better senses. He'll believe me.

Or he won't. That's an uglier part of me speaking now. A weaker voice, that I thought I killed but was resuscitated by Ruvan's actions. *None of what's happening between you two will matter once the curse is broken.*

Was last night an exploration for us both that culminated into nothing more? Was it mere satiation? Will it mean anything when all this is over?

Or was our lovemaking the consummation of a genuine marriage?

I look back over my shoulder and into the gloom that lives in these empty, haunted halls. Maybe he's right. Maybe I should stay and we should talk further. But the mere idea of going back there has panic worming up my throat. I imagine him digging in further. Neither of us is in a good enough place right now to talk productively. I'm going to need more proof if I want him to listen to me, which means I'm going to have to figure this out on my own.

Sighing, I turn back to the frigid air howling in the night.

Drew might be wrong about Ruvan's and my future, but he wasn't wrong about me being different now. I have the magic of the vampir within me—Ruvan's magic strengthens me, protects me even when he's far.

I leap into the air and land with confidence on the beam.

Even though the snow is just as thick—thicker—than the first time I crossed and the ice is just as perilous, I move with ease. A gust of wind tries to knock me over; I crouch low and stabilize myself. The ground below tries to rise up and meet me but I won't let it. I won't let the monster of fear consume me.

Back on the other side of the castle, I exhale in relief. Traversing that icy path was all the proof I needed that I have changed. For all I *want* Ruvan, I don't *need* him. It's oddly reassuring to know that these feelings don't stem solely from gratitude over the protection he's offered me.

I move to the room that I was first taken to, the same one that Drew occupied a day ago, to stand in the same place I stood in my dream. I look over my shoulder at the fireplace. I can imagine the bookshelves full of the same trinkets I saw in my dreams.

"Was this room yours, Loretta, or Solos's?" I say to her ghost. I wonder if she still walks these halls. I can almost feel her here with me. I cross to the bed and lie down. This was where I received my first dream. I can make no sense of how I get them, or why, but I'm going to retrace my steps, even if I must go all the way back to the old castle to do it. "Though let's hope it doesn't come to that," I say to the ghost. "If you want me to know the truth, now's the time."

I close my eyes and wait.

At first, I'm keenly aware of everything. Small shifts in the air, the way my body twitches just before it falls asleep, the growing ache in the back of my head that threatens to become unbearable in short order. I'm hardly tired, but this specter isn't going to come to me in the waking world.

Except, she did once.

I sit up and reach down to my hip where the blood silver dagger is holstered. I bite my lip and twist it in the moonlight. Do I dare cut myself with it again? Ruvan's sunken face flashes before me. If he needs more blood, I'll give it to him. He also has the Hunter's Elixir. This will be worth it.

The cut on my forearm is small but it saps the pain from my mind. I hold the dagger to my chest and feel its power focusing me. Lying back down, I take a deep breath, and focus on my feet. I force the muscles in each of my toes to relax, then in the arches of my feet, my ankles. I work my way up my body, one muscle at a time. It's a trick Mother taught me. The smithy is relentless, and sometimes you ache so badly that you can't even sleep, not even when you know it would make you feel better.

Somewhere between my abdomen and hands I drift off.

I don't realize I'm asleep until the dream hits me. I'm still in that bedroom. Except it's not the same, I'm back in an earlier time when the castle was still pristine.

It's night here, too, and Loretta fumbles about. She runs between the bookcases and a desk positioned underneath the window—a desk no longer present in my own time.

"They're not here." She curses under her breath. It's then I notice that three books are missing off the shelf. "Damn him."

She's back at the desk, quill moving frantically over parchment. I approach. It seems the more aware I am of these dreams, the more autonomy I have within them. Or perhaps I'm just stronger every time. Perhaps it's the magic of the dagger drawing power from the recesses of my body.

She's writing a letter, a few short words:

Tersius came back even after you banished him. He stole our work. I'm going to get it. Don't follow me, it's too dangerous for you to move across the Fade with Tersius as he is. He'll hurt you if you come. But don't worry, I'll be safe. I'll return soon.

"I should have known," she says softly. "I should have seen what you had really become and let Solos kill you when we had the chance."

Loretta hunches over the desk, tears streaming down her cheeks. Wiping her face and composing herself, she goes back to the bookcases. She lifts a short sword from a stand and unsheathes it halfway. Red and black lines squiggle across the metal. It looks almost like my own dagger.

She sheathes it with purpose and straps it to her hip. I can tell from the way Loretta moves that she's not a combatant. She's going to die. All signs point to that tragic truth.

A woman, loved by two men, betrayed by one in anguish, it would seem.

Loretta goes to the corner of the room and puts her shoulder into the bookcase. To my shock, it swivels open. She descends into the darkness. I try and catch up to her, but the moment I take the first step, the darkness swallows me.

Jolting awake, I fly to the bookcase and push just like she did. It refuses to budge. I keep pushing. My legs and arms strain. With a groan, the ancient hinges slowly loosen and the door to the secret passageway cracks open. I keep pushing until it's open wide enough for me to squeeze through. I need to suck in everything to fit and, even then, it's a tight push, but I make it. I silently thank Mother for all the times she pushed me to lift more heavy ingots, coal, and water. Without the strength she helped me build, I could do none of this.

The stairs round down, before opening to what appears to be another workshop, though this is far less stocked than the one in the depths of the old castle. Through another room, I suddenly recognize where I am. I catch my bearings and head right. Sure enough, at the end of this passage is the study I found the letters in—the one that connects through forgotten halls down to the workshop.

I wonder if Callos has had a chance to read those yet. He was going through everything brought back from the workshop so slowly. I wonder, if he did, if he would have found more concrete proof of a relationship between King Solos and Loretta. I'm beginning to affirm and expand my theories as I walk through these abandoned halls, a forgotten corner of a mazelike castle.

Loretta *was* human. Solos kept her hidden because he knew his people wouldn't accept her and, since he only spoke through Jontun, that was an easy feat. These were her chambers and secret passages. She was the castle's unseen presence. Solos took all the credit for her work on the blood lore. And yet…she loved him anyway. Despite all odds, she did; I can feel the emotion so vividly in the brief moments that I see the history of this world through her eyes.

And now I have another piece of the puzzle.

Tersius, the first hunter, stole the first three books of blood lore—the ones Callos has been after. Her initial work with Solos. They were the books I saw the statue holding in the underground hall of the fortress. Those tomes enabled Tersius to lay the curse, which he did in vengeance. Maybe if I can figure out what was in those books, I can find a way to identify the curse anchor or nullify the curse without it.

I stand back at a crossroads, looking up the passage I came from, and down farther still. Loretta had said that she was going after Tersius. That means she had some way to leave the castle and cross the Fade, even though she wasn't a vampir. Maybe it was even something that could get Solos himself across, too. She said it was too dangerous for him to go, not that he *couldn't*.

Perhaps that same pathway is what the Succumbed use. Another mystery explained. Everything is falling into place and soon enough I'm going to have all the proof I need. Ruvan will listen to me, then. He'll have to.

Down it is. If there's a way to make it easier to get across the Fade for the vampir, they're going to need it. Maybe then I can get across myself, too. If Loretta was a bloodsworn and had a way to make it across on her own then I should be able to use that same method as well. If I can't find alternative records of her initial work then I'll go back to the hamlet myself, sneak in, and somehow steal them from the fortress.

My heart is racing. It's all coming together. I'm so close to the truth—to figuring out the last pieces we all need to break this curse once and for all. I can feel it in my marrow and I will do it whether Ruvan and the rest of them believe me or not.

I enter a large, subterranean space. There are rows and rows of what appear to be small casks. I'm reminded of all the casks in the secret hall of the fortress. I run my fingers along the racks, leaving deep lines in the thick dust. Another confirmation that Tersius stole her work; he used it to make the Hunter's Elixir.

My stomach curdles with disgust at how this woman was treated. I ache for her. Erased from history, her life's accomplishments used against her and the man she loved. Hidden by that same lover. I shake my head. If I survive this, if the curse is broken…I will erect a statue in her honor in Tempost, in Hunter's Hamlet. *Both.* I will forge it out of silver steel. And I will write her name for everyone, and for all of time, to see.

Loretta. Bloodsworn of King Solos. Woman who gave the vampir their strength and Hunter's Hamlet the ability to defend itself.

I'm so lost in my thoughts and my anger that I don't see the movement until it's almost a second too late. A monster scampers across the ceiling, emerging from the darkness into my periphery. It launches itself at me. I tumble back, landing hard to avoid its claws.

The Fallen crashes into the racks of casks. Old blood, inky black, the same shade as the Hunter's Elixir, explodes, coating the monster. It shrieks with what sounds like beastly glee. A mottled and shriveled tongue laps over its face. Its all-black eyes gain a speck of gold to them.

It stills.

It looks around, jerking its head left and right, as if confused. The Fallen lets out a mighty shriek that seems to rattle the very foundation of the castle. It grips its head. Its stomach distends and shrinks from underneath its ribcage as it heaves breaths.

The Fallen are just vampir that were lost to the curse. Blood, fresh and preserved, help stave off the curse. I wonder if this bath of potent, ancient elixir has returned a semblance of awareness to this poor creature. I wonder if it's confused, searching for an answer, a shred of consciousness that was once lost.

Slowly, as it screeches and cradles its head, I reach down. I unsheathe the dagger from my hip. I drag it through the elixir on the floor. It glows so brightly that the Fallen and I are now in a halo of crimson light, the same shade as the Blood Moon.

That gets the monster's attention.

But rather than lunging for me, it scrambles away. Is it afraid of me? Afraid of this power? What does the shred of consciousness lingering in this ancient beast remember? While I pity the creature, I don't give it a chance to flee. Allowing it to do so would give it an opportunity to attack someone else in the future. I'm putting it out of its misery here and now.

I leap. My blade sinks into its chest. Its claws reach up for me, but it doesn't have a chance to strike before my blood silver has pierced its flesh. The Fallen dies instantly. I free the blade from the monster's ribs. The metal is no longer glowing, the magic gone.

The Fallen Ruvan and I fought in the old castle had a tolerance for silver. This creature died with a single jab. So the blood silver both stores power, and unleashes it with lethal effect.

As I'm inspecting the weapon, movement distracts me a second time. Deep power stirs in me.

"Ruvan, good, I'm sorry for earlier. But I must tell you what I've—"

I turn and freeze.

The shift in power is not from the vampir lord, though it is equal to his might.

Stalking through the darkness is a monster so horrible that it was previously unimaginable to me, even in the worst of nightmares. It has the body of a man with gray skin, the color of a corpse, stretched thin over powerful muscle. There's not a stone of fat on this creature clearly designed by Death himself.

His fingers are turned into claws. Fangs so large that they can't fit in his mouth extend past his chin. Horns ring his head like a crown. Two, massive, batlike wings extend over his shoulders, arcing around his body.

I have never seen anything like it before, which leads me to believe that this creature is the third monster Ruvan told me about. The worst of them all.

I'm face-to-face with a Lost.

forty

THE MONSTER DOESN'T MOVE LIKE THE OTHERS. It seems almost conscious. The shadow of the man it once was still lives in its gaunt, haunted face. My gaze drags down its horns to the voids where its eyes once were.

Am I looking at the remains of King Solos?

I imagine him chasing after Loretta. Even though she told him not to come. I wonder if the curse consumed him while he was down in these forgotten halls—the passages that he hid her within ended up being his tomb. Abandoned. Left behind. Left for dead as he still wandered.

But whomever this creature was, Solos or some other lord who made it as far as I did chasing Loretta's trail before the curse got them, it doesn't matter. He's still a Lost now. And he's still coming to kill me.

I adjust my grip on my dagger and slowly lean down. I need to charge it again. I could use my own blood, but the elixir is stronger and I don't want to risk Ruvan's wellbeing again.

I've made a terrible choice.

The Lost moves as fast as the wind. In a second he's behind me. I don't have enough time to charge the blade; I swing wildly, spinning. I slash into his arm, little good it does. The creature seems more curious than hurt. At least its curiosity gives me a moment to get away.

I drop to the ground clumsily and scramble backward. In the process I rake my dagger along the elixir-coated stone. Red light shines once more, but I'm not fast enough.

The creature descends on me. Teeth and claws. I try and get away, but I'm not fast enough. Its fangs dig into my shoulder. I let out a scream that echoes through the castle and my head spins violently. I bring up my dagger and slash across his chest. He reels back, letting out a sound akin to dragging a sword across metal. It makes my hair stand on end and temporarily freezes me in place.

Blood pours down my side, soaking my clothes. I'm already dizzy from the loss. I wipe my dagger in my own blood, summoning the light once more. I wish I had spent more time studying blood lore, instead of just the metal applications of it. If I had, maybe I would've harnessed my dreams sooner; maybe I wouldn't be here now. All those hours with Callos, wasted. The light of the dagger does nothing to the Lost. I see what Ruvan meant—this creature is something different, not vampir, not human, not even one of the other monsters of the curse, just evil and hate, spun together by magic.

"All right then," I snarl. "If this is going to be it then I will take you down with me. Come at me, fiend!"

As if he can understand me, he obliges.

I duck, avoid his first strike, and slash up across his chest. The creature reels, roaring. I use the opportunity to wipe the blade on my shirt again; it soaks up my blood. I take another jab at his arm. If I can somehow incapacitate his arms, I might get the upper hand.

The creature moves, proving that I never had a chance with one mighty flap of his wings.

The Lost launches himself forward, gliding across the ground and slamming into me. We crash through casks of elixir. Inky blood flies everywhere. My dagger is glowing again, little good it does me when I'm pinned against the far wall.

This monster is going to be the last thing I see. I lick my lips, stretching my tongue, ignoring the foul taste of the liquid for whatever power this forgotten elixir can give me. *I'm not going to die here.* I won't let myself die here. I have so much left to do. Ruvan flashes before my eyes. *So much left to say.*

I dig up strength I didn't know I still had. There's a well in me, deeper than I ever thought or imagined. I draw from that power. I bring up my knees, kick, and pivot. Just like grappling with Drew, I use training and leverage to throw the beast off me. I bounce to my feet.

Blood loss is another battle I'm fighting and losing. I put a hand against the wall for support. The monster is already getting up. The beast doesn't feel pain, doesn't know exhaustion, all it knows is instinct. And that instinct is telling it to kill and consume me.

The monster lurches. I brace myself.

A mighty roar fills the space. There's a blur as an object crashes into the Lost. The two tumble. At first, I think somehow a Fallen has come to my aid against all odds. I realize that doesn't make sense and get a better look.

It's Ruvan.

My heart seizes.

He rears back with a silver sickle, going to hook the creature's neck. It moves. He misses. Ruvan grabs and descends with his teeth. He catches the monster; it squirms away.

"Killing you to end your nightmare might be my duty as the vampir lord." Ruvan slowly stands. He spits up blood. I search for a wound on him until I realize it's the Lost's blood. "But it will be my pleasure to kill you for laying a hand on her."

Ruvan lunges for another attack. The two roll, scramble. I'm too stunned for a moment to do anything. Then I think of that putrid blood filling Ruvan's mouth. *The curse*. He was already teetering on the edge before.

Panic spurs me to move. I jump back into the fray. The Lost is fearsome, but for a time it seems like we're gaining the upper hand. Ruvan and I move as one body rather than two separate people. I can sense his intentions, his movements, before he makes them.

I plunge the dagger into the Lost's stomach, all the way to the hilt. The beast grabs for my hands, catching me with its claws as I pull away. I'm not about to let it take my weapon. The monster stumbles back, looking worse for wear but still moving. Still lethal. "How are we going to kill this thing?"

"I'm going to have to use my blood lore." Though Ruvan doesn't seem happy about that in the slightest. I think back to what he did to the Fallen and how much energy that took from him.

"What can I do?"

"Just don't let it out of this room; we can't let it live."

"I had no intention of that."

Ruvan turns my way. He's about to say something when a soft, humming noise comes from the creature. This is unlike the screams, guttural noises, or clicks that the other monsters have made. This sounds…almost like singing.

"What is it doing?" I ask, looking between the monster and Ruvan. The latter has gone perfectly still. Ruvan's eyes have glazed over; he sways slightly in time with the Lost's humming. Color is draining from his face. He's turning gaunt, ashy, cursed right before my eyes. I sprint over and grab his left arm. "Ruvan?"

His right arm flies up with the speed of a viper. He hooks my chin between his pointer finger and his thumb. Spinning, he slams me into the wall. My head snaps against the stone. It should hurt more. If I were still completely human the force of the movement might have knocked me out. Thanks to the elixir and our bloodsworn magic, it doesn't.

Our bloodsworn… He shouldn't be able to hurt me, not even if he tried. Whatever this beast is doing to him is turning Ruvan into something else. He's closer to a Lost than he is the man I knew.

"Ruvan," I wheeze.

The Lost hums its tormented and eerie song even louder. I can almost feel the creature in my own mind, scraping against my skull with those claws, trying to find entry. Maybe it can't because I'm not a vampir. *That's right*, Ruvan had said the Lost could hypnotize with sound.

I stare into Ruvan's eyes, looking for the man I knew, the man who claimed to be falling in love with me. His grip tightens around my throat. I fight to breathe.

"P-Please," I gasp.

He doesn't release. He doesn't relent. There is nothing in his eyes to make me believe that the Ruvan I shared a bed with mere hours ago, is still in there. All I see is hatred and the curse, running rampant.

I tighten my grip on the dagger.

If you're ever face-to-face with a vampire, fight! Drew shouts from the recesses of my memories. *Fight with everything you have. Fight like your life depends on it.*

I draw the dagger across my leg. Red light flares, illuminating Ruvan's emotionless expression. It makes his usually ethereal face all the more sinister.

Don't throw your life away. Mother now.

I can see the Lost moving in my periphery. It's approaching both of us. It's going to have Ruvan fully fall to the curse, kill me, and then they both will feast on me at their monstrous leisure. At all costs, we were to kill the Lost.

The dagger shakes in my hand. I can't let Ruvan succumb to the Lost and the curse. I won't let him turn into one of these monsters. If I have to kill him then so be it.

This is the destiny I stole from Drew that night—to kill the vampire lord. The destiny I thought I'd escaped coming back to haunt me in a way I never expected.

Forge your own destiny, Ruvan's voice, louder than the rest, echoes.

I pull back the dagger. I press my eyes closed. To my surprise, my hand moves. This is unlike before; there are no invisible hands holding me back. No barrier stopping me. Ruvan is no longer the man that I am bloodsworn to. I could stab him. But I stop short.

He's still in there.

My dagger clatters to the ground. My hands go limp at my sides. I can't do it. I can't hurt him. Not because of the bloodsworn… but because I can't. I stare at Ruvan through tunnel vision that grows thicker by the second.

"You're still in there," I rasp. "I know you are."

His grip tightens further. I continue to stare. I don't fight.

"Ruvan, come back to me." If Drew could break through the hold the Raven Man had on him, then Ruvan can beat this. The creature is drawing close. I lift a hand and gently rest it on Ruvan's cheek. Even this simple motion is hard, my muscles are screaming for air. "You swore—you swore to me that you would never hurt me. Not just because of our bloodsworn. But because you never would want to."

Words are harder by the second. His hand around my throat begins to quiver. I can't tell if it's from the strain of slowly choking me, or if it's a result of my words actually getting through to him.

It's then that I notice tears streaming down his cheeks. Even though his eyes have no emotion, even though he's still very far away. He's fighting.

"I'm…sorry," I rasp. I wasn't enough. Whatever we were, or were becoming, wasn't enough to break him free. I press my eyes closed. The pain is leaving my body. Cold is setting in. "The truth is I—I love—"

His hand tightens further. I choke as no more air can make it through. Everything tilts. I can only see his eyes now, fading, farther and farther away from me.

A distant roar accompanies the edge of reality speeding back. There's a blur behind us that isn't from the Lost. A flash of silver in a wide arc; Ventos's broadsword lodges into the monster's chest. The humming stops.

Ruvan releases me instantly. I sink to the floor trembling, coughing. I almost feel sick but I stop myself. Retching would be the worst thing possible right now. I need the elixir's strength to heal my wounds and give me strength.

"You will pay!" Ruvan shouts from the very pit of his stomach. The castle shudders with his rage. He balls his hands into fists and throws his head back. The elixir pulls up from the floor in droplets, as if the world has been turned upside down and the ceiling is now the floor. It begins to swirl around Ruvan, faster and faster, a tempest of blood lore.

Winny and Lavenzia speed into the room, screeching to a halt just inside the door. They look on in shock. Ventos stumbles back.

The Lost rises to its feet—to the challenge Ruvan presents. But the fight is already over. The elixir coats the monster as Ruvan magically commands it, sinking into its flesh. It screeches and wails. There is a vortex of death and when the noise stops the Lost is on the ground, unmoving.

Ruvan collapses.

Even though every muscle is on fire, I crawl over to him. I pull Ruvan from the wet ground and into my arms. His head dips back. But his skin is gnarled, wrinkled. His breathing is shallow and his skin still hasn't regained its luster.

The curse has him now.

forty-one

"We have to end this," Lavenzia looks between her sword and Ruvan. "Before he becomes one of them."

I clutch Ruvan tighter and glare up at them. "I won't let you harm him."

"Riane, you know what's going to happen." Lavenzia's eyes are wide with sorrow. "It's a kindness to him. It's what he'd want."

"No." I look down at Ruvan, smearing the blood on his cheek as I caress his face. "Wake up, please, fight this."

"Floriane—" Ventos starts.

"I'll give him more of my blood! I'll give him what he needs!"

"There is nothing we can do to stop the progression of the curse." Ventos shakes his head slowly. His eyes are shining. Have I ever seen him cry? I find I can't bear the thought of it.

But his sorrow jars a thought. An unlikely, improbable possibility. "There is something we can do."

"What?" Lavenzia shares a suspicious glance with Ventos.

"We have to take him to the chapel." Neither of them move. "Please, if you're going to kill him what does it matter if you do it here, or there. But at least we can try to save him!"

Ventos is the one to move.

Everything seems to happen slowly. Ventos scoops up Ruvan. We're running to the castle. Winny is sprinting ahead as she usually does, scouting for any other enemies. Lavenzia is at the ready.

And I…I find myself focusing on the strangest of things.

Ruvan's arm sways limply, in and out of my vision, blocked by Ventos's body. I'm hyper focused on the hand that mere hours ago ran through my hair. Caressed my body. Brought me to the heights of passion that I had only ever imagined before him. His hair is stuck to his face, dirty. But there are patches of white, as bright as the moonlight that streaks through Loretta's room as we reemerge.

Sounds are distant, drowned out by my racing heart and heaving breaths. Every gulp of air hurts. But that's not why my eyes are burning.

Seeing him like this is an axe to my sternum. My ribs are split. Heart oozing out. Did he hear me when I said I was sorry? Did he know what I was apologizing for? Did he hear me try to tell him of my love? Did he understand?

Don't go, my heart pleads with every beat, *don't go. There's so much more left for us. We're still in progress, still working, fighting, learning…bettering ourselves… Don't go, Ruvan.*

Wind and snow jolt me back to reality.

Lavenzia rests a hand on my shoulder. "Do you want help across?"

I fight the urge to tell her no. Now is not the time to be proud. Now is not the time to try and prove to myself or anyone else that I can get across this icy beam on my own. I did that earlier. All that matters now is Ruvan.

"Please," I say.

She kneels in front of me, bending her arms. Like a child, I hop onto her back, arms over her shoulders, gripping my elbows. Lavenzia stands and sways slightly.

"Am I too heavy?" I know I'm not a light woman.

"I'll be fine; I didn't exactly get roughed up back there." Lavenzia glances over her shoulder. "But if I topple, jump from me. Focus on saving yourself."

"Don't topple," I say deadpan.

"Certainly going to try not to." Lavenzia dashes across with the same grace I've always seen from her. It reaffirms my decision to rely on her help.

Just because I *can* do something alone, doesn't mean it's the best way. Even the greatest vampir lord needs a covenant. Even the strongest hunter needs brothers and sisters in arms.

There's so much still I have left to learn from you... Don't go.

We're back in the castle. I jump from Lavenzia's back and race ahead. Ventos is already down the stairs, Ruvan still in his grasp. They're out of my sight. I can't stand having Ruvan where I can't see him. Like any second and he'll disappear from my life forever.

I come to a skidding stop in the hall of blood lore.

Ruvan has been laid atop the altar underneath the statue of Solos. Ventos is nowhere to be seen, though I hear clamoring coming from the stairs leading to the main hall we occupy. He must've gone to get Quinn and Callos.

I take Ruvan's hand gently. "Callos is going to help you, he'll know how to make it work," I whisper. "You said it yourself, Callos is one of the greatest minds alive when it comes to the blood lore."

I'm not speaking for Ruvan's sake right now. I know he's too far gone to hear me. I'm trying to reassure myself. As if I could, through words alone, push away the reality crashing down around me.

Ruvan looks worse than on the night of the Blood Moon. His skin is hard, fingers bony. They've always been long, but they seem longer right now. I lay my hand over his, trying to remember how large it was last night. Is it larger? Is he already growing claws like the Lost? How much longer until one of the people most loyal to him shove a blade through his chest?

Winny and Lavenzia flank me. They look on solemnly. I swallow. My side is already mending. The vampir magic we share is able to heal me but not him.

"Take my magic," I murmur. "Take it back, take it from me, give it to him."

"Unfortunately that's not going to help the progression of the curse." Callos's voice cuts through the room, echoing off the high ceiling. His footsteps are quick to follow. Quinn is behind with a box that clanks softly—the elixir he was working on, I suspect. Callos halts at the altar. He doesn't ask for vials of blood. He doesn't move. He just stares.

His stillness prompts motion in me. My hands fly to his collar. Winny's hands are on my shoulders. I don't budge as she tries to pull me away.

"Give him the elixir." I demand with a shake.

"I don't think that will be enough." Callos answers me but his eyes are still on Ruvan. "Not this time."

"My blood, then." I release Callos and step away. I go to get my magic dagger, realizing it was left on the floor in the room. That's fine, it was a weapon for killing—for taking. I doubt it would help Ruvan now. Maybe it was because of my nicking myself to summon Loretta that Ruvan is in this position. The things I craft bring death. I don't make anything that saves a life. I draw a dagger from Winny's belt and slice my forearm. "Take it."

"It's not going to be enough." Callos shakes his head.

"I am his bloodsworn, of course it's enough."

Callos just looks at me with sad, shining eyes. He slowly shakes his head.

"The Hunter's Elixir and my blood together, then."

"He fought a *Lost*," Callos says softly. "It's a wonder any of you got out of there alive." He looks back to Ruvan. "He exerted himself too much. The curse has progressed too far; it'll claim him at any moment."

"I will not let any of you touch him." My voice rises with emotion. None of them move as I hover by the alter, unarmed but ready to fight for the man behind me.

"And what do you think you can do to stop this?" Ventos barks. "What do you think that you can do as a human that generations of vampir couldn't?"

Generations. I think of the academy and the hundreds of vampir still slumbering. Giving off an unnatural red-tinted light, the same shade as my dagger, as the Blood Moon, as everything I've come to associate with power when it comes to the vampir. It's the one idea I had, though I was hoping something else would work since I already know what I'm about to suggest is a long shot.

"Can we put him to sleep?" I whisper.

"To sleep?" Quinn repeats.

"You don't mean…" Lavenzia abandons the thought in shock.

I focus only on Callos. "The stasis slows the curse. Do you think it would work now?"

"Of course it won't work." Ventos is always the first to shoot me down. Always the pessimist. "When we entered into the long night, it was part of a great ritual that we were not the leaders of. And we used our own magic—our own life blood—to encase ourselves. You can't perform that kind of ritual on another person."

"It was a great ritual because so many were being encased at once. This is just one man, we have enough strength between us," I insist. "And his life blood… I'll substitute my own. I'm his bloodsworn after all, our lives are intertwined. I'll be his proxy."

"Would that work?" Winny asks Callos. He strokes his chin.

"We are not the great scholars that lived in the academy and studied from Jontun's original pupils," Ventos grumbles.

"Speak for yourself." Callos looks over his shoulder at Ventos, giving his companion a pointed glare. "This is exactly why the academy chose me to wake this late. They knew the protections on our people might be beginning to waver. They chose me to inspect the state of the long night and fortify as needed. I was given insight into the ritual, top to bottom."

"So you think we can do it?" I ask, trying not to let hope get too far ahead of me.

Callos meets my eyes. There's a fire in him I've never seen before. I've worked with Callos for weeks in the smithy and saw nothing like this. These are the eyes of a man rising to the challenge. Rising to the moment.

"I think we should try. And if we're going to have any chance of success, we need to move quickly." He takes the lead, beginning to bark orders. "Lavenzia, fill the silver chalice with water. Winny, Quinn, the two of you begin preparing a collection in the golden chalice. As soon as that's in hand, Winny, I need you to go to my room and collect the crimson shroud I've been working on. Ventos, get as much of the elixir from him as you can, we don't want it diluting things."

"Crimson shroud? Have you been preparing for this?" Winny sees right through Callos. She knows him better than the rest of us, after all.

"Let's just say the human thinks a lot more like a vampir than we give her credit for. She's as resourceful as our ancestors." Callos gives me a respectful nod. One I return. "I knew one of us was going to get caught by the curse, sooner or later. I was thinking this wouldn't hurt to try."

What else do we have to lose? I can almost hear him say. I look back to Ruvan; he's barely breathing now. He looks nothing like the man I knew. The man I… I try to keep my focus on the present.

We move like soldiers, like healers, like desperation.

Every one of Callos's orders is followed to the letter. I do everything he tells me, and yet I can't think of a single order after the fact. My body is moving but my mind is far away. It's wherever Ruvan has gone to, searching for him.

The bond we share is still…so horribly still. Everything stopped for me the moment he collapsed.

Ventos diligently wipes the elixir from the old castle off Ruvan's body. Winny lays a shroud overtop him, up to his chin. On it is a familiar marker, one I've seen many times. It's the same symbol that was on the silver door deep in the old castle.

"What symbol is this?" I ask Winny as the others continue to prepare themselves.

"The symbol of Solos."

I point up to the book the statue is holding, what I can only assume is the first tome of blood lore. "It's different from that one."

"That's the mark of blood lore."

Loretta's mark, I think, but don't say. Our focus needs to be on Ruvan right now.

"Is everyone ready?" Callos asks, interrupting my thoughts.

"What do I need to do?" I ask.

"What you've been doing," he says to me. "Exactly as I say." Callos holds the silver chalice aloft over Ruvan. "Blood of ancient kings, pure as moonlight, we seek to fortify, we seek to strengthen." He tips the chalice and pours the water over Ruvan.

Like a hot weapon submerged, the water hisses, bubbles, and evaporates. I lunge forward.

Ventos grabs me. "Don't."

"It's hurting him." Ruvan's skin is charred in some areas. The shroud continues to steam.

"It's purifying," Ventos says with what sounds almost like a note of sympathy. He knows I didn't witness the first great slumber. I wonder if he sees shades of himself in me, watching as his bloodsworn encased herself. "If he dies from this, he won't survive the rest."

I grab my shirt over my heart. I force my breathing to slow.

Somewhere, Ruvan is still in there. If my heart beats, so does his. I must be calm and steady for him. I must be stable.

Callos passes the silver chalice to Quinn with his left hand. He extends his right to take the golden chalice from Winny. "Blood of the guardians, blood of the covenant, blood of those who will watch over the long night," he intones as he laps around the altar, pouring the blood in a circle around Ruvan.

The four others fan out around me, positioning themselves at each of the points of the altar. Callos is still at its center; he motions for me. He speaks softly, just for me to hear, not for the ritual.

"Blood is parchment and life a quill. Everything we do, everything we are, will be, and could be, is all written upon us in our blood. When you became his bloodsworn you were both irrevocably marked. You entwined yourselves. Find the part of him that lives in you. Be a vessel for him in this moment." Callos meets my eyes. "Save him."

"But what do I do?" I ask frantically.

"You'll know." Callos smiles sadly. "We all encased ourselves. The ritual started with the others, but we were the ones to end it, and it was different for each. I can't tell you what to do and I can't do it for you." He moves to the altar opposite me.

They all place their fingertips lightly on the ring of blood around Ruvan. They close their eyes in unison, and magic fills the air. It sparks like red lightning across the blood, rising like embers.

I stare, dumbfounded. *You have to do this, Floriane. You still have so much to tell him.* He might not be my forever, but I want the chance to find out.

I close my eyes and inhale deeply. I think of him. I think of his hands on my body. I think of the moment that we became bloodsworn, the feeling of his magic—all he is, was, and would be—rushing through me.

Take it, I want to say. *Take it all. I give it back if it means I'll save you.*

Invisible hands slide from my shoulders down my arms. My skin puckers to gooseflesh. I shudder. I inhale. My eyes open.

Overlaid on the present is the past. Portraits of the vampir, collected in the great cavern underneath the academy, flash before my eyes. I see them as though I am Ruvan. I feel his nerves, his fear, anticipation.

Through those eyes of his, long ago, I see the vampir that stood in a circle at the center of it all. The first guardians. Those who laid the long night and said farewell to everyone they ever loved.

Goodbye, he whispers to the world he left behind.

"Goodbye," I say to him. *For now.*

Magic, blood, life, and power, take shape. It's a simple command, but a clear one. *Guard me from the world; let there be not another marker on my blood—on his*. There is no room for the curse. Only him and me.

I hold out my hands and slowly open my eyes.

Crimson threads unravel from my forearms, hands, and fingers. They wrap around Ruvan. The glow from the covenant cements them into place. Crystals begin to form like ice on the side of a water bucket, left forgotten outside the smithy. The ruby coats his body, thicker and thicker.

When the spool of magic runs out within me, I collapse before what looks like a coffin of red glass. Ruvan has been made perfect once more, the curse at bay, held in a sleeping stasis within.

forty-two

NO ONE MOVES.

We're all in awe. Suspended animation. As frozen in place as Ruvan.

It worked. It's a thought we all share. I can feel it in the magic that still hangs in the air, glittering like fireflies around the glassy stone of what looks like a ruby coffin encasing Ruvan. I can see it written on their faces. Ventos is the most shocked; his mouth hangs completely open. He's also the first to try to speak, and just ends up blubbering.

Callos runs his hands over the smooth ruby. Seeing him touch it prompts me to stand. No one stops me as I approach. My hands hover over Ruvan's stony tomb, trembling slightly. The pads of my fingers meet the faintly glowing crystal.

No… It's not quite crystal, in actuality. It's not stone, or glass, metal, or like any other substance I've ever encountered before. My fingers sink into the magic slightly. The haze that surrounds Ruvan is almost like jelly. After a point I meet firmness. It is smooth, silky almost. The magic is warm, inviting, like the radiant heat of a forge in winter. But it won't allow me to pass any farther. I cannot touch Ruvan.

"Did it work?" I whisper. It looks like it did, but I'm no expert in magic, and I want to be sure. I have to hear he's all right or I might not believe it.

"It did," Callos says. "The seal is solid. The color is right and the magic is strong." A faint smile graces his lips. "Just look at him."

I do. He looks exactly like he did before the curse. He looks better. "If we free him…"

"The curse will return in full force." Callos picks up on my poorly worded question. "This stasis preserves things as they should be—not necessarily as they are. Like a mirror, it's a window into a person's true nature, void of illness or curse. But it's not real; it doesn't reflect the true state of his physical or magical being, only what's in his soul."

A glimpse into the soul. My chest tightens. He looks far more perfect than I've ever seen him. I can't tell if he really is different or if I'm just so relieved to see his skin its usual pallor, his frosty hair, his smooth brow relaxed.

I've never seen him so peaceful. My fingers spread across the barrier. I want to see him this peaceful, time and again. I want to give him a world where this is his reality, inside and out. Where I can come to know him as he *should be*.

Even though it's something I want to give him, I want it for myself. Yes, I want to protect my family, my brother, Hunter's Hamlet. I want to help my friends here on this side of the Fade. But all of those are wants for others.

Ruvan is the first thing—person—I've ever wanted for myself.

His people will say I shouldn't have him. They have said as much already. If I can prove his covenant wrong, if I can win them over, then I could win over the rest of the vampir if I so chose. And maybe I won't choose. I've never much cared for what others thought of me. Even when they had control over my life, I didn't care what their *opinion* of me was.

I'm the one holding the hammer and forging ahead.

My hands ball into fists. I keep staring at his perfect face. I don't know what the future holds for us, or even what it can hold, but I intend to find out. No curse is going to stop me.

"We should get to work," I announce.

"To work?" Winny tilts her head to the side. "What are we supposed to do?"

"What we were already planning on doing: ending the curse."

"There are rules," Quinn begins uncertainly. "There must always be a vampir lord or lady to guide the covenant and protection of the people. We're not permitted to do anything without one."

"Our lord is right here." I motion to Ruvan.

Quinn folds his hands before him. "I do not think that is the intention of the rules that the council of lords and ladies set out before the long night."

My lips press into a firm smile. "Quinn, you're mistaking me for someone who cares about the council of lords and ladies and what they said three thousand years ago."

"For us, that council was merely a year ago," Ventos says.

"I understand. But that doesn't change the actual passage of time." I straighten, trying to command the same presence that Ruvan always did. His magic and essence are within me, there's no reason why I shouldn't be able to. I was able to do it when Drew was here. "It might feel like it happened so recently for all of you. But that's not the truth. Those people are long dead. Honor them, but do not tie yourself and the present to the past at the expense of moving forward."

"If we don't have lord or lady to guide us, how are we supposed to know what to do?" Lavenzia folds her arms.

"You're all smart and capable; I've seen how much freedom Ruvan gave you. He was never interested in dictating your every action and he never did. You don't need him or any lord or lady to tell you to do what's right."

"The next leader that's awoken is going to be cross about this. We might not be exempt from punishment," Quinn murmurs.

"What are they going to do? Kill us? We're all dying anyway so is that a real threat?" I'm surprised that it's Callos who points out that grim truth. But he was always pragmatic, always focused on the reality before him. "If we have an opportunity to end the curse, we have an obligation to try. It could take weeks to brief another lord or lady and convince them of our plans."

I give a nod to Callos and look to Quinn. "And if you awaken another leader, they're not going to be friendly to me."

"You don't know—"

"You're right I don't *know*," I interrupt his protest. "But think about it. At best they will send me back to the Natural World. At worse they're going to kill me. And when they do, Ruvan is dead. I won't be around to help feed magic to this barrier that's holding him in stasis."

Even now I can feel my energy being sapped. Quinn says nothing and Callos doesn't object to my assessment either. I use their silence as a chance to rise to the occasion.

"Give us one month," I plead directly with Quinn, with all of them. "Give yourselves one more month to finish this. We have the lead on the Raven Man. We have a plan. If we succeed then the curse is broken and Ruvan is king. Tempost returns. If that happens I'm certain it won't matter what the other lords and ladies might think of our methods—you will be their saviors and their king will be on your side. We've come this far, I know we can do it. And, if we fail in our mission, Quinn, you'll be the one to stay safely here in the castle. In one month, you can awaken the next lord or lady. The cycle will begin again."

But we won't fail. That's what I don't say. I'm not going to accept failure, not when we're this close and so much hangs in the balance. I look at each of them. Conflict is written on their faces, all of them except for Callos's.

"You know where I stand," he says. "I want to end this, and I think Floriane is right. I think we can."

"If Callos thinks we can do it, then so do I," Winny speaks up.

"I don't see how a month could hurt." Lavenzia's arms fall to her side. "With Quinn as our backup, if something happens to us in this final mission, the vampir will still be protected."

Ventos has about as much expression as the stone wall behind him. His brow is furrowed, arms crossed, muscles bulging with tension. He shakes his head and looks apologetically at Quinn.

"You're supposed to be the one who has the best sense." Quinn sighs at Ventos. "Aren't you supposed to be a castle guard who follows orders above all else?"

"I am. But I'm not mindless. I believe this is the best way to protect this castle, our people, and…" Ventos's gaze softens; he stares through all of us. "And if I have a chance for Julia, to give her the world she deserves, I owe it to her to take that chance."

Quinn resigns himself. "Very well. *One month.* I will go to the academy and stay there. I'll barricade the doors, just in case things go truly awry and the Raven Man is able to come for us."

"He hasn't until now," Winny says hopefully.

"But that's still a smart idea," I say with a nod to Quinn. I think about my vision of Loretta. There's still a path in and out of the vampir territory that we don't know about. One I'm going to find. And if I can find it, then it's possible for the Raven Man—Tersius—to as well.

"Very well." We all watch as Quinn departs.

"He'll come around, I think," Callos says. "I suspect seeing Ruvan that close to fully succumbing to the curse has shaken him to his core."

"It's hard when the foundations of your world, the people that act as its cornerstones, are threatened." I should know. They all will, in time. "That'll make it all the better when Ruvan returns as king." I look at each of them, still surrounding the vampir lord. The covenant I am now a part of, and somehow, despite all odds, seem to now be the leader of. "All right, let's get to work."

We stand back before the stairwell that leads into the depths of the old castle.

"Are you sure you want to do this?" Ventos asks.

"There is a way out of the castle, a simpler way than mist stepping through the Fade," I insist. "If we find it, then we don't have to wait until the full moon to go and attack the Raven Man. We can catch him off guard. Moreover, if we mist step then we'll be exhausted when we arrive back in the Natural World. We'll need all our strength to combat him so this could be a better alternative for that as well."

I know my rationale is sound and that this is the right course of action. That's why none of them argue with me. But I still hesitate. I still stand at the top of the stairs looking down into the gloom that I just emerged from mere hours ago, that claimed Ruvan.

I'm doing this for him, for myself, for all of us. I clench my fists to keep my hands from shaking and I start down the stairs. Winny, Lavenzia, and Ventos are at my back. Even Callos came. He's positioned himself next to me, surrounded by the other combatants.

"If we find another Lost, there's no way we'll bring it down," Ventos murmurs.

"Are you getting more cheerful by the day, or is it just my imagination?" Winny mutters with a glare in his direction.

"I'm being realistic."

"You've always been a bit of a pessimist, but you have been worse than normal lately," Lavenzia chimes in.

For whatever the reason, Ventos always seems to take her more seriously. "We haven't exactly had a lot going our way lately."

"Think of all the information you brought back from the workshop," Callos says. "We've made leaps of progress in our understanding of the blood lore."

"Now you're going to know the path to the workshop and it will be another place for us to secure and I'll never see you again." Winny seems a little perturbed by how much time Callos has been spending with the records and experimentation.

"Outside of the records, we do have a human. That's certainly something no other covenant has had, and it's worked out pretty well," Lavenzia points out.

"Pale moon above, the vampir are never going to be able to live down the shame of a *human* being the cause of the curse breaking," Ventos grumbles, though there's a sarcastic note that's never been there before.

"I'm right here, you know." I glare back at Ventos. He has the audacity to grin. I roll my eyes. "Besides, if it's a human that made the curse, then it should be a human that breaks it."

"You have a point."

"Of course I do, now, we should focus." We're back before the stairwell that leads to the room of casks. I can smell the elixir wafting up from the depths. I brace myself.

The remnants of the fight are everywhere, in the blood on the floor, the splintered shelves and casks. I stare at the spot where Ruvan fell. I expected it to hit me harder, to shock and numb me the same way that returning to Hunter's Hamlet did. Perhaps this wound is too fresh; I don't yet know all the ways it has damaged my psyche. Or perhaps I'm not slipping into the void of despair because I know that he still has a chance as long as I can keep pressing on.

I cross over to where I dropped my dagger. Now that Ruvan is in stasis I wonder if using it won't injure him. But it might not be a risk I'm willing to take—drawing our power could break the barrier that's protecting him by siphoning my magic.

"Old blood and orchids," Callos whispers, kneeling by the Lost.

"Nasty monster, isn't he?" Ventos grumbles.

"No. Yes. Yes he is. But that's not…" Callos gently reaches to the Lost's neck, grasping a fine, silver chain I hadn't noticed in the previous chaos.

"What is it?" Winny asks, kneeling at his side. Callos says nothing, turning a small, tarnished pendant over in his hands, smearing off grime and blood with his thumb. "Callos?"

"Jontun."

"What?" Lavenzia steps forward.

"It's—he's Jontun." Callos slowly looks up. "This was the pendant of the king's archivist. They modeled the ones at the academy after it."

"We have to go deeper," I declare, sheathing the dagger on my thigh. This discovery only supports my earlier theories of these halls.

"I'll take you to the study we found." Winny offers Callos a hand. He takes it with a nod. She looks to the rest of us. "We'll meet back with you later."

"Be on guard," Ventos says, and we part ways.

In the back of the room is another staircase. Down Ventos, Lavenzia, and I go, descending farther, farther than I ever have before. It is as though we're walking into the very center of the Earth.

Eventually, the sloping descent becomes less extreme, before it completely levels out. We walk for what feels like an endless amount of time through a rough-hewn tunnel deep within the earth. Our ears pop, and the walls become drenched with water, seeping from unknown sources. The water is so deep in some areas that we're wading through. But we carry on.

The one good thing about the tunnel is that it's impossible to be ambushed. Thanks to that, we make good time.

We come upon a section of the passage that is so thick with inky shadows that our eyes can't see through it. I slow to a halt, Lavenzia at my side. Ventos takes up the rear.

"Is that what I think it is?" I've only known this curling darkness through mist stepping.

"It's the Fade, there's no doubt about that," Lavenzia says. "I'll scout ahead."

"Be careful," I say.

She grins. "You realize how amusing that request is, right? Considering how nothing we're doing is careful at this point?"

"Do your best." I return the grin.

Lavenzia dashes ahead. Ventos and I wait with bated breath for her return. It seems to take forever. And yet, I know it was only a few moments.

"It's a straight shot," she says on return. "No difficult maneuvering of the barrier. Not sure how whoever set this up did it, but they definitely found a weak spot in the Fade and exploited it."

Or made one themselves. I think of Loretta and her power over the blood lore as I step into the Fade with them. The stone walls disappear, even though I can still feel them on either side of me, the atmosphere thick and heavy. It's almost like trying to breathe underwater. I keep pushing ahead. And all at once, we're on the other side.

The tunnel slopes upward, ending at a platform in the Fade Marshes.

"Well, I think this discovery alone is worth not immediately waking up another lord or lady," Lavenzia says.

I stare out over the marshes, reminded yet again that I'm giving the vampir knowledge of my world, my home, easier paths in and out. If I fail, Hunter's Hamlet is certainly doomed because of me. It doesn't matter what notes are left for the next lord or lady, especially not with Ruvan incapacitated.

"Come on," I say, starting ahead. Neither of them move. "I want to show you the arena we're going to face off against the Raven Man in."

Ventos tilts his head skyward. "The moon isn't full right now, it's not even out. We're not as strong. We should head back."

"You're strong enough, there are no hunters out at this time of day. Now is the best time to go." They exchange uncertain looks. "Trust me, there won't be hunters; I haven't led you astray yet, have I?" I wonder if this was how Ruvan felt with me constantly doubting him. Something else I need to apologize for when he wakes.

This time, when I move, they follow.

I'm driven on instinct through the marshes. One ghostly tree means no more to me than any other. But I still feel a pull to the ruins I fought Ruvan in for the first time. I'd come to think that it was the elixir in me on the night of the Blood Moon. I could sense Ruvan's great powers as a vampir lord. Now my logical mind wishes to think that it is my connection to my twin drawing me to this spot.

Blood is a marker, after all. History, time, experience are all written upon it.

The fog parts and we stand in the ruins of an old tower. Drew has made a makeshift hovel with supplies Lavenzia brought for him. He's curled into a ball, but his head snaps up the moment he hears us.

"What the—Flor!" He jumps to his feet and runs over to me. I wrap my arms around him tightly. "I wasn't expecting you for weeks."

"Plans have changed." I pull apart, holding onto his shoulders. "We're going to attack the Raven Man—Tersius—within the week."

"A week?" Lavenzia says, surprised. "It will be the new moon then; our powers will be at their weakest."

"Exactly."

"Tersius?" Drew echoes me. "The Raven Man is the first hunter? Truly?"

I nod. "I'm still piecing together the exact history, but I'm fairly certain he is." I turn to my covenant. "When your powers are at their weakest, his will be as well. But that's all right, we'll have preparation, numbers, and surprise on our side. We'll have the Hunter's Elixir to fortify you all—something he hopefully won't think to take. Drew and I won't be affected by the moon at all. Attacking then will be our best shot."

They all exchange a look. Ventos is the one who finally speaks up. "A week it is then."

"Good. Because we're going to need every hour from here on to prepare our trap."

forty-three

I HARDLY SLEEP NOW. It's a change that's been happening for a while, one I noticed weeks ago. But it's never been more apparent than in these final days leading up to springing our trap. I might not be fully a vampir but I'm not completely human anymore, either.

Some nights, as I'm awake and working in the smithy, I try to untangle my feelings on the matter. At first, I think I should be more upset by the idea of no longer being as human as I once was—as though it is a betrayal to everything I've ever known to become something different, to become like them. But then I realize that is just the elders of Hunter's Hamlet and their conditioning talking through me. The same people who taught me to blindly hate and follow the path that they laid out for me.

Hunters have been using the blood lore for generations; it's a part of us as much as it is a part of the vampir. I'm just a progression and extension of that long history. A history that gains more context by the day.

Callos and I spend hours poring through the old notes. At my insistence, he prioritizes studying the letters. He is of course utterly shocked when he discovers the connection between Loretta and King Solos. I intentionally didn't tell him. After how Ruvan handled my suspicions, I knew it was best for Callos to reach that conclusion on his own. Then the discovery comes from within the vampir. Let him handle the shock and disbelief that will no doubt ensue. He'll have an easier time convincing the others than I will, anyway.

There's not much information about who Loretta was. So far as we can tell, she appeared in King Solos's life shortly after the last Blood Moon before the creation of the Fade. But this doesn't prove that she's a human, given that the festivals during the Blood Moons in Tempost were allegedly world-renowned and attracted attendees from across the known world at the time.

While there are still gaps on who the woman was, her records hold a wealth of useful information on blood lore that is going to give us the strength to take on, and take out, Tersius and his curse. There's more information on the blood silver, too, among the notes. It supports our previous theories and Jontun's public writings.

"The smith was going to make hundreds of these blood silver daggers to harvest the blood of those who came to Tempost to have their futures told." Callos is scribbling away as I hammer, continuing to work on weapons and armor for our final assault on Tersius. "People would come and offer up their blood to the vampir. They would have their fingers pricked by daggers, and the daggers would store the power to be released later as the vampir needed it. Since blood freely given is more powerful than blood that is stolen, it would be potent enough."

"If as many people as you say came to Tempost for the festivals, there was no shortage of blood being given," I agree.

"I don't yet know how they planned to get the stored magic out of the blade later." He stands and goes to the window, staring out over Tempost. "But it's an elegant solution. People offered their blood freely, the vampir gained their power, and the people still received their insights into the future."

"Something still doesn't sit right with me." I pause to wipe my brow. "If blood lore is all about blood being freely given then it doesn't add up for Solos to have created magic relying on voluntary blood by experimenting on people he held captive." It's difficult sometimes not to outright tell Callos things. *But he has to come to the conclusions on his own*, I continually repeat to myself.

Callos hums. "I had always wondered that myself. In truth, I assumed it to be the worst and ugliest part of his process that led him to the discovery of the real blood lore."

"Unless he didn't trap humans?" I suggest, glancing his way.

"Do you think the humans helped willingly?" He cleans his glasses.

"It would make more sense," I dare to say. "Loretta is already an assistant we didn't know about." *And was a human*, I want to shout.

Callos wanders back to his notes, staring over them and the journals. "She does seem like a rather important figure. Which makes one wonder why Jontun never mentioned her."

"Curious, indeed." How can someone so smart be so dense?

"Another thing I've been wondering is about the group of humans that escaped—the one we suspect Tersius was a part of. If we're correct in assuming that he was the vampir they created…" Callos has a hunch to his shoulders. His eyes are still distant. Even though he scans the pages, he lacks his usual enthusiasm. "Why would Solos want to make a human a vampir at all? I always thought it was part of the general research on fortifying a body, but I'm not so sure."

"Is there record of that ritual?"

"Unfortunately, the only one who knows is Ruvan as one of the lords. Some blood lore is guarded only for the descendants of Solos. If there's a written record of it somewhere, its location was never told to me." He looks at me with haunted eyes.

"We can ask him about it when he wakes." I resume my hammering but Callos doesn't resume his reading. He continues staring listlessly at the notes. I pause. "What else?"

"Nothing."

"You're as bad a liar as me." I sigh, putting the metal back in the forge and setting my hammer on the anvil. "Tell me."

He pulls his spectacles off to rub his eyes. "I'm afraid that we're still missing something and all of this preparation is for naught."

"What do you mean?" I ask softly. I can't have him beginning to doubt now. We still need him—all of us have to be working together to make this plan happen.

"I've always said, the curse anchor can't be tethered to a living person."

I remember Ruvan going after Davos, thinking the Master Hunter was the curse anchor, and Callos's smugness on our return. "This is no ordinary person…this is a vampir—or human turned vampir. Either way, he has access to the first three blood lore tomes and very likely has powers we can't even imagine. And he has lived thousands of years. If any mortal could be a curse anchor, surely it's him."

Callos gives me a smile. I think it's meant to be encouraging. But it doesn't reach his eyes. My chest tightens.

"I hope you're right."

"I am. I must be," I murmur and return to my work. I've been right about Loretta and Solos. And my dreams… The curse anchor is Tersius. It has to be. And if it's not, then we'll make him tell us where it is.

Who else would lay the curse but him?

Day and night, we work, we plan, and we practice.

I want to spend more time with the rest of them in the chapel—our makeshift training grounds—but my duty is where it has always lain: in the smithy. I imagine the song of my hammer echoing up to Ruvan. I wonder if he can hear me over the clatter of blades and the hum of magic in that distant place where he sleeps.

We're doing everything imaginable to ready ourselves. And yet, when the time finally comes, I worry we're not prepared at all.

The Fade Marshes are drenched in an unforgiving night.

Even in summer, I shiver as we traverse the bogs. I carry with me the chill of the sleeping world of Tempost to what will hopefully be the final battle to determine its fate. The four of us move in armor that I've carefully designed for strength and speed. A difficult combination to achieve using mostly metal. But blood silver is unique. I've only begun to scratch the surface of its power. I could've made so much more if I'd had months, or years, to prepare for tonight.

We come to a stop at the edge of the ruins. Drew has tidied his camp, just as I told him to during one of my visits during the past week. Our arena is clear of obstruction.

"You're a sight for sore eyes," he says, pushing away from the wall he was leaning on.

"It's only been a few days since you last saw me." We've been running back and forth between the two worlds now that we have an easy passage through the boundaries of the Fade.

"It is painfully boring out here." He shrugs. "Is that for me?" Drew points to the armor that Ventos is carrying.

I made two types of armor leading up to tonight. The kind Drew and I have magnifies power. It'll work with our blood to become stronger—the protective barrier I made for Ruvan gave me the idea of using blood magic to create powerful armors. The other kind is what my covenant is wearing. I used my own blood—human blood—in their armor to help mask their presence as vampir. If I'm right, they'll be invisible, or mostly invisible, until Tersius is right upon us.

"Yes. It should fit." I help my brother into his armor. It fits, for the most part. But his measurements have changed slightly since I was last crafting for him. He's lost weight. I remind myself that when I sent him here—sent him away from Midscape but not all the way back to Hunter's Hamlet—I knew we were both making a sacrifice. Things weren't going to be easy for him. But it was hopefully a short-term struggle for a long-term gain. "There you go."

He adjusts the armor and says nothing of the places where it could be a little tighter. My brother doesn't want to be seen as weak, either. A stubborn trait we certainly share. "Do you have the elixir?"

I retrieve a small obsidian vial from my pocket. Callos isn't out fighting with us, but the preparation he gave us is going to prove invaluable. "Made from your own blood."

"I wonder if it'll taste different than a fresh cut." Drew accepts the vial.

"Knowing you, it'll be more bitter with aging," I tease.

"You realize we have the same blood, right? Any insult you give me is on yourself as well."

"I have it on good authority that my blood is quite sweet," I counter and immediately realize what I said when Drew goes still. I can almost hear everything he wants to say but doesn't. I shouldn't be reminding him that I've let vampir drink from me. Even if he has figured it out, or assumes as much, it's something entirely different to present him with the information so plainly. I try and move past it quickly. "Do you have any questions about what you need to do?"

"Being the bait is easy enough." Drew continues to stare at the vial in his palm. He's scared. Even after all the fighting he's done and all the training he's had, battle is never easy.

I rest my hand on his shoulder. "This armor will protect you. And we're here, waiting. We have him outnumbered; we'll strike fast and true. This all ends tonight, not with a drawn-out battle but a targeted attack. You'll be back in Mother's kitchen eating fresh, hot rolls from the baker before you know it."

Drew huffs softly and gives me a tired smile. "You know, I always knew you were incredibly tough. When did you start letting the rest of the world see it?"

"I had some good advice that maybe I should choose my own destiny."

"Who told you that?" He looks rather smug.

"Some people I trust."

Drew's smugness fades a little at the plural. I just give him a confident smile and say nothing more. We're going to have much to discuss when all this is over. That much is certain.

"We'll be waiting," I say encouragingly.

My brother starts off into the marshes. I squint to keep my focus on him for as long as I'm able. But eventually the night and the fog consume him.

"All right, let's get in our places." Ventos is the one to return us to reality. Otherwise we might have continued to stare at the hunter turned vampir ally until Tersius arrived.

The three other members of the covenant and I position ourselves around the ruins—behind the crumbling walls and nearby trees. We each hold an obsidian vial. The waiting is the worst part. My muscles begin to ache from tension. A strange and overwhelming urge to scream, just to break the silence, struggles in my throat.

But I keep still. I wait. And I continue to run over the plan we've been working on all week. My knuckles are white from clenching my vial, palms sweaty, when I finally feel it.

forty-four

There's a sudden and sharp buzzing coming from the direction Drew left in—the direction of Hunter's Hamlet. He's drunk his elixir. I know the rest of them feel it too because I see them each open their vials. And if we all can feel it, then hopefully Tersius will sense Drew as well. He'll come, lured by the opportunity to tie up a loose end.

Tersius will never know what's waiting for him.

After about an hour, Drew's presence draws near. He's running at a breakneck speed through the marshes, the elixir helping propel his legs. I hold up my hand so the rest of my covenant can see, and my eyes meet the golden orbs of each of the other vampir. *Hold*, my palm reminds them, *wait until the last possible second.*

Drew emerges from the mists; a raven soars overhead, letting out a cry.

I drop my hand. We all drink.

The raven banks hard. With the elixir flowing through our veins Tersius can sense us; he's going to try and flee. Luckily, it was easy to assume he would, and we are ready.

Winny pricks her finger and throws a dagger. Thanks to her blood lore, the woman never misses her mark. The weapon lodges through a wing and the bird lets out a cry, spiraling toward the ground. Lavenzia is there to meet the raven—she drives her rapier through the other wing, pinning the man-beast to the ground.

Ventos and I emerge as well. My armor lets off a faintly

glowing light from the blood I've smeared on it, activating the magic within. I draw my dagger against the back of my exposed palm. My skin knits but my weapon is aflame with magic. I point it down at the bird.

"Enough struggling. You've lost, Tersius. This ends tonight."

At his name, popping and snapping fills the air. The raven feathers disappear into mist that unravels to form the shape of a man. He's ancient, harrowed, scrawny, and as naked as the day he was born. The full cost of the curse and time is laid bare on his flesh—a series of gnarled scars from bloodletting and the ravages of magic I do not want to understand. Lavenzia's rapier is still stabbed clean through his arm. Winny's dagger is in the other. No matter how powerful he is, he can't mist step with that much silver in him. But for good measure, Ventos holds him at sword-point.

"So you know my name." His voice is as thin as his skin, breathy from not being used for centuries. "But if you seek to kill me, then you clearly don't know why I fight."

"I know everything," I lie. Certainly there are still gaps, but I know enough.

"If you knew everything, you wouldn't dream of fighting alongside them."

"I know the stories of King Solos and the early humans. But, perhaps more important to you, I know he stole your lover, Loretta."

Tersius howls with laughter. His stomach and chest heave. We allow him to get out his amusement, even though it sounds like daggers on glass.

"My *lover*? No, you clearly know nothing." He grins widely, fangs on display. They're slightly different from the curved fangs of the vampir. These are shorter, their points more triangular. His eyes are still emerald, only ringed in gold. A human turned vampir is a different creature altogether.

It's the color of his irises combined with the wispy bits of his dark hair that have me filling in his cheeks, the well of his eyes, to sculpt the picture of a younger man. A dream returns to me with a sting of recollection. I've been a fool.

"She was your sister," I realize.

"She was a magical scholar, the best of them all. She was the one who said we should go into the mountains for the Blood Moon festival. She wanted to see the magic. But it wasn't enough. As soon as *he* read her future, she wanted to help them like a woman possessed." He shakes his head, weak breaths straining against his ribs. "I was an apothecary; I knew the body. She couldn't help the vampir without me. *I* was the true founder of the blood lore. I was the one to uncover its uses and applications and I reaped its benefits before they judged me for my brilliance."

"You…you made yourself into a vampir," I whisper.

He smiles wickedly. "I knew the cost of greatness. I accepted the price. But my sister was soft. She took my work and made it more palatable. She lowered the cost and democratized it." All the stories of humans being brutalized make sense—they were, but not by Solos. By one of their own. Tersius turned against his own kind to develop blood lore to serve only himself. Two blood lores—one by force, one by free will. Tersius was the father of the former and his sister the latter, the one Solos would recognize. "So who did Solos give the credit to? The only woman he had eyes for. The bastard even named it after her."

"Blood lore," I whisper. "*Lore*tta."

The vampir might not have been ready for their king to be bloodsworn to a human, but that didn't stop Solos from honoring her. That information changes my other assumptions. The halls of the castle, while secret, were immense. Solos was giving her everything he could, trying to find as many ways as possible to integrate her with society until they accepted her outright. He kept her close, where he could protect her. He likely was starting to introduce her to his attendants and advisers to win them over first—like Jontun. His archivist kept records of Loretta's work and tried to frame them as best he could…they just didn't have enough time.

"So you took her work—"

"It was *my* work," he insists. "They just couldn't stomach the cost. The vampir were weak, they will always be weak. But we—you and I, you have it too, I can feel the magic in you—we can be stronger. We are the next evolution of vampir and human. You've seen it, you felt it. Together our blood-lore-fueled armies will rule not just the mountains, but all of Midscape. We can usher in a new age."

"You know nothing about me." I brandish my weapon. "Now tell me how to break the curse."

Tersius bursts with laughter again. "I was hoping you could tell me."

"Don't play dumb."

"It's not my curse." He shakes his head. "I've been trying to figure out who made it all these years so I could perfect it. A brilliant design, clearly just not good enough to end the vampir. And not good enough to end me, as I suspected was the intent."

"You thought the vampir made the curse to attack you," I whisper. Tersius only smiles wider.

"You're lying!" Ventos thrusts his broadsword toward Tersius's neck.

"Someone else hates you as much as I do." Tersius's gaze roves around each of us. "And that enemy will live much longer than I. Whoever he is, he's clearly very clever if none of us have found him yet."

"Stop lying," Ventos demands.

"I don't think he's lying."

"Everything you ever loved will burn to the ground," Tersius seethes. "My only regret will be not being the one to do it. The vampir throne should've been mine and I would've ruled all of Midscape. I would've sat on a throne of your bones and populated the world with the help of your women."

Ventos lets out a roar. He snaps. And thrusts his blade down.

"Ventos!" I can't stop him.

In a moment, it's over. The first hunter is dead. And with him, all the secrets and wisdom he might have held.

"What's wrong with you?" Lavenzia shouts. "We needed him!"

"He was just going to waste our time. He—He was stalling for something. An attack must be coming. He didn't come alone," Ventos says. Though I'm not sure how much even he believes it.

"He had information." Winny stares down at the remains of Tersius. "He might have been able to help."

"That man would never help you," Drew says.

As much as I want to scream at Ventos, what's done is done. I don't agree with his actions, but I agree with Drew—there's no way that Tersius would ever help us. I stare at his old and shriveled body. So much strength and magic, withered and whittled away by time and hate. The once mighty hunter—no, brilliant blood sorcerer—now reduced to nothing.

He was only ever strong because he held the upper hand. He held the secrets. Now that those were undone, he had nothing.

"How do you all feel?" I look to the vampir. "Does the curse still feel intact?"

"I don't feel any different." Lavenzia lifts her arms and looks at her body.

"Neither do I," Winny says. Ventos shakes his head. "Though I've never really had a curse lifted before, so I've no idea what it would feel like."

"There's one way to find out." But first, I turn to Drew. "You need to go back to Hunter's Hamlet, quickly."

"What? Why?"

"The search for a new master hunter will be beginning soon since the raven took flight. Go back and say that you were taken captive by the vampir. But you managed to escape when the raven came to aid you. Unfortunately, the vampir killed the bird."

"It's not a full moon, there wouldn't be vampir—"

"You're going to be coming back from the dead, I think they'll stretch their belief." I take Drew's hand and pull him to me. "I need you to do this. Whatever it takes, be the master hunter again. I need you on our side for whatever is to come next."

"All right." We pull apart.

I turn to the rest of them. "Use the empty vials and collect as much of his blood as you can. Callos might need it for study." I don't know anything about curses, but I know blood holds power, and this is our only chance to get Tersius's. "Then, we're going back to the castle. There's one way to tell if the curse lifted with his death or not. Hopefully Ruvan is waiting to greet us."

And if he's not...we might be out of options.

forty-five

My feet are weighed down with every step we take. There is no excitement for me as we head back to the castle. The rest of them are restless with anticipation. I can hear their thunderous heartbeats over our racing steps.

They're hopeful. I don't blame them. If I were them, I would be, too. But I'm just far enough from this whole situation to see it more objectively.

It was too easy.

I had *hoped* it would be easy. And part of me wants to think it was because of our preparations. It was easy because Tersius was an old man, tired and failing, who had clung to life with stolen magic as the centuries ate him away. He was only a shell of whatever strong and capable wielder of blood lore he'd once been.

He had cursed himself with his own hatred, that much I think is true. But he hadn't cursed the vampir. He was telling the truth. I can feel it in my bones that if he had been the one to lay the curse, the vampir would've been long dead.

We arrive back in the castle, breezing through it, sprinting down to the chapel. I know nothing has changed from the faint red light that glows up to us as we round the stairs. But they don't slow until they see the coffin itself.

The three of them stand in the center of the chapel, arms at their sides. Callos turns from where he was keeping vigil. Quinn is already at the academy; he has been for a week.

"Well?" Callos asks when none of us say anything.

I want to answer but there's a lump in my throat that I can't quite swallow. My chest burns. Ruvan still lies in stasis, as perfect as a statue, as cold as death.

Ventos falls to his knees. He slumps. I expect him to shout, to yell, to turn his anger at me. This was my idea, after all. What I don't expect is him to raise his large hands to his face, and shield himself from the world. I don't expect his shoulders to tremble with tears he tries to hide.

Lavenzia turns her eyes skyward, saying nothing as Winny runs into Callos's arms. I wonder if Lavenzia is trying to give us all privacy in our mourning. Herself included.

"I see…" Callos says softly as he strokes Winny's back. "I sometimes hate being right," he murmurs.

I walk up to Lavenzia's side and pat her on the back as well. She doesn't look at me. I meet Callos's eyes. "We got the Raven Man—Tersius, the first hunter. He's dead."

"Ventos killed him before we could get him to tell us where the curse anchor was!" Winny seethes, spinning to face the grieving man. "Your temper has always held you back! You never know how to rein it in and now we can't break the curse because of *you*."

Ventos flinches, but doesn't show his face.

"Winny, I don't think it's fair to blame Ventos," Callos says softly.

It makes Winny's expression crumple and she hides back in the safety of Callos's shoulder. "Sorry, Ventos," she mumbles, barely audible.

"Tersius couldn't have told us where the anchor is, anyway; he wasn't the one who laid the curse." I truly believed him when he said as much.

"If not him…then who?" Callos asks.

"I don't know," I admit, as painful as it is.

"So, that's it then…" Callos sighs. In the most outward of affection I've ever seen from him, he places a gentle kiss on Winny's temple. "It's all right, we did our best. The next lord or lady will accomplish the task." Callos doesn't sound convinced of the idea in the slightest.

"It's not all right," Lavenzia murmurs. "Every road, every path, every piece of information we ever had led to here, to him, to this. We came so far—farther than anyone else. If the curse wasn't from him, then who? If not from Hunter's Hamlet, where? What have we been fighting all this time? Was there even a point of any of it or was it just some forgotten, bitter person who cursed us all because they could, and now we'll never be free?"

Lavenzia's voice rises as she speaks. It reaches a pitch that echoes throughout the chapel, deep into the castle, as though it's a question for all those who came before. Silence is her only reply.

At least until Callos is the one brave enough to respond for all of us. "The point is the same as it's always been—surviving. Meaning is what you make it. We'll go to the academy, and we'll wake the next lord, we'll pass on all we know. We'll ultimately rest knowing that we did our best. And with any luck, the next round will do better."

"Julia," Ventos whimpers softly. We all pretend we don't hear.

"We have until the full moon before Quinn wakes the next lord," I say. "Let's wait until then."

"What's the point?" Lavenzia looks to me with hope in her eyes. I suppose I have been the one who has come up with insane ideas at the last possible second. But I'm all out of improbable schemes.

"I don't know." I don't have an answer that she's going to be satisfied with and I know it. But I tell her the truth anyway. "I'm not ready to say goodbye yet. I don't know what the future's going to hold for me either. I doubt I'll be here much longer...but I don't know where I'll go or what I'll do next." I look to Ruvan. He'll keep me tethered to Midscape for the rest of my mortal days. Am I to wander this earth without a home? Will I try and help the next lord or lady? Or will I return to Hunter's Hamlet fearing at any moment that someone will learn the truth? Hiding the mark between my collarbones for the rest of my days? "Give me a bit more time, please."

"I agree with her." Ventos lifts his head and meets my eyes. He gives me a small nod of understanding. He knows what it's like to long for someone who's right in front of you and yet impossibly out of your reach.

"Fine. What does it matter?" Lavenzia shrugs. "Two weeks."

Ventos picks himself up from the floor and begins to head down into the main hall. The rest of them follow. But I stay, my feet moving in the opposite direction, away from them.

"Are you coming?" Winny asks.

"Go on without me. I want to spend a bit more time here."

They oblige, leaving me alone. I walk up to the altar, domed in power. I place my hand over where Ruvan's face is.

If this were a storybook, I would be able to lean forward and kiss him. He would wake up. It would be proof that we were truly in love. Our union would be ordained by a force greater than us.

But I know the only way to save him is with action.

"And I'm all out of ideas," I say softly. "I'm sorry, Ruvan. I tried. I really did. I wasn't trying just to save Hunter's Hamlet. I wanted to help everyone—but especially you. Maybe this is what I get for reaching too far outside of all I was made of." A bitter smile crosses my lips. "You're right, you know, that you forge your own destiny… I guess I didn't have a skilled enough hand to make it happen the way I wanted it to. And I don't think I get any more practice runs."

My voice wavers. The words choke in my throat.

"I'm sorry for what I said to you when we last parted. I've been so scared. I've been angry and confused—at myself, at the people who raised me." I shake my head, and tears spill over from my eyelashes and onto the ruby casket. Ruvan continues to lie there, as still as the magic stone encasing him. "Even though I've known this—*you* are everything I wanted, I was still afraid. And that fear made me try to find every reason to say that this won't work, that I don't feel anything for you, or that it's not important. I'm sorry I wasn't better, that I wasn't braver or stronger or smarter or more eloquent. Maybe if I had been I would have a better idea now. I would've figured it all out sooner."

My nails dig into the magic, as if I'm trying to break through and reach him. It doesn't work.

"But the truth is… The truth is, Ruvan… Even though I was scared. Even though I feel like I've never been enough. I still want to try. For you, me, us. Because…because you weren't the only one developing an attachment—love. I'm not good at all this; I don't have practice in romance. But I think…I think I would like to, if it were with you. No, I *know* I want to. Because, Ruvan, I love you."

The words hang in the air. I imagine them sinking through the magic and reaching his ears. I hope he hears me. It's the only thing I hope for now. This is my last wish for him and me.

"I love you, Ruvan. I'm still learning what that is, means, and how to do it well. But I know it's true. So you have to… You have to come back to me, all right? You need to wake up; you need to not be cursed. You need to lead the vampir like I know only you can do. You need to save them because I wasn't enough." I double over, resting my forehead on my forearms. My nose touches the smooth barrier, which quickly puddles with tears. "Ruvan, please. You said you'd never hurt me, but this is agony. So please, *please…*"

My words become muddled. They finally break into sobs. I weep for everything that could've been. For a life I could've had that ended before it even began.

I go through the motions for a few days. We all do. We're like ghosts drifting their familiar halls, doing things by habit. We hardly say anything because there's nothing to be said; we share nothing more than despondent glances.

Most of my time is spent in either the chapel or Ruvan's bedroom. It's too painful to lie there the first night. I can still smell us on the sheets so I sleep on the settee. But it's so lonely and cold there. The second night my emotions break and I flee to the comfort of the bed we last shared. I envelop myself with the blankets. I toss and turn, fighting for sleep. It doesn't come until morning. And when it does…

He's not there.

I try and force myself to sleep for two full days. I hardly eat. I want to slip away into a dream world of memory. I try and summon Ruvan like I did Loretta. And just when I've given up hope, he comes to me. I relive our night of passion, again and again. I become so good at calling him from the recesses of my mind that the memories are there as soon as my eyes close.

One evening I'm interrupted by a particularly loud thumping on the main door. Cursing, I pull myself from the bed. All four of them are there. Winny holds a plate of food.

"I know you don't need to eat as much as you used to, but you still need to eat *something*."

"Thanks." I take it and go to close the door.

Callos stops me. "I was reading through more of Loretta's notes and there are a few things I want to go over with you. She had some interesting applications of blood magic—a ritual, well, more of a theory for drawing out one's inherent ability. Ruvan had mentioned that was something you were curious about so I thought you might be interested in—"

"I'm not interested in Loretta or blood lore anymore." I shake my head. "Thank you for the food." And I close the door on them. I place the plate down in the main room, next to the vial of blood we took from Tersius.

That's when it hits me.

These dreams...visions of the past...they started after I drank the elixir on the night of the Blood Moon. It wasn't Ruvan, the bloodsworn, Midscape, or this castle that caused the dreams—it was the elixir.

"Blood is a canvas..." I whisper. "It records the sum of our experiences..."

There are basic magics of the blood lore, Ruvan's voice explains to me from a distant place. *Everyone can summon different abilities, do different things with it, but some are truly talented. Some have innate gifts.*

I had begun to think mine was forging. But what if my innate gift is something different? What if my dreams aren't some strange byproduct of the bloodsworn? I was using the blood to see the canvas of another's life...but it wasn't Ruvan's.

I pick up the vial and race out of the room.

"Floriane?" Lavenzia calls up to me. Winny's fiddle playing stops.

"I'm fine, don't worry about me." I close the door behind me loud enough that they hear. They're going to assume that I'm going to mourn Ruvan again. They'll give me space.

Except I don't stop in the chapel, I continue up the stairs and across the beam. I pass through the rooms and hallways that connect to Loretta's old quarters and down into her secret passage. I know it's dangerous to go alone, but I have my dagger with me, and this is worth the risk.

This might fail. I don't entirely know what it is I'm trying to do. But right now is the closest I've felt to hope in days. I don't want to give it up. I have to try. Callos said that a part of blood lore is instinct. The magic is always in us. So I trust my gut and attempt to claim my power.

At the very least, I'll see the truth of what happened to Loretta, Solos, and Tersius…through their own eyes.

I open the tap on one of the ancient kegs, and elixir *plops* out. I hold my head under the spigot and take three drops into my mouth. Holding them there, I race back up the stairs to Loretta's room. I close the secret passage and stand at the edge of the bed.

Well, here goes nothing. Cheers. I raise the obsidian vial I carried from Ruvan's room in a toast to the past and drink.

Loretta's blood was the basis for the Hunter's Elixir. The vial we took from the fortress was likely mixed with Tersius's blood as he continued to experiment. I theorize that the original elixir in the old castle was mixed with Solos's blood, since she was working with him. And, even if it didn't, they were bloodsworn.

If I'm right, if any combination of my theories is correct, then I should have the blood of all three of them in me now. Those markers—those memories—I should be able to access them in dreams, even if fragmented.

Holding up my dagger, I lightly nick my skin between my collarbones—right over Ruvan's mark. Just like before, the pain that creeps up the back of my neck at the mere thought of trying to recall my dreams abates. A door has been opened within me and I walk through by lying on the bed.

As soon my eyes close, I'm whisked to a different place and time.

Loretta races through the night, wet up to her knees in the Fade Marshes. I can feel her heart racing as keenly as I can feel the anger that burns around Tersius's ears. His eyes are ringed in gold and shining in the low light.

"Don't run from me!"

"You took my work!" she shouts back.

"It was my *work," Tersius seethes.*

"Our work."

"You stole and bastardized it!"

She clutches three books to her chest—the three journals that had been missing from her bookshelf in my earlier dream.

"It was mine!" he roars. "Now come back here. Loretta! Listen to me. I am your brother!"

"You are a monster." Loretta glances over her shoulder, her eyes growing wide.

"I am the future of the vampir, of humanity, of all of Midscape. Humans will return across the Fade. We will no longer be the weaker species, preyed on by the others. I'm doing this for us, all of us, Loretta."

"We were never preyed on." Loretta shakes her head; tears spill over her cheeks. She ducks her chin and barrels into the night. "You could've worked with them—with me—but you went too far."

"Don't pretend like I still hold a place in your heart! Did you even weep for me, sister, when your precious King Solos banished me?"

Loretta stumbles, glancing back. That wound is still fresh for her. I can see the longing in her eyes—feel it in her heart. She misses her brother. Misses the man he was.

"Go, run back to him, do his dirty work of fetching my stolen breakthroughs." His words are bold, but I can sense a deeper panic in Tersius. He's afraid of Solos. I wonder if he's freshly turned, if his powers aren't as great as he thought. "No matter what you do, you know he will never respect you. Jontun will never write about you and Solos will never command it. You will be his hidden whore!"

The entrance to the secret tunnel is ahead. In this time, it's protected by a wall and gate. I can feel Loretta's panic. Her belief that if she can get there, she'll be safe. She clutches the books tighter.

But she slows to get one last look at her brother. "When I am queen, I will ask for fairness when they judge you for your crimes against humans and vampir. But I will not ask for leniency."

Tersius moves as fast as a vampir. He grabs her wrist, looming over her. The books topple to the ground. "I can't let you do this."

"Let me go."

"He is close enough with the Elf King that he might be granted permission to bring his armies across the Fade if you tell him of my plans." Tersius's face relaxes slightly; his voice becomes pleading. "Don't you see? I'm doing...I'm doing this for us. *For our people. We will claim Midscape and I will be a benevolent ruler. You can sit at my side and help me, just as you always have. Why can you not trust me?"*

"I don't know who you are anymore." Loretta rips her hand from his and goes to grab the books.

"You will not touch those!" Tersius shoves her. Perhaps it's the rage

surging through him. Perhaps it's his newfound power making him stronger than he realized—stronger than he can compensate for.

He barrels into her with the force of a charging boar. Loretta barely lets out a gasp as all the wind is knocked from her. It's not a cry. It's not a howl of agony as her ribs collapse inward. Her eyes widen slightly. She hardly realizes what's happening.

She's thrown like a ragdoll into the gate behind her. There's a sharp crack followed by a smear of blood. She's propped up, impaled on the ironwork as her head hangs limply.

There's a long moment of silence.

"No," Tersius whispers. "No, no!" He rushes over, trying to lift her face. Tears stream down his cheeks. But the softness quickly vanishes, replaced by rage. "I told you...I told you not to go. But you had to. Why did you have to?" He shakes her and then suddenly releases. Loretta falls to the ground. Tersius backs away, as though he's been burned. "It's his fault," he whispers. "The Vampir King...the one who twisted your heart against mine. This is his fault." Tersius begins to laugh.

The world shifts.

We're back in the underground hall of the hunters' fortress. Tersius reverently places the three books on the statue of himself for safekeeping. He positions tools of ritual on the altar.

He makes the elixir from Loretta's blood and his own.

I blink, and things are different again.

Tersius addresses a small crowd underneath the bell tower of Hunter's Hamlet.

"Do you see? Do you see now? The Elf King lied about the Fade keeping us safe from the powerful magics of Midscape. They will come and they will kill us all if we do not kill them first. We must protect our land or we will perish at their hand, just as my dear sister did," Tersius shouts to a group of young hunters. "Kill them. Kill them for humanity—for our future."

The memories are becoming hazy, the blood is running thin. The images blur.

A battle of fire and silver.

Solos is outnumbered. Loretta was a secret. He couldn't bring his army to defend his human lover. Only the small contingent of sworn guards who knew about her—the few he sent across the Fade to "collect the humans who ran away." Men and women who all took the secret of the true founder of blood lore to the grave with them.

I follow Tersius into the fog. We race through the crimson night. Deep within me is a thread, pulling me forward. Pulling me to a tower, not far from the secret entrance to the Castle of Tempost, a stopover on the road that was cleaved in two by the Fade.

Solos is there, wounded and fleeing.

Tersius launches into an attack. He and Solos exchange blow for blow. Despite Tersius's earlier fears, they're surprisingly well matched. His elixir has worked. But not well enough to win.

They're both bloody, wounded.

Dying.

Tersius grabs the carcass of a raven from the muck of the marshes. He bites into it and his skin rips. Bones crunch. Feathers sprout from where there were once none.

He flies away.

"Damn you, curse you," Solos growls toward the sky. He turns to the dagger in his palm, the dagger he had been using to fight, a dagger with the same luster as Loretta's blood silver. "A curse upon you. A curse of vengeance, a curse wrought in blood for blood."

Solos retreats into the tower.

I jolt awake. My heart is racing, but not faster than my feet carrying me back deep into the castle. Down into the passageway that leads through the Fade.

I know who laid the curse…and I know where—and what—the anchor is.

forty-six

SOMETIMES, WHEN A WOMAN STEPS INTO THE SMITHY, A CAULDRON OF INFINITE POSSIBILITY, SHE DOESN'T KNOW YET WHAT SHE INTENDS TO MAKE. She has her tools, her supplies, and most importantly her skill. A whole world of opportunity is before her.

Sometimes, what she ends up making is astounding. It's new. Different. Like Grandmother's lock. Sometimes, it's nothing at all, just a mess of metal—practice. And sometimes what's made isn't what she intended at all. It's something different. Maybe not good, or bad, just different.

This is one of the first lessons Mother taught me about the smithy.

Creation will happen for its own sake. Things happen, regardless of our intent, and all we can do is judge the result. We were helpless to change it in the process.

I stand before the ruins. This is where I was drawn to on the night of the Blood Moon. This is where I was pulled to when Drew was staying here. Every time, I had an excuse, a reason to find myself attracted to this spot. At first it was the power of the vampir calling out to Ruvan. Then it was my connection with my brother, pulling me toward him after so much time apart.

But now I know, there was an undercurrent all along. There was *something else* drawing me to this place time and again. *Loretta*, the woman whose blood I drank in the elixir that was supposed to be for Drew. She was calling out to her own bloodsworn, to the man she loved. The man she has been separated from for thousands of years. Regardless of whether it ends the curse or not, it's time to put an end to their story.

I arrive at the ruins of that forgotten tower. There's not much. I've seen all of it before. But now I look with new eyes. I remember the shape of the tower, the small room off to the side.

I search the ruins from top to bottom. I spend hours combing through muck and mud until I find what's been calling me. The cellar door is completely rusted. Heaving it open takes all my strength. Like a primordial monster, it's resurrected from the mud. Water flows down into the earth below.

If King Solos had gone up in the tower, his body would've been found long ago. There would've been some record from those who patrol this wasteland, some mention passed down in the lore of the hunters. I would've heard it from my brother. There would've been no way that Tersius would have let Solos die without gloating into eternity that he was the one to kill the mighty Vampir King.

No, Solos had the upper hand on Tersius. He had bested the hunter. The only way Tersius escaped was by assuming his raven form. And Tersius seemed to think that the curse might have been placed on the vampir because of him. I believe he thought Solos had made it back to Midscape.

So I'm led to think that Solos's body was never found. I laugh to myself as I stare into the abyss before me. Tersius was hunting for the king that defeated him, the one that had eluded him, the one he thought was constantly pulling the strings, extending his life unnaturally just as Tersius was. Maybe he even thought Solos was behind the curse himself.

But what Tersius didn't know was that even though Solos was gone long ago, he never really left.

I start down the stairs and arrive in a basement. There's not much; whatever was stored here has long since rotted or turned to dust. The walls are thick with algae and moss. The swamp is determined to consume this place. Thank goodness it has lasted long enough for me to find it.

In the corner is the withered and mummified remains of the once great king.

The last of the true line of Vampir Kings. A man who fell in love with a human and knew his people weren't ready to accept his chosen bride. A man who tried to honor her as best he knew how, for good or ill. Who tried to write her into the history by hiding in plain sight. I wonder what he would think of a human as the one to uncover the truth.

He might have preferred it this way.

I walk over to the remains of King Solos. He doesn't look anything like the man in my dreams. His long, moonlit hair has vanished. His lips are curled away from his fangs, still pearly even after all this time.

Stabbed through his chest is a dagger.

A misplaced curse created by a broken heart.

"A curse of vengeance, a curse wrought in blood for blood," I echo his words.

He had intended to curse Tersius. He had wanted to cut the man down. To curse his blood for spilling the blood of his beloved.

But what Solos had failed to consider was that Tersius had turned himself into a vampir. Even though he was different from the rest. He had still become a vampir.

So when Solos had lain a curse on Tersius's blood…he had lain a curse on his own people, too, on the blood of *all* the vampir. The curse was finalized in this place. Paid for with Solos's life. The memories didn't show me the terms, but I can suspect what they were.

A curse of withering. A curse of death. A curse from which there was no escaping, not ever.

And no one did. Not even Tersius, in the end. And not Solos's own people.

I take the king's mummified hand and hold it in both my own. "It's all right," I murmur. "It's time to let this go."

I slowly release his hand and grab the dagger stabbed through his chest. The moment my fingers touch the metal, a jolt surges through me. I shudder. Coldness sets into my body. This is an item of great magic. An item marked with blood.

This is the curse anchor.

I wrench the dagger from his chest. A popping sound crackles behind my ears. I stare at the weapon in my palm, not so unlike the one I crafted. I wonder if, in her own way, Loretta was guiding me in the smithy those nights. If blood is a marker, I've written her life, her brother's, her love's onto my own. I will carry them with me into eternity. I will keep their memories for however long I have left.

I get back to the castle, but I'm not sure how. My head is in a daze. Perhaps I'm overwhelmed by everything that's happened. Or perhaps it is the deep magic that is seeped into the blade I carry that's blurring my awareness.

Before I know it, I'm in the main hall. All eyes are on me as I descend the stairs, ancient dagger in hand.

"Floriane?" Winny asks. They're still around the table as if nothing has happened, even though the entire world has changed.

"I need you to do something," I say, pausing at the hallway that leads down to the smithy. "It's going to require all four of you."

"All four of us?" Callos is surprised; he's not used to being sent out.

"Yes, I want you all to see it," I say cryptically. They need to discover things on their own. I've already taken the dagger from Solos's body, but they'll piece together the important parts: there's still the hole in his mummified chest that I took it from. A vampir must be the one who passes on the truth. As much as I want to do it, it has to be one of them. Because I will never be believed. Solos knew it, as did Jontun, even Loretta.

The people who are frozen in time are only a generation and a half away from King Solos. They're still the direct descendants of vampir who couldn't even fathom their king taking a human as a lover. Ruvan will have a hard enough time convincing them to accept my role in all this as it is.

"See what?" Ventos asks.

"The truth. Go to the ruins where we trapped Tersius. You'll find a cellar door there; I left it open. Go into the depths, find the truth."

"I'm not really a fan of all this dodging," Lavenzia mutters.

"Please, do this for me." I need them to leave. I don't want an audience for what I'm about to do.

They all pause. I don't know if I've ever asked them to do something so earnestly, so plainly.

"It couldn't hurt," Winny says.

They all reluctantly agree, stand, and leave. I descend to the smithy with a sigh of relief.

The forge is hot. It takes no time to fire it up to a workable temperature. All the while I loom over the dagger I freed from Solos's chest. I stare at it, willing it to tell me its secrets. Maybe I have two gifts when it comes to the blood lore. One is an innate gift unique to me—to see the past written in blood. The other is perhaps one passed down to me from my family through the ages, and that is my gift of understanding the union between metal and blood.

I place the crucible in the forge, allowing it to get hot. Solos's dagger is a beautiful piece indeed. A shame so much evil and heartache has been tied up with it.

Without a second thought, I toss it into the crucible.

"I will remake you into my own shape." I hold my arm over the crucible, my own blood silver dagger in hand. I draw it across my arm just above my elbow and bleed into the melted metal from Solos's dagger. "I take ownership of this curse. Let it be bound to my will and to my blood. I will take its burden from here on. It is enough, Solos. You can rest."

I pour out the molten metal into a mold. While it is still red-hot, I lift it with tongs and place it on the anvil. Keeping it steady, I begin to work.

This will not be my finest piece. It doesn't need to be. It just needs to be sharp and strong enough for this one final act.

When the metal has been quenched and cooled, I pick it up with my bare hands. It's a basic dagger, nothing fancy or special. I have taken what Solos used to create the curse and I've made it my own. I have shaped it into my design and merged my blood with it. I have gained control…I hope.

I hold the dagger outward, looking at it in the early dawn. So simple. So elegant. To think so much rides on this little bit of nothing.

I point the dagger toward myself.

"A curse, wrought in blood, a curse on the people of Hunter's Hamlet, and the man who led them. A curse in search of vengeance. A curse in search of retribution," I say to the dagger. Though, in reality, I'm speaking to Solos. "*I* accept the punishment of Tersius as a descendant of his kind. I accept your curse. I will pay in blood for the blood that was spilled unjustly. Let it end with me."

I take a deep breath and plunge the dagger into my chest.

forty-seven

A WAVE OF MAGIC BURSTS OUT FROM ME AS THE DAGGER PLUNGES BETWEEN MY RIBS.

I collapse to my knees as the glass from the windows rains down around me. Rumbling is heard in the distance, as if the city is waking with a mighty yawn. A new sun is rising over Tempost, and the shards from the smithy windows look like ice, finally breaking free after a long slumber. Magic continues to pour from me in waves, wracking my body and spilling out over the city.

Groaning, snapping, crunching, rumbling from deep within. The earth itself is being liberated from this long night. I double over, the dagger still in my chest, one hand still around it, the other supporting me. I wheeze and cough. Blood splatters onto the ground.

Old gods, I didn't intend for it to end up like this. I grin bitterly, digging my nails into the stone of the forge as if I am clinging on to life. Maybe I didn't intend for it to end like this…but I suppose that part of me is glad it did.

I reclaimed what was lost, for the vampir, the humans, and for myself. And if I'm honest, if I'm going to die anywhere it might as well be on the floor of a smithy. I'll die as I lived.

Pushing myself away from the ground, I lean back, and look at the sky. There are worse deaths, less noble ones. I can be content with this. But I wish that just once more I might have had the chance to—

Movement draws my attention to the doorway.

I blink several times, trying to force my eyes into focus. I don't think that he is an illusion—a trick of my dying mind. But if he is…I'm grateful.

Ruvan is there. Breathless. Stunned. Lips parted and brows raised. With a whisper of wind he is at my side. His arm is around my shoulders. His other hand frantically moves over the dagger, too panicked to break my grip from it.

He looks as perfect as he did in slumber. *So, so perfect.* He's everything I imagined.

"What—what the—what did you do?" He brings his eyes to me. They're glassy with confusion, panic, and about a hundred other emotions.

"I did it," I whisper, blood dribbling down my jaw. "It was a curse bound in blood. A curse demanding life for life. We already killed Tersius. Someone…someone had to pay the price."

"No… No." Ruvan shakes his head. "I won't accept this, I refuse, I don't understand."

"There's not much time left." I sink into his arm, allowing him to pull me against his chest. "I have so much to tell you. So much I want to say…"

"I heard it all."

"What?"

He caresses my cheek, tears falling onto my face. "You are my bloodsworn, my chosen one, the woman to whom I have bound my life, for whom I draw breath. No curse, not even death, would take me from you."

I smile weakly. "And what if death takes me from you?"

"I will not let it…if you permit me."

"This wound is—"

"It's too deep, and too magical," he agrees before I have to say it. "Just having my blood and my power isn't going to be enough for this. And the curse must be broken, it must claim its price. There is no way to save you without letting you die. However, you could be born again." His eyes, the same color as sunrise—red and gold—shine over me. "But I will not save you without your permission. I have taken you once from your world. I did so without your permission or your blessing, and I changed your life forever. I will not change your life again without your consent."

"Ah." It all makes sense to me, what he's saying—no, offering. "Will it hurt?"

Ruvan smiles tenderly and caresses my cheek. "My darling, I swore I would never hurt you. I swore it in an oath and as a man. I promise you, it won't hurt in the slightest."

I close my eyes and think of home, of Hunter's Hamlet, of my family's smithy. I wonder if it will go dark. No…a forge always finds a way to keep warm. Mother will continue to work, and then whatever young woman she's already no doubt begun training will take over after that.

It will be a new family of smiths, one that doesn't know forge maidens but just a passion for heat and metal. The young woman will grow up making practical things—locks, horseshoes, hinges, nails. Because there will be no more need of silver or weapons. The long night has ended.

The war of humans and vampir is finally over.

"One other thing," I rasp.

"We don't have much time," he cautions.

"We don't need much more." Even though it hurts to move, I grab his hand. "If you do this—*we* do this—I will not be hidden. It will be hard, but we will not make the same mistakes as our forefathers. We will live together, out in the open. We try this in earnest, or not at all."

Ruvan chuckles. His smile is brighter than I've ever seen. This is the smile I was fighting for. "I do not think I could hide you if I tried." He's absolutely right, of course.

"All right then. I'm ready; the iron is hot. Make me into something new."

"Brace yourself." He grips the dagger firmly. Running his lower lip along his fangs, he cuts lines into it. Blood dribbles onto my face and lips. Ruvan leans forward and presses his mouth against mine.

My head tilts back as he deepens the kiss. His power flows into me as he withdraws the dagger. Blood pours from the wound, as hot as sunlight. Life leaves my body; my tethers to this world are beginning to fray. All I can do is hold on to him, and hope.

Everything slowly goes dark. It is as if the sun is being eclipsed. I don't know if this fading is part of the ritual, or if it's the ritual failing, but either way, Ruvan will be the last thing I see and feel in this life.

As everything dissolves into nothingness, all light gone, a new spark takes hold. As red as the Blood Moon that started it all, a new spark of life rises within me from the ashes of the woman I once was. It illuminates every memory etched on my blood. It burns through my veins.

I inhale sharply and open my eyes to a world tinged in crimson. Everything glows, held together by threads that connect to people long gone, to the blood of those forgotten but not lost. In my mind's eye, I see my sternum mending. Tissue reconnects in impossible ways.

Thump.

Thump.

Just like when we became bloodsworn, my heart beats anew. Different. Stronger. Deeper. I remember to breathe.

I turn my eyes to Ruvan, still holding me, mouth still bloody but healing. I lean up and drag my tongue along his lips. His blood tastes different now, sharper, even more delicious than I thought possible. Memories flash across my mind, access to parts of his history that I don't unpack now—that I won't ever unless he decrees I may.

"How do you feel?" Ruvan asks.

"Like I could conquer the world."

"Good. We'll start with conquering the hearts of the vampir of Tempost. Then we'll discuss the world, my queen."

forty-eight

I STILL MAKE DREW UNCOMFORTABLE WITH MY GOLD-RINGED EYES. But I suppose that much is to be expected since most days I experience some amount of my own discomfort when I pass by my reflection. It doesn't come from the way I move, or learning how to deal with strange cravings, or sudden magical surges…just my eyes. They're the only thing that serves as a physical reminder that I am different.

Fortunately for me, Ruvan seems to be much more adept at turning a human into a vampir than Tersius was. But the blood lore has evolved and become more sophisticated over time. Tersius was an initial attempt. I'm the process after much more practice.

Drew returned the three missing blood lore tomes, giving Ruvan the opportunity to continue ensuring my recovery went smoothly and Callos the opportunity to piece together most of the fraught history of the early humans and the vampir. Frankly, even if it's not as bad as Jontun made it out to be, it's still messy, ugly, and complicated in many ways. Most of the freshly awakened vampir seem to be glossing over the details.

They left a world dying. Governed only by chaos and constant squabbling. They left a world where answers were few and conflicts were plentiful. And they woke up to a place of hope, where those that made it through the long night can look toward a future.

So no one seems too keen on fussing over the details from thousands of years ago. Whose fault the curse was, why it happened, *how* it happened, none of that seems too important anymore to any of them. They're ready to move on. Those finer details are important to the Vampir King, however. Ruvan has made it a point to make it clear *who* broke the curse. And that seems to keep most of the skeptics about me at bay.

For now.

"You seem to be doing well here," Drew says. He's perched on one of the tables of the smithy like usual, like he always was. He wears the robes of the master hunter again, even though it seems to be the consensus back in the hamlet, among those who have even a portion of the details of what's transpired, that the Hunter's Guild will dissolve sooner rather than later.

"I have few complaints." I give him a knowing smile as I wipe my hands on a rag.

"Sister to the master hunter, queen of the vampir, and settling in quite well. No one would believe me if I told them the full truth."

"Nothing is official yet on the queen front." I tap my forehead. "Still lacking a crown."

"Now tell me. Is that only because you haven't got around to making one?"

I laugh and shake my head. "You're unbearable. Remind me again why I should escort you across the Fade so often?"

"Because you would be heartbroken if you couldn't see me whenever you wanted."

"Would I be heartbroken, or would you?"

"Both?"

We share a smile. I put the rag down on the table and look out the windows. The glass was replaced a few months ago. It turns out that Callos and Ruvan weren't exaggerating about the skill and craftsmanship of the vampir.

To think, we once hunted them, a people of scholars and artists. We have so much more to learn by working with each other. I can only hope to see such a day in my lifetime.

"Here." I toss him the small, circular, steel pendant I was working on.

Drew turns it over in his palms. It's smooth on the back and marked with five dots on the front. "What is it?"

"A good luck charm. Callos has been teaching me about them. The vampir catalogued the stars and I found out what shape we were born under." I pull on a leather cord around my neck and show him a similar pendant. "I figured we needed a replacement for our rings. Apologies it's not silver this time."

Drew laughs. "No need to apologize. I wouldn't want my vampir sister accidentally killing herself." I smirk and begin cleaning up the smithy. "What does our star shape mean?"

"You're not going to believe me if I tell you."

"Tell me." He hops off the table.

"Dagger—the shape of swift and irrevocable change." We share a laugh. "Now, we should get you back. Dawn is breaking and we don't want to raise too many questions."

"No one will ask; I told them I was going to inspect the new gate and make sure the foundations were settling well."

The secret pathway into Tempost is guarded once more, the final duty of the hunters. Drew has the young hunters working around the clock to build the walls and roof around that "mysterious place." Mother was the one who forged the gate and lock. I was there to help her install it. Other than her and Drew, the rest of Hunter's Hamlet thinks I'm dead and that Drew really did slay the lord of the vampir when he was kidnapped, which is why the attacks during the full moon have stopped.

Though, I suppose technically I *did* die. So they're not wrong. I chuckle to myself.

"What is it?" Drew asks.

"Nothing." I shake my head. "Nothing at all. Let's go to the receiving hall and get you back."

The armory is now orderly, even if most of the weapons are still unusable. Ruvan has been adamant that the rest of Midscape doesn't need to know that the vampir have returned just yet. As long as we're a secret, we don't need to worry about weapons for protection, so he has me focusing on smithing tools to help us rebuild.

He's worried that the vampir still won't be on good terms with the lykin. Though, I try and remind him that the squabbles were three thousand years ago and brought on by a curse that's now gone. Everyone who fought in them, or even remembers, is long gone. Ruvan is still cautious.

Up the hallway that's now lit by polished sconces and into the main hall, noise bounces off the rafters, harmonized by Ventos's booming voice. He has a firm hand on the new castle guard and Julia is constantly busy patching up new recruits being put through Ventos's gauntlets. Even though he and I have always had an up-and-down relationship, I've never felt safer than with him at the charge of my guard. Winny at his right hand doesn't hurt either in that regard. Plus, Julia is an unexpected and utterly welcome delight.

Drew and I don't leave through the chapel. There's no more balancing across snowy beams.

Instead, we head left, out into what once was the old castle. Scars of the long night remain. They whisper to me, tinged with the smell of blood spilled long ago. If I wanted, I could reach out and pull a memory from the remnants of the blood of the lord or lady or vassal who sacrificed themselves to try and bring us to this moment. But I refrain. My powers are still fresh and I'm still learning how best to manage them. Moreover, it seems intrusive to peer into people's pasts without their blessings, so I avoid it for that reason too.

Drew keeps up his hood as we move through the castle. His hunter's robes don't mean much to the recently awoken vampir. But his not-gold eyes will.

I'm an expected anomaly, at least within the castle. And people know of my existence beyond. I move freely, just as I wanted. Ruvan has not hidden me in the slightest.

We're almost to the receiving room when we nearly bump into someone. A half-shaved head, bright golden eyes. Lavenzia.

"Sorry! Oh, it's you." She smiles.

"Talking with Ruvan?" I ask.

"Getting orders to take back to the city." She pats a folio. Lavenzia has been an incredibly worthy head of city planning. I never realized just how organized the woman was until she was tasked with leading up the rebuilding of Tempost. She's as clever and capable with a pen and architectural drawings as she was with a rapier in the old castle. "We're going to start in on the museum shortly, I have an idea for a new expansion to house relics from the long night."

"Museum?" Drew echoes. I bite back a laugh, understanding his confusion all too well.

"You should see it when it's finished," I say.

"I could take you," Lavenzia offers. "If you're interested, that is." She tucks some hair behind her ear, almost shyly. I've never seen Lavenzia look even remotely close to what I would call *shy*.

"Certainly, when it's finished I would love to see it."

"With me?" Lavenzia hesitantly seeks clarity.

"I'd love that." My brother is perpetually oblivious. I bite back laughter as Lavenzia speeds away, fighting a massive smile and losing. "What?"

"Nothing." I shake my head. I'm going to watch this unfold from the sidelines. There are some things that it's best not to get involved in. And Ruvan and I have enough matchmaking on our plate leading up to Callos's impending proposal to Winny.

In the receiving hall, Drew takes my hand and I step between the folds of the world. The darkness reminds me a little bit of the Fade. I almost imagine myself wandering through it every time I mist step.

"What are we doing here?"

I understand his confusion. Usually, I take him deep into the tunnel, right at the edge of the Fade. It's far enough away that it's no longer in the castle's barriers. But this time, we stand along a rocky beach, cliffs reaching up behind us, cradling my new home.

"It's the sea," I say softly, squeezing his hand.

He beams. "Just like we promised."

Today has gotten away from me. After returning Drew to the edge of the Fade with a hug to pass on to Mother, I returned to the smithy. Callos, as the new head of the academy, has requested a great deal of my blood silver for study.

It keeps me busy until the sun has vanished. But I'm not the only one who's working late.

I lean against the door frame, arms folded. Ruvan sits behind a desk, the moonlight framing him just the way I like it. Even though vampir can exist in the daylight, the night is so much kinder to them. No matter how much he objects, my bloodsworn is a creature of the night. The pale light caresses his cheeks, cuts sharp shadows, and highlights the hair that spills into his eyes—hair he's constantly brushing away.

"If you're going to keep staring like that, I'm going to expect a portrait." He sets down his quill.

I smile at his running jest. "I didn't want to interrupt."

"Yes, you did." My king wears a lazy smirk as he leans back in his chair and away from all the papers littering the large desk in what he's made as his office. The castle is large and there are still a lot of rooms to reclaim. Most living spaces are makeshift right now.

"Maybe a little." I shrug and push away from the door, slowly crossing the room. "It's getting late. Should I go to bed without you?"

"I *should* say yes." He taps the papers. "There's not enough hours in the day to get it all done. I need to burn more of the midnight oil if we have any hope of getting up to speed to hold a festival celebrating our return within the fortnight."

"Who would've thought that being king would be so glamorous?" I lean against the edge of his desk at his right and motion to the papers. "I imagined it to be a lot more thrones, capes, crowns, and commanding people."

"I will take hours locked behind a desk, a thousand times over, if it means my people are safe and I am with you." He takes my hand.

"Are you sure you want me? I'm pretty stubborn, you know."

"Oh I know."

"Unbearable, really, just ask my family."

A slow, seductive smile creeps across his face. He pulls me toward him. I fall into his lap, shifting until I'm positioned just right. "Perhaps, but you're my kind of unbearable."

"Good." I plant a firm kiss on his lips. Ruvan doesn't miss the opportunity to deepen it, his hand wandering down my torso. I know his thoughts are wandering with it, dragging mine along with them. "So, to bed then?" I pull away with a grin.

"Well, when you put it like that, how could I argue?"

I stand and make an effort to lead him by the hand away from the desk, but he doesn't move. "What is it?"

"There's one thing here for you." He picks out a leaf of paper and passes it to me. On it is a rough sketch of iron points and rubies. "Just a rough idea, of course. I want to make what you like best—I want it to be your choice."

"Are you sure?" It's sooner than I expected.

Ruvan wraps his arm around my waist and steps closer. He runs his fingers along my jaw, tilting my head back to look up at him. "I have never been more sure. You are the destiny I choose."

"When will it happen?"

"If you're in agreement to make this official, I'd like to hold your coronation before the first festival come winter. I want to present you to all of Midscape as the queen of the vampir."

I try to fight a smile and lose. There's much to be done. But right now, in these stolen moments that we make for just the two of us, it's nothing but pure bliss.

He whimpers as I pull away.

"Down, my king." I push him back into his chair. "Now we both have work to do." I plant one more teasing kiss on his lips. "The seasons are turning and the festival will be here before we know it. So pick up your crown and your quill, and I shall get my hammer. Together, we shall make something wonderful."

How about a bonus scene?

Want more of Floriane and Avian? A glimpse of the Tower of Stars and Floriane continuing to learn her vampir magic? Head over to my webiste to learn how you can get a special bonus scene from Davien's perspective that takes place after the end of the book. It also has some hints about what you can expect from the next books in the Married to Magic universe.

Learn how you can get the bonus scene for FREE at:

https://elisekova.com/a-duel-with-the-vampire-lord/

Do you want more?

Married to Magic is not a series, but a world. Each stand alone novel set in this universe will be championed by its own heroine who encounters magic, romance, and marriage before reaching her ultimate happy ending. If you enjoyed *A Duel with the Vampire Lord* and want more, then check out the other novels in the **Married to Magic** world on the next pages...

a DUET with the SIREN DUKE

a MARRIED TO MAGIC *novel*

Learn more at

https://elisekova.com/a-duet-with-the-siren-duke/

VICTORIA IS THE BEST CAPTAIN ON THE SEAS. There is nowhere she can't go... thanks to the siren magic she bartered for. But all debts come due and when a handsome siren comes to collect her, Victoria's payment will be more than being a sacrifice to his God of Death; her payment might end up her heart.

a DANCE with the FAE PRINCE

a MARRIED TO MAGIC novel

Learn more at

https://elisekova.com/a-dance-with-the-fae-prince/

KATRIA SWORE SHE'D NEVER FALL IN LOVE. When her hand in marriage is sold, her new, mysterious husband makes that resolution very difficult. But what's even harder is surviving after she learns he's the heir to the fae throne in hiding. After accidently stealing his magic, she's taken to Midscape where she learns the truth of the fae and her heart.

a DEAL with the ELF KING

a MARRIED TO MAGIC novel

Learn more at

https://elisekova.com/a-deal-with-the-elf-king/

NINETEEN-YEAR-OLD LUELLA HAD PREPARED ALL HER LIFE TO BE HER TOWN'S HEALER. Becoming the Elf King's bride wasn't anywhere in her plans. Taken to a land filled with wild magic, Luella learns how to control powers she never expected to save a dying world. The magical land of Midscape pulls on one corner of her heart, her home and people tug on another... but what will truly break her is a passion she never wanted.

About the Author

ELISE KOVA has always had a profound love of fantastical worlds. Somehow, she managed to focus on the real world long enough to graduate with a Master's in Business Administration before crawling back under her favorite writing blanket to conceptualize her next magic system. She currently lives in St. Petersburg, Florida, and when she is not writing can be found playing video games, watching anime, or talking with readers on social media.

She invites readers to get first looks, giveaways, and more by subscribing to her newsletter at:
http://elisekova.com/subscribe

Visit her on the web at:
http://elisekova.com/
https://twitter.com/EliseKova
https://www.facebook.com/AuthorEliseKova/
https://www.instagram.com/elise.kova/

See all of Elise's titles on her Amazon page:
http://author.to/EliseKova

More books by Elise...

THE AIR AWAKENS SERIES

A young adult, high-fantasy filled with romance and elemental magic

A library apprentice, a sorcerer prince, and an unbreakable magic bond. . .

The Solaris Empire is one conquest away from uniting the continent, and the rare elemental magic sleeping in seventeen-year-old library apprentice Vhalla Yarl could shift the tides of war.

Vhalla has always been taught to fear the Tower of Sorcerers, a mysterious magic society, and has been happy in her quiet world of books. But after she unknowingly saves the life of one of the most powerful sorcerers of them all—the Crown Prince Aldrik--she finds herself enticed into his world. Now she must decide her future: Embrace her sorcery and leave the life she's known, or eradicate her magic and remain as she's always been. And with powerful forces lurking in the shadows, Vhalla's indecision could cost her more than she ever imagined.

Learn more at:

http://elisekova.com/air-awakens-book-one/

Air Awakens:

Vortex Chronicles

THE COMPLETE SERIES

A sweeping magical adventure, filled with royals, romance, family bonds, and sacrifice. Perfect for fans of Sarah J. Maas and Holly Black!

Vi Solaris is expected to rule an Empire she's barely seen... but her biggest problem is the dangerous magic that's awakening within her.

Now, alongside her royal studies, she's training in secret with a sorcerer from another land. From his pointed ears to enchanting eyes, he's nothing like anyone she's ever met before. She should fear him. But he is the only one who knows what's happening to her.

As Vi fights to get her magic under control, the Empire falters from political infighting and a deadly plague. The Empire needs a ruler, and all eyes are on her as Vi must make the hardest choice of her life: Play by the rules and claim her throne. Or, break them and save the world.

This coming of age, epic fantasy is a story of family, sacrifice, sorcerers, slow-burn romance, wrapped up in a magical adventure that will ultimately take readers to places they never imagined.

Learn more at:

http://elisekova.com/vortex-visions-air-awakens-vortex-chronicles-1/

Listed by Bustle as one of 15 fantasy series for Game of Thrones fans!

LOOM SAGA

What does an engineer with a dangerous past, a Dragon prince, and a trigger-happy gunmage have in common? One dangerous mission to assassinate a king. Perfect for fantasy fans looking for something different. Step into this dark and divided world today.

Learn more at:

http://elisekova.com/the-alchemists-of-loom/

"I HIGHLY recommend this and can see it easily placed on anyone's bookshelf, right next to the likes of Brandon Sanderson or R.A. Salvatore."

- Emi, 5 Star Amazon Review

Acknowledgements

To all the people on Social Media who told me this book was coming out around their birthday — Happy Birthday!

Melissa — I so appreciate you being flexible with the editorial process to make sure a book always gets what it needs. This book needed every single pass you were willing to give it.

Robert — My love, thanks for always being willing to help me with my stories… from storyboarding to kissing inspiration.

Danielle — The best author friend one could ask for. Thanks for always being there to talk about anything and everything. You are so immeasurably appreciated and I'm so lucky to have you.

Amy — I cannot thank you enough for all the feedback you gave me during my major edits of this book. You really helped me find the heart in Ruvan and Floriane!

Robert of Wrought Iron Arts, Largo — I cannot thank you enough for all the time you spent answering my questions during our day in the forge. It was a wonderful experience to learn the basics of blacksmithing from you and really helped me bring Floriane to life!

Michelle — Let's get more words done on the high seas soon!

Katie — Thanks for being a body double when I need to double down and get work done, as well as good for a hang out when I need to relax.

Rebecca — Another one for the books, pun intended. Thanks for helping me pick apart all the problems I was making for myself in the overcomplicated mess of a back story I had created.

Kate — Thank you for the encouragement and for making sure there's as few pesky typos that sneak through as possible.

Marcela Medeiros — I appreciate the time and effort you put into bringing the covers of these stories to life. I know this one went through a lot, but we got there and it looks incredible!

Merwild — Your character art as always is incredible. Thank you for bringing them to life.

The Tower Guard — I'm so lucky to be surrounded by such supportive people. From going live and chatting with you all, to our weird discussion posts, I love having an opportunity to be on this journey with you.

Leo & the whole Urano team — Thank you for bringing Married to Magic to Spanish speakers. It's been a delight seeing new readers engage with this world and I couldn't have done it without you.

My Patrons — M Knight, Kate R., Kelly J., Raven B., Jennifer G., Marissa C., Monique R., Ru-Doragon, Claribel V., Sarah L., Nicole M., Anna T.G., Ren, Lisa, Sorcha S., Jessamyn H., Shelby H., Tea Cup, Caitlin P., Bec M., Delilah H., Rebecca T., Madi, Paige E., Tessa J., Rebekah N., Gracie S., Tiffany G., Kate R., Skylar C., Halea K., Alexandria D., Katelynn M., Taylor., Bridget W., Olivia S., Sarah [faeryreads]., Macarena M., Kristen M., Anna B., Kelly M., Audrey C W., Jordan R., Allison S., Keshia M., Chloe H., Donna W., Renee S., Ashton Morgan, Mel G., Mackenzie S., Kaitlin B., Amanda T., Kayleigh K., Shelbe H., Alisha L., Katie H., Esther R., Kaylie., Heather F., Shelly D., Hazel F., Nutmeg 1422., Tiera B., Andra P., Melisa K., Serenity87HUN., Liz A., Nichelle G., Sarah P., Janis H., Giuliana T., Chelsea S., Carmen D., Alli H., Siera H., Matthea F., Catarina G., Stephanie T., Heather E., Mani R., Elise G., Traci F., Beth Anne C., Samantha C., Lindsay B., Lex., Sassy_Sas., Eri., Ashley D., Amy P., Stengelberry., Dana A., Michael P., Alexis P., Jennifer B., Kay Z., Lauren V., Sarah Ruth H., Sheryl K B., Aemaeth., NaiculS., Lauren S., Justine B., Lindsay W., MotherofMagic., Hannah., Charles B., Kira M., Charis., Tiffany L., Kassie P., Emily C., Angela G., Elly M., Michelle S., Sarah P., Asami., Amy B., Meagan R., Axel R., Ambermoon86., Bookish Connoisseur., Tarryn G., Cassidy T., Kathleen M., Alexa A., Rhianne R., Cassondra A., Mick H., Emmie S., Emily R., Tamashi T., Patricia R., BookishAmyLeigh., Alisa T., Xyvah., Amelia S., EJ N.,

Angel K., Betsy H., Liz R., Malou7., Nicola T., Kat S., Esther., Bethanie E., Bianca N., Kaitlyn., Disnerdallie., Fran R., Melissa F., Pamela F. — thank you for being with me on the journey of bringing this book to life. From your support, to feedback, to watching as the first chapter transformed before your very eyes. I appreciate every single one of you immensely.

To all the readers, reviewers, booktokers, bookstagrammers, book sellers, and everyone else who reads, shares, reviews, and talks about my books — I couldn't do what I do without all of you. While I don't have as much time to respond to all your beautiful posts as I wish I did, please know that you are seen and very much appreciated.

CPSIA information can be obtained
at www.ICGtesting.com
Printed in the USA
LVHW012248160822
726102LV00002B/131

9 781949 694406